DOUBLE SHOT

DOUBLE SHOT

WILLIAM W. JOHNSTONE
AND J.A. JOHNSTONE

PINNACLE BOOKS
kensingtonbooks.com

PINNACLE BOOKS are published by

Kensington Publishing Corp.
900 Third Avenue
New York, NY 10022

PUBLISHER'S NOTE: Following the death of William W. Johnstone, the Johnstone family is working with a carefully selected writer to organize and complete Mr. Johnstone's outlines and many unfinished manuscripts to create additional novels in all of his series, like The Last Gunfighter, Mountain Man, and Eagles, among others. This novel was inspired by Mr. Johnstone's superb storytelling.

Kensington Books Hardcover Printing: October 2026

Pinnacle Books Trade Paperback Printing: November 2026

ISBN: 978-0-7860-5238-7

ISBN: 978-0-7860-5239-4 (ebook)

10 9 8 7 6 5 4 3 2 1

Printed in the United States of America

The authorized representative in the EU for product safety and compliance
is eucomply OU, Parnu mnt 139b-14, Apt 123
Tallinn, Berlin 11317, hello@eucompliancepartner.com.

DOUBLE SHOT

Chapter 1

"Majors."

"Yes, mum."

Mona Starret sighed, shaking her head. "Why is it you people from England always insist on calling every woman you meet 'mum'? There is no way on earth or in the heavens above that I am old enough to be your mother. In fact, I think you will find I am your age or younger."

The man to whom she spoke, Dalton Majors, was her manager of operations out there in the tantalizing, promise-filled West. Despite his intention to appear to be a hard-handed, rough-and-ready character, she knew he had been born into British nobility.

It amused Mona to know that Majors's mother had been a lady or a dame or whatever they called fancy women in society over there, and his father had been a lord or a duke of some place or other.

Starret didn't really care about where or to whom a person was born, but as with all unusual facts about anyone she met, she tucked it away for further consideration and possible use. And the fact that Majors bore some shade of royal blood might well be useful to her on down the road, perhaps when she decided the time was right to broaden her business presence overseas.

Majors had told her that his family still owned the estate, but because he was the youngest of three sons, he was obliged to leave home and explore and carve his own way in the world. It had not been particularly easy, he had told her when she hired him, but he had risen to the challenge.

Mona had rolled her eyes. "Mr. Majors, do you honestly think I would not have your background thoroughly researched? I know far more about your . . . explorations, shall we call them, than you might think. And that information shall remain where you prefer it to be—hidden. Unless there comes a time when you will have forced me to exhume it. Do I make myself clear?"

Majors had nodded. He'd nod to anything she said, and if there were a directive behind it, he'd make it happen. Even though it was rare for her to pay him any form of compliment, particularly one that seemed offered out of kindness, Majors figured that any attention from Mona Starret was good attention.

"Mr. Majors—"

"Dalton, please," he had said, hoping to encourage her somehow into noticing that he was roughly her age and that he was a reliable, perhaps even friendly soul.

She regarded him over her spectacles, which she wore pulled down onto the end of her long, pretty nose. "Mr. Majors," she continued. "What I am paying you for is to help me secure ownership of as much of that Texas ranchland as I am able to procure. I am not paying you to be anything other than that, which certainly includes being on familiar terms with me.

"I have plenty of acquaintances, some of which I daresay I might call friends. If not, then so be it. Beyond that, at present, I have no need for such familiarities and niceties in my life. I have money to take care of that. If that should change, I will certainly let you know. Am I clear enough for you on that matter?"

Dalton Majors nodded and thanked his stars he was endowed with the capacity to absorb blunt talk in life. He had always had the ability, one of the few useful traits he inherited from his father. There was precious little else that came his way from the old duke.

You bet, thought Majors, for a solid paying job like this, I can put up with a whole lot of insufferable behavior.

He had never had trouble nibbling away at brick walls, no matter how seemingly solid and high, that stern-seeming women built up around themselves. That was due in part to the fact that he was English, well-educated, and, judging from his considerable past successes with women, he was not a homely man to look upon.

Yes, he would wear Mona Starret down. Eventually. And he suspected that this Texas whim might well provide him with the very opportunity for that to happen.

That Mona Starret was the wealthiest person he had ever known personally and was also one of the more attractive women he had ever met, well, these twin traits certainly did not hinder his urge to keep on working for her.

Yes, sir, he would keep his mouth shut and a smile on his face, and he would endure whatever coldness and insults she might lob his way. Majors smiled and nodded, doing his best to absorb the information she was imparting. If it was important to Mona Starret, then it was important to Dalton Majors, too.

"This region of Glen Rose"—she bent once more over the topmost of a stack of maps on her massive oak desk—"looks the most promising. There is ample water and ample grazing. The river I see here"—she traced it on the map with a fingertip—"the Paluxy, looks like it might well be the solution to a lot of potential problems. What do you think, Majors?"

She looked up and caught him staring at her again. She sighed. "Look, Majors, if we are going to make this new venture work, you have to pull yourself out of this infatuation you appear to have with me, understand?"

"I . . . I don't know what you're talking about, Miss Starret!" But try as he might, and despite his best intentions, Majors knew he was on the losing end of this conversation. It had been that way since he had, nearly a year before, answered her advertisement for a position for which he felt himself quite qualified.

He recalled the brief, terse wording and smiled.

Old and established firm seeks intelligent, forthright, strong person with better-than-average education to help formulate plans of expansion. Position offers long-term potential. Dolts will not be tolerated.

It was that very forthright, no-nonsense nature of the advertisement that had intrigued and amazed him and convinced him to apply for the position. That and the fact that he had recently burned the last sagging bridge of tolerance—and thus money—between himself and his stuffy English family.

Majors also bent low over the map, pushing his luck, he knew, by seeming to cozy up to her. But his defense, should he need to express it, would be that the map was only so large and they both needed to give it a thorough going-over.

"According to my research into this matter, Miss Starret," said Majors. "Much of the region you seek to purchase is already inhabited."

"What?" she said, looking at him with wide eyes and shock writ large on her pretty face.

It appeared as if she was truly surprised that anyone might dare settle on land that she had of late determined to be of use to her.

"Yes, ma'am. This entire riverine landscape, perhaps we can call it a valley, that stretches from here"—he tapped a long forefinger and dragged it eastward along the blue painted line of the Paluxy River—"all the way to here, and beyond, really, is the most desirable land thereabouts. And as such it has attracted settlers for a good long time, well before. . . ."

"Spit it out, man!" she snapped, clearly not liking what she was hearing from him.

"Well, before you came along, Miss Starret."

She did not flinch, did not do much of anything save for stare at the big map and drum a couple of her lovely fingertips on it. Finally, she drew in a deep breath and said, "Mr. Majors, I want what I want, and I will have it. I have my mind fixed, immovably so, on the pursuit of building the largest cattle ranch in the world. That is my intention, and therefore that is what will happen. I am Mona Starret, and I deem it so."

Majors held his tongue a moment, then said, "I never doubted that for a single moment, ma'am, but. . . ."

"But, man? But? But nothing! You, as manager of this bold new plan, will represent me there, in person. Yes, this is how we shall begin." She rubbed one hand along the other, over and over, as if she were washing them.

This was a trait Majors recognized as indicative of excitement in his employer. He liked seeing this, for it meant she was about to smile. Even if that dazzling look was not directed at him, he reveled in its reflection.

"You shall travel to this Glen Rose place, and you shall interact with the local populace, such as it is, and you shall proceed to purchase as much of the land from them as you can in person, without arousing ire or suspicion. Never that. We must entrench. From there, we shall usurp. This has been my method in every business dealing I have ever had, and so it shall be with this."

"Yes, ma'am. Pardon, but what do you suggest as a course of action when a landowner will not sell up to me, er, you?"

For the second time in that conversation, Mona Starret looked at him as if he had suggested they try swimming nude together under a full moon. "Frankly, Mr. Majors, you disappoint me. What is the use of having ample amounts of money, you dolt, if you don't use it? Whatever the cost, make it happen. And do not take no for an answer. We shall return together and deal with any holdouts. For surely there will be a few fools whose greed will lull them into thinking that if they wait, they will receive more compensatory money.

"Nonetheless, promise them anything, offer them more money. Pay them as little as possible but make as many purchases while you are there as possible. Attract as little attention to yourself as possible. And for heaven's sake, do not mention my name."

"Shall I take anyone else with me?"

"Why? Is the task I've assigned you so very onerous and perplexing that you feel you might need assistance?"

"Well, no, ma'am. What I meant to say was—"

"Mr. Majors, you appear to be operating under the delusion that my plan is open for discussion. It is not. I am your employer; you are my employee. You will therefore do as I command. The initial foray will be made by you. Secure the land, Mr. Majors. At all costs. At some point, there will be no more resistance. That is the magic of money, Mr. Majors. Perhaps someday you will learn this.

"In the interim, while you are there, inquire as to the availability of workers. I have a detailed list of needs in this packet." She patted a thick sheaf of papers folded double and wrapped and bound in tooled leather.

"Very good, ma'am," said Majors as he bowed, took the bundle, and backed toward the door. As he took his leave, tucking the paperwork under one arm so that he might open the door, he heard her voice reach him from back by her desk.

He turned. "Yes, ma'am?"

"I doubt I need to remind you, Majors, and yet I shall: Failure to accomplish this task, Mr. Majors, is unacceptable. By this, I mean that if you fail to do as I wish, then I will find someone who will succeed. Therefore, my intentions will not fail. Weak people fail. Prove to me you are not one of them, and I see no reason why we cannot both enjoy a long and fruitful relationship. As employer and employee, that is."

CHAPTER 2

Jedediah Stark, tall, lean, and muscled, raked a steel poker over a bed of hardwood coals. His faded blue, salt-stained shirt, worn beneath leather braces, was a study in how a hardworking man sweats. Particularly when he's faced with the twin devils of the budding heat of an early morning in April in Texas, and the pulsing barely tamed beast of the fire in his whiskey still.

Jed was the third generation of Starks to live his days and nights on this one-thousand-acre patch of Texas soil, with its woods and water, grass and gravel, that the family fondly named Whiskey Woods.

He heard a soft popping sound and knew even as he turned his head that it was their dog, Redeye, breaking wind in his sleep.

"My word, dog," said Jed. "You are the rankest old beast to ever draw breath on this fine earth."

The big whiskey man's words did not rouse the hound. Very little did, in fact, save for the whiff of dinner—he was partial to a mess of baked beans, which accounted for much of his odious offerings. Other than that, it was the appearance of a stranger down the lane traveling to and from Whiskey Woods that had the ability, when little else could, of raising the dog's head.

"Yes, ma'am. Understood, Miss Starret."

"Good." She dragged another stack of papers before her and seated herself once more behind the massive desk. "Now, on to the ice hauling enterprise on the New England coast." She regarded him once more. "You may leave now, Mr. Majors."

"Yes, Miss Starret." He smiled and bowed slightly and closed the door behind him. Out in the hallway, he readjusted the bulky bundle and proceeded on down the long, carpeted hallway that led to the middle of the mansion. As he walked, he glanced left and right.

Yes, sir, he thought. When I am the man of this house, then we shall see who orders who about.

He grinned. "Just a matter of time, my good man," he whispered to himself. "You heard the woman, Majors. Do the job or else. So I shall most certainly do the job. And soon enough, all of this shall be mine for the plucking."

By the time he reached the first floor once more, Dalton Majors was whistling.

The old, graying hound somehow seemed to sense the impending arrival of visitors long before Jed or his mama, Minnie Stark, were able to see them as they traveled down the long lane that led from the high road running from Grindle to the east to Glen Rose to the west. In this manner, Jed and Mama always trusted the dog's gaze first, and their own second.

It was one of the very same traits the raw-boned hound shared with all his predecessors, a long line of much-loved dogs of varying abilities and sizes and shapes, but all long-lived and equally loved by whichever Starks were in residence at Whiskey Woods at the time.

Just the year before, Redeye had been drawn close to the brink of death by a vicious gun blast doled out by one of Merlin Sheldrake's death-dealing hirelings. But he had recovered, albeit with a limp in the front end, and he didn't have to live through another day of his life without someone at the ranch recalling his bold, protective spirit and doling out extra meaty treats.

"We're dog folks," Minnie would say to Jed over the years of his growing up, as if to affix in him the notion that he had no choice in the matter. He was a Stark, therefore, he was a dog lover. But there was never any question on that matter where Jed was concerned—he couldn't imagine life without a dog about the place.

He loved having at least one dog close at hand, even one as seemingly dead to the world as ol' Redeye. Up until the day he'd nearly been murdered, and every day since, that old hound had not given anyone a reason to be concerned about him or to question his value about the place.

He helped corral chickens. He slept. A lot. And he ate enough to sustain his underworked, overtired self. His biggest and most valued contribution, however, was how he came to life when strangers with ill intent showed up. The dog could sniff them out a mile or more off.

Once Redeye worked up that low-throat growl, twitched a

lip that rose high enough to reveal a glimpse of white fang, and posed his lithe frame set to pounce, Jed and Minnie knew they had best keep a sharp eye on whoever the stranger might be.

Redeye never failed to prove himself of great worth to them, as a member of the family and as a protector.

And although they were a singular and independent lot, it was still to Glen Rose that the Starks felt they belonged. And yet at the same time, they knew and took quiet confidence in the fact that they were apart from the bustling town, a town that prided itself as being "built on whiskey," which was largely due to the Starks.

Sure, Jed's grandfather, Hawcliffe Stark, had trekked westward from Tennessee many years before and had established the town. But he had also been cautious throughout his life about keeping his distance from prying, nosy interlopers, as he thought of them, who, to him, were anyone who might stomp all over his hard-won and well-protected freedom.

His grandfather, his grandmother, his mother, and now Jed were of the same mind—if folks wanted to live in the laps of other folk, then they should have at it. Never had a Stark done such a thing, from way back generations before generations, in the hills of Tennessee, to the rolling country of the middle of Texas, and no Starks were about to break with that, or any other Stark tradition.

They worked hard, they made the best whiskey they were able to make, which, as it turned out, was some of the best whiskey made anywhere, and they were fierce in protecting their property, their freedom, and their own, which included friends as well as family. And family was family, no debating it.

Their potential friends were slow for the Starks to warm to, but once they were accepted as friends, they might as well be family, too. The bonds the Starks formed were as tight as the bark on trees, as Mama always put it.

And so when wealthy businessman Merlin Sheldrake had

fancied himself a titan of the liquor world, he blustered and blathered and bought his way into life in the region, plunking himself in Glen Rose. When he did so in the quiet, not overly prosperous town, it didn't take long before he made a whole lot of folks happy because he spent a whole lot of money building up the whiskey end of his empire, which began in the upper Midwest with shipping and trains and reached eastward, too.

For reasons known only to Sheldrake, and perhaps not even clear to himself, Merlin Sheldrake lusted after anything that was denied him. He felt that his vast wealth could and should give him access to everything. And when he found out that the Starks made the best whiskey to be found anywhere, he wanted to buy it.

Time and time again, he made offers to do so. He wanted the recipe, the still, the stock, all of it. But he didn't understand that what made Stark whiskey so good were the passed-down methods and recipe, never written down but passed along from one generation of Stark to another.

The other crucial ingredient in Stark's Whiskey Woods whiskey was the sweet, clean, clear spring water that sat in the midst of their ranch. It was the very thing that Tennessee whiskey maker Hawcliffe Stark had sought all along on his journey from back East to the vast promise of the West.

Once Hawcliffe Stark tasted the steady flowing waters of that sweet natural spring, he knew he had found what he had left his beloved but increasingly cramped hills of Tennessee for. And in that fingersnap moment of time, he swore he would carve out a life for himself and his heirs right there on that spot or die in the attempt. He did not yet know he would one day take as a sweetheart and marry a hardy spitfire of a woman, Bethelza Hubbard.

But in those early days as a loner, he was determined to make it work. And it was a good thing, for he had had his hands full for years, battling attacks from Apache, who resented the white man and his claim-staking ways.

In truth, Hawcliffe had felt a little bad about moving on in and setting up a life on land that they had always used. To make the sting more painful to them, he laid claim to a rare local freshwater spring, much coveted by the beasts and by the humans who all had used the land and the spring forever and a day before he arrived.

The thought of it had caused him a few nights of deep consideration and turning and harrumphing when he should have been sleeping.

He eventually managed to come to some slice of ease over it, at least in his mind, and at least where the spring was concerned. He widened the basin from a shallow, grassy, reedy thing pocked with mud and scat and paw- and hoof- and footprints into something they might all use, and channeled some of the flow off for his own use, still leaving ample flow for others to use.

But the Apache had not liked this, and after a number of bloody encounters with them over the following months and years, the native people had ceased to use that stretch of land as a point of passage to the Paluxy River, which flowed lower. This bitter victory provided another well of confidence to Hawcliffe where the land was concerned. He'd made a wise choice, he felt, in settling there.

He built up a place, down lower, along the river, yet high enough to avoid much damage should the river flood. And in his experience living alongside and traveling through regions in which rivers and streams flowed, it was not really a matter of if they flooded, but when they did so.

For he knew that a river is fed from somewhere and that somewhere would always receive rain that would be seen or felt far downstream, eventually.

And so it had been that Grandpa Hawcliffe Stark had established Whiskey Woods, the home, so he hoped, of the Starks forever and a day from then on. And so it had been. And now Jedediah Stark was the man of the place, and his mother, daughter of Hawcliffe and his bride, Bethelza, was the ruling Stark thereabouts.

A diminutive old chicken of a woman, Minerva was nonetheless one of the toughest critters to be raised up in the region. She was not one to suffer fools or anything that might one day consider a foolish notion, with anything less than a sharp tongue and a cocked single-barrel shotgun, which she referred to as Ol' Shredder, and which she toted with her more often than not.

She lugged the thing, once her father's favored weapon, as she made what she called her "patrols" to see if anything or anyone dared to ruffle her feathers. It was a rare occasion when such a thing happened, for Mother Stark, as she was known far and wide, was not one to be tampered with, even in jest, unless the daring party wished to stagger away with a tongue-lashing, at best.

She'd birthed Jed late in her life, long after her parents had all but given up hope that she might ever settle down and wed, and thereby carry on the established family line of work, whiskey making.

Jed's father, a traveling man, had somehow done what so few men had dared to do. He had wooed Minnie Stark enough to form a dalliance, however brief. Before the rascal, by all accounts a handsome gent with less ambition than a split of firewood, could make his exit, Hawcliffe caught wind of what had happened betwixt his beloved daughter, Minnie, and the drifting drummer of a stranger.

Papa Stark cocked Ol' Shredder and nudged Arthur Bigelow-Watts behind the ear one fine morning and explained a few things. The handsome fellow had merely smiled and nodded and agreed to whatever Mr. Stark told him. A wedding date had been set in the very near future.

Before that might happen, Arthur, who had been allowed to

borrow a horse and ride to town for a visit to the tonsorial parlor, he being particular about his looks, had availed himself of the very fine whiskey his soon-to-be family distilled.

Alas, he availed a little too deeply on the ride home and slipped from the horse's back, striking his head on a rock, and dying with his eyes closed, a wide smile on his face, and his handsomeness fully intact.

And with that turn of events, Minerva Stark counted herself among the luckiest women ever to have drawn a breath. She wasn't saddled with a no-account for a husband, she got to keep her treasured name, and she found herself with a fine and handsome strapping, bawling, lusty young bairn less than eight months later.

Jedediah was named for Hawcliffe's very own father, dead these long years and laid to rest by Hawcliffe himself back in the hills of Tennessee.

Jed also inherited his grandfather's tall, lanky, muscled frame, his own father's handsome visage, and a blend of his grandfather's and his father's mild temperament. Any fiery aspects of his personality, all attributed to his mama and her mother, Bethelza, bubbled to the surface whenever he was in sore need of them, which was not often. But when he was, his mother's traits of quick, decisive action and a *no-fools-spared* approach were well employed by the big whiskey maker.

But of excitement or reason for timely action on this day, there was little. It was a fine, blue-cloud day, and worry and hardship seemed a hundred miles off. Jed stood from leaning over the whiskey still and stretched his back, dragging a bare wrist across his sweat-stung eyes.

He also noticed a small yet surprising thing: Redeye had been roused from sleep and stared up the long roadway into Whiskey Woods, although he did not expect to see much. He was not disappointed by this lack of minor revelation, however, for he knew that Redeye's continued attentiveness would bear fruit at some point in the near future.

And in this he was also not disappointed, for he recognized who it was, or rather who he thought it might well be. Jed's somewhat keen eyesight revealed the familiar shape and slow pace of the incoming visitor, and Redeye's resumption of his napping pose confirmed Jed's guess. After all, the old hound would not behave in such a manner for too many folks.

Sure enough, within twenty minutes, Jed spied his old friend from town, Loudon Paley, journalist and owner and editor and sole employee of the *Glen Rose Gazette*, a weekly single-sheet that was a challenge for the back East newspaperman to fill, so dozy had Glen Rose once more become.

Loudon, or Loud, as most folks who knew him well called the slightly portly fellow, reined up on his new mule, Alice II, replacement for the original Alice, and slowly climbed down from the saddle.

It had been a good week since Loud had ridden on out to Whiskey Woods, and Jed felt a little bad about that, as his friend had for most of the six or so years since he'd come west, ridden on out several times a week.

But Jed and his longtime sweetheart, Lilly Chu, owner of the Glen Rose Café, had been spending a good deal of time together of late, not least of which was because she had finally pinned Jed down to committing to a wedding date, and that date was creeping closer with each picnic and conversation they had.

"Well, hey there, Loud. I thought you'd given up on us." Jed strode across the dooryard and shook his chum's hand. And within minutes, as Jed resumed his labors and Loudon perched on the edge of whatever somewhat comfortable surface offered itself to him, they were back in their old routine of easy conversation, with most of the chatter on Loudon's part and with Jed offering the occasional brief remark or grunt.

After plowing through the usual snatches of gossip and stale news, a silence settled. As Jed knew, it did not last for long.

Never, he thought as he poked his fire, had a man been born who abhorred the peace and quiet more than Loudon Paley.

Loud whistled, high and easy. "It's something, it surely is," he said.

Jed guessed what his friend was referring to. He based his guess on the fact that since it had been a good week and more since Loud had been out to visit to talk, or as Loud called it, to confabulate, Jed knew he would have to give in, against his own wishes, and let the newsman talk through the well-chewed topic of the Sheldrake mess one more time. But this had to be the last time. Jed was far beyond sick and tired of hearing—and thinking—about it.

Jed finished pouring off the mash. He glanced over his right shoulder at his pal. "What's that you're saying, Loud?"

"I said . . . it is something, it surely is."

"Oh. Uh-huh."

There was a quiet moment. Jed knew what was coming. And he was not disappointed.

"Aren't you going to ask me what the 'something' is that I'm talking about?"

"Hmm," said Jed, not pausing in his work. "Nope, guess not."

"You have to be joshing me!" The wide-eyed Loudon rubbed his forehead.

"Nah," said Jed, not daring to turn around and show Loudon the budding smile he was hiding. "I guess I'm just not in a curious mood today." He shrugged. "It happens."

"Not to normal folks," said Loudon, shaking his head and slumping back down into his seat. "And certainly not to journalists."

Jed shook his head and chuckled, facing his friend. "Loud, you know I'm fooling with you. But I do have to say that I get a little tired of plowing the same old patch of earth that we plow near about every time you wander on down here for a chinwag. Don't you?"

"Sure, I guess." Loudon sighed. "And I suppose that the Merlin Sheldrake episode is well and truly behind us. And put to rest. But, and I doubt you'll believe me, I actually was not about to talk of Sheldrake again."

"Good to hear," said Jed, resuming his task.

"Not today, anyway," said Loud. "No, there's another topic I wanted to chat with you about."

"You don't mean there are other items of newsworthy merit afoot in Glen Rose!" Jed's raised eyebrows and look of mock surprise raised a grin on Loudon's face.

"In fact, there are, Mr. Stark."

"And I'm sure you'll tell me about them," said Jed with a chuckle.

"Well, I feel I should, don't you? I mean to say, after all, there's not much else to chat about." But Loudon cracked a smile himself. "Except that there's a newcomer who's driving around the countryside hereabouts in a fancy buggy, making cash offers on ranches, land, and such. *Big* cash offers."

Jed could not help himself. He rose to the bait, knowing full well he was going to pay for it for some time to come. "What's that, now?"

Loudon smiled and leaned back against the stacked grain sacks. "Yeah, I thought that might tickle your curiosity bone."

"Okay, okay, I admit it," said Jed with a sigh. "Just don't lord it over me, eh?"

"Aw, Jed, you know that's a futile request!" Loudon smacked his pants leg and laughed.

Whatever it was that Loudon was set to tell him about, Jed reckoned it would likely be nothing that would amount to anything anyway. Folks were always coming and going in these parts, ranches were being bought up, parceled out, sold off. He figured it was the way of the world. Still, it might be worth knowing of. "Okay, Loud, let's hear it."

"Well, now, here's what I know."

And for twenty minutes, Loudon Paley, the newspaperman, told his best friend, the whiskey maker, all that he knew of a certain fellow by the name of Dalton Majors, an English dandy, as it happened, with deep pockets and tight lips.

He told Jed about which of the local folks had been approached by Majors, and who among them had succumbed to his promise of copious amounts of cash should they agree to sell their homes, lands, and more to him.

The conversation left Jed bothered and irritated. He was less convinced of the innocence and fleetingness of the stranger's appearance and doings in and around Glen Rose and more concerned that there might well be something odd and potentially worrisome in the air.

Then a thought came to Jed. "At least we have you to keep an eye on things." He looked at Loudon then, square in the eye. "I'm not kidding this time, Loud. This sounds like it could get troublesome. You know how Glen Rose folks are about money, if that cursed Sheldrake episode is any yardstick. Anyway, I'm glad to know you're marking this Englishman's progress, if you can call it that."

"Thanks," said Loudon. He shrugged to show, he hoped, that it was no big deal, he was just doing his job, but he was blushing, too, because he knew Jed Stark didn't dole out praise for little reason.

And even though they were both men of roughly the same age and each accomplished in his chosen profession in life, Jed's opinion of Loudon mattered much to him, more, he suspected, than did his opinion of his big, whiskey-making friend.

CHAPTER 3

Once again, Jed Stark was up to his elbows in grime and soot and all manner of glass and metal parts and pieces. The day was turning off hot, and he had an itch at the end of his nose, but his hands were filled with other odds and ends. Sweat would not stop dribbling down his forehead and through his eyebrows and into his eyes, stinging away.

No matter how many times he blinked or blew upward, it would not stop the sweat droplets nor quell that annoying nose itch.

Jed was not a man prone to giving vent to his frustrations, but he was sorely tempted to bark an oath that he would not utter before anyone else, especially not in front of a lady. Not Mama, and especially not Lilly. The woman was his longtime sweetheart, and now they were set to be wed, and he did not want her to think he was an uncouth heathen.

Lilly had been fairly understanding and kind about his reluctance to choose a date for the event, knowing that he assumed it would happen in due time. After all, he reasoned, they had spent the previous six years as sweethearts, and that had been just fine, so what on earth was the rush?

But Jed knew the answer to that as surely as he knew that he would have to let go of the copper tubing in his left hand and itch his nose . . . no, wait, he figured out that if he shifted his weight from his right knee and leaned forward a pinch more he could scratch his nose against the nearest side of the cold copper boiler. And what a relief it was. . . .

"Aah," he said, continuing to indulge in this gentlest of scratches. It would not do to work the nose right off his face if he could help it.

No, this wedding was, despite his efforts, not working out to be the vague, sometime-in-the-future affair he had assumed it would be.

When he'd asked Lilly to marry him, it had been admittedly an ill-timed question, offered as it had been when he was fresh off a fistfight with the now-former corrupt marshal of Glen Rose. If he'd only known what sort of trouble was soon to follow on that day a year back, he would have . . .

"Would have what, Jed?" he whispered to himself as he groped with his fingertips in the dark, hard-to-reach place where just a few more twists of the threaded end of the pipe sat, any second now, and it would be freed up.

As he fussed with it, he worked on the thought he'd just raised. He knew, of course, the answer had to be that he'd marry Lilly all day and every day from here until the end of all time. That much was certain.

But when his dear old mama pressed the issue, Jed felt himself bristling and wanting to do the very opposite, just because he did not like being pressed on a thing. Especially not on a matter that was so important and so final as a man's marriage.

Besides, he thought, it was none of Mama's business. And he had vowed that if she raised it again with him, he would tell her so. Somebody had to put the crotchety old matriarch in her place, and Jed reckoned that if he didn't, there was nobody on earth who could.

But that would have to wait, because he had to finish dismantling the still he'd cobbled together in some haste following the fire a year back. He'd limped through with the smaller still down by the family camp along the river, but it had not been sufficient for his needs.

Even though Merlin Sheldrake burned the place down, the ranch house, the barn, and his whiskey-making shed along with it, Jed had been determined at the time that he would do everything in his ability to get the place back in top order in plenty of time for the wedding.

Now that they had chosen a date, in just a couple of months' time, Jed was beginning to feel the pressure of it looming ever larger with each passing day. But first, he had to get this improved version of his still operating before the day's light left him.

He was motivated, too, by the fact that he wanted to resume his favorite task, which was the making of Stark whiskey, first, last, and always. The only other thing he enjoyed as much, and perhaps more, was spending time with Lilly Chu, his sweetheart.

Why he had never tired of her company or she his, apparently, he'd never know. But it had been six years since they'd met, and he was glad of it every day. And if they were lucky to have children, why, he couldn't imagine that his life could get any better.

How could it, he wondered? A little one to teach the family trade to—ensuring that Stark whiskey flowed as smooth and tasted as fine as it had always, well on into the future.

That's when he heard Redeye growling. It took a long moment for Jed to place the sound, for it was a slightly higher-pitched growl than their old dog usually offered.

Redeye continued his growling, and Jed reluctantly slid his arms free from the inner depths of his still's cold fire chamber. He knew exactly what he wanted to do with the firebox, how he might improve it for airflow and expand it in the doing, and he was anxious to get on with it.

He'd spent far too much time this morning chasing his own

tail, so to speak, and now that he had the various hastily built parts and pieces apart, he wanted to get cracking.

The last thing he needed was a stranger poking about the place. He glanced over at Redeye and regarded him seriously for the first time that day. The dog seemed to have even less ambition than he had possessed before. Indeed it could be said the old hound had become a master of . . . *laziness* was not the precise word, more along the lines of . . . being permanently calm.

Well, except when there were strangers about. And in particular, strangers who Redeye determined had the potential to be unsavory. And Redeye always seemed to know somehow when a stranger was lurking about the place, and if the stranger was somehow bent on ill intent, well, heaven help that stranger.

The dog had kept up the growling, and Jed had risen to his feet because of it. He was but half concealed behind the neat piles of whiskey-still parts and gear, and still had to snake his left leg free of the remaining bits—the old fire pan and the wire that had held up the dangling stovepipe.

Jed's top lip also curled as he kept working. He was not a short man, standing north of six feet tall, and he was forever smacking his head against low-hanging tools and such in the shop. Raising the height of the walls, and thus the roof, was one of a number of improvements Jed had been working into his rebuilding of the whiskey shed.

The interior of the building was open to the roof, rafters forming an A-frame high up, at least higher than his head might ever reach, by a full couple of feet at the lowest height.

The old whiskey shed had been built many, many years before, by Mama and her old daddy, Jed's grandfather, Hawcliffe. It had been a solid structure, and Jed had grown accustomed to it being just so, but once every so often, he'd knock his bean on a beam end, and he'd groan and rub his poor head and fantasize about having a taller roof.

And while he was at it, he put a whole lot of thought and effort into making various improvements to not only the Stark family distillery and barn for their livestock, but to their home, the big old family ranch house, which was soon to be his and Lilly's home.

Mama was content—and had made it known to him early on—that she wished to live on her own down by the river in the old family camp. It was but a couple of minutes' walk from the house and barns proper, anyway.

But she had insisted that she wasn't going to be "one of those pesky old women who tells her daughter-in-law what to do all the time!" And she had raised a finger to Jed's nose in case he was tempted to say what was on both their minds—she already was that pesky old woman. But he appreciated her intentions and would honor them.

It helped ease his mind on the matter that the family camp, over the years, had become more of a small year-round home than a drafty getaway.

Had the main house not burned, he would be far more reluctant to make any changes to it, even to suit Lil's wishes. He would have, of course, but it had been his home, after all, the place he'd hung his hat his entire life. And Mama's before that.

It had been built by Grandpappy Stark, the same man who settled the place and who brought with him the knowledge to make what a whole lot of folks, not just the Starks, called simply, the best whiskey they'd ever tasted.

Granted, that opinion was offered by folks who lived within a day or two from Glen Rose, but over the years, word had leaked out in an ever-wider area, and for many, many years now, decades in fact, the Starks had not had to do much at all in the way of drumming up business.

They had more than they could handle, and regularly turned down inquiries from folks who were opening saloons and fine dining establishments from as far as Finchley.

They turned them down not because they didn't like the folks, but because the Starks had, from the start, realized that the only way to keep something pure and of the highest quality was to keep the offerings to a strict minimum. This kept the task pleasurable and not something that, over the years, he would grow to despise.

It also meant that Jed didn't have to hire anybody from outside the family to help him. Mostly because he didn't want help.

Mama had turned over the entire whiskey-making affair to Jed years before and had only stepped back into the role when he had gone off to fight in that foolish mess of a war. In the end, he had been gone far longer than he had wanted or thought he might. Three and more years of his life had been ripped from him. At least that's how he still felt about it.

He knew lots of other folks chose to look at their time in the war as largely years well spent, if not wholly enjoyed. But in Jed's experience, such men who glorified war and fighting and violence were the ones who had not had to spend their time in the thick of the brutality of it. But he'd come back from it, and tending the still had been a longed-for and soothing relief.

To hear Mama say it, Stark's Whiskey Woods whiskey was certainly the finest whiskey in the greater Glen Rose region, a place long established as the heart of whiskey making. But, Mama would argue, Stark's Whiskey Woods whiskey was the best, the absolute best, whiskey ever made in the history of whiskey making, and thus the best in all the world.

It had long been a source of amusement to Jed, who, whenever this topic reared its odd head, would mention that perhaps those Scottish whisky makers might well have something to say about such a proclamation.

"Bah!" he'd always spit. "Those gobbledygook-talking Scots, what do they know?"

But that was all thinking from the past. Now here he was, up to his neck in grease and grime and soot and with more chores than five men should have, and from the looks and sound of him, Redeye the old hound was telling him that a stranger was soon to be in their midst.

Jed straightened up and tugged an already begrimed rag from a hook on the nearest support post. As he wiped his hands, he angled over toward the open face of the new whiskey shed. It was a corker, and he couldn't help admiring it as he worked in it. The smell of freshly milled timber still wafted in the air, and he pulled in a nose full.

"What's got you all worked up, eh, boy?"

The hound twitched his near ear to let Jed know he'd heard him, but otherwise kept his gaze steady on up the long lane leading toward the place. He also kept his growl long and low. Jed hadn't felt any urgency, knowing the tone of the dog's throaty noises.

When it escalated to a higher pitch and louder volume, he knew the dog was then seeing something approaching.

But Jed also knew that all of this activity, significant for Redeye, plus the fact that the dog was slowly pushing himself up to a sitting position, was remarkable for a dog who spent the majority of his days and nights sprawled as if clubbed in the head with a mallet.

"My word, Redeye, you are getting riled. I guess that means I had better take your warning seriously, eh?"

Following the mess of last year, Jed Stark had once more sworn off having guns in his life, save for making meat. Anybody who kept them around for other purposes must surely have their reasons, and he wasn't about to think for other folks. Some of them felt the need for protection, and chose to do that with a gun. Fine by him, live and let live, but he wasn't much interested in having a gun in plain sight about the place any more than he had to.

The odds of the foolishness of a Merlin Sheldrake type of

situation descending on all their lives again were so minuscule that Jed felt good and safe with nothing nearby but hand tools—axes, hammers, tongs, a hatchet, and a bucksaw.

And he wanted nothing on his person but his big old hip knife and his folding Barlow in his pocket. They each served him well several times a day, and unless he was attacked by a rogue lion or deranged bullock wandering free from a local ranch, he reckoned he was plenty protected.

He'd seen his share of death in the war, more than any man ought to, in his estimation. And he'd caused the demise of men, too. It was bad enough to have to take a fellow creature's life for food.

It was a thing he always felt sorry for, watching that same treasured thing he had within himself, life's light, pinch out in the eyes of a deer, a rabbit, a chicken, didn't much matter. He always figured that each of those beasts valued its life as much as he did his own.

Oddly enough, it was Mama who'd taught him that, and he'd grown up learning to be grateful for so much in his life rather than to take it all for granted, as if humans had some sort of dominion over the rest of life.

No matter what the thumpers said, he did not think that was true. Let others have their beliefs, but he had been through war. He had been told it was all right to kill on one day and then that it was illegal and he would be punished the next. Why, that sort of fickleness, he reckoned, was what led humans to all manner of heartache, misery, and woe.

All that and more flitted through Jed's mind as he gazed up the roadway, visoring his eyes.

The sun was blazing, and he realized he needed to fetch his hat, the old felt beater he wore while working in the whiskey shed. It was more stains and holes than hat, as Mama was wont to say. But she also knew that Jed would never give it up, and she was pleased to know it. Because the hat had been her father's whiskey-making hat. She'd worn it when she was the family's chief whiskey maker, and then she had passed it to Jed when he assumed the role.

By then, it was more of a floppy, barely shaped thing to wear on your head, but there was something about it. Oddly enough, it had escaped burning that day of the big fire because Jed had worn it out to the spring to check on the flow earlier that day, and he'd taken it off to run a couple of palms full of water over his face.

Uncharacteristically, he'd left the hat behind, dangling off the nub of a branch where he always hung his hat whenever he was at the spring, checking it and clearing away debris and slaking his thirst.

"It's a sign!" Minnie Stark had said after the fire when he brought it back and showed her. "Sure as I'm a crotchety old woman, it's a sign that you can't keep a Stark down!"

Jed didn't normally buy into such things as signs and belief in things he couldn't rest a hand on, but at that moment, and seeing how happy Mama had been, he held his tongue and even nodded in agreement. "Might well be," he'd said.

"Might! Might? Bah, boy, it's a sign!"

And so he had left it at that.

And now he ducked back into the whiskey shed to retrieve the hat from its peg. As he reemerged from the shed, he saw Mama tromping across the yard, cradling her favored weapon, her father's single-barrel shotgun that she had inherited and had long ago named "Ol' Shredder."

As she walked up, she nodded at Jed, then toward the dog. "Heard him growling and figured that with any critter as lazy as this to get worked up, there might well be something to it."

"Yep," said Jed. "Same here."

They both looked up the long lane that led, after a long fashion, roughly a half mile, to the primary roadway connecting Glen Rose with its nearest neighboring burg of any size, Grindle, to the east.

"You hear anything?" she said, cocking an ear.

Jed did the same. "No, nor can I see anything." But they both had long known that a dog's hearing and sense of smell were so much more powerful than a person's that they would do well to keep quiet and pay attention to the dog.

"Deliveries all set?" said Mama, knowing before she asked it what the answer would be. Jed Stark had never missed his weekly delivery of whiskey to the handful of local saloons.

"Yep," said Jed.

Another long moment passed, then Minnie said, "Can't be Lilly. This dog dotes on her more than he does me!"

"Naw, it's not Lil," said Jed, wishing it was. He could use a look at her pretty face just about then. It had been a long, hot day, and it wasn't done yet, not by a long chalk.

"Loudon?" said Minnie. Then just as quickly, she shook her head. "Nah, Redeye here, he likes him just fine, too. I reckon it's because he knows a fellow lazy critter when he sees one."

"Mama," said Jed. "Loud's a good man."

"Sure he is! I ain't saying otherwise. But you have to admit he isn't starting any fires as he moves through his days, now, is he?"

Jed smirked and shook his head.

At that moment, Redeye rose to all four feet and took one, two steps forward until he stood, tense and lock-legged, between the two Starks.

"Will you look at that," said Minnie. "Dog's not careful, he might expire from all the excitement."

"There," said Jed, squinting and nodding up the road. "I see something. Coming closer, but slow, sure is slow."

All three of them, the whiskey man, his mother, and his dog, stood watching the lane as whatever it was, whoever it was, advanced at a tortoise's pace toward them.

"What do you reckon?" said Minnie, shielding her eyes and leaning forward, as if that might somehow help her sight.

A few long moments passed, then Jed said, "I do believe it's a buggy of some sort. Single horse, can't tell how many are in it. But it is moving some slow, and not like you'd expect, at least not in a straight line. Odd, that."

"You don't think somebody's in there but has somehow come to harm, do you?"

It was Minnie who asked this, but Jed, too, had been thinking that same thought. "I don't know, Mama, but I think I should investigate. Nobody moves that slow."

"Except for Loudon and this here dog," she said.

"True." Jed strode forward, and had walked perhaps fifty feet when the buggy seemed to smarten up and began proceeding toward them, but this time keeping to the center of the lane and advancing at a closer to normal speed.

Jed slowed, laid a hand atop the handle of his big hip knife. He kept his eyes on the slowly advancing rig. Now he made out that it was steered by one person, a man in a light-colored suit, if he was seeing things right. Light-colored hat, perhaps straw. He didn't see anyone else in the buggy besides the man.

Jed walked back toward Mama, keeping one eye on the odd new visitor's approach. He resumed his place, stood with his feet slightly apart, and his big, begrimed hands on his hips.

With his left, he untied the rawhide keeper holding the knife in its sheath. He didn't want to think of violence, but the Sheldrake episode of last year had made him jumpier than he would have liked to live.

"Well?" said Minnie.

"Looks to be a man, didn't see anyone else in there. A buggy, two-wheeled, single-horse. Man's wearing a light-colored suit and a light hat, maybe of straw."

"Well, that ain't much to go on," said Minnie.

"You could always ask the dog," said Jed, but with a tinge of humor in his voice.

"Bah," said Minnie. "Here he comes now."

The buggy clopped down the last swell before reaching the outer edges of the ranchyard proper. The lower half of the horse slipped from sight, as did the bottom half of the buggy.

Jed kept a sharp eye on the man, who he now saw looked to be perhaps middle-aged, trim, white of skin, and smiling and staring straight at him and Mama.

Redeye kept on growling, a low, steady rumble, and stood stiff on all fours, tense and ready to do what needed doing, whatever the situation might require. Whenever Jed or Minnie should call on him, they knew he would spring into action.

The man was rolling toward them at what Jed figured was a considerate pace, and he hoped it was because the fellow did not wish to kick up dust. There didn't feel to be a breeze, but the momentum of the buggy would carry some slight cloud of road dust toward them. If that was indeed the stranger's intent, Jed appreciated the gesture.

Beside him, Minnie thumbed back the hammer to half cock and transferred Ol' Shredder from one cradled position to a less comfortable but more immediately useful hold. From there, she need only heft it aloft six, eight inches, finish off the hammer, and dole out a dose of peppering pain.

The fellow angled to his left, roughly broadside to them, and eased the sauntering horse to a stop. "Whoa, whoa there."

He set the brake, loosely knotted the lines, and laid them over the brake's handle.

"Good day to you fine folks," he said through as wide a smile as Jed had ever seen on a man's face.

"English," said Minnie loud enough for Jed to hear. She growled low down in her own throat, matching the dog's sound for a moment or two.

"Yep," said Jed, eyeing the man. To him, he said, "Hello. Can I do something for you?"

The man's smile seemed to bloom as his eyebrows rose. "Perhaps, perhaps. Or perhaps it might well be the other way around!" He seemed to find this amusing, for he offered a soft chuckle that dwindled as he took in the two non-smiling folks on the ground before him.

"May I step down, then?" The man's wide smile did not slip as he said this. If anything, it widened.

"Why?" said Minnie.

"Mama," said Jed in a lowered voice. No sense in digging at the man before they found out what he wanted. Might well be there to do them a favor. "Light down, then," said Jed, hoping he sounded more welcoming than his mother.

For a generally kindly person, she could certainly be a surly old thing at times, generally if she felt prodded somehow.

"Thank you," said the stranger, stepping down out of the buggy.

Jed pasted on a slight smile and gave the man a once-over. He appeared to be about in his early thirties, in decent trim, perhaps the same size as Jed, that is to say, a pinch north of six feet tall, and fit.

The man's hair was light colored, sandy in tone, short, well-groomed, and he wore no facial hair. His suit was also a light-colored thing, topping a white shirt with a tall collar and a bow tie. Atop his head, the man wore a light, short-brim hat with a cleft in the crown. A rancher's hat, Jed had heard them called.

But the man did not look to be a rancher. More like a back-East banker or some such. He also wore a false smile that did not share intention with his eyes. One of the things Mama had told him many years before, when Jed was a boy, was to look for smiling eyes when meeting someone. If their eyes don't rhyme with their mouths, then you have a false person in front of you.

It was a simplistic way of assessing someone, to be sure, but Jed had to admit that over the years it had proven to be a surprisingly effective way of judging a person. At least on initially meeting them.

Now, Jed had to admit that part of the man's odd look might well be because Redeye was still in full throat-growl mode, albeit with his big toothy mouth closed. The dog, Jed thought, somehow knew he appeared even more menacing that way.

On top of that, Mama stood there, no bigger than a minute, but holding Ol' Shredder, her deadly single-barrel shotgun, its business-minded snout aimed right about at the stranger's crotch.

"Please allow me to introduce myself." The stranger extended his left hand. "My name is Majors. Dalton Majors."

"That's all fine and dandy, Mr. Majors," said Mama before Jed could interrupt her. "But again I say, why? Why are you here?"

The stranger smiled, canting his head to one side as if she were an addled child. "Why, ma'am, I am here to make you wealthier than you can possibly imagine!"

His smile, Jed noted, looked to be even more false. And then the meaning of the man's words drizzled in on his work-weary mind. Jed felt his eyebrows rise. He looked at Mama, who looked as wide-eyed as he felt. Before either of them could reply, the man spoke again.

"I can see by the looks on your two faces that you are both astonished by my offer!"

"Hush now, stranger!" snapped Mama. She glanced at Jed. "You thinking what I'm thinking?"

Jed shifted his glance briefly to Mama and then right back at the newcomer standing before them, the stranger's brows beginning to draw close in puzzlement.

"If you're thinking 'here we go again,' then yep," said Jed.

"That's about it, yeah," she said.

"Now look, stranger," said Jed.

"Dalton, please," said the man, extending his hand again and taking a step forward toward Jed.

Redeye's growl increased in volume and lowered in pitch to a menacing level. His lips rose high, whiskers twitching, to reveal wet, yellowed teeth. The dog's eyes did not blink. They were narrowed and unwavering as they remained fixed on Majors's face.

The old hound stepped forward with one paw. As he set it down, Jed said, "Easy, Redeye," and the dog held that pose, his scarred, short-haired coat pulsing and rippling with the tensed muscles beneath.

It was as if he was silently begging Jed to let him continue the move, which Jed knew would be a hard and fast leap straight at the man's starched white collar. A collar that would soon be red.

"Mister," said Jed. "Put that hand down slow and easy and step back even slower and easier."

The man swallowed and gulped in silence, his smile all but faded, his eyebrows high. He almost nodded agreement with Jed but appeared to think better of it, not willing to risk any further unpredictable movement. He did as Jed bade him and eased back to his former spot, his hands held near his waist, fingers slightly cupped and trembling.

"Good," said Jed. "Now, I speak on behalf of me and Mama and all the other Starks hereabouts"—he motioned with his head to the sides and back and front, without taking his eyes from the man's, as if they were at that moment surround by dozens of folks—"who are all weaponed up and not inclined to listen to foofaraw, that we are none of us interested in anything you are here to peddle. Now, you'll consider this if you are as smart a fellow as you think you are . . ."

At this Majors's eyes narrowed and Jed knew the man understood he'd been insulted. Jed could not help it. Back door digs, he thought of them as. But he only doled them out to folks who had gone too far down the road of annoyance with him. And this Dalton Majors was a prime example.

Minnie spoke to Jed but kept her little hawk eyes on their uninvited guest. "I'll give him this, Jed. This dandy man don't give up on a thing."

"That's right," said Majors, licking his lips, his eyes widening with his smile. "That's right, ma'am. I . . . I don't give up on a thing! Precisely because there is no way you can lose on this proposition. Please just hear me out. And then I'll leave you in peace to discuss the matter, that much I promise. Now—"

Jed held up a silencing hand and sighed. "Mister, we've been through all this before. Not with you but with someone, in tone and intent anyway, who might well have been your twin. Some fancy man shows up in his little dandy buggy, promising the moon, the sun, and the stars, and it ended the same way. . . ."

Jed didn't feel inclined to dwell on nor go into for the benefit of this ignorant stranger the events of the year before. "With us saying no, no, and no. Now, if you'll take your leave without saying another word, I won't turn the dog or Mama on you. That much I promise."

The man opened his mouth to speak, but Jed raised a long, work-begrimed finger and canted his head. The move shut the man's mouth.

Majors eyed the three of them—man, dog, and woman, then swallowed once more and nodded slightly. At the last moment, he pulled in a breath, mouth open, and looked yet again as if he were about to speak.

"Dog or Mama, which first?" said Jed.

The man shut his mouth, backed the few feet to the buggy, and with surprising speed climbed into the seat.

He glanced once more at them, his face still wearing a look of shock and confusion, as he wheeled and steered the buggy around to make his way back up the lane he rode down not but a few minutes before.

As they watched him make a speedy little departure, Minnie said, "What was that business about all the other Starks?" She was grinning as she said it. "Didn't raise you to be a fibber, did I?"

"No, ma'am," said Jed, eyeing the dust that mostly hid the retreating buggy. "Not much of a lie. Seeing as how your folks are buried here, and then there's you and me, the chickens, the turkeys and geese, the cattle, the mules, the horses. . . ."

"Aren't you forgetting Lilly and your young'uns?"

Jed's eyebrows rose. "Haven't even gotten married yet, Mama."

"Oh, you will." She wagged Ol' Shredder for emphasis. "You will. And then you and Lilly had best get to work filling that fancy new house you built."

Jed pulled in a big breath and let it out again. "Yep," he said.

They were silent a moment longer, then Minnie said, "I reckon I'll just dose him with a little pepper for his backside, eh, Jed? One squeeze is all it'd take. If I angle up a bit, it'd still reach him."

"Mama, no. For all we know, the man's ignorant of the past doings around here and just looking to buy himself a choice ranch. At the very least, it shows he's got good taste."

Minnie sighed and spat. "I reckon," she said, snarling and grumbling as she turned to make for the steps of the newly rebuilt Stark family home. She still hadn't taken to living in it, instead preferring to spend her time at the camp. But she did use the new house's kitchen to fix vittles for Jed.

"Come on, dog," she said. "We can complain together while I finish mixing these muffins. Might be, I could scare up an egg for you. We can talk about how empty this new house is. And how much fun you'd have with a passel of bairns hanging off your lazy hide."

As if he understood every word the somber little old lady

had said, Redeye turned and ambled behind her, loose-limbed and with a hanging head, looking as though he had just run five miles without cease.

Nearly to the steps, they both turned to look longingly back up the lane toward the retreating dust cloud that had been their source of expected sport for the afternoon.

Jed grinned a tired grin and walked back to the whiskey still, determined to finish cleaning and refitting the thing before he quit for the day.

CHAPTER 4

Dalton Majors set the brake, looped the lines, then sat in the buggy seat a moment and surveyed the scene before him. What he saw was a sad mess, but nonetheless promising.

Especially after the frightening encounter at the Stark ranch, which he learned was called Whiskey Woods because of the Stark family's proclivity for distilling some sort of moonshine on the premises.

But this place, the Englishman thought as he looked about himself, this is little more than the smoking wreckage of a life gone wrong. He smiled. This one would be easy. And perhaps he could save Mona Starret a little money in the bargain. Not that she seemed to care about such things. Money to her was a piffling concern.

Dalton giggled as he climbed down from the buggy and approached the house.

The porch was a leaning affair, one of the uprights appeared to have been knocked to one side. The base was now barely touching the earth. He saw a stack of flat stones, which he assumed was the original base for the post. Behind it sat the porch floor itself, an equally sad affair that looked to have been stomped by a heavy giant in several places where planking was snapped and holes gaped.

The roof of the house, low and shingled with a scatter of gappy shakes, didn't look as if it would do much to deter rain, not that a whole lot of it fell in the region anyway. Certainly not like in Old Britannia, where it rained just about every day, it seemed.

As he looked about the place, then advanced toward the house, Majors heard a squeak ahead. From the shadows beneath the sagged porch roof, an angle of deeper shadow widened.

"What d'you want?" barked the voice, a grating thing, as if the man had just awakened and had yet to clear his throat.

Majors held up his gloved hands raised to chest height, palms out, to show he was no threat. This was always the most unnerving part of his job. But if he didn't wade in at some point on each visit, then what was the point in pursuing a goal in life?

"Mr. Chiswick?"

"Who's asking?"

"Mr. Lawrence Chiswick?"

The voice sighed. "Said . . . who's doing the asking?"

"I am, sir. Dalton Majors, here on behalf of my employer."

"Who's that, then?"

"Ah, that person by request has asked for the time being to remain anonymous."

The door squeaked open wider. Within the lightening shadow of the widening gap in the doorway, Majors spied a thick, bearded face atop a tallish fellow who looked to have once had a decent physique but had let himself go to seed. The man coughed, brought up whatever was in his throat, and spat it on the dusty porch puncheons before him.

Majors suppressed a grimace and kept his smile pasted on.

"Anonymous usually means a body has something to hide."

"That can be a wise rule of thumb, but I will say in this case, the opposite is true. It is because my employer is being so, shall we say, *generous*, that I am sworn to protect this person's identity."

"I don't really care one way or the other. What is it you want, mister?"

Majors cleared his throat. "In short, sir, I am here to make you an offer I suspect you will have a difficult time in refusing."

The door opened wider. "I will be the judge of that, mister. Keep your hands up and come on in if you care to. I ain't got nothing left to hide." With that, the man turned and disappeared inside.

Majors pulled in a deep breath, in part because he did not know what to expect and in part because if his guess were correct, it would be musty and smelly in the man's hovel.

Once inside, he let his eyes adjust to the dimmer light. The surroundings were a clutter of items—a clot of two broken chairs piled atop one another, their caned seats shredded and many of their legs snapped.

A picture frame with no picture hung at an angle on the far wall, between two smudged, gunk-clouded windows, the glass panes in each surprisingly intact. The resident had turned and was about to assume a sitting position in a leaning, torn, maroon wingback chair. Horsehair stuffing bloomed from its armrests and seat and back as if it had been savaged by angry cats.

He dropped into it and dust clouded up from it.

"Have yourself a seat, mister," said Chiswick. Or who Majors assumed was the man he'd come to see. All aspects thus far of the man, as described by the various folks he'd discussed the former marshal with, seemed to be on full, unabashed display.

Majors looked about himself, saw a wooden chair off to his left that appeared to still have four legs somewhat the same length, and a seat that had been planked over instead of thrown in the pile of chairs across the room.

Majors sat on the edge of the chair, his hands still held up by his armpits. "You are Lawrence Chiswick?"

The man shrugged, then barked a raw laugh. "Who else did you expect to find in this rathole, anyway?"

"I'll take that as a yes, then."

Chiswick sighed. "Yes, yes, that's me. Now what do you want of me?"

"I want," said Majors, leaning forward, his hands still held up. "May I lower these, please?"

Again, the rough man chuckled. "Sure, yeah. Just don't shoot me. Been a long day already. I don't need to die on top of it all." He leaned back in his chair and closed his eyes a moment. "Or maybe I do. I don't know." He opened his eyes. "I'd offer you a drink, but I'm fresh out." He leaned forward. "Say, you don't have any on you, do you?"

"A flask, you mean, Mr. Chiswick?"

"Sure, yeah!" The man's eyes widened.

"No, I am afraid I am not in the habit of carrying liquor on my person."

"Oh, too bad," said Chiswick, leaning back once more.

"However," Majors held up a finger. "If you could round up a couple of glasses"—he looked around himself—"preferably clean, then I am in the position to remedy the situation. I happen to have a bottle of whiskey in my buggy."

"Say it's true!" said Chiswick with a giggle. He popped up from his seat, eyes wide once again. "Go fetch it and I'll do the same with glasses. Clean, sure, yeah, clean."

He chuckled as he walked across the room and entered another room off to one side. Majors presumed that was the kitchen.

He took his leave and returned within a minute bearing a leather-wrapped box with a strap lid and buckles. It was roughly bottle length and rectangular. He sat once more, with the box on his lap. By that time, Chiswick had returned, holding two mismatched, cloudy-looking glasses.

Majors regarded the glasses briefly, then unbuckled the leather box. He figured the whiskey would kill any germs the glasses might harbor. He didn't really fancy a drink himself, but he knew it would be inhospitable for him to not sip with the man.

He began to pour out the drinks into the glasses the man held out before him with shaking hands. Chiswick made no effort to control them, and when the first was poured, Majors switched to the second.

Chiswick upended the first glass and swallowed back the contents in a single gulp. Then he held out the glass again and breathed out a shallow blast of fumes as his eyes watered. He was smiling.

"Mr. Chiswick," said Dalton Majors, tipping a smaller amount into the man's glass, then drawing the bottle back to himself. He accepted the second glass, albeit with a pinch of resistance from Chiswick's grimy, gripping fingertips. "That whiskey is not easily procured in the United States."

"Rare is it?" said Chiswick, barely taking longer with his second drink. "Mind if I look at the label?"

Majors raised the bottle, then brought it back to his lap. "I think we should discuss terms first, don't you, Mr. Chiswick? Now, please trust me. Have a seat and then once you have heard what I have to say, terms I am confident you will find most agreeable, we can resume our celebratory drinking, no?"

Chiswick's eyes never left the bottle, stoppered and standing upright on Major's right thigh, the neck gripped firmly in the Englishman's hand. Chiswick backed up and sat down in his chair. Then, with effort, he looked up at the stranger in his house. "Uh, sure, sure, whatever you want to tell me, I'm here, I'm listening."

Majors smiled and nodded. "Good, good. Now, a few preliminary questions, if you don't mind. Is this your home? In other words, do you own it? The house, the outbuildings, the land?"

"This place? Yeah, yeah, I grew up here. Been in my family for a while now. That all you want to know?"

"Not quite, but it is a promising start. Now, as I mentioned, I am in the employ of a certain person who is interested in procuring ranches in the region. Specifically, this person is interested in land. Much land, in fact, in order to help establish a sizable cattle ranch."

"You buying today, then?"

"Well, in a manner of speaking, yes, I am," said Majors. "I don't have the full cash on my person, if that's what you're asking. However, I do have a copy of your deed with me. Oh, and the details of your loan against the property."

Chiswick's breath halted in his throat, and the smelly, dim, little room was silent a moment as he stared at this stranger, who looked back at him with a calmness that the wreck of a former marshal found unnerving.

"Just how much do you know about me, anyway?" said Chiswick.

Majors smiled. "Oh, you would be surprised what information I can manage to unearth about people."

"Not sure I like you sniffing around my life."

"With all respect due to you, of course, Marshal Chiswick, but you don't have much say in the matter. By that I mean the information I dig up is used purely to base business decisions on, and it is available to most folks with an urge to know something."

Chiswick kept staring at the man through narrowed eyes. Finally he grunted and knocked back the rest of his whiskey. Then he looked with what appeared to Majors to be genuine sadness at the empty glass in his hand. As he gazed at it, he said, "Ain't a lawman anymore. Surprised you don't know that, Mister Knows-Everything."

Still smiling, Majors said, "Ah, yes, well, I actually did know that, but apparently it slipped from my mind. I stand corrected."

"About that loan against the ranch."

"Yes," said Majors. "The one you have had difficulty in paying for some many months now, yes?"

Another awkward silence followed, then Chiswick said, "Yeah, well, that's my business, ain't it?"

"Actually, if we come to terms, it becomes my business."

"You keep talking about terms and such. What are you on about, anyway? Take a long time to get around to the meat of the matter. All Englishmen that way?"

Majors smiled. "No, well, I don't know, to be honest," he chuckled. "I don't know them all. But I will tell you that should we strike a deal"—Majors held a hand up to silence Chiswick, who looked to be pulling in a breath to speak—"I will explain what I want in a moment, but should we come to an agreement, your loan will be wiped clean, and you will be paid full market value for the property you own."

"How does that work, then?" said Chiswick, showing interest once more in the conversation.

"It works," said Majors, "precisely because my employer will soon become sole owner of the Glen Rose Bank, which incidentally is the office you have your loan through, no?"

"Right. Well, it sounds like I can't lose."

"That's exactly it, yes,"

"My father, he wasn't much for kindnesses, but he was a worker. Sometimes he told me things that I recall. One is to never trust a deal that sounds too good to be true."

"Wise man," said Majors, nodding.

"Yeah, well, sometimes even a blind dog will sniff onto a rabbit track."

"But I should say that while this deal does sound quite lovely, on the face of it, it is not a one-way situation. We expect something in return for what could be a rather generous offer."

"Now we're getting to it," said Chiswick. He leaned forward. "Before you go on," he waggled the empty glass in the air between them. "What say you help me out here, huh? All this talking is hard work."

Major nodded. "Certainly." He poured more whiskey into the man's glass. Not as much as before, however, as he did not want to impede the fine points of their discussion.

"Now," said Chiswick, leaning back in his chair as if he were a king granting a subject a private audience. "Let's hear it." He hoisted the fresh drink and gave it an indulgent swig. His face began to glow pink, as if life had been breathed back into a corpse.

His closed eyes and slight smile told the man seated before him, Dalton Majors, a whole lot. As if the rest of Chiswick's surroundings and appearance hadn't already filled him in on the man's plight.

The former marshal of Glen Rose was a genuine, double-barrel soak, as Dalton had heard one of those crude Yanks describe a dedicated boozer in a bar room back East. But that was before he'd had the pleasure of meeting Miss Starret and becoming . . . respectable once more.

The moment of silence was broken as Chiswick popped his eyes open and said, "So, what'd you have in mind, then, Mr. Majors?"

"What I have in mind all depends on if we are able to come to solid agreement on the purchase of your fine property here." Majors waved a hand at the hovel in which he sat. He recognized that at one time the home was likely just that, a home, well-appointed and tidy, as women were wont to make an abode for their families.

But as it stood now, the place was as he initially suspected, as he rode up—a dump, inside and out. And as such, he had suspected the state of the man who was said to dwell within would be much the same, perhaps worse.

In his experience, people who, for whatever their reason, had given up on taking care of themselves could certainly be counted on to have abandoned any obligation they felt to tending their families, their homes, their businesses, their livestock, all of it. This also made them ideal candidates, mused Majors on his way out there, for plucking by way of a cash offer.

He knew what they wished for, what they wanted to happen, expected to happen—that somehow, magically perhaps, this new bulging coin purse would give them the fresh start they needed. He knew they pined for this. He also knew that it never worked that way. Left to themselves, they would continue their old, slovenly ways, but with more vigor, fueled by new cash.

He smiled at the thought. People were the same the world over, for he had seen this elsewhere in his travels, notably in his youth in travels on the Continent and throughout England, too.

In his current situation, it was a good thing, he suspected, that this truism was in place, that people were predictable, for it made his job easier.

There were holdouts, of course, people who could not be tempted by increasing amounts of money. In their situations, he found he had to raise the stakes by way of pressure in the form of threats, lies, subtle blackmail.

Dalton Majors knew himself well, and he considered one of his strengths, perhaps his mightiest, was that he was honest with himself.

Could he live with himself knowing he had sacrificed some poor, ignorant fool's happiness for his own betterment? Yes, yes, he could. Because through it all, he kept a twin vision blazing bright in his mind: the pretty face of Mona Starret, and her vast, deep wealth. And if he could but stay true to his course, which meant her directives, then Dalton Majors knew in the very pinpoint core of his heart that he would be her husband and thus would have for the taking, for the reveling in, both aspects of that vision.

But as he sat there in the run-down hovel of a ranch home about him, with the bloated, leering face of Chiswick before him, Majors knew he had a whole lot of work to do before he became Mona Starret's husband.

"Very well," said Majors. "I have been authorized to purchase various local properties on my employer's behalf."

"Who, it seems, is too weak-kneed to do it himself." Chiswick offered a sly smile, clearly feeling confident, thanks to the liquor warming his veins.

For the first time since he arrived, Majors's smile slipped away, descending into a frown. "Perhaps I misjudged you, Mr. Chiswick. I assumed you were a man willing to deal with me on a certain level, one of civility."

"I am, I am! Don't let your manners get all knotted up. I didn't mean a thing by it."

"Nonetheless, Mr. Chiswick, once you hear what it is I am after from you, you will see that comments such as the one you made about my employer are wholly inappropriate and will not be tolerated."

Chiswick didn't lose his grin, but shrugged. "Fine. Pay my bills and take the place, I don't much need it now anyway."

"Very well, then," said Majors, smiling once more. "We are, as I indicated, prepared to waive penalties or fees associated with your delinquent loan, and even willing to overlook the loan entirely in favor of paying you a full fee for your ranch. In return, I would like to talk with you about the possibility of you working for me."

Chiswick snorted and sipped, then looked over the glass at the strange Englishman. "You aren't fooling me, then?"

"No, I assure you, Mr. Chiswick, there is a time and a place for tomfoolery in life, but it has no place in business dealings."

"Huh. It's just that, as you can see, I am not what you might call, by any stretch, a fellow who folks want to hire for much of anything these days."

"Nonetheless, I don't make idle offers of any sort."

"Okay, then, so, what is it I'd be doing, if I worked for you, that is?"

"First things first. I would like you to sign a paper I have brought with me indicating your willingness to sell your property to me, and for the amount indicated."

Chiswick looked as if he wanted to hesitate, deliberate, and Majors wanted to talk with other ranchers that day. But most of all, he wanted to get out of this drunkard's close, smelly, little wreck of a house. He leaned forward with the papers in one hand and the whiskey bottle in the other. "And then we should have another drink, don't you think so?"

Chiswick grunted and leaned forward and held out a hand for the papers. "Yeah, let's get on it, then."

He read the paper while the Englishman stood and carried the plank-seated chair he was sitting in over before Chiswick, so that the man might use it as a hard surface on which to write. Chiswick was still at it, squinting at the paper, his lips shaping each silent word he read. He held up his right hand, and Chiswick placed a pen in his hand.

"What's this, then?" said Chiswick, staring at the implement.

"That is a fountain pen."

"But where's the ink?"

"Inside itself."

Chiswick held it up and eyed it. "Huh," he said. "That's something."

He signed, then paused, his hand still resting on the page. "Now, I am playing this game your way, as you see. But what I want to know, before you take this paper, is how do I know you ain't going to just steal the place from me? And when do I get my money?"

"The money will be forthcoming, I assure you. And we would expect you to, of course, stay in residence here for the time being. Until the purchase is formalized and finalized, I have been authorized to advance to you sufficient funds to allow you to live. And perhaps purchase replacement firearms."

"How did you know I sold my guns?"

"Again, my friend," said Majors. "It is my job to find out information. Now, let us seal the deal with a drink and then we shall discuss terms of your employment."

"What is it you want me to do?" said the drunk as he licked his lips and watched as Majors poured a generous amount of whiskey into his glass.

"What I will require of you is this: Soon, after a few more visits, I will be returning for a short time to my employer's offices, back East. But I will return here forthwith.

"In the interim, I find I have need of someone who knows his way around the region, as it were, a former lawman with intimate knowledge of the doings hereabouts, not just in Glen Rose, but also in Grindle and Finchley and Tularetta, for starters. And that seems to be you, Mr. Chiswick."

"Okay. But what will I be doing? You do have a way of talking circles around a thing."

Majors smiled and leaned forward, lowering his voice. "I find I have need of someone who will be here, as it were, in my place while I am away. Someone to, shall we say, persuade the more reluctant landowners to forgo their recalcitrance."

"You mean there are folks who don't want to sell to you and your boss—"

"Which would be *our* boss, should you choose to accept this offer," said Majors.

"Right, okay, then, my boss, your boss, whatever you want to call him. But how much of a strong arm should I show these folks? I got to live here, after all, you know."

Majors leaned back. "That depends on you. I leave that up

to your discretion. That said, I am uninterested, and my, or rather *our*, employer is uninterested in anything, um, how shall I put it? Unlawful that might occur during your own visits to these ranches."

Chiswick smiled. "So if I'm hearing you straight, I can do pretty much whatever I want, or let's say whatever I need to in order to persuade these folks to sell up to you. That about right?"

For a long moment, Majors stared at Chiswick, devoid of expression, and finally said, "Yes, Mr. Chiswick, that is more or less what I am saying." He held up a finger. "No foul play, mind you."

Chiswick kept on with his wry grin. "At least not traceable back to you and this mysterious employer."

Majors nodded once.

"Well, who are the fools on this list of folks who don't want to sell, anyway? I ask so I can get to thinking of how to deal with them, you see."

"Yes, of course," said Major. "Well, I guess it wouldn't hurt to mention a few of the names. It's a relatively short list, actually. Mostly because our terms have been more than generous with our offers."

"Yep, sure. No complaining here," Chiswick said, taking the bottle from Majors's hand. "If what you offered them compares with how generous you all have been in my situation, well, the way I see it, they deserve a shove in the right direction, if you *comprende* my meaning. They might even thank me later!"

"Yes, well, perhaps a nudge would be more appropriate to begin with. Let's see, as far as these holdouts are concerned, there are a few. Just now, there are three that come to mind. The first is a young family, apparently new to the region, with the name of Brighton. Come to think of it, I have nudged them quite a bit already.

"Then there's an older couple, the Albersons. And that Deke Frakes fellow. Oh, and another, a fellow and his mother. Founders of the town, apparently. I visited them but alas was unable to make my case before they ran me off the place, at gunpoint, no less."

Chiswick said, "Jed Stark and his mother, Minnie."

"That's right! I really shouldn't be surprised that you know to whom I refer," said Majors. "After all, you have lived here your whole life."

"Yep," said Chiswick, sneering as he looked off into the shadowy corner of the far ceiling. "And it don't surprise me none that Stark and his mama are on your short list. There is no way they're going to sell up, I can tell you that right from the start. I know you said something about starting up a cattle ranch, or some such, but as for the Starks, they were founders of Glen Rose, and they're whiskey makers, and everybody loves them."

"And you? How do you feel about the Starks?" said Majors.

"I hate them," barked Chiswick, rising forward a bit in his chair. "Hate everything about them!" He leaned back and pulled on the bottle for comfort while Majors regarded him, suppressing a smile.

"Everything about the Starks rubs me raw." Chiswick's sneer deepened. "Oh, I look forward to convincing him to take your money and move himself and his sweet ol' mama on out of town. But just so you know, it won't work. Never in a hundred years will it work. They ain't going to sell the place."

"I'm afraid that is unacceptable." Majors leaned forward, and when next he spoke, his voice was low, level, and clear. "If we do not purchase the Stark parcel, all the deals are off, everything. Let me reiterate: There will be no deals made for anyone, to anyone. We will have no interest in this region without the Stark place. You will be unemployed, penniless, and living as I found you earlier, here for a time, and then you will be evicted by the bank for lack of payment."

"Hold on now, hold on." Chiswick tapped his fingertips on the bottle's neck and sucked his teeth. "It'll be a tough old sell, sure, but I didn't say impossible. I got ways of making even Jed Stark give in. You wait and see."

"Do they involve the use of weapons?" said Majors.

"You never mind about that! You hire me on to do this here job you have in mind, which I might add is not a small thing, no sir, but if you hire me on to do this . . . *convincing*, let's call it, for you and your high-and-mighty employer, then, man, you got no say as to how I do the job. That clear? Now, no matter what I do or how I do it, that's none of your affair—"

"I must say, Mr. Chiswick, that all sounds fine, however, let me reiterate that there can be no trail that will lead the law to me or to my employer, who, I might add, is not high and mighty."

"Now don't get your knickers knotted, Majors. Ain't going to be no trails leading no one to nowhere, you have my word. And what I can also say is that I can make it all come out as you want to. And that's a promise."

"Well now," said Majors. "Fine, then. That is good to hear, good to hear, Mr. Chiswick. Because—"

Chiswick held up a hand. "Now don't go into all that, threatening to call-it-all-off business again. I said I'd make it work, right? Just give me money and go on your merry way, and it'll all work out. Just like you want it to."

The red-eyed man leaned forward, the bottle still resting atop one thigh, his other hand extended outward, palm up. "But let's make one last thing clear: There ain't a thing going to happen without money. Right here and now, as a good-faith deal, if you understand me, Mr. Dalton Majors."

The Englishman regarded the former lawman before him for a long moment. For the first time in a long, long time, and certainly since he arrived in this part of Texas, on behalf of the most lovely Miss Mona Starret, Dalton Majors felt a ripple up his spine of doubt. And of something else, too. What was that?

Ah yes, something he'd not felt in a long, long time . . . fear. And the feeling became more intense as Lawrence Chiswick nursed the bottle of whiskey again, upending it, glugging back a massive swallow, but not taking his eyes from Majors's face.

Then Chiswick leaned back in his chair, winked, smiled, and barked a coarse laugh. "Looks like we understand each other just fine, Majors. Just fine. Now get to counting out my money."

CHAPTER 5

"There she is," said Jed, smiling and straightening from tending the still. It had been a long ol' morning of getting the thing set up just right. He'd been able to produce batches, and they had all seemed to come out right.

Yet something had gnawed at him about how he built the new still, something he wanted to get just right, because as Mama had told him over and over as a child, because her father and mother had told her the same—anything worth spending your time on was spending it to the full, wisely and with all care.

So his reasoning had been that just because the still had been, if anything, built far bigger and better and stouter and tighter than it had been, did not mean he hadn't somehow overlooked one crucial little element in the process.

Of course, it was a newly built tool and would take time to settle into its role, but he felt there was something that could be, should be better. But no matter how much time he spent using it and thinking about it when he wasn't using it, Jed Stark could come up with no reasoning behind his feeling.

But it was there nonetheless.

"Are you still fussing with the still?" said Lilly, hopping down from the saddle atop her sweet-tempered mare, Poppy.

"You bet," said Jed, walking over to meet Lil halfway across the yard. They embraced and shared a quick smooch before they were met with what they assumed was coming, and they weren't let down: Mama.

"What are you two lovebirds doing out here?" said Mama from the steps of the new ranch house. "As if I didn't know!" She giggled and smacked a wooden spoon against her leg.

"Come on in here and get yourself something to eat. I have tea water on the boil! And a molasses bread I'm trying out. Looks like dirt. I sure hope it tastes better than it looks. I need your thoughts."

"You're not working very hard to convince me it's something I ought to eat, Mama."

"Oh, hush, you big brute!" said the bristling old woman with a sly grin. "You know as well as Lilly and I do that you are going to tuck right into that bread with both hands and then think of how it tastes later!"

She turned to Lilly. "Am I right about that?"

The woman who was to be her daughter-in-law in but a few months' time, grinned. "That is what they tell me about him, yes."

Jed and Lilly smiled at each other and walked to the house, hand in hand, having to skirt Redeye, who was sprawled in the dust smack dab centered at the base of the wide porch steps.

"Who is this 'they' anyway?" said Jed, striding ahead and holding the door open for Lilly.

"Oh," she said, stepping into the house and smiling as she looked about the place. It was to be her home. The home in which she and Jed would finally live together as wife and husband. The home where they would raise their children. She hoped. "Nobody you'd know, Jed. Why, jealous?"

"Yep," he said, winking at her.

Lilly liked how, even after knowing Jed Stark for six years, the man could still make her feel so warm, so special, and all with a mere wink or a word or a gesture. Nobody had ever felt that way to her before.

They weren't wed yet, and for as much as she loved him, and she knew he felt the same about her, Jed Stark was not a man to be pinned down to a thing, at least not without a whole lot of squirming and wriggling and occasional escaping altogether.

Still, the day was bright, the sky was blue, all the troubles of last year seemed to be behind them, and Lilly reminded herself to enjoy the day, the moment, and the fact that she, Lilly Chu, daughter of a Texas ranch woman and a Chinese railroad blasting master, had for years now been welcomed into the Stark family.

The Starks were an institution in these parts as much for their justifiably famed whiskey as for the fact that they, that is to say, Jedidiah Stark and his mother, Minerva Florabelle Stark, were the last of a long line of Starks, at least in this part of the country.

It had been Minnie's father, Hawcliffe Stark, who had roved West by himself from the Stark valley in Tennessee to seek more freedom for himself. He brought the family whiskey recipe with him, in his head, in his bones, and in his hands and eyes.

And he discovered the land he'd stopped on, in Texas, by the Paluxy River, was also rich in something more, a good flowing spring offering up water of such pure and sweet and tasty quality that for a few moments, Hawcliffe had thought perhaps his entire journey west had been but a dream and that he was sipping Tennessee mountain water once more.

But no, the spring was indeed on the land in Texas, and what's more, the spring seemed to be quite ample, able to continue to provide a drink to the wild critters that visited with frequency. It was a small, shaded pool where it emerged from the earth, bubbling and pure. Enough for him to also run a pipe to, say, a whiskey still.

Hawcliffe had thought long and hard about this. On the one hand, he wanted to make whiskey, but there weren't that many folks in these parts, and selling enough of his own whiskey to justify the effort and expense of making large quantities of it was not something he had decided on yet.

Was this even the right land on which to settle? He'd encamped down by the river to explore and rest and think things over and through. Within days, he had seen the soft, rounded imprints of human feet up by the spring seep. He had known, of course, that there were tribes of native folks about, but he had not been molested in the least on his way west. He also knew that this had let him grow sloppy and far too trusting of the fact that everyone was friendly enough.

But on that morning, not but three or four days after he'd stopped on the spot and had slowly begun to consider setting up a home and living there, Hawcliffe had seen those imprints and his concerns solidified and his innards tightened. He'd bent low, his palm had drawn up to rest atop his big pistol hanging at his side.

It turned out that despite that feeling, and then a mounting suspicion that they, whoever "they" were, certainly knew he was there. Hawcliffe had begun to feel as though he was being watched, no matter what he did, and no matter where he went on that riverbank patch he had, without knowing he was doing it, begun to think of as his property.

It had not fully come to him until he'd been there some days that this thing, this place he felt himself growing to covet, was also the home and water source of many, many other beings, critters of the four-legged variety, for certain, as well as birds and bugs far beyond measure.

And then there were those human footprints. They appeared

to have been left by somebody who likely didn't travel a long distance for their water, for he had seen no horse hoofprints on any of his scouting forays into the surrounding region. So that told him there was at least one Indian who was likely watching him.

And maybe it was just the one, and friendly, too. But more than likely, it was a whole tribe. It would be a region he'd settle in if he were an Indian. At least it made sense to him.

And since he had not taken pains to live in a cold camp down by the river, that meant, too, that he was sending out smoke and smells—coffee cooking, bacon crackling and snapping in the pan, and the scents of other meats brought down by the thundering and echoing of his gun's shots.

And then it had come. Late in the day, an attack by a party of warriors. What tribe they were, he did not know at the time. He later found out they were Apache. But in that moment after the first arrow whiskered in to smack quivering, head height, into a tree close by where he had been standing sipping a tin cup of warmed up coffee, in that moment, nothing mattered but staying alive.

He'd dropped low and snatched up his rifle, his canteen, and a saddlebag that held, among other useful items, his spare bullets, and fire-making bits and bobs, and a half dozen hard-as-rock biscuits he'd made days before.

He clambered fast, keeping low, his long legs stepping with caution and yet ease, too, up the long, gentle slope away from the river, deeper into the trees that he had not yet fully explored beyond.

He knew that the land sloped up in that direction, but he did not know how much, or if it was passable or would offer him protection, something to hide behind while he reloaded. Still he had little choice but to flee, because other missiles began parting the air all about him, whistling in left, right, center, from seemingly all directions.

He ran, keeping his tall body bent low and in half, and stepping fast. He made it into the bushes, past a random scatter of trees, and saw that, yes, the land ahead did indeed slope, right up to a raw cliff face. He saw the jags of dark gray rock poking through, showing between long, thick curtains and veils of vines and thick vegetation growth.

He glanced left and right, but saw only more of the same, as the land, by no means impassably steep, led to this, the hill at the top. Still, it was tall enough, perhaps fifty feet, if he had to guess.

At that moment, Hawcliffe Stark didn't much care. He knew this was the best he was going to get, and he rushed to the rock and brambled mess before him, leapt around a boulder, then another, tumble-downs he guessed, from long before. And he looked for a place to back up to, some protected spot from which he might drill lead at his attackers.

He held little hope that he was going to survive this onslaught, for they had him all but cornered, but he had to try. After all, he reminded himself, Starks nor nobody never got anywhere by not trying.

He heard whistles and hoots that could be mistaken for critter and bird calls by someone who was not familiar with forest sounds. But that was not Hawcliffe. He was a backwoodsman, through and through, from his days roving the hills of Tennessee, skirmishing with neighbors and with various bands of Indians who were not keen on being eyed as they made their way west and south.

But through it all, it was the creatures of the burrow, the air, and the woodland pathways that kept him company, and he knew each call of a hawk, jay, crow, finch, and chickadee, each rattle of a thicket branch by a rabbit, the quick flash of a twitch of tiny nose and whiskers, and the glint of small black eyes of a chipmunk and squirrel.

As he roved westward, Hawcliffe, who tried in life to never

be in a hurry, had enjoyed nearly every step of his trek, choosing to walk beside his horse and pack mule much of the way.

There had been so much to see, so many unfamiliar sights, strange plants, and odd bird and critter calls that he had almost been disappointed when he had arrived in Texas and his daily moments of wonder had eased off.

But as different as many of them had seemed to him, they were, for the most part, also quite recognizable.

He had arrived there mere days before, and now he found himself pinned, his back against the coarse jag of rocky cliffside. He made certain he tucked himself as much as possible into the hanging vines and thick mat of brambled vegetation.

Facing outward, with that barest of protection behind him, Stark knew he had mere seconds before the warriors would be on him, right there before him, and no doubt to either side, fanning about him.

He did not doubt that he could and would kill whoever he was able, should it come to that. But that was not what he wanted, never had been. Killing another person only ever brought misery, to yourself, to the dead person, and to that person's friends and family. That said, Hawcliffe knew he would do what he needed to.

And avoiding it did not seem a possibility.

Just then, he saw the tops of one, then two heads appear. He shoved himself back as far as he could go. His right bootheel came up short and hard against what he knew was the solid rock wall behind him.

As he eased his weight onto his left boot, slowly now, for he could be seen, he was certain of it, he felt not the expected resistance of the stone face of the cliffside, but rather his left boot found no resistance. It kept going. Hawcliffe did not understand what that meant, but realized it was something he could explore later, should there be a later.

And then his leg kept moving, back into what he assumed

was the barest of grottos. But it felt wider. How tall was it? he wondered. Tall enough for him to crouch down within and hopefully buy him precious inches so that he might peer through the hanging vegetation and remain somewhat unseen. Unless the attackers looked dead at him, he began to think he might have some success with this seemingly paltry hiding spot.

And then he angled his bent left leg farther to the left, and he found that the recess was wider than he expected it to be, and deeper. How much so, he did not know. Yet.

There was a pause when the advance braves had dropped back a couple of paces and appeared to be discussing something with someone he could not yet see. This might be his only opportunity to duck down and use that little niche he found with his left boot to hide within.

The thought of acting as though he was a coward and could only hunker down and wait for them to either pass him by or discover him and kill him there, squatting and wide-eyed, ground his teeth together hard, but Hawcliffe knew that there were at least twenty men looking for him. He might be able to take down one or two before they got him, but get him, kill him, they would.

No, if he wanted to live a life of his own choosing, it had to begin then and there.

Hawcliffe grabbed the brief moment when he hoped all eyes were not on the cliff face. He dropped down fast to a squat with his left hand groping behind him. With his right shoulder and side, he felt the rock there, but it angled slightly, and the more he groped it in the dark while still keeping his eyes looking outward, he felt that the rock formed a cornice of sorts.

He kept inching backward, and soon knew he was tucked well beneath the viny mat. But then he felt the constraints of rock to either side of him. He paused there and held still, for he heard voices once more, and footsteps approaching the rock face.

Here it comes, he thought. If ever he was going to be spotted, it was right there and then. And surely given the number of men reaching his hiding spot and fanning out to either side, Hawcliffe knew he was in a very poor position to offer protection to himself, but defend he would, should it come to that.

And then he lost his balance and flopped backward. Even as he fell to his backside, his feet untangling and kicking outward, he noted they were still within his seemingly thin gap of safety.

But his head, the thing that had flopped farthest back into the gap, had remained unhindered. With no more thought than that, Hawcliffe shoved himself backward with his bootheels, even as a warrior, then another and another walked by slowly, creeping, eyeing the earth, which, he thought fondly, was all rock chunks and gravel, nothing easy for him to have left a bootprint in.

In the end, Hawcliffe waited and waited for what felt like hours before they finally seemed to give up the close-in quest for him.

Could it really be that easy? he thought. Just sit here in the dark and hide? No, of course not. They were Indian, and Hawcliffe had had enough experience with them throughout his life to know that they never really gave up on a thing. And more than likely, they were encamped close by with lookouts eyeing the entire region about him.

No, he decided. He would stay there for as long as it took for his gut to tell him he could think about crawling on out of there.

Soon enough, he groped in the darkness, not to his right, as he sat with his back to the rock wall. The rock facing him was close enough that his knees touched it. After an hour in this cramping position, he decided he had best try to stand. He was able to, although bent over and only if he kept himself angled sideways.

The outside lay to his left, and he could see daylight through the vegetation. It was waning. Good. He didn't like the idea of leaving his animals and goods unattended, but there was not much he could do about it just then. To his right, in the darkness, the hollow gappy space went on as far as his arm and tapping boot could reach.

The air was not overly stale, and the floor, although a dusty affair, was firm. It felt as if it were hard-packed dirt, which made sense, as any cave he'd ever been in had seemed formed the same way.

It took another hour before Hawcliffe felt ready enough to risk more sound, which he avoided by creeping slowly, hunched down, into the darkness of what he was convinced was definitely some sort of cave.

From what he could tell, there were no animal scents, nothing on the floor save for gravel and packed earth—no bones or hair. And soon enough, too, he realized he needn't hunch over as he progressed slowly into the space. The ceiling arched up, up until it was beyond his fingertips.

The more time he spent in there exploring in the dark—he did not dare risk kindling a flame lest the glow from within be seen from without—the firmer a notion formed in his mind.

This could be a safe place, to be sure, at the very least a spot to retreat to should the attacks continue. And that is just what it became for Hawcliffe Stark.

In fact, he made it his home for quite some time until he was good and certain that he was not going to be molested by any local Indians. The cave had turned out, too, to be an ideal place, as he would discover in later years, to store barrels of whiskey, as it offered the perfect year-round temperature and dryness for letting the whiskey mellow.

And that is just what his daughter and his grandson used the cave for as well, and no one save for Lilly had ever been told of the cave.

* * *

What Hawcliffe could not know that day of the attack was that the warriors rode away, battle-worn but grateful that they had remained alive in a fight with a white demon such as this. They had referred to him as a half-living creature who must not be sought, who must be left alone. No other mortal man could have disappeared as he had, one moment there before them, and the next . . . gone.

This, had Stark known, would have suited him right down to the ground. The last thing he wanted was to fight anybody. But that would be the first thing he would do should it come to it. Particularly since he had, unintentionally, fallen in love with this place, this patch of land.

He fully intended to explore it further and then decide on how much he wanted, how much he needed—which he knew were two different things ("only gluttons and fools don't know the difference, son," his dear old mama had told him long ago). Then he would stake a claim to it. However that worked. He still wasn't certain, nor did he much care.

In his mind, if he resided on it, it was his place, a new spot to call home. He'd not felt that since leaving the family hill farm back in Tennessee. That had been a most painful day, the actual departure from the old Stark homeplace.

It was far more than a mere place, though. It was a home, a beautiful patch of land, a scratched-in and dug-in and whittled-down, downright cozy home. That was as he reckoned it should be for a family that had been there, as his granny used to say, "since Moses was a baby."

But the Fever, a terrible affliction that had swooped down through a handful of valleys in their part of the hills, had laid low nearly all of his family. He'd seen robust uncles and aunts and cousins one by one drop to their knees behind their team in the fields or topple down a hillside hunting up ginseng, never to walk under their own steam again.

It began as an off feeling, then fever came in, then chills and uncontrollable twitching and shaking and sweating. The afflicted had by then taken to their beds, and no amount of broth or herbal remedies, no poultices or teas, made a difference in the least.

Boils rose on their hands, faces, scalps, all over the body, then did the same inside the mouth. They filled with something vile and then burst, leaving a bloody trail that crusted over but did not heal. It went right on oozing and barely forming a lesion.

One by one, Hawcliffe's family, with whom he had shared a life in all its peculiarities, the ups and downs, the good and bad, fell victim to the dreaded Fever. And then, one by one, they all fell away.

He and his papa buried Papa's own parents, then buried Hawcliffe's mama. And then two days later, as they worked together digging up the last of the taters, Papa stood up quick from bending low over a row nearby. His eyes widened and his breath hitched. He locked eyes with Hawcliffe, then coughed and blood spattered his hand.

Papa staggered as if he'd been caught from behind by a swung club. "Son!" he cried, then he stiffened and pitched forward between the half-dug rows of the late-season patch. He lay still, eyes wide and gnawing dirt with his last breath.

Oh, but that had been a raw moment, a time when all the miseries of the previous months had seemed to descend like Death itself, flapping brittle, black wings that fanned no breeze but smothered all.

Hawcliffe barely recalled burying Papa there on the hilltop mound in the all-too-busy family plot overlooking the orchard. He did recall that it had rained that day, and kept on for a week straight. By the end of that week, Hawcliffe had made his decision. Save for a few straggling cousins and such tucked here and there, cousins it had to be said he was not overly fond of to begin with, he would leave that place and seek his fortune elsewhere.

He was young, barely into his twenties, unmarried, and possessed of skills such that he had confidence to survive in the world of his preference—at the periphery of man's inhabitation.

He had his confidence, in the way of an asset, and not much else, certainly not much in the way of worldly goods. He looked about the place, a homestead he had known all his life, and other than tools he could use in hand—Papa's stoutest axe, his own skinning knife, a hammer, a bucksaw, two chisels, and other such odds and ends, there was precious little he felt inclined to bring with him wherever it was he made for.

That part of his decision was still wide open. But he didn't care. For once a Stark decided on a thing, a direction, a path, it was a certainty. All that remained, he thought as he roved about the homestead, was to gather what he could take with him on his horse and atop Bet, the mule. He would not overload the beast, for that would be cruel, but he would need to make a pile of goods and then whittle it down from there.

He did this, gathering items from about the place into the sagged front porch, doing his best to keep from glancing up the hillside, past the orchard, toward the mounded graves of his beloved parents. They were side by side, and snug also beside his little sister, Demelza, who had died at age six of her own singular sickness some years prior.

Without them, he reckoned, life could be an empty thing without hope, yes. But it could also as easily be an empty thing akin to a vessel, waiting to be filled with promise, with hope, with new adventures, and, perhaps, if he found himself lucky enough one day, a life shared with someone he loved, and who loved him back.

All of that seemed so very far away, but while he was alive,

Hawcliffe knew he had to depart from there, and he had to stay away from other people for as long as he could, in case he carried with him unseen baggage in the form of disease, vestiges of the vicious and foul Fever.

Two days later, Hawcliffe Stark departed from the Stark homestead carrying what he felt he needed to carve a new life elsewhere, wherever that hazy land might be. It was a drizzly Tuesday morning, the sun was rising, offering a dour, low, gloomy glow, enough to see the muddy roadway.

He took with him the family Bible with all the names marked down, to which he added, on their own lines of the tree, the full names of his father and mother.

Later, he told himself, at night, he would jot notes about the various relatives he had known back in the holler. But not yet. Thoughts of them, of home, were all too fresh and raw.

He led the two beasts, Punch, the horse, and Bet, the mule, attached with a lead rope and following behind, and they stepped slow and purposefully away from the Stark place.

He reached the last crest in the long, rutted, narrow lane way, a spot he knew from past experience when he would venture up there and sit, gazing out over the world beyond their wee valley, wondering what life beyond the Stark's holler might be like.

That last morning, however, he paused there and thought for a full minute and more. If he turned to look one last time at the old homestead, he might well be far too fragile still to continue. He might make his way back down the muddy track and unpack the beasts, return to the house, and resume life there.

He also knew that if he did that, he would never think of himself in full kindness and pride, for he would always be aware of a burr of disappointment in himself. It would be a disappointment that showed itself like a painful canker, and it would continue to do so more and more as the years passed. It would become a thing of regret and shame and fear and cowardice.

That would not, could not be tolerated. But neither could the cowardice of the moment be tolerated, and so Hawcliffe had turned to gaze down upon the place, and he had had to offer the world a quick snort of bitter laughter and a shake of the head.

The rain, which he appeared to be heading on out of, had seemed to congest over their homestead, the house and barn and coops and sheds and whiskey still. All of it was well draped in the dark, gauzy scrim of gray fog that he saw when he had been living beneath. He pulled in a deep breath through his nose.

"No more," he whispered, and turned his back on the place for the last time. Somebody else can have it, he thought. And best of fortune to them.

He had not tried to sell the place, all eighty acres of it. He had thought it would be something his parents could understand. And if not, then that told him perhaps he did not know them as well as he thought, and that it didn't really matter, for they were dead.

He found himself having conversations with the dead, at least in his head, and when they arced back to where they began, he shook his head and mumbled, "No more, you've done enough," and that is where he would take his leave of them, at least in a debating form of conversation.

He would leave them to it and good riddance. He would not regret this, he told himself. And he wished the next conversations he had with them, his deceased family, to be words of hope and promise.

And that is what he did as he walked on, making his way to where the land told him to stop, guiding him first southward, then angling west. West, it is, then, thought Hawcliffe Stark.

As he walked, he thought about the one thing that had always made the Starks, particularly his household of Stark, different than any other. It was the family whiskey still, far more of a religion to the family than any church, purported to be the most wonderous of its ilk.

And so by the time he reached the vastness of Texas, he had decided without knowing he had done so, that he would resume whiskey making and that one day it would be the thing he did nearly to the exclusion of all else.

What Hawcliffe Stark could not know then was how accomplished at it he would be. Nor how successful and dedicated to the art of whiskey making his grandson would become.

Chapter 6

Lawrence Chiswick watched the English dandy's buggy disappear at a measured, sometimes halting pace on down the lane that led back out to the road to town. It almost looked as if the man was stopping to look around, which, now that Chiswick thought about it, made sense. He was going to buy the place, after all.

He looked about him at his home, the modest ranch house and scatter of barns, loafing sheds, and a chicken coop marking the place he'd grown up and had lived his entire life.

His mother had died when he was but a boy, and his father, Lawrence Senior, had died thankfully a couple of years before last year's mess in town. Thankfully, thought Chiswick, because he didn't have to live through the disgrace that Lawrence had felt when he'd been stripped of his job as marshal of Glen Rose.

He was alone now, had been for years, save for the few times he'd been able to coerce a dance hall girl back to his place for a day or two. Inevitably once the liquor dried up, he and she would sour of each other's company, and they would have a joyless, headache-filled, tooth-rattling ride back to town in his work wagon behind his old nag, Ethel.

The wagon and the horse were long since gone. They had

been the only two items of any value, save for a withered old mule and the land and buildings, that he had left. The ranch itself was mostly owned by the bank once more, and the feeble amount of money they had loaned him against it hadn't been enough to keep him from once more facing ruin and starvation.

He'd had to sell off his double-gun rig and shotgun and rifle, all his good tack, and then he'd worked his way through the chickens, eventually killing and eating even the last of the layers. And then, just this very day, when he had been out of booze for nearly two days, and out of food for twice that long, an angel had arrived, as his old long-dead mama would have put it.

An angel in the form of a dandified Englishman who wanted to offer him a whole lot of cash money for the land and such. Land and buildings that Lawrence did not tell the man were more the bank's than his these days. Didn't have to tell Majors that because the man apparently already knew it. That was annoying, but there it was.

And then, as they had chatted and the man saw Chiswick's plight, he went back out to his buggy and returned with a bottle of fine liquor, not the vile tincture Chiswick had been forced to drink when he could come up with cash.

And Majors had given him the bottle and said he had a thought, a proposition, he'd called it. And that's when it seemed to Lawrence that daylight had flooded on into his foul little home for the first time in a year.

Since that vicious lying braggart Jed Stark had beaten him for no reason, gotten the drop on him right there in front of his people, the very citizens of Glen Rose. Then Stark had worked more of his lying ways and got all those people to rip the badge off his chest and hired that little mama's boy, of all people! His wet-nose deputy as the new town marshal.

Kid was just that, a kid, but hey, Glen Rose deserved what it got. Nothing but misery and poor service and no laws being upheld, that's what, he just bet. He just knew it.

He also knew what folks thought of him now. They didn't have to hide it—he saw it on their faces when he went to town. Didn't even bother to hide what they were thinking anymore. Just came right out with it and stared at him. Some of them, mostly old biddies, they watched him from the safety of the other side of the street and shook their heads, their eyes narrowed as if they were sending witchy curses right on over at him.

It was unnerving and sometimes a little spooky, if only because he didn't believe in such foofaraw. His mama had, and she was forever going on about how there were always witchy womenfolk around. Said they were everywhere in the world, and that he'd do well to know who they were and then stay away from them.

He'd asked her when he was a lad just how he was supposed to know what women were that way, and all he got in response was a clout on the right ear from his pap. Set that ear, that whole side of his head, ringing for a week.

After that, he never did ask about such things again.

But man, he never forgot it. The pap part, whompings and such, for certain. And he never forgot what Mama said, either. The witchy thing was always nested in there, deep in his mind. It would come out now and again when he was a man, full-grown and working as a deputy at first and then as a marshal, after a lot of glad-handing and such, and then help from that fat, rich man, Merlin Sheldrake.

When Chiswick would make his rounds in Glen Rose, he'd often think on what Mama meant when she talked of witches and other spooky notions. Oh, but he missed those days and nights as marshal. He'd stop off for a nip at the Happy House or The Money Tree, then move on, dealing with some drunk or other, showing them a bit of what Pap taught him was how a man had to deal with what he had called "surly others."

To his father, that meant men, and sometimes a woman, who would not do what needed to be done. Maybe they would have too much wine or rum or beer or whiskey and then there would be trouble.

Chiswick admitted to himself sometimes that he prodded folks a bit much, and then there would be a fracas. But most of the time, he reckoned he was the settling force.

He sighed and returned inside the house. He walked across the room, making for the bottle, but stopped and looked about him, suddenly aware that this was the room the stranger, Dalton Majors, had just been in.

Chiswick looked about him at the sagging window, filmed with dust, grime, spiderwebs, dead flies, the cracked panes still hanging in place. The walls at one time bore plaster, at least in what his mother had called the "family room," even though theirs was, in his estimation, not much of a family. Especially after his older sister ran off in the night with a neighboring ranch boy when Lawrence was eleven years old.

Nobody ever heard from her again. He'd thought of her now and again through the years, wondering how she was, where she was, was she even alive, had she become a mother, all of it.

At some point, he discovered what his father had learned for himself as a youth—the early glories of whiskey. Now it wasn't glory so much as it was a big ol' chain wrapped tight around his neck. And it felt like it grew tighter a smidgin with each week that passed.

He saw the plastered walls now, more crumble and hole and lath than smooth plaster, curls of drooping wallpaper sagging here and there or bubbling off, torn in places.

Yet even then, he could still make out, when the day's light angled in just enough through the upper panes of the window, the once-yellow background on which rested tiny white and blue flowers with even tinier green leaves.

He remembered how pleased his mama had been once she'd put it up. Standing right there, he recalled, glancing at the warped brown and scuffed floorboards about two feet to his right. Just there was where his mama had stood, how many years ago?

Lawrence had been a boy of maybe eight or so years old, and she'd rested her big, work-rough, red hands on her wide hips and had smiled as she looked at the walls.

That moment had always stuck in his memory like a dart. He supposed because it had been so rare for her to smile, wide and long like that. Certainly he couldn't recall his pap doing much to cause her to smile.

Yet Chiswick mused as he stood there in the dusty, buckled little hovel of a room, there must have been a time when they had been happy together. Must have been.

He pushed out a breath of finality, as if he had decided something, and shook his head as he picked up the bottle and eyed it. Still a good third of it left. And money in his pocket—"Payment against services to be rendered" was how Majors had put it when he'd laid the cash in Chiswick's palm.

Before the man had let it go, however, he'd looked Chiswick hard in the eye and said, "You understand you will have to be sober some of the time, right?"

Chiswick had returned the stare through his glassy, bloodshot eyes. It had galled him hard, the man's bold comment, but it was the truth, and more than that, Majors knew that Chiswick needed that money bad.

Chiswick had snatched the money from the man's hand even as Majors grinned.

"Yeah, yeah, you'll get what you pay for, Majors. No worries there. Besides, you'll be buying my ranch, that there is another sum that is a separate deal.

"Sure, you know that I am land rich and money poor, and I am a drunk most of the time, to boot. But that don't mean I'm stupid. You play me false, Majors, or your fancy boss, and . . ." Chiswick thumbed through the cash, then stuffed it into a trouser pocket. "Well, we'll just leave it at that for now, won't we?"

Chiswick knocked back another long pull and continued looking about the room, empty now of the stranger whose brief visit had reversed Chiswick's fortunes, perhaps his entire life. However long that was going to be.

The room, Chiswick saw and thought, for the first time in a long time, was a small, broken, dingy thing, just like the rest of his life.

"What a mess," mumbled Chiswick, as he turned to head on out of doors once more. And he stepped out onto the broken, sagging porch, the porch where so many long years before, his mama used to sit and rock and knit after the day's work was done.

Her rocker was long gone, busted up for burning for heat one day last winter. Or was it the one before? Still, it had served its purpose, and it was a rickety old thing anyway, sitting unused as it was for years inside, and then outside, after Mama's death.

He'd asked the doctor what he thought Mama had died of, and the doc had looked at Chiswick over his half-moon lenses. "Lawrence, that woman never knew a day's peace in her life. Came from her folks' place as a girl, barely into her teen years, to live here with your father, just shy of ten years her senior.

"She left drudgery and hard work behind at her folks' place and stepped right into more of the same here. If she had thought maybe her life was going to be different somehow, that notion pinched out like a snuffed candle flame after she married and moved here.

"Didn't take long for her to have two babies that died, then your sister, then another one that died, then you. By then she was old, Lawrence, life old, work old, trudging through her days because your father was such a devil of a man."

The doctor narrowed his eyes and looked away, breathing deep for a moment. Then he looked back to Chiswick. "I'm not telling you a thing you don't already know, Lawrence Chiswick. So don't give me that look of surprise or rage or whatever look it is you are trying to conjure. And don't even think of acting surprised when I tell you that your mama, Bess, died of exhaustion brought on by a lifetime of too much hard work!"

Chiswick had wanted to lay the doc out flat for that, but he'd known the man was right. Mama had just collapsed from hard work, years and years and years of it. Without letup.

"Sorry, Mama," he said to the yard, leaning on the tender, angled upright post of the porch. He nibbled back the last of the bottle, then tossed it aside. Then he stepped off the porch, walked to the half-collapsed shed where he kept his mule, and only remembered once he'd gotten there that it had died, looking starved, he recalled with a wince, the month before.

Before the mule, he'd also had a dog, Rex, an odd-looking critter with a scarred neck from fighting or some such. Even though the dog had lingered and provided companionship for Chiswick for a good many months, it, too, had left him.

He remembered seeing the dog just walking on up the road, westward, one afternoon. He'd called to the dog, who looked back at him briefly, then turned and kept on going.

Chiswick couldn't blame him. He'd leave himself behind if he could.

He sighed and began the long walk to town, cursing himself for not cadging a ride with Majors.

It was going to be a long ol' walk into town, but he had money, and that meant he would soon have more whiskey. And these days, mused Chiswick, that was always a welcome thing.

And then once he had that, he would get himself a bath, hot food, and the company of a woman.

He would follow this up with a horse, some guns, and better clothes. And then, by golly, he was going to set to working on the folks on the English dandy's short list.

He wasn't certain just what he was going to do by way of convincing folks to sell to the man. But as he walked, Chiswick mused that a no-nonsense approach to most any situation was always the best way to get a job done. No wasting time. Get it over with and move on.

He giggled at the thought of taking on a position of power once more. He'd show them all. Kick him out of office, eh? Chiswick chuckled. "You bet, you bet," he said as he kicked on down the road toward town.

CHAPTER 7

The shot whistled in from the northeast. It caught the rancher low on the right boot, shredding the stacked leather heel, and drove his leg out from beneath him. For that finger snap moment, Henry Brighton did not know what had happened, did not yet know that only his boot had been wounded, and he did not know that it had been hit by a bullet.

He only knew that one moment he was looking ahead, walking down the long line of field he still had to plow that day, his mules, Bess and Beau, lumbering forward slow and steady, the share slicing deep, bold furrows one after the other, all day long.

It was, by the angle of the sun, late afternoon, perhaps four of the clock. He still had plenty to do, and he did not need another thing in his day to slow him down. He thought this even as he flopped to the fresh, dry earth, not yet knowing what had caused this oddness, this interruption. And he certainly did not know why.

Henry had gotten a late start that day because the morning had been full of unexpected occurrences—their bullock had gotten loose, somehow. He still wasn't certain how the young brute could have done it without knocking down rails and tearing through the short runs of wire Henry had been able to buy and string up.

It was precious little safeguard, he knew, between himself and his family and the ornery young bull. But he trusted it would all work out as it needed to, because he had so much to do. And if it required better fencing, he would see to it after the plowing.

But none of that had mattered this morning. What had been a goodly early start to the day had dwindled with every growled curse and random dash as he chased the brute. In the end, it took him the better part of two hours to catch the young, headstrong bull.

His wife, Maeve, had tried to help, as always, but she was not used to such dealings. As a back-East city woman, Maeve had even less agricultural experience compared with Henry's meager background in ranching matters. Although spunky and filled with the best of intentions and an eagerness to be the best helpmate she could to him, Maeve was nonetheless more accustomed to life in a city and was still learning about life as a rancher's wife out on the range.

This was a life Henry had also not been born into, but having grown up close by a noisy freight yard in St. Louis, he had from an early age yearned for the freedom of open land and the quiet of the country. It was this idealized vision he held in his head and heart, to be his own man and work his own land. This had been his dream for as long as he could remember.

Texas had seemed to be the one and only place he might find the freedom he sought, freedom to breathe as much fresh air as he wished, to own acreage, and the animals on it, and to have a home filled with a wife and children, as many as they might be blessed with.

Henry didn't think these were outlandish notions. But he had not counted on it taking him so long to make into a reality. Yet after years of deep, dogged labor as a younger single man, he had come to acquire debt after losing much of his hard-saved money following one bad decision sealed with a handshake in a bar. And that had been that.

Henry had to build up all over again what the old timers and sourdoughs called a grubstake. But he took grim satisfaction in the idea that he had at least learned something. It had been a painful lesson, to be sure, but there was no changing it. The past was a written page, the future did not exist, and so he set to work in the present to attain his dream. And it was a flame within him that burned hotter and brighter with each precious new dollar he squirreled away.

And then he had met Maeve, a refined young woman from a good, if humble, home back East. She had been brought to America when she was a child by her Irish parents, who had doted on her and made certain she had the best education they might afford.

This desire had paid off well for them, for Maeve had become a well-educated, sought-after governess teaching the children of one of the wealthiest families in Newport, Rhode Island.

Henry and Maeve met one day at a pier in Narragansett, where she had taken the children on an outing. Henry had been enjoying a rare few hours of time away from the coastal steamer he had been working on.

He recalled it was a Sunday afternoon and he wore his best clothes, a light-colored linen suit he saved for just such occasions. He had been about to indulge in a spot of ice cream, flavored with vanilla bean from Madagascar, or so the sign had read, when he heard a woman speak from in front of him. It was a soft, but firm voice with the slightest hint of an Irish accent, worn proudly, he would come to know.

The woman was ordering some of the same flavor from the man in the booth, and was reluctant to let go of the little boy and little girl gripping tight to each of her gloved hands. And yet she had to in order to pay the man and then help the children with their ice cream.

Henry hesitated but a moment. It would be awkward for him to say something. And for her, no doubt. And yet, there was something about her, something that he would later learn was the kindness and charm that surrounded her, something she could no more control than the sun could keep from rising each morning.

Henry cleared his throat. “Allow me, ma’am,” said Henry.

The pretty young woman glanced at him as she fumbled with the small purse dangling from her left wrist while trying also to free a hand and tend to the two struggling imps, who he saw now were sensing an opportunity to take their small cups of ice cream and run off, perhaps.

“No, no, thank you, kindly, sir. I am fine, I assure you.”

But as was his way, Henry Brighton had already begun to do as he intended, permission or no. He paid for the ice cream while the pretty woman, whom he now regarded with bright-eyed fascination, turned red as she struggled with the tots, doing her best to not lose her temper.

That had been the first time they met. He had followed the riled woman and the two tugging children at a distance that day, all the way to the gated private drive of a grand mansion. Henry thought about this situation for some time and came to several conclusions that day.

She was far too young and tender-looking to be the mother of children who looked to be five to seven years old. And since they had disappeared up the gated lane to one of the mansions thereabouts, he guessed without any further proof that she was some sort of governess to the children.

And as a governess, she would likely take the tots on another outing the following day. And furthermore, since his ship was to be docked for minor repairs until early Wednesday morning, Henry’s onboard duties were limited. He would follow the woman on the morrow. For somehow, he knew, just knew, that his guesses were correct. And they had been.

Once she discovered what he was on about, and recognized him as the kindly but intruding man from the day before at the ice cream stand at the pier, the woman's temperament that second day proved far more sharp and intolerant with him.

But on that day and the next, something within Henry, that inner voice that usually murmured to him, guiding him to the good in a decision over the bad, fairly shouted to him. It told him that in no uncertain terms was he to abandon the notion of talking with, and hopefully getting to know, this beautiful young woman.

And so, as with everything in his life that had ever offered the whiff of promise to him, Henry Brighton made a bold decision and quit his well-paying job on the steamer. The captain liked him and told him not to be a fool.

"Brighton, a woman is a woman! If you need to know one that badly, spend a few coins and work it out of your system. My word, man, there are plenty of them about nearby the docks to help with such a situation!"

But no, Henry was not to be dissuaded. This, he told the man, was different. The captain sighed and shook his head. "They all are, my boy. They all are. Until the next one in the next port."

Henry shook his head then, smiling and brimming with confidence and with the knowledge that by then he had more than enough money to embark on his dream life as a man of the earth far to the West. He was determined to get to know the pretty, fiery young governess. If it came to naught, then so be it, but he had to try. If he did not, Henry knew himself far too well, and he knew that her face would remain in his mind, vexing and taunting him to the end of his days.

That was as far as Henry Brighton traveled in his memories, trekking with much pleasure along the trail of among the happiest of his life's remembrances. At that moment, when he would normally recall the day, nearly a week after his steamer had left port without him, that she had almost smiled when he spoke to her. . . . At that moment, a second bullet whistled low over his plowed field and whiskered in at him.

It traveled straight and true, as with the first, also from the northeast. This time the shooter corrected his aim, raising the rifle's barrel a pinch. The delivered lead nugget interrupted Henry's eyeblink-fast moment of happy reverie as he struggled finally to stand upright once more on his blasted heel, still not comprehending what had happened to his boot.

The second bullet drove fast and hard into Henry's sweat-sodden workshirt just below the arc of his ribs on his right side. It bored a brutal tunnel through cloth, skin, lean flesh, nicked a rib bone, and nested as if exhausted deep within the working man's vitals.

That second shot did not knock Henry to the earth. He stiffened, arching backward, and his huffing breath whooshed from his mouth as if he had been punched between his shoulders by a huge man's fist.

His right hand jerked down out of instinct and snatched at his side. Even as he struggled to draw in a breath, droplets of cold sweat stippled his forehead and his clean-shaven face.

"What . . ." He tried to puzzle this out, wondered if he had been stung by bees. . . . It made no sense—what was happening? He felt himself beginning to stagger, his legs wobbling as if they were too weak to hold him up.

He raised up his right hand, the fingers and palm bright with a dripping redness—blood. His blood. His very own blood! But what did this mean?

Before Henry Brighton could ponder this conundrum further, a sound from far away came to him, a single quick crack, as if a dry tree branch had been snapped over a man's knee.

This third bullet also found a home in Henry Brighton, this time within his head, drilling in tight below his hat band, through his short hair, his scalp, and skull, and burrowing into his brain, where its presence soon rendered that organ a dead thing.

In fact, Henry Brighton's body all but died before the top of his head smacked hard against the smooth-worn left hickory handle of the plow before the rest of his body slopped to the side and lay, face down on the fresh-turned furrows of his dream.

With their young daughter, Maisie, traipsing along beside her, Maeve strode slowly up the last rise before the field where she knew she would find her husband, Henry, once again working too late, ignoring the time. He was eager, she knew, to make up for the lost hours this morning.

Maeve lugged a tall, narrow, stoneware crock with a cork stopper and cradled in a wire basket that rose up to form a wire and wood bail handle. Maeve walked slower than she would like, but little Maisie was beside her. Together they sang a pretty little Irish ditty her own mama had taught her so many years before.

It was lovely to be able to teach her own child such things, and oh, she had so much more to share. Perhaps one day, if they were so blessed, little Maisie might find herself older sister to a wee Henry. One day. But for now . . . Maeve topped the rise and visored her eyes against the bright orange ball of the setting sun. "Come along, Maisie. Papa will be thirsty. . . ."

She looked to where she thought he might be, and yes, she saw the team, but they were standing still, and the field was far from finished. There was the plow just behind, and . . . where was Henry?

"Maisie, come along now."

The child kept singing and trudging along.

"Now!" But Maeve did not wait for the child to reach her. For she had seen something behind the plow, something low, a shape darker than the rill of turned, dry earth. It was Henry, perhaps resting, yes, that would be it. It had to be! If anyone deserved a rest, it was her Henry.

But Maeve knew, in that sliver of a moment, that this deepest wish was mere folly. Something was wrong, and dear Henry was down, on the ground, and nothing minor could do that to Henry Brighton. Not the Henry she knew and loved.

She dashed the last fifty feet, shouting his name, saw his hat, upturned some feet from him. She flung the water jug away as she scrambled the remaining dozen feet to him, grasping him, seeing the blood on his right side, wondering as she worked to flop him over, to face her, if perhaps the handle of the plow had somehow hurt him. . . .

His head slipped to the side, showing her a bloodied welt in his short, dark hair. What did it mean? Blood on his head? Then she saw blood and dirt clogged and clotting on his face, beneath his nose, his mouth, his chin.

"Henry! Henry!" She chanted this as if a prayer, over and over, and was not aware as she worked her fingers in his mouth, smearing away the dirt and blood from his handsome, sunburned face, that little Maisie stood beside her. The girl's tiny hands rested on her mama's heaving, working shoulders, patting her, telling her not to cry, Mama, Daddy's sleeping, only sleeping.

Maeve worked that way for long minutes, long enough to realize that her dear Henry was no longer alive, that the sun was going down, that Maisie was now crying, too, and that her life, their lives, were to be different, so very different, from that moment onward.

Chapter 8

As Jed worked that day, sweat building and dripping off his nose tip, he reflected on life and, in particular, how lucky he felt about his lot in it. After all, a whole lot had happened since that cursed time a year back when the Whiskey Wars, as the protracted fracas was known locally and even far and wide, had boiled, then ruptured, causing terrible grief and tragedy. Few Glen Rose folks escaped its foul effects.

Mostly, however, that grief and tragedy was felt by Merlin Sheldrake and the band of killers and thieves he'd hired on to help him grab what was not his. In the end, the rich, fat Sheldrake had resorted to murderous intent.

The Starks had not given in to him, however, even though it almost meant the death of Minnie, aka Mother Stark. In the end, Sheldrake died, crushed by barrels of whiskey, his own swill, in the crass distillery he had built outside of Glen Rose.

And then, as if that had not been bad enough for the fiendish, rich brute, Jed's sweetheart, Lilly Chu, a half Texan, half Chinese woman who owned the town's much-loved café, had lobbed one of her dear departed Chinese railroad blaster father's precious sticks of dynamite into the rich man's warehouse and distillery.

Topping that, the citizens of Glen Rose seemed to finally

awaken and shake off the four-year, greed-induced slumber they had been lulled into by Sheldrake.

They had dealt with Sheldrake's handful of the bullying hired guns in their own frontier fashion—by stringing them up in the center of Glen Rose. This act put a hard and brutal close to the Whiskey Wars.

Jed and Minnie had retreated to their fire-gutted ranch, Whiskey Woods, to recover. Jed spent the year since rebuilding where possible—which turned out to be precious little—and building a new and better ranch house and barn and whiskey shed and still. He also finally got around to agreeing to a date to marry his sweetheart, Lilly, right there at Whiskey Woods, and now they were happy as he could ever imagine anybody ever being.

Well, except maybe for that pesky eatery she owned in town. The Glen Rose Café. He loved the place, for certain..

Curiosity had driven him in there one day as much as had his urge to taste home cooking that wasn't Mama's, whose kitchen skills were second to none, but a man had a hankering for pie made by somebody else once in a while. And he'd thanked his stars every day since that he had followed his nose that day.

But now? Now that café was set to be a wedge in their lives. Jed wanted Lil by his side, day in and out, at Whiskey Woods, and he knew, just knew, that she wouldn't want to give up the café.

Funny thing was, before they'd officially discussed getting hitched, he had been just fine and dandy with her living there over the café and running her own business in downtown Glen Rose. He had visited often.

But now? Things were different. He fully expected her to be his wife, in all ways, and that meant living with him, and not running off on her horse every morning and being gone all day long, working at the café.

Trouble was, she didn't seem in any mood to let go of the place. It was a vexation, to be sure.

Still, he didn't think at that moment that anything could change how he felt about her. He would later think back on this time and wonder how very wrong he had been.

And so, when Lilly rode into the dooryard of Whiskey Woods later that day, the first thing he'd said, almost without giving it much thought, had been, "How was the morning trade, Lil?"

He knew it was with extra effort that she rode out here to visit, and he appreciated it. After all, this was the in-between time following the breakfast rush and the late afternoon into evening stretch when she served up copious amounts of belly-filling, savory-smelling foods.

It was during that time when Lilly would most often clean the place, prep a bit for the afternoon flood of growling bellies, and then retreat to her own humble dwelling upstairs, over the café. She owned the building, which made this convenient. Once there, she would nap for a spell to help, as she told Jed with a wink, "build up her strength."

No matter what Lilly Chu did, she always did it with gusto, and that was but one of the many things Jed admired about her. Ironically, it was the Glen Rose Café, her place of business, that first brought them together.

And it was now the very thing that had wedged itself between them, and had become the only thing of any importance that had done so in all those years.

Jed sensed, from the way Lilly looked just now, that the café was about to become the thing they were going to discuss again, right then and there.

He sighed and tried to make his smile seem genuine. But the thought of that topic coming up was a mighty tough nugget to crack in his mind that day. He was hours from winding up his work, and already he was dog-tired.

"Funny you should ask, Jed," she said, giving him a quick smooch on the lips, the sort of kiss he would settle for but always left him hoping for more.

"I have Maggie's help for the rest of today, so she's getting everything prepped for the dinner trade."

"Huh," he said. "That's great. But why is that funny?" He somehow knew he should have stopped there, but he didn't. "She's getting to be quite a hand. You're not careful, she'll put you out of work." He smiled to let her know he said it in jest.

But she didn't take it that way.

"And I suppose you'd like that just fine, wouldn't you, Jed Stark?"

His smile slipped a bit. "Well, Lil. You know what I meant."

"Do I?"

He sighed. "Lil, look—"

"No, why don't you just go ahead and tell me exactly what you mean, then, Jed? Because it seems to me, we should have had this all out in the open a whole lot earlier than now, don't you think?"

There was that fiery side of her that he claimed to like. And he did, but just now, on this day, heck if he was honest, on most days, it was something he could do without in any measurable quantity.

"Okay, Lil. You want me to be honest? You know how I feel about it. I'm proud as punch that you are the proprietor of a successful business, you bet. But once we're married, I would hope you'd do the right thing." He saw her eyes widen and quickly held up a hand. "All right, all right, the *logical* thing, okay?"

"And that would be?"

Jed sighed. Here we go again, he thought. The beating heart of the matter. "Come on now, Lil. You know where I stand on this. I haven't said any different than when we first started talking about getting married."

"*Talking* about it?" she said. "I thought we had already decided it. But now I guess we're back to talking about it. Pardon me, but I thought we had even discussed and settled on a date and pretty much everything else about it," she said.

"Now look, Lil." Jed laid a hand on her shoulder, but she shrugged it off and turned from him.

"How on earth," he wondered aloud, "did we ever get to this point? We were so much happier, for years, for Pete's sake, when we hadn't ever talked about getting married. You had your place and I had mine and we'd see each other pretty regularly. And now this." He raised his arms and let his big, work-hardened hands drop to his sides.

"Happy?" she said, "Sure, you were happy. You got everything you wanted. A nice home with your mother and a nice, comfortable place to visit when you were lonely. And hot meals at both ends!"

"Is that what you think?" he said, his voice rising with hers. "You think that's all I was after?"

"It's beginning to look that way, Jed," she glared at him.

"Look? No, no, Lil. We are way off the point we started with here, which is—"

She tried to jump in, but Jed spoke louder, shaking his head, "Which is that you don't want to move in here and live with me and give up the café once we get married. What's so wrong with me wanting my wife here with me?" he said, arms wide, as if asking the whole of the sky.

"After all, a man has a right to want his wife to live with him and do all the things a wife does. And I'm building a decent home, aren't I?"

She stared at him in silence for long moments. Finally, she said, "I never said I had trouble with those things, Jed. Except for the little *woman-as-servant-to-her-man* part. But you never asked my opinion. You just assumed I was going to do all those things because you want it that way."

He began speaking again, but this time it was her turn to shake her head and hold up a halting hand. "That is something I cannot and will not put up with. You've made me angry a few times in the past, Jed, and I am quite certain I have done the same to you a few times. I know I can be a bitter tonic at times, but this time, mister. Oh, this time you have really . . . oh, boy!"

With that, Lilly turned and stomped back to her horse, with a slack-jawed Jed a pace behind.

"Lil, hold up now! You can't just say those things and walk away!"

"I'm not going to walk away, Jed," she snapped over her shoulder as she reached Poppy and swung up into the saddle. "I'm going to ride away!"

Jed grabbed the horse's bridle and held her in place. "Lil, whatever I said, I'm sorry! I didn't mean anything by it. . . ."

"That's just the problem, Jed. You don't even know what it was you said that was so . . . so wrong! I can't talk right now, Jed. Just leave me be."

"But Lil—"

"And let go of Poppy!"

With wide eyes and great reluctance, Jed let go of the mare's bridle and backed away a step as his wife-to-be, if he could still call her that, turned the horse hard and thundered on up the lane, back toward Glen Rose, or so he presumed.

"What in the name of all that is sacred was that all about?" said Jed out loud, half to himself, half to Redeye, who was lounging not far away, but with head raised. The dog also looked suspiciously as if it were judging him.

"Not you, too," growled Jed.

"Yes, him. And me, too!"

Jed spun, saw Mama approaching from the house with her hands on her hips. He suppressed a groan. "Mama, it was a conversation between Lil and me, that's all."

"That's all? You call that a conversation? I'd hate to think what you call a right full-on fight, mister! My word." She strode on up, shaking her head as if she'd just heard the most shocking, melancholy news of her life. "Heard that one all the way on over to Grindle.

"I could swear I raised a boy with a brain, somebody who wasn't so thick as to think that he could make assumptions and decisions for his soon-to-be wife without telling her. Better yet, without asking her what she might want!"

"I know what it's all about, Mama. All she had to do was say she wanted to keep the café, and we could have worked out something." He snapped his words, squinting up the long drive toward where Lilly would still be visible had she not ridden hard and fast on out of there.

"Jed," said Minnie. "You really, really in your deepest heart think that she wants to keep the café and not be with you? My word, boy, she rode all the way out here just to see you! It's a three-quarter-hour ride at a steady clip! She did that because she wants to be with you, you . . . you idiot!"

"Mama!" said Jed, turning wide eyes on his mother. "You never called me such a thing before!"

"You never deserved it so much as you do right now! Might be I should have called you that a few more times over the years, might be it would have knocked sense into your feeble Stark bean!"

Jed grunted and looked up the empty lane once more. "Maybe I should go after her."

Minnie shrugged. "Up to you. O'course I wouldn't. But then again, I'm not that dim. Or a man. Same thing, I reckon." She turned and walked back toward the house. "I'd say the only male around these parts with any notion of how to behave is Redeye. And just look at him."

She waved a hand at the motionless dog. He broke wind and twitched in his sleep. "Proves a point right there." She resumed her walk toward the house. "Just what the point was, I have no idea."

Jed did his best to ignore what she was mumbling, but he knew she was a wise old hen, even if she could be annoying about it. Still, maybe he'd hold up on trailing after Lil. After all, he thought, she's the one who stormed off, not him.

Maybe they both needed time to cool. He walked back to the whiskey shed, half wondering how his fire was faring. It was possible that Lil and Mama were right. Could be he should have talked it all over with her beforehand. But man alive, didn't a fellow have the right to expect his wife would be close by of a day's time? And not gone off to her place of business, which took much of an hour to get to and then back from, each and every day. Just didn't make any sense. And what about when they had children? How would that work?

No, he thought. She knew he was right, she was just . . . just what, Jed? he asked himself.

"Just jittery," he said with finality, as if he had decided a thing. She's all worked up because she's going to be wed, and she doesn't want to give up the life she's led up to now. She's had all manner of freedoms, and now maybe she's thinking she'll be tied to this place. That's what it must be."

Even that line of logic, as sound as it seemed as he thought it, did not really make sense to him. He sighed and snatched up the steel poker, thrusting it into the glowing coals and snarling because not only had he not come to any resolution about the odd mess of an encounter he'd just had with Lil and then Mama, but he'd also managed to burn the grains he'd been trying to toast.

"What I get for trying to come up with a variation on the Stark whiskey recipe," he growled. "Should know enough to leave things alone. If they work, leave them be!" He slammed his long-handled tongs down on the grate and walked off.

CHAPTER 9

Maeve Brighton and her little daughter, Maisie, drove their pony trap southeastward to the downtown of Glen Rose, a stout half an hour's ride at a rigid clip. She eased up only when they came abreast of Milchner's Tonsorial Parlor and Tooth Pulling.

But it was not Milchner Senior's barbering or dentistry skills she sought. It was those of his son, Jacob, whose cabinetmaking shop was located out back.

It took her mere minutes to pay the kind young man. He had built a solid coffin for the man she had loved more than she had thought was possible in this, or perhaps any other life. And then she had buried him, her unexpected sweetheart, the father of their young and only child, little Maisie.

Maeve did not know what to do with herself, but she knew that her husband had been gunned down, murdered, and she would find out who had done this thing. She would not rest in the least until she had.

And even then, she thought, I shall rue the day I let him talk me into moving to Texas to buy land and a home. But it had been his lifelong dream, and so she had said yes, of course, my love, this we must do.

And now here she was, a widow with a young child, debts to pay, and no notion of how to do so.

* * *

Loudon Paley welcomed the new widow and her small daughter into his office. "Please, do come in, Mrs. Brighton. We were all so saddened to hear of your husband's untimely death. It was a truly tragic accident."

"Accident?" she said, her red-rimmed eyes glinting with a sudden fire. "This was no accident, Mr. Paley."

"Oh, but it wasn't a hunter?" said Loudon. "Has Marshal Thompson found out who did it?"

"Oh, I know who is behind the killing of my husband, Mr. Paley." Maeve Brighton stared at Loudon Paley, the newsman, founder, owner, editor, and sole employee of the *Glen Rose Gazette*, the Texas town's one and only newspaper.

She looked hard at him with cold brown eyes. "At least I have a very good idea of who is behind it. And I will not let him win."

"*Him*, ma'am?"

Maeve Brighton nodded. "That is why I have come to see you."

"Me?" Loudon Paley gulped. "I . . . I am not certain I understand, ma'am."

The pretty young widow seated before him said, "Neither am I, yet, Mr. Paley. I had been on my way to the marshal's office to see what progress he has made in his investigation. Then I had intended to see you, depending on what I learned from him.

"But as the marshal was not in his office, and as you were, and as your office was on my route, I determined to rearrange my visits."

"Yes, ma'am." He still didn't understand what was happening. "Well, again, I am so very sorry, Mrs. Brighton." He spoke in a lowered tone, afraid that the woman's sweet young daughter might hear him.

"There's no need to do that, Mr. Paley," said Mrs. Brighton, glancing over at her daughter, who was rearranging her doll's skirts on the chair several feet away. A tired smile appeared on the woman's face. "Maisie and I have talked. I am not certain how much of this she understands. However, she was with me when . . ."

She looked to her left, and Loudon saw tears welling in her eyes, and could not help but realize, once more, what a pretty woman she was, despite what a trial the last few days must have been for her. And what a trial the future, the near future at any rate, would also be to her. To them both.

"Is there anything I can get you, ma'am?" he said, standing and looking about the office. He realized he really should keep the place tidier. And he should be able to offer visitors something more than a cigar and a nip of Stark whiskey.

Then he realized he could. Coffee, he would offer her a cup of coffee. "I . . . I have coffee, ma'am. It won't take very long to heat it up on the stove. Oh, once I kindle a small fire. . . ." He made a move toward the potbelly stove by the back wall.

She looked at him as if he had just shouted to attract her attention. "What? Oh, no, no, Mr. Paley. Thank you. I am sorry. It's just so new, so fresh, you see."

"I understand. I really do." He offered another weak smile. "I lost someone recently. Oh, but it's not the same, not the same thing. Not at all." He realized he should shut his mouth. Losing a mule to old age was hardly the same thing as finding one's spouse dead in a field. And shot, to boot!

He was relieved to hear that she did not ask him questions. A mule! What was he thinking? Sure, Alice was a wonderful mule, in many ways she was as stalwart and as true to him as a boon dog companion might be, but a mule was decidedly not the same thing as a husband or a wife.

Sure, Alice was likely his best friend, except for Jed and

Lilly, that is. But they were preparing to be married themselves, and he didn't see all that much of them these days.

"Oh, cheer yourself up, Loudon," said Minnie Stark, Jed's mother, aka Mother Stark. She had said it with a wink one day when he had ridden his new mule, Alice II, out to Whiskey Woods, the Stark ranch and home of the world's finest whiskey, a truth accepted rather widely by anyone who had even the remotest taste for whiskey.

Loudon had made his way out there, as he used to in the old days, before his chums were set to be wed.

He didn't visit as much these days as he had no desire to put himself or anyone else in an awkward position by being in the way. Why, just today, he knew that Jed and Lilly were off together, enjoying a rare picnic alone down along the river somewhere.

"They ain't any different than any other soon-to-marry couple," Minnie had said. "Give it time, things will simmer down and get back to normal." She cackled, then grew serious. "They better! He needs to finish that house before the babies start coming. I raised one, and that's enough. This here granny"—she jerked a work-hardened thumb at her chest—"is not about to share her home full time with his son and his wife and their brood, no sir! I'll have the camp to myself, thank you very much, and that is the way it's going to be!"

As usual, Minnie's bold and frank demeanor was disarming and not without its refreshing aspects, but Loudon still found himself uncertain what to say some of the time around the tough old bird of a woman, despite the fact that he had played a primary role in saving her from likely death at the hands of Merlin Sheldrake the year before.

Loudon took solace in the fact that most folks of his acquaintance in and around Glen Rose felt the same way when the topic of the infamous Mother Stark came up.

"Mr. Paley?"

"Oh, yes, ma'am," said Loudon, shaking off his reverie and looking once more at the bold eyes of Mrs. Brighton.

"I have come to ask you what you know about . . . that man." She gritted her teeth and paused before resuming. "That Dalton Majors, the one who has been buying up so much land around here."

"Ah, well." Loudon looked at his desk. It was a mess, as usual. "Um, let's see now, sure, yes, I know about him. That is to say, I know of him, haven't had personal dealings with him. And since he left town, let's see, just about a week ago, I am not certain I will have the opportunity to talk with him again."

"Hmm," she said, eyes narrowed. "That sounds convenient for him. Do you know where he went?"

"Not specifically, no, I don't. Not yet, anyway."

"Very well, do you know anything of use about him, then?"

He nodded. "Yes, let's see, as far as I understand it, he works for a certain someone with a bottomless coin purse, if you know what I mean." He leaned forward over the desk, aware from her expression that he had not likely told Mrs. Brighton anything she did not already know.

"It's interesting that you should ask about him, ma'am, as I have recently unearthed, as it were, information about his employer."

He saw Mrs. Brighton's eyebrows rise.

"Yes," Loudon continued. "It took some doing"—he tapped the side of his nose—"and I had to tug a few dangling strings, don't you know, but that's a reporter's life."

"What is, Mr. Paley?"

"Oh, that of favors and confidences and letter writing and such. But as I am from back East myself, I have managed to maintain alliances with a number of newspapermen there. And politicians, too."

"Back East, you said?" she asked. "Yes, that's interesting, Mr. Paley. But as to Mr. Majors, as you may well have gathered from my reaction, I am acquainted with him. But what is this about his wealthy employer?"

It took Loudon a few moments to come around to comprehending what it was she had just said. He was momentarily lost, slightly adrift, looking at her unwavering brown eyes. And that, he told himself, would not do! Never, never, never, Loudon Paley. Now pay attention, man!

He nodded. "His employer is not a he, as one might suspect, but as far as I have been able to discern, he is a she." He liked her reaction—raised eyebrows. "Oh yes," he said, in a lowered voice. "A very wealthy and thus very powerful she."

Mrs. Maeve Brighton regarded him a moment, then leaned back slightly. "I do not care if this she happened to be the Queen of England. Dalton Majors and therefore she are guilty of murdering my husband."

It was Loudon's turn to pause, then lean back. "Well now, ma'am, that is quite a claim. Do you have any way to back that up? Any proof? I ask only because that is what the marshal will or has perhaps already asked you. And I'm afraid that without proof of some sort, well . . ." He shrugged.

She stood with a suddenness that surprised him. "Very well, then, Mr. Paley. I won't take up more of your time, thank you."

"Oh no, ma'am. I didn't intend to offend you, nor take lightly what you've told me!" He saw her hesitate. "Look," he said, coming around the desk and making a broad gesture to seat herself once more. "Why don't you tell me what you know, from the beginning, and I'll see if there's some way I might be able to help you."

She stood drawn up, tight seeming, her lips pursed, her eyes red, and for the first time, she looked to him to be truly tired, so truly tired. Finally she nodded. "But I have to get to the marshal's office."

Loudon held up a finger and looked out the glass top half of his office door, down the long street. "He's still out." Loudon looked at her. "Most of the year, he always keeps the door open when he's in, and it's still closed."

"Very well," she said, sighing. "Very well." And slowly she began to tell him about the encounters she and her husband had had with Dalton Majors.

And this interested the newspaperman Loudon Paley very much. Very much, indeed.

Chapter 10

"It all began," she said, leaning forward, "with that foul man's first visit."

And Loudon Paley found he had to concentrate extra hard on the words, delivered as they were in that entrancing Irish lilt, and the meaning behind them coming from the tired, sad, beautiful face of the recently widowed Maeve Brighton.

The newsman knew he should be reprimanded by his own conscience for this, for not considering her as a citizen who had consulted him as an impartial possible authority on matters of importance in Glen Rose and the surrounding region.

Stop it, Loudon, he told himself. Stop it right now and listen to what she is telling you.

"Mr. Paley, are you . . . are you quite all right?"

"What? Oh yes, yes, ma'am. I am fine, I assure you. I merely want to concentrate on what you are telling me. It's just my way." Here I am, flustered and found out, he just knew it.

"I see. Well, yes, where was I?"

"You were about to tell me how this all began. The events that led up to . . . to . . ."

"To my husband's murder. Yes, Mr. Paley. As I was saying, it began some weeks ago, we had been living at our ranch, well, we call it that, but really it is more of a small ranch, or a farm, oh, I don't know. But it makes . . . made Henry happy. It was always his dream, you see, to live here and grow crops, raise animals, that sort of thing."

"His dream," said Loudon, "but not yours?"

"Oh, as long as he was happy, really, that's what I wanted. A good, safe home for us all, and for my baby, you see." She looked to her left at the pretty young girl playing quietly with her homemade cloth doll.

"You mentioned Dalton Majors?"

"Yes," she nodded. "He visited us the first time some weeks ago. It was just as we had finished breakfast. I was clearing the table when Henry heard a horse and buggy outside. We all went to the door to see who it might be. We hadn't had but two visitors in the five months since we had moved in, you see. So it was exciting.

"And what we saw was a handsome man, sandy-colored hair, neat of appearance, in a fine linen suit, driving a small but lovely buggy. I hadn't seen one like it since back home, that is to say, back in Rhode Island."

Loudon wanted to interrupt her, to get her to talk about Rhode Island, which was, after all, quite near where he was from himself, back in Providence and Boston, but he decided he should keep his mouth closed and merely nodded for her to continue.

" 'Wait here,' Henry had said. 'I'll see what he wants.'

"They talked for a few minutes, and I saw Henry smile and nod. Maisie and I stayed on the porch and presently the two men approached the house. My husband introduced us and said the man's name was Dalton Majors."

She looked at Loudon. "I know you already know who he is and why he was there, Mr. Paley."

"Yes, ma'am." Loudon nodded.

Majors had been a frequent visitor to both the *Glen Rose Gazette*'s office and, consequently, within Loudon's pieces in the newspaper itself.

"And I bet he made you an offer he said you could not refuse."

She nodded. "That is precisely what happened, Mr. Paley. He insisted that Henry accept a gift of fancy whiskey from him, and that he listen to what Majors had to offer. The man was overwhelming, really, and very difficult for Henry, who is . . . was so polite."

She paused and dabbed at her eye corners. "The second time he showed up, perhaps two weeks later, my husband was in the field he had been working on improving, far from the house. It was almost as if Majors had been waiting for my husband to leave so he could talk with me.

"He thought he sensed a weakness in me, perhaps because I am a woman. But I can assure you, Mr. Paley . . ." Maeve Brighton drew herself up from a slight slouch in the chair, straightening her shoulders. She looked even more impressive to Loudon then.

"I assure you I was in complete agreement with my husband. The ranch had grown on me, you see. It . . . well, it was home."

"Was, ma'am?"

She offered a faint smile and shrugged. "Oh, now, I . . . I don't know. It's all so different. Everything has changed."

"I understand," said Loudon.

"At any rate, we had no reason to suspect that man would turn up on our doorstep yet again. But he apparently was not one to take no for an answer."

"What did he say, ma'am?"

"Well, first, I heard his buggy, the same fancy one as before, so I walked around to the front of the house. I had been hanging laundry to dry along the side where I was also hoping to coax flowers to grow. I remember holding my hand up to block the sun so I might see who it was.

"I recognized him and that same feeling I had had during

his first visit, when he had offered me that false smile, that same feeling of doubt and mistrust, returned. Even before we spoke, I felt it.

"He saw me, but he stayed beside his buggy and appeared to be jotting notes in a small book of some sort. As he did this, he looked around in various directions, then he would write more. Finally after a minute or two of doing this, he closed the little book and tucked it into an inner coat pocket. He looked at me for the first time and walked toward me, still wearing that same false smile.

" 'How do you do, ma'am? I hope you remember me—Dalton Majors.'

"He nodded, offering a bow with his head. I said, 'Yes, I remember you, Mr. Majors. What brings you out here today?' I asked this even though I well knew.

" 'I tell you, ma'am, oh, is that coffee I smell?' He closed his eyes a moment and sniffed.

" 'No,' I said. 'It must be something else. I don't have any on the boil. What can I do for you, Mr. Majors?'

"He was trying to make me comfortable with him, as if we were in league against my husband. That is what I was thinking at the time, anyway.

"Well, he must have taken the hint because his mouth's weak smile faltered, and he looked around himself again at the landscape. 'I will tell you then, ma'am. I am here to estimate the worth of the place that you and your husband reside on.' "

" 'The ranch that we own, you mean. All one hundred fifty acres of it, sir.' "

" 'Own it, yes, yes. So you say. But I have to tell you, ma'am, that unfortunately a discrepancy in the original deed has been discovered by a team of attorneys.'

"As soon as he began telling me this, and explaining the situation in great detail, I wanted to slap him, to shout at him to leave, and to saddle the horse and ride for my husband. What

Majors was telling me was awful, and deep in my heart, I knew he was wrong. 'As wrong as wrong can be,' as my husband says, or used to say.

"I shook my head. 'I'm sorry, Mr. Majors, but you are wasting your time. You have been misled by someone. The attorneys you spoke of, perhaps. I can assure you that we own this ranch, the entirety of it, home, barns, animals, water rights, and the acreage itself. It was all thoroughly researched, and the deed was found to be satisfactory, according to our lawyer.'

"He offered me that same dead smile again and rocked back on his heels, his hands in his pockets. 'You are incorrect, ma'am, this much I know. Would that it were not the case, honestly, because I respect you and your husband mightily.

" 'You see, in my work, I rarely come across a young couple who show so much dedication to themselves and to their home, but be that as it may,' he said, 'I have been sent here by the true owners, rightful heirs of the land, to make you a last offer. It is not something they need to do, believe me. But they are generous people, and I do believe it would be in your best interest to take them up on this fine offer, extended to you just this one time.'

"Well, Mr. Paley, as you can well imagine, I was flummoxed. I am an educated woman, Mr. Paley. I was a governess before marrying my Henry. And I don't mind saying that, as such, I was privy to all manner of emotions, but I knew enough to keep them in control.

"At least until I had made quite certain Mr. Majors was gone. I asked him what his proof was that what he was telling me was true. He offered me a condescending smile, and I swear he looked as if he was about to pat me on the head and tell me to toddle along!"

" 'I believe I should talk with your husband, ma'am. These are matters best left to the head of the household.'

"I am afraid, Mr. Paley, that I let my anger get the better of my reason. I ground my teeth together hard and told him that my husband and I share in all decisions and that he would do well to show a little more respect. Furthermore, I would appreciate it if he would refrain from arriving on our property unannounced, and instead, to send a letter, preferably via his attorney, if he wishes to pursue the matter further."

"What did he say to that, ma'am?" said Loudon, leaning forward and enjoying every moment of this conversation. Not only professionally, for what it was beginning to reveal about Majors, elements of which he had been suspicious of for some time, but also for the impressiveness of the woman herself.

She was bold and intelligent and . . . well, he could plainly see what it was that had attracted her poor husband to her in the first place. Her face was lovely and her poise was its match.

And speaking with her . . . it was an unparalleled moment in Loudon's experiences talking with women in Glen Rose these past few years, since he'd arrived from back East seeking adventure and fodder for his writing.

He'd found adventure and inspiration, and more, to be sure. But he had only ever really been dazzled in this way by conversation with a woman once before, and that was with Lilly Chu, his best friend's sweetheart.

But Lilly had quickly become not unlike a sister to him, or better yet, a good friend.

But Mrs. Brighton was . . . oh, Loudon, he almost said it aloud. She was a widow, yes, but so fresh and new to the role it would be a year and more before she might even deign to talk with him outside of his professional capacity.

"Mr. Paley? Perhaps I should come back another time."

"Oh no, no, ma'am. I am listening with all my heart, that is to say, I am concentrating on what you're telling me, ma'am. I am, um, integrating it in my mind with the other information I have gathered, as it were, about Mr. Majors."

"Oh? Does that mean that what I am telling you might not come as such a surprise to hear?"

"That's about it, yes, ma'am. I don't like to speak off the

record, you understand, as I must maintain what journalistic integrity I have managed to cobble together here." He raised his hands to feebly take in what he hoped conveyed the town.

"But yes, what you are telling me echoes the experiences others have reported having with Majors, and this confirms suspicions I have been having for some time now. As I say, you are not the only people to be harangued by Mr. Majors."

"Do you mean to say he has shot other people?"

"What? Oh no, I mean that I don't know that, ma'am. That is to say, I don't, well"—he leaned forward—"do you have proof that he shot your husband, ma'am?"

For a moment, Loudon thought she might rise to her feet, snatch her child's hand, and storm out of his office. But she swallowed hard, and looked toward a corner of the ceiling. "No, that's not what I meant at all. I . . . but it's far more than coincidental, don't you think?

"That the only real interaction we have had since moving here, other than meeting a number of very kind and helpful people, of course, has been with Dalton Majors and the unpleasantness and lies he brought our way."

"Lies," said Loudon. "So you were able to disprove his assertion that your place belonged to someone else?"

"Of course we were able to disprove it. It was a lie from the start and we knew it. We also had, or have, a copy of the deed to prove it."

"You own the place outright?" As soon as he spoke, Loudon realized this sounded too nosy, too probing.

"We do, as a matter of fact. Or rather I do, now."

Loudon nodded, then a thought came to him. "You'll pardon me for asking, ma'am, but well. . . ."

"You can ask anything, Mr. Paley," she said. "After this week, which we're still very much in the middle of, I doubt there's a thing you can say that might surprise me."

"All right," he said, nodding. "Are you certain your name is on the deed, too, ma'am? I ask because there are a good many men whose names are listed solely on the deeds. And when they . . . pass on, their families are left to deal with so very much."

She offered a light smile. "I made certain, as did my husband, that both our names were on the thing. But we hardly thought we would need such protection. Not this soon, not like this."

She looked at Loudon hard, those pretty brown eyes seeming to burrow right into his soul. "Tell me, Mr. Paley, is it . . . is this place, the West, always so savage?"

How to answer that? he thought. "When I first moved here from back East myself, what, five and more years ago now, I confess I had hoped it might be, well, less tame than what I knew. And I was not disappointed. You have surely heard of the events of last year in Glen Rose. They rose to an awful and final close mere months before you and your husband and daughter moved here."

She nodded.

"All right, well, I admit that when I first moved here, I was hoping to find what I'd read about in dime novels. I admit it, but it seemed so exciting and so very different than the life I led back East.

"And when I got out here, I was disappointed, for the most part. Life was, well, fairly quiet, sedate, and . . . *pleasant*, for the lack of a better word for it. And then the events of last year took place. Oh, the situation had been building up for some time."

Loudon closed his eyes and shook his head. "I had no idea people could be so ruthless in so many ways. Most often, it is men, and most often, it is because they feel they don't have enough money or power. Most confuse the two as being the same.

"It was eye-opening for me, I can tell you, Mrs. Brighton. And it changed me. I don't care to relive that level of brutality again in my life. And if I can help to lessen it or remove it from others with my paltry efforts through my ability, which at the moment seems only to be journalism"—he offered a weak smile—"then, so be it."

She sat silent a moment and continued to look at him.

"I'm sorry, that tangent was uncalled for, especially given what you're going through. Please forgive me."

"No, Mr. Paley, on the contrary, it was well said and well taken, I assure you."

"Mrs. Brighton, what makes you so certain that Mr. Majors did this . . . this horrible thing to your husband, you both?" Loudon nodded toward her and the little girl, who was now looking at them. A sad little waif, he thought. And now fatherless.

"I only ask this because Mr. Majors, to my knowledge, anyway, left here recently. He indicated to everyone that he would be back soon, and with more of his promised money. Money to purchase from folks more ranches and businesses—"

"And their lives and freedom," she said, a dark tone to her voice.

"Yes, I'm afraid you're only too right in that assessment, ma'am."

"What makes me think he is behind it?" she repeated. "Only what I have told you, Mr. Paley. Other than that, very little. I have found no real evidence. But call it instinct, intuition, call it what you will. His visits and subsequent disturbing lies were far too coincidental." She shrugged. "Perhaps you're right. Perhaps it is all just happenstance, nothing more. Perhaps it was as the marshal seemed to think when he first came out to the ranch that it likely was someone out hunting, someone with the sun in their eyes who shot several times, thinking they had . . ."

Her eyes welled again and she shrugged.

"I am going to see the marshal again, and go to the shop for . . . oh, something, I forget what."

She looked so sad and helpless to Loudon that he felt a renewed rush of empathy, and an idea came to him. "I tell you what, Mrs. Brighton, if you have the time, well, I have the inclination to treat you to a piece of warm pie and a cup of fine coffee at the café owned by my good friend, Lilly. Have you been there before?"

"No, no, I'm afraid, we never frequented eateries. We were saving, you see, for the ranch."

"I see. Well, it's perfect, then, as you will be there as my guests."

"Oh no, I'm afraid that's impossible, Mr. Paley. But thank you just the same."

"No, no, now I'm not a terribly disagreeable person, ma'am, but where it comes to food, and especially pie at the Glen Rose Café, why, I have no shame in shrugging off my nosy reporter's demeanor. What say you?"

"No, really. We have much to do in town and then we must go back . . ."

"Home, I understand, sure, but, oh, please do let me take you." Loudon looked at the little girl, who was staring at him. "Wouldn't you like that, Maisie? A treat? Perhaps some pie and hot cocoa?"

"Oh, Mommy! Let's go!" The child brightened and popped to her feet, dancing in a circle with her dolly.

Mrs. Brighton smiled a weary smile and looked from the girl to Loudon. "That was unfair, Mr. Paley." But she said it with that slight smile still in place. "It seems I have no choice, Mr. Paley."

"Good," he said, rising from behind the desk. "I promise you it will be the best pie you have ever tasted. Oh, unless your own mother was a fine baker, or yourself." He reddened. "I have a habit of talking too much and too soon, I'm afraid."

"Not at all, Mr. Paley. In fact, if I might prevail upon you for one more favor?"

"Of course, of course," he said, eyes widened in curiosity.

"I have to stop at the marshal's office, as I mentioned, that is, if he is back in, to see if he has learned of anything new. Would you possibly. . . ."

"I am more than happy to accompany you, ma'am. Absolutely. Yes, let's go."

As it turned out, the marshal had not yet returned, so the trio proceeded on toward the Glen Rose Café.

As he opened the door for her, Maeve Brighton said, "The woman who owns this place, is she your . . . sweetheart?"

Loudon blushed and his eyebrows rose as he looked over Mrs. Brighton's shoulder toward Lilly, who was moving from table to table with a coffeepot. "No, no, just a friend. In fact, she is engaged to be wed to my best friend."

They moved to an empty table, and Loudon pulled out chairs for mother and daughter. Lilly brought them all pie, and coffee for Loudon and Maeve, and hot cocoa for Maisie. As she came by to top up cups, Lilly lingered, and she and Maeve talked as if they had known each other for years. Lilly stood beside Maisie, rubbing her arm and looking quite at home with her new friends.

As they rose to leave, Lilly walked around the table and bent low, hugging the little girl. "Will you come back to see me, Maisie?"

"Yes, please!"

"I would like that very much," said Lilly. She stood and then hugged a surprised Maeve Brighton. Still holding her at arm's length, Lilly said, "Trust Loudon. He's a good man and a good journalist. If there's something to be dug up, he will be the one to find it."

Loudon turned red and looked down at his hands resting on the chair back.

"And he blushes so easily!" said Lilly.

"Seriously, Maeve. Don't be a stranger here. Perhaps one day you can meet my husband-to-be, Jed Stark."

"Stark?" said Maeve. "Stark, yes, I believe we have heard of that name. A founding family of Glen Rose, is that right?"

"One and the same," said Lilly.

"Yes, there was an older lady who visited after . . . well, after. She brought food, a basketful. She told me her name and said that if we needed anything, we were to track her down, as she said it. Then she hugged me, too, and left."

"That would be Minnie, Mother Stark. She's Jed's mama."

"And if she ever heard you calling her 'older,' she would make your ears burn!" Loudon laughed as he said it. "But you didn't hear that from me! I don't have any urge to get on her dark side."

Lilly said, "Oh, Minnie's not a demon. You just need to know how to . . . um . . ."

"Exactly," said Loudon, chuckling again.

Lilly handed him a heavy, large parcel wrapped in oilcloth and tied with twine. "Help the lady to her buggy and put this in there," said Lilly, handing the thing to Loudon.

"Yes, ma'am," said Loudon, knowing it was likely a parcel of tasty food for Maeve and Maisie.

Chapter 11

"Well, don't take this the wrong way, but I was hoping you'd be Lilly," said Jed, glancing up at Loudon.

"Sorry to disappoint you, Jed," said Loudon with a smile. "I guess you haven't seen her in a few days then, eh?"

"Nope," said the big whiskey maker. "I've been holed up here, making whiskey and working on the house, trying to get it into some sort of order before . . . well, you know."

"The wedding?" said Loudon, grinning.

"Yeah, yeah."

"Gosh, don't sound so enthusiastic, Jed."

"Oh, I am. Don't worry about that. So, anything come of that dandy Englishman who was drifting around a few weeks back? I can't imagine he'll make too many inroads."

"You'd be surprised. There have been a number of folks who I've heard have taken him up on his offers."

"Really? Huh, well, good riddance, then. At least we have that new family that moved out onto the old Kirby place, what was that, pushing a year now, eh? Beston? Beeton? Something like that. Any idea how they're doing?"

Loudon's eyes widened. "Well, in fact, Jed, that's what I was about to tell you. That couple, their name is Brighton. Henry and Maeve Brighton, actually. And what happened to them concerns that Dalton Majors fellow. I think."

"What is it, Loud?"

Loudon sighed. "Well, you see, that man, Henry Brighton, he was shot dead two days ago."

"What?" Jed looked up from his work.

"Yeah, it sounds to me like it could well have been a hunting accident, but Maeve, that is to say, Mrs. Brighton, she came to see me, and we talked. She was in town to pay for her husband's coffin at Milchner's and to talk with the marshal. Harley was out, but she saw my sign and came in and told me it was no accident."

"What is she thinking?"

"She is convinced her husband was murdered, shot by Majors, or someone working for him."

"Wow," said Jed. "And was he?" said Jed, rasping a big hand over his stubbled jaw.

"There's still no proof as far as I know, but Marshal Thompson has been checking into it. I must say, after hearing her side of things, it sounds plausible."

Loudon explained to Jed all he knew of the story, which was all that Maeve Brighton had told him, in addition to a few salient pieces of his previous explanation of the Dalton Majors situation.

"Where is this Majors fellow now?" said Jed.

"That's the curious bit in all this—he's gone. Left town about when all this happened, more or less."

"That's quite a coincidence. So it's possible, maybe probable, that he did this horrible thing and then disappeared."

"He might well have, yes, but that just doesn't make sense."

"How's that?"

"He made cash offers, even bought some of the places he offered on. And he swore to everyone he was returning in a few weeks."

"Was his money good?"

"Yep, apparently so. And that woman he's working for, that Mona Starret, who I mentioned a minute ago, she's a big wheel, make no mistake. Not the sort of person who might get mixed up in something like this."

"Or," said Jed, "she might well have gotten where she is, all that money and power, by being just the kind of person to do these sorts of things."

"True, true. But still, it's odd. Look, if somebody wants to own land somewhere and set themselves up in business of some sort, why would they commit a murder? It's not as if whoever did it took any pains to cover up what they had done."

"No," said Jed, his arms folded over his broad chest. He looked up at the sky. "What an odd and awful thing to have happen around here."

"Anywhere, really," said Loudon.

"Yes, it makes me think of last year. Killing for land, for money, for power." He let out a long breath. "I don't know, my friend. Every time I start to think life's righting itself again, some great big wave of water rises up and rocks the little boat we're all floating in."

"Yeah, it's worrisome. That's why I'm still looking into it, as much as I can from here. I have my friends back East digging around—they're the ones who found out that Majors works for Mona Starret. Harley's using the information, too. He's wired back East, but these big-money people always seem to be above the law somehow."

"Figures," said Jed. "Well, I have to head into town tomorrow. I'm overdue and I want to see Lil. I'll check in with Harley, see what he's thinking about all this. How's the widow, Mrs. Brighton? She bearing up okay?"

"Oh yes, her name's Maeve. And there's the sweetest little girl, three, maybe four years old. Doesn't seem to understand what's happened. She says she misses her daddy, but that her mother told her he had to go away for a while."

"I can't imagine how they feel. Did she say she's going to stay, then? She did reject Majors's offer, after all."

Loudon shrugged. "I think it's too early for her to know. I imagine it's so fresh to her that she isn't certain yet what she's going to do. I do know she's angry as much as she is in mourning, and sad. And I don't blame her. Imagine it, even if it turns out it was some sort of hunting accident and the hunter was a clueless coward, well, her husband is still dead. That might even be worse, come to think of it."

"How so?" said Jed.

"Well, at least with a murder there's a reason, nasty and foul-intentioned as it would be. But with a random hunting accident, well, that's just wrong, more a thing of raw bad luck and chance. That would leave a person feeling hollowed."

"Either way, her husband is dead, and she's alone now with a small child." Jed sighed and raked a callused hand through his hair. "I'll talk with Mama and Lil. Must be something we can do for them."

CHAPTER 12

"Hey there, fella! Long time, no see! Where you been keeping yourself, son?" Deke Frakes smiled and extended his right hand in a wave as his visitor rode slowly closer.

The man on the horse did not acknowledge the greeting, but kept riding at the same measured pace, moving toward Frakes as if he had not heard or seen the man.

The miner-turned-rancher let his hand drop and rested it back in its usual spot, slung in the bib of his overalls. He spat a stream of chaw juice and dragged a grimy cuff across his spittle-wet lips and waited.

After another half-minute, the man on the horse plodded right on up to Frakes and halted the beast. Then he shifted his gaze from looking forward to looking down at the man.

He did not smile, even when the rancher looked up and said, "I knowed it was you, Larry Chiswick. Heck, I thought you was sore with me or something, the way you rode on up and didn't even give me one of your big ol' howdies. You funnin' me, boy?" Frakes squinted up at the man and offered a hesitant smile.

The man on the horse, Larry Chiswick, indeed, continued to look down on the man he'd come to visit. He wore neither his usual past smile whenever he dropped in on his old drinking pal, nor did he wear a scowl. On this day, his face offered an impassive gaze.

"What's ailing you, boy? Everything all right? Something I can do for you?"

Still, he did not respond, but shifted his gaze to the leather satchel slung over his saddle horn, hanging down the horse's right shoulder. He lifted the unfastened flap top and lifted out a half-empty bottle of liquor.

"Oh, Larry, now you ain't still sore about being ousted as marshal of Glen Rose, are you? I told you when you was last here that they was all fools, blinded by that Stark and those other goody-minded folks, nothing more. You bide your time, wait it out a while longer, and that whelp you trained will flail, you mark my words. Then the townsfolk will all come to their right minds and wonder why they did that terrible thing to you. Mark my words or I ain't Deke Frakes!"

The rancher held up a finger as if making a grand declaration on the election trail.

A weary, sagged look settled on Chiswick's face, and he almost smiled. Holding the bottle by the neck, he swung his right leg over the cantle and dismounted. When he had righted himself, he straightened up before Frakes and finally offered the man a tired grin. "How you doing, Deke?"

"Hoo-wee!" said Frakes, popping his right hand out and shaking Chiswick's. "Had me going there, Larry, I don't mind saying so. As for me, I'm good and fine. Got my place, got my health, what else does a man need?"

"Your place and your health, huh?" Chiswick glanced about himself, eyeing the buildings and close-up terrain. "You been doing work here, I see."

Frakes turned, smiling as they surveyed the scene before them. His home was a modest, white-painted, lumber-built affair with a long, low shade porch.

Across the way, to their right, sat a weather-grayed barn and rail corral. Two horses, one brown, one a mottled blue-black roan, stood at the rail, eyeing the two men who were at that moment eyeing them.

"Yeah," said Frakes. "Had to do something with my time since I give up on the booze."

"Say what now?" said Chiswick, staring hard at his old friend. "You ain't drinking no more?"

Frakes shook his head. "Nope. Got to liking it too much, and when you do that to a thing, it usually don't end as you might like it to."

"Shame," said Chiswick. "I brought this bottle here to share with you. Just like old times."

Frakes looked down at it, rocking back on his heels. There was the slightest glint in his eyes, and he realized he also licked his lips. "I see you did, yep. I also see you tucked into it a mite on your way out here!" He chuckled and looked back to his house.

"No call to make a man feel badly about himself, Deke."

"What? No, no, I was just crackin' wise, that's all. Sorry if it bothered you, son."

Chiswick turned to face his friend. "You know what's always bothered me, Deke?"

"Huh?"

"Yeah, I'll tell you. You always calling me 'son' when you ain't but what? Ten, twelve years my senior. You ain't old enough to be my pappy, never was."

"Larry, I . . . I am sorry to hear of it. Never knew! I will stop it right here and now. Okay, then. I apologize for all them times. Say, how about we head on inside and have ourselves a cup of hot coffee? I still have a couple of biscuits left. Ain't been much in the way of baked sweet breads and such in the house since Maria passed on to her reward, oh, what was it? Ten years now?"

Chiswick thumbed the cork off the bottle and let it fall. He swigged deeply and then thrust the bottle toward his friend. "That's another thing, Deke. You always went on about your dear dead Maria this and sainted Maria that. My word, to hear you tell it, she was the sun and the moon, and you weren't nothing but mud."

Frakes backed up a step, pulling his big-knuckled hands from where they rested in the overalls bib. "What's got into you, Larry? You have no call to say such things about my wife, nor anyone else's, for that matter!"

Chiswick's wry, sour sneer slipped, and his face seemed to turn to stone before the rancher. "What do you know of wives? What do you know? You talk with mine, did you? Talk with her, maybe even spend a little time with her before she up and left me? Huh?" He advanced on his old friend. "Come to think on it, that bawlin' brat she whelped bore a whole lot more resemblance to you than it did to me! Huh? Ha! Now we come to it, I reckon!"

Before the wide-eyed Frakes could utter another word, before he could remember to step backward and pull his arms out before his face, his visitor, his longtime friend, Lawrence Chiswick, Larry to his chums, whipped that *more-than-half-empty* bottle up and around in a tight, quick sweep that caught Frakes high up, between his left cheekbone and temple.

The sound that burst from Frakes's mouth was less a cry than a guttural shout clipped off as he dropped to the earth, face down. His right shoulder jerked up and down and his head twitched.

Chiswick backed up a step and regarded the man on the ground with a hard glare, his teeth set tight, his bottom jaw canted to one side as if he had been interrupted chewing a hunk of steak. He grunted, then hoisted the bottle up before his face, eyed the meager contents, then upended the thing and swallowed what was left.

By then, Frakes had begun moaning. Within moments, he

was shoving himself up onto his knees, but leaning forward with his palms resting on the gravel. He held that pose, his chest working as if he had run a mile. Bloody spittle drooled in a string out of his mouth and hit the ground beside his hand. Finally, he said, "Ahh, what . . . why you do that, Larry?"

"Because you disgust me, that's it and all about it. Whining about your dead woman, giving up on drink, keeping your place so tidy. Man alive, you're just packing salt into the seeping wound that is my life, man!"

Chiswick didn't move as he said this. He glared at Frakes, who rose on shaky pins to his feet. He swayed there a moment, then slowly moved his head from side to side. His vision settled and he raised his glance to Chiswick, who now stood three or four paces back from him. Frakes raised a hand and tenderly felt his head with his fingertips.

"My word," he said, eyeing his old friend. "Never thought I'd see the day." He shook his head and began walking to the house. He stopped after a dozen or more feet and looked back to Chiswick, who had not moved, save for his face, which now wore a wide smile.

"We are through, Larry Chiswick. Forget we ever was friends, 'cause I have. Now get gone from my spread. And don't come back."

He wanted to shout all this, but the side of his face began to throb. He resumed walking to his house. "Git!" he managed to all but shout, without looking back.

Deke Frakes had almost reached his house and the still-open front door when he heard the bootsteps closing in fast behind him. He turned in time to see Chiswick sneering once more, but now he was bent low, as if he intended to barrel straight into Frakes.

And that is exactly what Chiswick did to his old friend. The force of the hit from behind whipped Frakes's head back, wrenching his neck and sending a bloom of fast lancing heat from the stalk of his neck up into and over his scalp, as if he had had scalding water poured over his head.

He shouted, whipping out a sound that wasn't a word, and managed to raise his left hand as he pitched forward. His hand crabbed for something to grab, anything, and it found purchase on the doorframe. It wasn't enough to stop him from pitching inward, but he did manage to maintain his grasp, however meager, pivoting him to his left, spinning him so that he ended up slamming to his back just inside his kitchen. His already battered head bounced once, twice on the worn, swept plank floor, and he grimaced wide.

That was all he had time for, because Chiswick was on him, snatching up the fellow's shirt front and balling the blue chambray cloth in his left hand, lifting the addled Frakes's shoulders and head up off the floor. Chiswick's right hand snatched out his revolver from its holster, and as he raised it, he thumbed back the hammer all the way to the deadly position.

Frakes was not so stricken by the attack that he didn't see the gun and guess what might be coming. He howled, a harsh, phlegmy "No!" that tailed off in a wheeze as Chiswick began shaking the man with that balled left fist.

The attacker dragged the man into the room, shoving his head into the back of a chair, then raking at the chair with his gun-filled right hand.

The barrel fetched up between two narrow spindles of the chair's back and required both of Chiswick's hands to free it.

He shoved Frakes hard to the floor and, spitting out curses and growls of frustration, the crazed ex-lawman jerked the chair in his seething rage, thrashing and whipping the chair side to side. Then he raised it up, the chair's feet smacking the painted planking of the ceiling before he brought it down hard to the floor, where it splintered, cracking and coming apart in three places in his hands.

During this brief moment of madness playing out before

him, Frakes had enough sense left to shove himself with his bootheels hard and fast to his right, scooching around the far end of the table toward the stove, which still held the barest glow of warmth from his early morning breakfast fire, over which he had made coffee and then fried up two eggs and bacon and buttered bread.

The cast-iron fry pan sat above his head, canted out enough that its black handle jutted, sticking out where Frakes always held it in his right hand while he hummed and poked the frying food. He used a worn, burned-ended wooden spoon that had been Maria's favorite. Therefore, he used it daily, washed it clean, dried it right away, and oiled it often. He did this to keep it in good health, something his Maria had not enjoyed herself in the last two years of her too-brief life.

All this and more flashed through Frakes's mind as he reached up with his left hand and snatched that frying pan's jutting handle. He began to slide the pan off the stovetop just as Chiswick rounded the table and brought the revolver to bear on his friend's wide-eyed face.

"Well, now, old friend," barked the man, his chest heaving. "Just what is it you are planning to do with that there fry pan? Huh?"

Frakes did not give voice to the question hounding him—why? Why are you doing this? Why is this happening?

Instead, he gritted his teeth and finished dragging that fry pan off the stove, fast. Chiswick took one last step closer, planting his worn boots right beside Frakes's supine form. The addled rancher yanked hard on that fry pan and thought, even as he swung the thing with all the strength he could muster, that he might as well do this, because he was going to die in the next moment anyway.

That thought flicked into his mind with no more alarm than as if he had been hoeing his food patch and had looked up to see a mass of dark clouds low and sliding his way. Yep, that meant it was going to rain. Can't change it, so there it is. All right, then.

This meant, you bet, you're going to die and a whole lot sooner than you had hoped. There it is.

Even as he swung that fry pan with all his solid, stiff-armed strength, he heard two sounds at once, although he could not be certain. It might well be more than that. But each of the, for certain, two sounds was accompanied with a feeling.

The first was the sound of his madman visitor and old friend, Larry Chiswick, screaming a sudden, harsh, sharp shriek as the hefty steel pan slammed with brute force into his left knee.

Barely a pinch of a moment later, Frakes heard the world explode all about him. He thought for certain the fool had set off some secret charge of dynamite he'd carried into the house with him.

Along with the burst of sound, Frakes saw a bright blast of light and felt it peel apart the room, his head, his life. Surely it had to be his end.

Then followed the stink of something raw, burned, and base, the stench of a gun blast. This all somehow made sense to him, and he knew that Chiswick had to be completely gone from his senses to behave this way. But what did it matter?

As Frakes came back to himself through the ringing and the smoke, he realized he was still alive and so he had to move, had to get away from Chiswick. With a gun, the madman was no man that Frakes could fight.

His slamming of the pan into the man's knee must have done something to slow him down. As if in answer to this, the smoke parted to reveal the wonder of all wonders—his brutal visitor still standing above him, but this time he was bent over, rubbing a hand on his left leg, right about where Frakes had landed his fry pan swing.

Frakes knew it would not slow down the brute for long. For

the man glared at him with live fire dancing in his eyes. The fires of hate. For what reason, Frakes did not know.

Through his ringing, muddled senses, the assaulted rancher realized that although he had been shot at close range by Chiswick, what had looked as if it was going to be a shot right in the face, Frakes could not feel it.

That's the way death works, he thought. Playing him false to the end. He saw Chiswick still sneering down at him, and what's more, the madman's voice was slowly buzzing alight, the sounds of him shouting as he looked on in raw anger at his captive, his gun again cocked and loaded and ready to kill. In fact, Chiswick looked more ready to kill than anyone Frakes had come across in all his years. Ready and angry.

"Now we get to it, you old fool!" barked Chiswick through teeth parted just enough to shout and blow spittle. "I come here ready to offer you cash money for your pitiful ranch, and you attack me with a fry pan! All right, then, you foul dog!"

He thumbed back his gun's hammer, the deadly snout end of the barrel but two feet from Frakes's face once more.

With his free hand, Chiswick snatched with viselike fingers, clawing and wrapping around Frakes's wrist of the hand that still held the fry pan. Chiswick spun his hand around to grip the underside of the man's arm.

With all his strength, he slammed Frakes's arm against the ridged, steel face of the cookstove, once, twice, and again. The fry pan dropped from the rancher's fingers, smacking upended on the floor.

The rancher howled as he felt small, needlelike pains in his arm, splintering, cracking, snapping. This was more pain than he had felt since that mad young bull had trapped him beneath the buggy so many years ago.

Maria had finally run the thing off with a broom, bless her, long enough for Frakes to scrabble on out from beneath the wagon before the bull took after him once more.

The brute chased him clear across the barnyard. He had enough time to stumble inside the kitchen and snatch down the shotgun from the set of muley horns he had it cradled in on the wall by the dining table.

He checked, and yes, there was a shell in it, for he had been having trouble at night with some varmint meddling with the chicken coop. And so, he had kept the shotgun at the ready.

Frakes had hurried back outside only to see the bull still frothing and pawing and bellowing with mad bull rage, stalking his sweet Maria around and around the wagon.

Just as Frakes emerged from the house, shakily checking the single-barrel iron, the bull rammed his mighty head against the small wagon's side, and then did it again, his powerful legs and chest rippling with the effort as he forced the wagon up onto the far side wheels.

"Get out of there, Maria! Cut wide toward the house! Cut wide!"

As he shouted this, she nodded and, still clutching her trusty broom, his wife ran for the house, cutting not nearly as wide as he would have liked, but making for her kitchen, where she felt, no doubt, safest in all the world.

The bull saw this and shoved his way away from the wagon and made for her. It looked to Frakes as though he might well reach her before she reached the safety of their home.

The haggard rancher dropped back, legging it wide himself, and set himself dead in the course of that bull, not wanting to waste the shot, knowing just then as the thought came to him that he had but one chance to drop this rogue beast.

For he had no other shells on him, and even if he did, he would not have time to break the barrel, snatch the spent, smoking, hot shell from it, and jam in another.

He set his feet and didn't bother looking to see that Maria was safe. He trusted she was. As the red-hide, blood-eyed brute tore at him hard and fast, closing the distance, Frakes finally sighted not on the bull's big, bony head, for a blast there would merely anger the seething beast. He dropped his barrel to the side and down, the barest of angles. He was not standing full straight on, for which he was grateful, but before the bull altered his course and changed that, Frakes knew he had to fire.

He tugged back on the trigger, and his slugs drove hard and fast and offered him the results he wished he had not had to force to happen on them.

The bull staggered, his left front leg peppered, yes, but the brunt of the lead had punched into the chest, between the neck and low on the shoulder.

The rogue bull screamed, a frothy, high-pitched sound Frakes had never heard from a bull before.

He had already darted to his right, spinning the gun around to hold the thing by the handle and swing it as a club should the bull come after him. But the bull had already slowed, then staggered to a stop, hoofing at the dusty earth and snorting. He rolled his riled, addled head in an odd side-to-side, then up-and-down motion, his big white eyes seeming to bulge even more, rolling in counterpoint to his head pivots.

This all happened so quickly that Frakes, still tense and unbreathing—without knowing so—was still very much ready to be slammed hard into by the brute even as it gouged and snorted and tore at the patch of earth it trembled upon.

Blood and great dripping gobs of snot and phlegm and saliva gushed from the big beast's bawling maw, its thick, wet, rubbery snout open wide with its confused, rage-filled bellows and its nostrils flexing, as if it could not pull in enough air.

Frakes glanced at the house and saw Maria in the kitchen doorway, half crouched and holding her broom, worry frowning her face and making it look all the sweeter and sadder to him than ever he'd seen in their years of marriage.

Sweeter to him because he saw her then as the true, fearless, bold, warrior-type of woman he began to know more and more as the years with her rolled by. And sadder because neither of them relished the thought of killing, even for meat and protection. And to have had to kill the bull, who they now and again referred to in jest as 'the boy' because they had raised him from a calf, oh, this was a hard one to swallow.

But they would, and literally, because caring they might well be, but foolhardy they were not. They knew that food was food. That did not mean it wasn't going to take some time to commit themselves to gut, skin, and render down all the beast's big frame.

But that didn't mean they didn't like the knob-headed beast. And until that day he grew lusty and rutty, he had never given them cause to question him, in the least. But a bull is a bull is a bull.

Frakes had heard that phrase from older, wiser ranchers over the years, and it echoed in his head. It was one of the many mantras a farmer or a rancher was expected to know, to absorb as the result of working with beasts for a living.

Ah, my dear, thought Frakes from the floor, so many memories of this place. And unless he could somehow keep Chiswick from killing him, then he, too, was going to end up dead there. Dead by the hand of another, someone he had invited in many times before. But only after Maria had been taken by death, in those few dark years when he was mired in mourning and sought the thin, false help of whiskey.

Good, thought Frakes with a sense of finality. Good and fine, then. There was a cold comfort in knowing he would die in his own home. For this means, he thought, that I will finally be with my Maria, in the place she believed in, even if he never had. But he believed in Maria, and her faith was such that he knew it would pull him along, too.

Frakes jerked once more to his right, hoping somehow to trip up Chiswick, upend the brute, and maybe that would give him time to bolt on out of the path of immediate and deadly danger.

But no, his left leg smacked into the near table leg, the very table that he himself had built, intending it to be a temporary thing until they could save up enough money to buy a bigger, finer catalog-bought table, or maybe to hire a woodworker to build one to Maria's preferences.

Alas, neither happened, and they continued using that cobby table he had made. Maria never once complained. In fact, it hadn't taken long for her to praise the table and proclaim she wanted no other. That was just like her, he thought from the floor. Truly, she was a kind and forgiving woman.

"You gonna sell the ranch to Mr. Majors or what, old friend?"

"Is . . . is that what this is all about, Larry? My word, my word!"

"My word, your word, ain't nobody's word is worth spit and none of it means a thing, you know that as well as I do, man. Now, wise up, and you might still make it through this mess all right, you hear?"

So many thoughts flickered in and out of Frakes's mind as he lay on his kitchen floor, writhing in an effort to get away from his death-dealing visitor and one-time friend. Frakes tried to move, to roll to his left, hoping to somehow avoid a gunshot a second time.

Chiswick's words peppered through his thoughts, and he could not understand what Chiswick, by all accounts a penniless drunkard these days, would want in bringing up that dandy's foolish offer on Frakes's ranch. That had been a week or two back. Frakes had almost forgotten all about it.

He tried to yank his legs and jerk himself up, away once more from Chiswick, but the man with the gun staring down at him from above with a harsh leer on his veined, ruddy, begrimed face, shook his big hairy head. "Nope."

There was a long, tense moment when neither man moved. Then just as Frakes was about to speak, to say yes, take it, I don't care anymore, at that very moment, Chiswick said, "Bah," and touched his trigger.

Chiswick's bullet split the air and drove hard and fast at Frakes. Even then, the addled rancher turned his head to one side. It was not quick enough of a movement to avoid the bullet entering his skull, but it was enough to prevent the lead vermin from creating a hole in his face. Not that Frakes would care.

As he thought all this and waited for Chiswick's bullet to do its intended job, the beaten rancher worked up the slightest of smiles. For he knew that without doubt, yes, Maria was waiting for him.

And yes, even the bull and all the turkeys and sheep and pigs and chickens and cats and dogs he had had to lay low over the years would be there, too. Yes, he would finally meet them all again.

After he had pulled the trigger on his old friend a second time, as had been his intention all along, Chiswick sighed and lifted the revolver. The end of the barrel smoked, and his ears pulsed and rang as if a dozen bells were competing in a volley. None of them pealed at the same pitch, all of them clashing with each other in a stinging, brassy sound. He did not care.

Once he figured out that he no longer cared about much, Lawrence Chiswick felt himself grow happier, he guessed, despite the fact that he did not think he had ever truly been happy a day in his foul life.

So perhaps he had not felt happier, he mused, now and again, but he for certain felt less weight on his shoulders. Maybe none at all. Why fight what he knew he could not change about himself? He was a hopeless boozer and so he would die that way. There it was.

And if that didn't get him in the end, then the bullet from a stranger would. As long as he could keep enough money in his pocket to buy whiskey—the job Dalton Majors had lured him into would do that for him just fine—then he would never wake up feeling hopeless and awful, because he would no longer be a hungover mess. Just always drunk. Okay by him.

"Well, as I'm here, I might as well see if I can't find his fancy papers, a deed or some such. Maybe the old skinflint has cash jammed away in a knothole somewhere. I could use a meal, too."

Chiswick pulled long on his cigarette and regarded the dead man. Blood still pumped from that vein on the fellow's head. Looked odd, but there you have it, he thought. Just when you thought your life couldn't get any odder, along comes something such as this.

Chiswick giggled. "Tell you what, Frakes. Should have made you cook me up something in that fry pan you are so fond of whipping around. Then I could have dropped you. I tell you, the older I get, the slower I am on the draw. Hmm."

The drunk upended his bottle and, still finding it to be empty, he let fly a curse and tossed the thing to the floor. "One of these days I have to find me a bottle that don't do that." He giggled and drew on his smoke while he rummaged in cupboards. Anything in his way was peeled on out of storage and dropped to the worn kitchen floor.

He found nothing of use save for a couple of hard biscuits. He bit one and ground it down to crumbs while he continued to stroll through the modest, solid structure. Then, on a shelf in an old dry sink along the northeast wall of the bedroom, he found a sheaf of yellowed papers bound tight into a curled bundle with a faded purple hair ribbon.

He figured they might be some sort of foolishness along the lines of love letters, but the bundle might also contain something of use, such as that deed Majors seemed to prize. He'd take the papers with him, and later, he'd see if they might have value to the Englishman.

Try as he might, Chiswick could not find much of anything of value that he could turn into cash or at least take and use for himself, except for a decent old hip knife.

It was older but of finer quality than his own, and he gladly strapped it on his belt, almost tossing his own hip knife to the floor, but then he thought it might be useful, and besides, he'd had it for many years, so when he made his way back outside, he stuffed it down into his saddlebag.

He mounted up and cast a last look at Frakes's place. He had to give the fellow credit. He'd tightened up these last years and had done himself proud. But work was work, and Majors was paying cash money for ranches and land, and Frakes had been a thorn in the man's foot, and Chiswick worked for Majors, so that's all there was to it.

Chiswick sighed as he lit another cigarette. He felt none of the regret he assumed he'd feel once he had done this thing. He hadn't given all that much thought to it anyway, the killing of an old friend. "Ah, well, I got money now. Who needs friends?"

He blew out smoke and urged his horse out of the dooryard and on up the long, narrow, straight lane. "Let's see who's next on the list of folks who just don't wanna sell."

Chapter 13

In town several days later, the haggard young Marshal Harley Thompson poured another cup of tepid coffee from the office's battered tin pot. "Lucky you caught me in, Jed. I'm here for a spell, then back out again."

"Harley," said Jed. "If you don't mind me saying so, you look like you can use this coffee more than me."

"Aw, I'm all right. Just a bit stretched just now, what with the Brighton shooting. And that's not all."

Jed paused, his coffee cup halfway to his mouth. "What do you mean, 'not all'?"

Thompson let out a long breath. "One of the folks from church found Deke Frakes dead out at his place yesterday."

"Deke Frakes?" Jed knew the man, not well, but enough to exchange a greeting should they meet on the street, which happened, at best, once a year. "Dead? But how?"

"A couple of the ladies from church rode out to visit him. They bring him a cake, that sort of thing, mostly checking on him now and again, something they do since Maria passed."

"Oh, that's right, his wife died, what was it, a couple of years ago?"

"Yeah, something like that. He's been okay, from what I know. But . . ."

"But?" said Jed.

"But the ladies found him beaten and shot dead in his own house."

Neither man spoke for a moment. Then Jed said, "Beaten? Then he didn't do it himself?"

"That's what I thought at first, that he did it, but no, it does not look that way at all. When I went out there, I saw unmistakable signs of a big fight, no gun at hand that he would have used. There were hoofprints and dung, cigarette ends, and an empty whiskey bottle."

"Whiskey? In Glen Rose?" said Jed. "One of ours?"

Thompson shook his head. "Nope, not Stark whiskey. Bold Branch, if you can believe it."

"That stuff is liquid poison. Who would voluntarily drink that? Frakes?"

"Lots of folks buy it, Jed. It's all they can afford."

"I know," said Jed. "It's still trash."

Thompson nodded. "I don't think it was Frakes. He's been teetotal for a long time now.

"I have to track down whoever did this, but I'm worn thin just now, what with the Brighton shooting and a few town matters, and now this." The young marshal rubbed his eyes, and when he let his hand drop, he was smiling.

Just like the kid I always knew, thought Jed. A one-man beacon of optimism if there ever was one.

"Can't you hire a deputy?" said Jed.

"Sure, I just haven't had the time." Thompson chuckled. "That's rich, huh? I need time to find a deputy so I can have more time to do the things I need to do!"

"Like . . ." said Jed, shaking his head and grinning. "Hiring a deputy."

"That's about it, yep."

Both men sipped coffee a moment, then the marshal said,

"Sid, you know, the barkeep from the Happy House saloon? He said that not long before Dalton Majors left town, the Englishman was in there asking directions out to Chiswick's ranch."

"Larry Chiswick's place, huh? Interesting," said Jed, musing on the various possibilities this news brought to the surface. Any bit of information involving Larry Chiswick, former marshal of Glen Rose and, at one time, Harley's boss and predecessor, was sure to carry with it a tinge of foulness. The man carried far more guilt than most in the town back during the Merlin Sheldrake affair.

The former lawman had never been a particularly good fellow, more of a bully and blowhard, even when he and Jed were schoolmates together. Over time, Chiswick became an even fouler seed, and the role of town marshal only made it worse. He had, over the years, wallowed more and more in the whiskey bottle and was ideally suited to his role of sycophant to the wealthy fool, Sheldrake.

The town's citizens had finally awakened on that fateful night a year and more before and had ripped the star from Chiswick's chest, forcibly ousting the man from his office. They replaced him with young Deputy Harley Thompson and had yet to regret their decision.

He glanced at Jed, a man Harley had long looked up to as a male figure in his life, long before young Harley had taken on the duties of a lawman. Today he valued Jed Stark's friendship mightily.

"We can only guess it was to make an offer on Chiswick's run-down mess of a ranch. Or a place that used to be a ranch, anyway, before he turned professional drunkard."

"That makes sense, for certain," said Thompson.

"Man has no money and owns land. Most everybody knows it, so someone new to town sniffing around for likely sellers would eventually find his way to Chiswick."

"I agree," said Harley. "Trouble is, shortly after that, Chiswick was seen in town by lots of folks, buying booze, of course, but also buying himself a nice pair of used revolvers and a rifle and shells. He even got himself a haircut and rented a horse. Then he rode on out of town, after he spent a few hours drinking at the Happy House. And all this by a man who has barely had enough money to buy his booze and scraps of food for the better part of the past year."

"Hmm," said Jed. "You think Chiswick was preparing to leave town? Dare we think we're shed of him?" said Jed, not hiding the hopefulness tinging his question.

Thompson shook his head. "I doubt it. See, I haven't told you everything yet. Sid also said that Chiswick told him he was going to go 'earn his keep' for his new employer. Then Chiswick patted his guns and giggled and rode on out of town. In the direction the Brighton place sits."

Jed's face lost any hint of jocularity it had had thus far in the conversation. In a low voice, he said, "Could be a coincidence." He looked the young lawman in the eye. "But you know I'm just being charitable. And that word *charity* is never used in the same breath as *Chiswick*."

Thompson offered a grim look and a nod. Both men knew, without dragging it out into the open again, that even before last year's events, Chiswick was a man on the edge. And being caught up on the wrong side of the mess with Sheldrake had pushed him right over that edge, giving him the rest of the excuse he needed to become a full-time drinker.

Jed had reluctantly fought with Chiswick a couple of times, goaded by the smarmy lawman, and after that, the townsfolk had finally turned on Chiswick and stripped him of his badge. Since then, Chiswick had done nothing but drink and glare and threaten anyone who might listen that one day he was going to get his revenge on the whole lot of them.

That promise included his once-deputy and now-marshal, Harley Thompson, and it most assuredly also included Jed Stark, who Chiswick loathed with a fever that burned hot and red. And it was a sentiment that was returned, try as Jed had over the years to think charitable thoughts about the man, to little avail.

"You think this Majors fellow just wanted to inquire about buying Chiswick's land? Because, given the timing of the Englishman's leaving, and the fact that he visited Chiswick and then Chiswick bought guns, and rode off in the direction of the Brighton place, well, that gives you two possible suspects."

"Yep," said Thompson. If he was offended by Jed pointing out the obvious aspects of this incident, which was his job, not Jed's, Harley didn't let on.

He nodded and looked at Jed, and in that moment, he felt to himself to be very much the kid and then the young man who had always idolized the large, silent whiskey man.

Thompson, raised by his mother, had always been a good, quiet youth, attentive to his mother, and despite Chiswick's abuse had been an affable and intelligent deputy who more often than not compensated for Chiswick's increasingly unreliable behavior on and off duty.

But now that his former boss was a potential suspect in a possible murder, the new marshal felt himself once more in the hot seat. It seemed as if he might never be shed of Larry Chiswick. Oh, but he sorely hoped that Henry Brighton's shooting would turn out to be little more than a tragic mess of a hunting accident. It sure didn't feel that way, or look much that way, but he knew that it didn't hurt to hope for the best even as he carried out his investigation into the rancher's death.

"I think I should ride on out to Chiswick's place, see how he's been keeping himself. I'm having a devil of a time finding clues to Brighton's shooting. And now there's Frakes."

"Sounds like a logical plan. After all," said Jed, giving Thompson a hard look, "if Larry Chiswick is involved, there's not much room for coincidence."

While Jed and Thompson were chatting in low tones, now outside the door of the marshal's office and with no one in earshot, the sound of pounding hooves from the east end of town drew closer and closer, aided that morning with a slight breeze drifting toward them from the northeast.

Within moments, a man on horseback in the midst of a boil of dust thundered into view. He did not slow but rode straight for the two leaning men.

Shoppers walked, in no hurry, from one shop to another along Glen Rose's main downtown street. As the hustling man drew closer, they halted their progress, one, two, then several at a time, and looked to see who this might be.

Jed held up a big hand, as did Thompson, to visor the sun's glare and help him to see.

They did not have long to wait, for the man still wasn't slowing and looked to be making, if anything, even more of an effort to get right up to them before he halted his heaving, lathered steed. And this he did.

By then, Jed and Thompson had moved close to the edge of the boardwalk. "You see who that is yet, Harley?"

The lawman squinted. "Looks like . . . Joel Funke."

"Huh, don't know him," said Jed.

"Sure you do, works for the Albersons."

"Oh, yeah, I'd forgotten about him."

Of course both men knew the primary reason Jed didn't recognize the man was that the whiskey maker didn't spend that much time in town. He was reclusive by nature and had always been the quiet sort. When he took up with Lil years before, folks began seeing him in town a whole lot more frequently than they ever had, although they heard about as little from him as they ever had. He spent his time with Lil and then rode on home again.

He still wasn't overly comfortable with spending much time away from Whiskey Woods, especially not since last year when he'd returned not once but twice to find the place in a righteous shambles.

The first time the buildings, including the rambling ranch home he and Mama lived in and that he and she had grown up in, along with the barn, a shed, and the whiskey shed and still, had all burned to the ground. In fact, they had succumbed to the torch by Merlin Sheldrake's hired brutes. They had been a pair of idiots who had met their rewards in various ways.

The next time the ranch had been violated had been when he had returned from making a whiskey run to the closest town to the east, Grindle, Glen Rose's nearest municipal neighbor. He had found that Mama was missing and Redeye was scratching at death's front door.

He still felt a clot of fear and worry in his gut when he rode to either Glen Rose or to Grindle to make his weekly deliveries. But he vowed to continue supplying the few saloons in each town that carried Stark's fine whiskey.

He also continued to ride to Glen Rose to spend time with Lil in her own building, either in the café or upstairs in her home above the eatery. Nonetheless, he was never certain what sort of situation he might find on his return to Whiskey Woods.

Would he find the place razed again? Would Mama be clubbed or missing? Redeye and the horses, chickens, cattle, and such, would they be well or slain out of spite?

Despite such widespread worry and fear, the year since Sheldrake's era had passed from their midst, if not from their minds, had grown slowly better. These days, Jed gladly spent part of his ride back to the ranch mulling over his fair Lilly, or ways to continue to improve the still he had had to resurrect and rebuild.

But now, seeing Joel Funke, largely a stranger to him, ride hard and fast right at him and Marshal Thompson, a ripple of fear washed through him.

Chapter 14

What Marshal Harley Thompson knew of Joel Funke was that he was a past-middle-aged bachelor, a German fellow who kept to himself, but who was nonetheless liked by all who knew him. As were his employers, an older couple from way up at the top of the country, near Canada somewhere.

The Albersons had come to Glen Rose many years before as a younger couple, seeking a warmer place than the snowy, cold, northern clime they had each been born into. They wished to ranch a small spread and live quiet lives, as most folks thereabouts seemed to want to.

Many years ago, they had recognized they could do with some help about the place. They hadn't been thinking of hiring a full-time fellow to help with such matters, but it had worked out well for both Joel Funke and for the Albersons.

He was new to the region, spoke very little English, and Mrs. Alberson, Roberta, Thompson believed her name was, knew enough of Funke's native German tongue that the three of them could squeak by in those early days. Now, Funke was an old hand with English, if not always with the correct words.

He was, by all accounts, an intelligent fellow, quiet, and also seeking a quiet life. He kept to himself but did enjoy singing at church of a Sunday. He also liked to carve wooden toys for the local children during the yule season.

And within moments of Thompson thinking all these thoughts in a rush, Joel Funke brought his horse to a lathered stop before them. The heaving mount, a big brown beast with a graying muzzle, looked to be more suited to trudging before a plow or stepping somewhat lively before the Albersons' Sunday go-to-meeting buggy than to being ridden far too hard and far too fast to town from their spread, he presumed, some twenty miles to the northeast of town.

What did this mean?

The young marshal would soon find out. Thompson grimaced and moved forward, along with Jed, to help the man, now pretty much an old-timer himself, as he all but fell from the saddle. He, too, was out of breath from the raging ride, although his poor old horse looked to have fared a whole lot worse.

"What's wrong, Joel?" said Thompson as Jed caught the sliding man from toppling and slopping into a heap beside the sagging, panting horse.

It took the man a few moments to come back to himself, and when he did, it was as if he had woken from a dream. Or a nightmare, for as he looked at them, with Jed's big arms about his shoulders, and Thompson standing before him holding him by the elbows, Joel Funke's eyes widened as if recalling some hell only he knew of.

This, as they would soon learn, was most decidedly the case.

"Harley the marshal!" Joel Funke looked to his left. "And Mister Jed Stark!"

By then, a good six or eight others, townsfolk who had been on the street nearby and who knew Joel and the Albersons well, all wore looks of grave concern. Something, they decided, was wrong, quite wrong.

A mild, kind man such as Joel Funke would not behave this way. Indeed the man had rarely been seen in town on his own over the years. They all began peppering the haggard man with questions, and soon the marshal had to calm them down and move them back.

"Now, then, Joel, why don't you come on inside my office, and we can see if I can't find you a chair. I have water, and there's coffee on the stove."

Funke began stammering and looking about with wide eyes, and his mouth trembled.

Up close like this, the closest many of them had been to the man in years, they realized Funke looked old, so much older than they thought of him as. He had not yet shaved his face that day, which he normally wore quite smooth, save for trim, clipped mustaches. Even in church, he sat by himself at the rear and sometimes stood at the back if the seats were filled more than he found comfortable.

Thompson managed to escort the man into the lawdog's office, as it was known affectionately in town. With a stern eye, he warned the onlookers off.

Jed had volunteered to take care of the still-heaving, lathered horse, and after it had slaked its thirst at the nearby trough, he led it slowly around the end of the short string of buildings to the livery the marshal always used.

Rudy Nelson, a former slave with a gift for interacting with horses so much deeper and more meaningfully than anyone in town had ever seen, owned and ran the small but highly thought-of stable.

When the old man saw the horse, he dropped to the floor the mound of tack he was lugging from one storage rack to another. "What has happened here, my sweet, lovely girl?" He stroked the horse's long nose, then massaged her eyes with cupped, work-hardened hands.

Without looking at Jed, in a gentle voice, he said, "Now I know, Jed Stark, that you never would do this to a sweet girl like Mabel here."

It did not surprise Jed to know that Rudy knew the name of

the horse Joel had thundered into town on. Rudy knew all of the region's horses about as well as most folks knew their neighbors' names.

"No, Rudy, it wasn't me. Joel Funke just rode in hard and about fell from the saddle. He's with Harley now in the marshal's office. I don't know what it's all about just yet, but I can't imagine it's too good. I should go back."

Rudy stood there, still stroking the calming horse, whose shudders and heaving were abating, but he looked at Jed with drawn brows. "Oh, I've known the Albersons a long ol' time. I hope nothing's happened to them. But I do fear something is not right in their world, for Joel Funke would never treat Mabel this way. Never."

"Agreed," said Jed, turning to go. "I'll come back as soon as I know something." He reached the door. "Rudy," he said, turning. "I'm sorry to just bring her here like this."

"Jed, I'd have had to track you down and take a round or two out of you if you didn't!" Rudy winked and turned his attention back to Mabel. "Now git gone. Me and Mabel have some talking to do."

Jed nodded and smiled. He left the stable and made his way back up the street toward the marshal's office. Clustered outside, a dozen folks crowded before the door, peering in the windows and trying—and not succeeding all that well, in Jed's opinion—to keep themselves from pressing an ear to the door and windows, which is what they really wanted to do.

He could hardly blame them, after all, it wasn't a usual occurrence in the least to see anyone thunder into town on an overworked, hard-ridden horse giving more than her all. And that the rider was a normally mild, quiet man whom they rarely saw—well, that made the situation even more troublesome. And of even more concern was the fact that Funke looked as if he had been chased for miles by Ol' Scratch himself.

Jed wasn't certain what he should do. He wanted to know

what all this was about, as did everyone here. He wanted to elbow his way on into the office, but Harley—Jed still had a tough time thinking of the kind young man as "Marshal Thompson"—was in charge, and Jed didn't think he needed to see Jed nosing in on his professional duties.

As if in answer to his concerns, folks in the tiny crowd saw him and naturally parted, seeing him as a close friend to young Harley and being the man who had helped ease Joel Funke from the saddle and held him upright while the poor fellow regained his senses.

Jed noticed that the curtains on the door were drawn, and the same with the half curtains on the two windows flanking the door. A person really had to stretch a neck to see over them, which a few folks were trying to do. Jed, too, wanted to look in there, and he was tall enough to do it without trouble, but he held himself back.

He was weighing the merits of just barging in when, as if he'd been awaiting him, the marshal opened the door and poked his head out. "Jed? Would you have a minute? I'd appreciate your thoughts."

"Sure, of course, Harl—, I mean, Marshal. Of course."

The young lawman eased the door open so Jed could pass by him into the office, then Thompson said to the crowd, "As you all know, Joel's rattled, but we'll figure out what happened and then I'll let everyone know what I can. Thank you for your patience, folks."

People in the crowd mumbled and watched as, with a kind smile and a nod, the lawman closed the office door.

Once he was inside, Jed saw Joel sitting sagged in a wooden armchair by the far end of the desk. The man now breathed at a more measured pace, and he held his work-thickened left hand to the side of his face, the fingertips resting tenderly there as his eyes stared past his knees, as if the floor might hold answers to whatever mysteries he was considering.

Jed kept to one side while Thompson drew two wooden chairs, arranging them with their backs to the door. They sat at a distance close enough to have a conversation with Funke, if he was up for it.

Jed saw that Thompson had set a glass of water at the edge of the desk, and half of it was gone.

"Joel?" said Thompson. "Joel?"

At the second mention of his name, the old man looked up, eyebrows raised, as if he had been startled from sleep. "Oh, Marshal Thompson, yes, yes." He nodded, then saw Jed and nodded more. "And Mr. Jed Stark. Good, good."

Then he fell silent again, and his eyes began to look downward as if he were about to descend into his trance once more.

"Mr. Funke," said Jed in what he hoped was a kindly tone. "Did you have something to tell us?"

Thompson said, "Something about the Albersons, maybe?"

The old man looked up again and his eyes widened, his bottom lip began quivering again, and tears formed in his eyes. "Oh, Rudolph and Roberta. Oh, it is . . . how did this happen?"

"What, Joel?" said Jed, leaning forward. "What happened?"

The marshal leaned forward, too, and both men watched Joel as he once more looked up and focused on them, one then the other. Then he looked at nothing once more and pulled in a deep breath and let it out. Then he began speaking in a calmer, quieter voice than either of them thought he might.

"They . . . they are dead."

Although they half expected to hear those words, the awful truth of them still caught Thompson and Jed by some surprise.

Funke nodded, still not looking at either of them. "Yes, oh, you see, each morning, I rise early, often before Clement the rooster, and I begin the morning chores, you see. Rudolph, he is an old man now, and although I am old, he is so much older. I finally convinced him several years ago to stay abed for a while longer and let me begin the chores. He is a good man, but hard"—he tapped the side of his gray-haired head—"hard up here, yes?"

Then his slight smile slipped as he recalled the man was now, apparently, dead.

He breathed deeply once more. "It was on this day, the same as all the others, that I rose, and I went through from my home." He looked up, realizing that the two men to whom he spoke did not likely know how he lived.

"Yes, you see, long ago, Rudolph and I, we built a fine little home attached to the far back side of the barn. It has its own door to the outside, of course, but I rarely use that. I spend so much time with the animals, you see, in the barn. But I have a nice home, two whole rooms! Mostly I am in the barn, you see, but I have a small room to sit in of an evening, and I like to read, and sometimes I play my concertina."

He smiled slightly. "Then when I am done, I go through into my bed chamber and I sleep. Oh, but I sleep so deeply at times. I find I am a little sore in the mornings, sometimes because I find I have not moved at all in the night.

"Rudolph, he told me once that he tried to rouse me in the middle of the night because he thought I should have been paying attention to Mabel. This was when she was much younger, and she was about to foal. But I knew she would wait another day, perhaps two. But Rudolph, he was worried, you see. But on that night, he could not rouse me from a deep sleep.

"And that night, which was some years ago, I slept well. He was annoyed with me and told me later he considered that he would send me away when morning came. But no, that did not come to pass because he saw that I was right. And the next night, Mabel foaled a pretty colt, and there you have it."

There was a pause, and then Thompson said, "I'm sorry, Joel, but I don't understand. What does that have to do with why you are here today? What happened at the Alberson place last night, man?"

Jed cast his eyes to his right and whispered, "Easy, Harley, easy."

The young, impatient marshal blushed and nodded, "I'm sorry, Joel. Please, do go on."

But Thompson's impatience didn't seem to have bothered the German fellow much, for he looked still to be dwelling deeply in his own mind. Despite the fact that his eyes were open, he was again not looking at either man.

"Rudolph told me many years after I began working for him that this was one of the things he liked about me. 'That I sleep too deeply?' I said. 'No,' he said. 'Because you said on the day we met that you sleep well on nights of big wind.'

"And he knew what I meant, for I did mean just that. Before I let myself slip into sleep each night, I walk through my day in my mind and make certain that everything that needs doing will be done, you see."

Jed nodded. He saw that the young man looked fidgety again, ready to blurt out to Joel to get to the point. Thompson glanced back at him, and Jed raised an eyebrow to convey that the marshal needed to calm down and let Joel go through this at his own pace. It would all work out.

Jed knew, of course, how Thompson felt. He had been much like that when he was Harley's age. He knew how impatient he had felt in such situations, and he knew it was little more than the silliness of youth. Most of it, at least in himself, had been bludgeoned and pounded down and beaten out of him in the war. The foul, cursed war.

The worst of it was that man's violence toward other men never seemed to go away. And now, it seemed that Joel was, that is, if he ever got around to it, about to tell them of some other violent moment in their midst.

As if his thoughts had been read by the man, Jed heard Joel Funke follow up on his shocking statement.

The old man sighed, a long, low, trembling sound. "I tell

you all this about sleeping deeply because it will explain why I never heard what has happened . . ." Joel's breath hitched, and he held a gnarled hand to his mouth, clutching at it as if it might scurry off should he move his hand. His eyes scrunched and watered.

After a few moments, he said, "Last night I went to bed with the sun, as I always do. And I did sleep well, of course. When I woke this morning, it was early, of course, before the sun, and before Clement the rooster. I did all the things I always do. I built a small, quick fire in my little stove so I might have early tea. While that takes, I check on everyone in the barn. There is much to do these days.

"We have mostly a full barn, and then many other animal friends outside. I find out that they all are as I left them, and some are quite asleep still. These, I do not wake until I have to. After all, cows and sheep and chickens should get the sleep they wish to, yes?"

"Then what happened, Joel? Please, I have to know. You said so yourself that the Albersons are dead. I need to ride out there!"

Thompson began to stand, and this time Jed did not try to calm him. It might be the shove that Funke needed to get on with his story. He, too, was beginning to get annoyed.

To the surprise of both men, Joel Funke leaned forward and laid a hand on the rising marshal's knee. "Calm yourself, son, calm. My story is not done, but the dead will wait, I promise you. I do not have much more to tell."

This went some way toward calming the lawman, but he sat on the edge of his chair and stared with intention at Joel, who had cleared his throat and resumed his story.

"I made my tea and had sipped it, and left it to cool as I always do, on the stall divider between Boss the Jersey milch cow and Puff the donkey. I am grateful that Puff does not bray in the mornings. It is not a pleasant sound that early in the day."

He nodded as if agreeing with himself. "Then I keep on with the chores, removing dung and freshening feed, watering the beasts and such."

"Then I attended to the chickens. I gathered the warm eggs and made to carry the basket of them to the house, the Albersons' house, that is. Mrs. Alberson, Roberta, she would have breakfast underway by then. Rudolph and I would sip tea at the stove and discuss the day, what needed our attentions, that sort of thing."

Jed nodded. Thompson fidgeted and all but glared at Funke, who had stopped talking and looked as though he was about to weep once more. Then he did, his breath hitching in his throat. A tear, then another, slipped down his cheeks.

"They . . . oh, I opened the door, but even before that I thought perhaps they were ill and still abed, for there was no puffing smoke from the chimney, no soft light in the kitchen window by the door. Nothing. Sometimes I hear one or both of them singing. They love to sing, the Albersons, both of them. Beautiful voices, and always the hymns. Which is nice, you know.

"But this morning, oh, it was terrible. For when I opened the door, I found an empty, dark kitchen and dining area, it is a small house, you know, and as such, there are but three rooms. There is the front room, which is the kitchen and dining place, with the woodstove and the big table at which we take the meals.

"Beyond that is a sleeping chamber. I have been in it a few times, helping to move furniture and such, but I do not normally go in there. But this morning, as I stepped into the house and looked about, all was still, not even snoring or some such.

"I set the basket of eggs on the sideboard as I always do, and said, 'Hello? Good morning, Rudolph? Roberta?' But I heard nothing. I paused and listened with the ears of a rabbit. But no, I heard nothing still. I looked hard at their bedroom door, but it remained closed, you see."

"What then, Joel?" said Jed. He hoped they were closing in on the end of the story, as he didn't want Thompson to leap up again. He could feel the tension rippling off the young man in waves.

"Yes, yes." Funke's lip trembled and a tear slid down his face. "I took off my boots, you see, because I did not want to track mess into the house. Roberta, she always keeps such a tidy home." He nodded and continued, looking down at his thick-fingered, knotted hands as they slowly flexed in his lap, palms up, the fingers curled as if upturned helpless creatures that did not know what to do with themselves.

"I walked to their bedroom door, the house seemed close and cold and still about me. And dark, too, you see.

"I gently knocked like this." The man imitated a single-knuckle rapping on an imaginary door before him in the air. "But nothing. I hear nothing. I tried again, and said, 'Rudolph? Roberta? Is . . . is everything well?'

"I waited and still I hear nothing. I try again. Nothing. My mouth is very dry then, for I put my hand on the wooden latch and thumbed it down. This I had never done, you see. But still nothing. So I gently pushed open the door a little. There was a dark gap there and I spoke into it, again asking if they were all right.

"Perhaps they are outside already, I thought. Taking a walk, yes, an early morning walk, yes, that must be it.

"Even as I said it, I knew I was thinking and talking foolishness. The habits of a life do not change so fast. These were not people to walk in the dark of a morning for no reason, you see."

"Not many people are," said Jed, gently, offering Funke a slight smile and a nod, to please continue.

The old man nodded in return, seeming to appreciate the small kindness shown by the whiskey maker. "I opened the door wider and saw, from the light from the kitchen window, as the morning was breaking through nighttime outside, that there were the two lumped shapes in the bed. These I knew to be my friends, the Albersons. They are sleeping hard, I remember thinking. They must have, perhaps, stayed up late talking, perhaps over tea and cake. Yes, that must be it. But even as I thought it, I knew that this, too, was the foolishness of an old man with more hopefulness than information, you see."

"Then what did you do, Joel?" said Thompson, in a voice that sounded to Jed as if it were tense, but as if the young man were trying. Good, thought the big man. He's thinking first instead of acting.

"Then, Marshal, I kept saying, 'Hello, hello, good morning, my friends,' even as I walked into the room and to the window on the wall to my left. It has wooden shutters on the inside, to keep out the light. I reached them and fumbled with the wooden slide, and I managed to open the shutters without looking. All this time, I kept my eyes on the bed, but my friends, they did not move.

"Then I opened the shutters wide, as wide as they can, and more light came in from that window, too. Enough to see that . . . oh!" He wept again, sobbing loudly, and held a big, work-thick hand to his face, his shoulders shaking with the effort of crying.

Jed reached over and laid a hand on the man's resting forearm and rubbed. "It's all right, Joel. You're with friends."

"But they weren't!" He looked at Jed, then at Thompson. "You see?"

"No, Joel," said Thompson, gently. "Not yet. What did you find?"

"They were both . . . dead there in their bed. I walked over and gently touched the larger shape; it was Rudolph, of course, as he was much bigger than Roberta. I poked him, gently, then harder, and I said, 'Rudolph! Wake up now!'

"But he did not, he could not. For as I looked closer, daring to tug back the quilt off their necks and faces, I saw that there was blood. Oh, so much blood!"

The old man broke down again, shuddering and sobbing.

"They were dead," said Thompson, doing his best to remain calm, but as the closest lawman, he needed to get out to the Alberson spread quickly.

Funke seemed to understand because he quivered and pulled in huffing breaths, then said, "Yes, yes, they were dead. It looked as if they had been shot. Shot in their heads! While they were sleeping, I think!"

"But . . ." said Thompson. "But aren't you and the Albersons all meeting folks? Quakers or some such?"

Funke nodded, his gaze fixed once more at nothing before him, his face a wet mass of tears. His cheeks were reddened, as were his eyes. Every few seconds, he shuddered and pulled in a huffing, stuttering breath.

"Do you know for certain that they were shot, Joel?" said Jed.

The old man nodded. "Yes, yes, for I saw the blood, and so as I said, I pulled the quilt back more and each I see, they were facing each other, with Rudolph below me and Roberta facing him. Each of them . . . each of them had the bullet hole here." He tapped his temple. "Small, but yes, this was done. And so terrible, you see. So terrible."

He fell silent again, and Harley didn't seem so agitated to Jed. In fact, he seemed shocked and little else. As if the full truth and shock of the situation had draped its cold, foul hand over him.

Finally, in a low, thick voice, he said, "Joel . . . did you see anyone about the place? Anything suspicious or . . . I don't know, out of the ordinary?"

"No," said Funke quickly. "No, this I know you were going to ask me, as you should, but no, there was nothing amiss that I could see. The place looked the same as always, even if I don't know their bedchamber so much."

"Did you try to rouse them, Joel?" said Jed, suspecting the answer but needing to ask just the same.

The old man nodded. "Yes, yes! I grabbed them by the shoulders and gently shook them, but even before I shook them, I knew they were no longer alive. No longer." He shook his head. "So sad. Each was cold, you see, cold to my touch, even through their flannel nightclothes covering their shoulders, their arms, they were cold . . . stiff. Their flesh was stiff."

"They had been . . . gone," said Jed, "for some time, then."

"Yes, yes," Joel nodded in a somber way, his tears still dripping.

"But this is unthinkable," said the marshal. "They are, were, so kind. I have been out there, not in some time, several years, I think."

"I remember," said Funke, smiling slightly. "You came out with your mama looking for a turkey for the table, as I recall. It was a nice day in autumn, and I showed you the barn, too."

Thompson smiled at the memory. "Yes, I enjoyed that, I did."

Funke, too, smiled. "It was more than a few years ago, though, young man," he said. "For you were still young then. Not in knee pants, no, but young enough that you were thin and small and a little afraid of what you were seeing. I understand because you were raised in town, and that is as it should be. Okay, then."

Short minutes later, Thompson stood behind his desk, setting boxes of bullets on top. "I'd appreciate your help out at the farm, Mr. Funke."

As soon as he said it, Thompson knew that Joel Funke was not going to accompany him back to the Alberson place. He also knew he had to get out there as soon as he could.

The old man shook his head slowly. "I've told you what I found, Marshal. I've told you what I know. Please go there and figure out who did this thing to my dear friends, will you? And one more thing, Marshal. I want you to lock me up here."

"Why?"

"Because I know how this appears. Who else might have done this thing?"

"But you came to us, Mr. Funke. And you were their oldest friend. I just can't believe you would have done such a thing." Thompson shook his head as if to dispel the notion once and for all. Even doing that, he knew the old man was right.

Funke nodded but kept his eyes closed a moment. "Yes, this is all true, but you don't really know this yet. And you are now the marshal, not the little boy and his sweet mama who used to visit us at the farm.

"Now you are the marshal, and even if you don't want to believe this thing, and this makes me happy that you feel this way about me, believe me, young man." Funke smiled a little, a rare thing for him on this day.

"What would all the people of Glen Rose think if you let me walk free among them? They would think you have failed them, and they hired you because the other man did that, you see. He let them down. You, Marshal Harley Thompson, you are a good man, too good to do that." He gazed at the young lawman with that sad little smile on his face, and Thompson replied with a slight, hesitant nod.

Jed said nothing, but Thompson turned to his big whiskey-making friend. "Sorry to ask, Jed, but if you're inclined, I believe I could use your help out there, just in case."

"Sure, you bet. I was hoping you'd ask, but I didn't want to intrude."

"Are you kidding? I'd be grateful. I've never had to face this sort of thing. Well, a little last year with the town lynchings of Sheldrake's men, but, well. . . ."

Jed knew Thompson still felt sore and guilty about that, but he also knew the young man hadn't been able to arrest the entire town, had he? He'd told him as much later, after the dust of the affair had settled a bit and Thompson had visited Whiskey Woods.

A thought came to Jed. "Locking you up might also be safer for you, Mr. Funke."

"Oh?"

"Yes," said Jed, looking at Thompson. "Whoever did this will learn at some point soon that there was another person out there, someone they left alive. Maybe they will think they should not have."

"They'll want to finish the job, so to speak," said Thompson.

Jed nodded. "And we can't let that happen."

Chapter 15

It took another few minutes, as Thompson asked Funke more questions. None of the answers added to the information he had, nor did they change his opinion of the situation.

He and Jed finally rode on out of town toward the Alberson place. By then a few folks had made for the place themselves, having guessed correctly that something foul and amiss had happened out there.

Once on the road to the northeast, Jed and the marshal rode hard and fast, and soon they saw men ahead who they recognized from town as heading for the Alberson place themselves.

"Look," said Thompson in a quick voice with a hard edge. "Mr. Cates and Felix, I know you mean well, but this is lawful business. If I need help, other than myself and Mr. Stark here, I will send for someone."

"Oh, and I suppose Stark—" Cates spat the word as if it were a hot coal in his mouth. "—is a lawdog, too?"

"Matter of fact, he has been deputized, yes," said Thompson.

"I have?" said Jed in a low voice.

"Well, you will be very soon."

Jed nodded.

"Were there any folks ahead of you, Mr. Cates?"

"Not that I know of. Look, I know the Albersons well. If something bad has happened out there, I have a right to know."

"How do you mean, 'something bad,' Mr. Cates?"

"I mean, well, I don't know. But well, Joel, he wouldn't have ridden into town like he did, all lathered and bothered now, would he?"

"That's what I'm headed there to find out. Now kindly leave us to it, all right? And when you get back to town, tell everyone to let me do my job. If I need help, which I likely will at some point, I'll come knocking, Mr. Cates."

Cates kept his scowl pasted on, but he began turning his horse. "Okay, then, Marshal. But don't you forget they are our friends! Heck, I have known them longer than you've been alive!"

Thompson sighed. "I really do understand, Mr. Cates. And I promise I will do everything in my ability to figure out whatever it is that needs figuring out."

The man nodded, slightly quelled, and turned his horse, saying, "Come on, Junior."

His son, Felix, nodded and smiling as always, followed his father on his own large horse. Junior Cates was a large, quiet, affable fellow, and while a solid ranch hand, was not able to live on his own. He was, as the locals referred to him when the Cateses weren't about, "slow on the draw."

As soon as the father and son rode on out of sight, Thompson turned to Jed. "As marshal of Glen Rose township, I deputize you, Jed Stark."

Jed nodded. "Okay, that's all there is to it?"

"I think so. It's been a while since I've seen it done, but that's the basic approach. Oh, I think you're supposed to raise your right hand and say something like, 'I accept and will uphold the law to the best of my ability.' "

Jed grinned and did as he was instructed.

"Good," said Thompson. "Great, in fact. I really do appreciate it, Jed."

"You're welcome. Now we should ride."

"You bet," said Thompson, already nudging his horse into a lope on up the roadway toward the Alberson place, not far away.

The ranch buildings came into sight a quarter mile ahead, and it all appeared as Funke had said—no smoke drifted up from the cozy-looking home's chimney, and they saw no movement, save for the slow walking of a corralled donkey to the far right by the tidy barn.

"That'd be Puff, according to Joel," said Jed.

Thompson nodded. "But I don't hear any livestock, Jed."

"Oh, that might be because Joel said he fed everybody before he lit out for town."

"Before he found them?"

"Some, yes, then after."

"You mean after he found the Albersons shot?"

Jed nodded. "Given how the old man feels about the farm critters, I don't think there's anything odd in it. Next to the Albersons, I'd guess the beasts are his closest chums. He's not about to let them go hungry, killings or no."

"I guess you're right."

They fell silent as they approached the last hundred feet to the house. Thompson wore his revolver and had insisted that Jed and he also each carry a rifle. Jed turned down the offer of a loaned six-gun and belt, but agreed to the rifle and boot, which he lashed to his saddle.

Now he and Thompson, each armed, slid from their saddles, and at half cock, eyed the place, looked in opposing directions. They approached the house, each standing to one side of the kitchen door, with Thompson at the latch side. He looked at Jed, nodded, received a nod in reply, and thumbed the latch.

It took them scant time to make their way through the cold front room. Jed left the door open to allow light in. Already, he thought, the house had taken on that distinctive musty, unoccupied smell, as if it had been vacant by anything living for many months, or longer, and not just hours.

With Thompson in the lead, they entered the bedroom, the door of which was shut. They assumed Funke had closed it behind him.

The marshal stepped in and noted with a grunt of satisfaction that the window's shutters were still open, letting in, by then, the late morning light.

Each man tried to breathe as little as possible, and when they did, they did so through their mouths. For when they smelled the air about them, it bore the distinctive tang of the presence of death.

It took them very little time to see what Joel Funke had told them, and it was all as he had said. The two old folks were side by side, facing each other, inward, and stiff and cold in death.

Jed left the room and returned with a lit oil lamp, which he had seen on his way through the kitchen.

The brightness of the honey-glow of the lamp revealed the crusted bullet hole in each temple and the stiff, white, slack, and seemingly frozen faces of their old friends. It was as horrible to view as each man knew it would be.

"Harley? I'm going to leave you here while I go look for clues, anything as to who did this and why."

"Dalton Majors," said the younger man in a low voice, not taking his eyes from the dead pair.

"Pardon?" said Jed, turning back.

The marshal looked up, finding it difficult to take his eyes from the two. "Majors."

"You think he did this?"

"No. Well, I don't know. But I bet he's behind it. I do know that Henry Brighton and Deke Frakes both died of bullet wounds."

"But I thought Majors left town before Brighton."

Thompson nodded. "Near enough, yeah, but what if he had someone working for him?"

"Could be, sure, but why would anyone want to shoot the Albersons?"

"For their land, if that Dalton Majors is in the picture."

"Or the money it would bring."

"Both, I'd wager."

"I have to finish looking them over, Jed."

"You up for it, Harley? Do you need help?"

"No, I'm not up for it. But I need to do this sort of thing sometimes. It's not like I've not seen dead folks before."

"Okay, then, I'll head outside to look around. If you need help, shout, and I'll come back."

"Okay, I appreciate it, Jed."

"You bet, Marshal." He offered the younger man a nod and a smile.

Outside, Jed pulled in a deep breath and walked past their horses. He bent lower at the waist and walked slowly about the barnyard. There were plenty of prints of horses, chickens, goats, and donkeys—too many of them to make much sense from them, if that was even possible.

He went back toward the house and decided to focus on boot marks instead. He found his and Thompson's and Joel's, who, Jed had noticed back in town, wore the low-cut, lace-up, hob-soled work boots of a farm laborer. His prints were easily discernible, dimpled and wide.

Then there were others. One set, slighter and narrower, but still boots, must have belonged to Mrs. Alberson. They reminded Jed of those of his own mother, solid prints, smaller than a man's, but he saw a good many more of them about the place, once he'd begun searching them out.

The lot of farm and ranch women, Jed decided, was one of constant work and movement, the very thing that wore them out also usually kept them alive longer than their husbands. Usually, that is. Unless someone laid them low in their sleep.

The thought of that, and the sight of the two kindly, and now very much dead people back in the little cottage in which they lived and now died, was a brutal thing that he knew would haunt his mind, awake and asleep, for a long time to come.

He had often thought of the Albersons as an idealized old couple to which he and Lilly might pay visits to now and again, perhaps for tea, and they would bring baked goods with them—as he recalled, Rudolph had a sweet tooth.

But now, as Jed and Lilly began their own lives as a couple making for their dotage together, they would not be able to visit the Albersons, nor learn from them, save in memory.

As these thoughts came to Jed, he continued to rove the yard, then circled back to the dooryard before the house. He spied another set of tracks, man's boots, that at first he assumed had been those of Rudolph Alberson, then Jed realized they were not. And they went to the house and then they led from the house. They were made by someone not in a hurry, and they were not in a straight line.

He followed them on up the narrow lane that led back toward town. Still within sight of the home and barn and barnyard, the tracks, now along the right side of the narrow, scrub-brush- and boulder-lined lane, disappeared. The tracking became trickier, and he lost his way several times due to the coarse gravel and grit pocking much of the laneway. He managed to always find another partial bootprint along the way, but then they disappeared, and it took him some time to figure out where they went.

Jed cut off the trail and pocked among the gappy boulders and such flanking the lane. He was eventually rewarded with another full bootprint, and then, deeper in, to his left, he saw fresh horse dung and hoofprints. And not far from that, an empty liquor bottle.

He toed it and found the label to be that of Bold Branch,

one of the lousier yet popular brands available due to its low price, and the very brand Thompson had found an empty bottle of out at Deke Frakes's place. The liquid inside, rank, headache-inducing swill at best, and more than likely gut-curdling poison, would never touch Jed's lips.

He'd rather never drink whiskey if that's all he could afford. He sighed. Easy for me to say, he thought, considering I make a decent whiskey myself.

Jed glanced about him once more, seeing little more than the scraggly scrub brush and here-and-there juts of taller growths. As a locally raised fellow, these were bushes at once familiar to him, but unfamiliar, too, for their location was not within the Whiskey Woods boundaries. Peppered about, too, were trees, robust pines and oaks and such.

Jed bent low, keeping a watchful eye on his surroundings, then hunkered and touched the bottle with the fingertips of his right hand, the left held the rifle at half cock. His gut—and his eyes and nose and ears—told him that whoever had left these tracks and the bottle were gone from here. Still, he palmed the partially smoked cigarette remnant he'd found hidden beneath the bottle when he rolled it to one side.

The cigarette was cold. Sneering, he tweezered up the ragged thing and dropped it into his left breast pocket, then he grabbed the bottle by the neck and regarded it once more, eyeing it all around, but saw nothing that might offer any food for deeper thought about it. Not yet, anyway.

He knew that it was possible its presence, or that of the cigarette, as well as the bootprints and the horse hoofprints, might lead to some revelation. And he had a certain ex-lawman in mind, but it was thin proof, he knew.

The odds were against them finding better proof, but they apparently had so little to consider here regarding the murder of the Albersons and Brighton and Frakes, that everything they found at the present moment bore weighted consideration.

He stood, once more glancing about him—it would be a regret he'd carry far into the hereafter if he allowed a moment of forgetfulness or worse carelessness to snuff out his life. He had too much to live for, so much that he was thankful for in each moment of the day when he allowed himself to think of something other than the task at hand—usually whiskey work.

He had Mama, his entire life at Whiskey Woods, his health, Ol' Redeye, and all the other critters, of course, topping them all was his lovely Lilly.

She was a wonder and a half, as he'd told her the second time they'd spent any time together. She had blushed, he guessed, from the top of her head clear on down to her pretty little toes. And that endeared her to him even more. And his love for her had only grown since then.

And now they were set to be wed, a notion and a commitment he had resisted for years, for all manner of reasons that had seemed fine at the time. But now, in hindsight, those reasons appeared to him to be foolish, stunted, and misguided, the thinking of a selfish child-man instead of a fellow who loved a woman and wanted to spend the rest of his days and nights with her.

So no, he thought with a warm feeling inside, there was no way on this earth, if it was within his power, that he was going to allow himself to miss out on all the wonders his life promised to hold. Certainly not for some vile creature who would lie in wait to murder two of the sweetest folks anyone could ever hope to know.

Who could kill anyone in such a cold way? What sort of vicious brute could do such a thing? Surely not even someone with a belly filled with this swill whiskey, he thought as he glanced again at the Bold Branch bottle.

Jed eyed the rest of the little spot, but it appeared as if it had been used solely to wait out something, or perhaps to finish off the bottle. For he saw no tracks leading anywhere else save for the intermittent boot tracks making for the house.

Jed retraced his route, and when he came abreast of the horse drops, he once more bent and held a palm low over them, but felt no heat emanating from them. They, like everything else about this particular possible trail of clues, were cold.

He reached the lane once again and looked up it toward the direction of town, many miles back, southwestward, and then glanced toward the now sad and cold-looking little farm. As he walked back toward the house, he saw Thompson emerge from the front door and walk from the house a couple of strides, rubbing his temples, then running his hands up and down his face, as if washing in a mountain freshet.

The young lawman stood full height and breathed deep, several times filling his lungs with air, then expelling it. He repeated this twice more. He looked to Jed, who remained unseen for the moment by the younger man, as if he were trying to push out and away from himself the stifling, choking scent of death from his very mind and soul.

Jed wanted to tell the young man that the smells, the feelings, the sights, the dead silence of the close presence of death, would never leave him. They would forever hover inside, rising to the surface when he least wished them to do so. The big whiskey maker had learned this the difficult way, mired as he had been for years in the vile thing politicians had labeled as a "just war."

The bitter, grim irony, as any man who had been forced to kill another for a cause, no matter how noble or necessary it might have seemed at the time, was that there never is a peace that comes to a man or woman for taking the life of another creature.

There is a negotiation with oneself, but that always ends with the man kneeling before his own conscience and trying to bargain for peace, a rare and precious thing that never fully comes back to a man for all his days.

Harley Thompson, a young man Jed had known all of Harley's life, was the best of the best as far as Jed Stark—and a whole lot of other folks in and around Glen Rose—was concerned.

He was raised by his mother, a kindly widow whose husband, Thompson's father, was lost in a skirmish with a rogue band of trail thieves on their way westward as a young couple. She had been ready to give birth to Thompson when the small group of travelers reached Glen Rose.

She was left there and had, after the child's difficult birth, stayed on, eventually becoming a much-loved and needed fixture in town as a teacher of music and languages and other topics. She had been educated back East in Connecticut, and so had assumed a role as schoolteacher quite naturally.

Thompson grew up under her wing, perhaps too tightly, she would be the first to admit this, but he had developed an independent vein to his personality. Although gifted academically, he preferred pursuits such as hunting and fishing and trapping and learning woods lore, peppering these passions with hearty doses of book learning and bookish ways.

He had also early on come to admire as a bit of a surrogate father figure the quiet, reclusive man known as Jed Stark. Thompson had spent many hours down at Whiskey Woods, doing his best to help Jed there, eventually becoming a useful, if sporadic, hand about the place.

Mama Stark doted on the boy, and Thompson's mother, Jed recalled, had in a quiet way expressed the hope that perhaps the big whiskey maker might reciprocate her timid yet amorous feelings toward Jed.

While he had been flattered, Jed did not feel that way toward the kind woman. But they remained good friends, and she had become a trusted pal of Lilly as well.

Nobody had been surprised when young Thompson had

pursued the post of deputy and had been taken on by Marshal Chiswick, but neither had anyone been pleased by the news. Not that they thought that Thompson shouldn't be a lawman. He had the makings of a solid fellow, albeit in a young man's package, but Larry Chiswick was not the sort of man anyone wished a good young man to endure much exposure to.

And yet while working for Chiswick, Harley Thompson had thrived in his own way. Indeed, he had quickly filled the increasing gaps in performance as Chiswick had become a more and more useless character as a lawman. It had been, Jed mused, perfect training for the young lawman.

Yet seeing him now, Jed felt little more than sadness and pity for the youth, saddled as he was with the full weight of the office of marshal of Glen Rose, Texas, and without a current deputy. Jed vowed, as busy as he was, to be that person to support his friend during what was quickly building up to be another time in the town's history that nobody saw coming and that nobody wanted.

Jed strode forward, hating to interrupt the young man's moment of calm, of reverie, before he must resume the role of local lawman. But interrupt him, he must.

"Marshal!" Jed intended it as a gentle, barely audible shout, enough to pull the man back from his moment of calmness.

Instead, Harley Thompson dropped to a crouch, spun, pivoting on his right boot, and shucked and thumbed back the hammer of his revolver, keeping his stature low, his torso turned sideways to Jed's location, and yet lining up the tip of his revolver's barrel with Jed's approaching chest.

Jed did what any man might do in that situation, without thought, he tossed the derelict whiskey bottle and, as Thompson was a friend, he raised his hands high, higher than his head, his rifle gripped in his left fist.

The lawman saw who he was pointing his gun at, and he, too, stiffened, drawing back. His eyes were wide as he stood, holding his gun up in his own hand, aimed skyward. "Jed! I'm sorry, I . . . you spooked me!"

"Don't shoot!" said Jed, offering a smile tinged with sheepishness. "Sorry, Harley, only meant to gentle you out of your musings." He walked over to him. "You all right? You look a bit gray and ragged, if you don't mind me saying so."

"Ah, no, I'm fine. It's . . ." He gestured toward the house behind him. "It's a lot to consider, you see. I know being marshal isn't something simple, but no matter how many times I see the results of depravity and violence, I cannot seem to get used to it."

He turned tired eyes to Jed, who decided that Thompson looked to have aged ten, twenty years in the time he had spent in that house, in that room, with the murdered old couple.

He also looked as though he had cried, and Jed knew that was a forthright and honest reaction, in fitting with Thompson's character. For the old folks meant much to him.

"The Albersons," said Thompson, "they were, in some ways, not unlike a pair of grandparents to me. My mother has no kin back East, and my father's people seem to have ceased caring about Mother and myself once he died." He snorted. "I know they are aware of my existence, for Mother wrote to them of me. But they never replied."

He sighed. "And so we came to build family members of a sort here in Glen Rose. It's the only home I've ever known, so it was natural and easy for me. I met the Albersons so far back that I can't recall not knowing them. And now this. Oh, I just thought of something . . . I imagine Mother will have heard by now. It's a raw thing, Jed."

"I know it, Harley, but if there's any man I know of who can make this turn out as it needs to, you're that man." He laid a big hand atop the young man's sagged shoulder. "Now, Marshal, what is it you'd like to do here? How can I help?"

Those words seemed to have a restorative effect on Thompson, for he pulled in breath, straightened, and said, "Right. It's up to me, so here's what I have been thinking needs to be done."

He worked his hands together as if washing them in a stream. "And Jed," he said, stopping and looking at the bigger, older man beside him. "Thanks. Thanks for all this, for coming along, for helping, for being here. It's tough enough, but . . . it's helped."

"You bet, son. Now"—Jed held up the bottle—"lest you think I've been drinking swill on the job"—he handed the bottle to Thompson—"and there's this." He fished in his breast pocket and lifted out the tattered remains of the cigarette. "Found these up the lane a ways, right-hand side, from here. Horse and man tracks around them looked fresh."

Thompson nodded and looked over the two items, sniffing the shreds of tobacco and singed paper. Then he held the bottle up to the sky, eyeing it toward the light. He seemed to see something there.

"Handprints, but I can't tell whose are whose."

Jed felt his ears redden, a thing that happened whenever embarrassment caught him in its snare. "I'm sorry, Harley, I didn't think to carry it so as not to smudge such things."

"No, they'd likely not be useful to me anyway. That sort of thing is beyond me. Just now, that is." He offered a slight grin. "Someday, maybe. When I'm not so green."

"I do think we need to figure out what all we need to do with the Albersons, Harley."

"Yes, I know. I'm not equipped to do this sort of thing myself. I did check them over as best I could without, well"—the young man shook his head and turned red—"you know."

"Sure," said Jed. "Maybe Doc Peters ought to come out, along with Milchner, if he has a couple of pine boxes already made. They both are used to having to deal with folks who are . . . who have been dead a while, let's say. You want me to ride back to fetch them, Harley?"

"Which would you rather do, Jed, search here or ride for the doc and Milchner?"

"Not my call, Harley." Jed saw that his comment was of slight disappointment to the marshal.

Jed drummed his fingertips on his chin. "If it was my call, and if I was you, I'd leave the old-timer—that'd be me—here to watch over things while I rode back to town. Not least because folks there will have gotten full wind of the doings here and will be agitated and confused, perhaps fearful. You don't want them jumping to wrong conclusions, especially about Joel Funke."

Thompson nodded but didn't make a move toward his horse. "You don't think Mr. Funke did this thing, do you, Jed?"

"No, Harley. No, I don't. But a person could be excused for thinking such, sure."

"You're not talking about me, are you, Jed?"

"Nope. And forgive me for thinking uncharitable thoughts about my fellow citizens of Glen Rose, but last year's events will take a while to wash off my tongue. A good lot of those folks, many of them I'd call friends, were lulled far too easily by Merlin Sheldrake. Because of money, they were willing to let too much drift for too long before they finally stood up and did the thing they should have done from the start."

"Well, let's hope it doesn't ever happen again in Glen Rose."

"Right," said Jed, thinking but not saying what they both knew in their hearts—oddnesses were popping up of late in Glen Rose and beyond, the killings and such, and this annoying and worrisome business of the out-of-towner named Dalton Majors.

Thompson rode on out with a wave. Jed watched the young man leave, noting how tight and hunched his shoulders were. The man was weighted down by the events, and who could blame him?

Jed walked his horse to the barn and unsaddled her, then fed and watered her. As he worked, he mused that if Loudon was correct, and Jed had no reason to doubt the man, then Majors's employer, some monied back-East woman named Mona Starret, was fixing to do something in the area that might not sit well with a good many folks.

On the other hand, maybe money was most folks' primary concern in life. And all they wanted really was to grab as much cash as they could with both hands, and if it was a land-greedy back Easter who was paying, well then, so be it.

He knew his thoughts were unkind for the most part, but at that moment, with two kindly folks lying dead, murdered, shot in the head while they slept in their marital bed, well, it was a raw thing, and he was feeling chewed up by it all.

Doubly so, he decided, because he was finding nothing else out of the ordinary save for hungry critters and an otherwise quiet place.

He made his way to Joel Funke's little home, the lean-to structure built on to the back side of the barn, and gently thumbed open the latch and swung the door inward.

It squeaked on pin hinges and opened wide, revealing not a dingy, dark little space fit for a man who worked in the barn and little else. Instead, he was rewarded with a pleasing sight—Joel Funke's front room was orderly, tidy, and clean. The small window beside the door, in addition to another larger window in the outside wall to Jed's right, allowed in ample daylight. Other than a half-filled teacup holding cold brown tea, nothing much seemed disorderly or out of place.

There were no drawers about, nothing within which the man might hide something, anything. Jed still didn't believe a wit of the thought that old Joel could have done this thing, but neither did Jed assume sainthood of anyone. It was best, he had found in life, to base one's opinion on hard memory and earned trust. Both of which he and just about everyone had of Joel Funke and of the Albersons.

"To come to that end," he whispered, shaking his head.

Jed sighed and searched the rest of the man's little home, then the entire spread, buildings and all, for the better part of an hour. By then, a good many of the animals—goats, sheep, chickens, pigs, turkeys, a donkey, and a horse—were beginning a chorus of clucking, bleating, and in general making a ruckus about the place. This was, in part, Jed knew, because of his presence. They regarded him as someone who would feed them, no matter that Joel had fed them all hours before.

"I can't blame you," said Jed to the populace in general, shaking out another forkful of hay to a little billy goat who was busy sizing up Jed for a sneaking, butting attack.

Jed had been around goats enough to know that any chance they were given to ram a set of curled horns into the backside of an unsuspecting human was not to be passed up. Jed kept an eye on the little brute.

Out in a nearby paddock, he fed the horse and donkey and two docile steers that looked to be more pets than food sources. They, too, weren't ravenous. But he felt better in putting the effort into taking care of the beasts, not being certain how long it might be before Joel Funke would return.

He would have to discuss the feeding of the Albersons' livestock with Thompson when the marshal returned, hopefully with the doctor and the casket maker tagging along.

Jed felt as if he should be busy with something else, but there was nothing he could think of, no other possible logical source of clues for him to follow.

He ended up out back of the barn, leaning on a low corral rail and running through in his mind yet again the day's horrible events. What was happening to their little community, once again? And once again, he came up with no answers, but far too many outlandish notions.

Then the sound of something distant but steady, a soft

sound, drew closer, and soon Jed knew that it was a horse approaching.

He straightened, stretched, and made his way around the near corner of the barn to await Thompson's return. As he cleared the corner, he shifted the weight of the uncocked rifle from one arm's crook to the other, then looked up again. And stopped short.

Jed seized in place, taking in what he was seeing, and then stepping back slowly until he was confident he was once more well hidden by the shadowy barn corner. He leaned there, the rifle ready, and eyed the scene before him.

Just walking into view in the dooryard was a slouch-shouldered man taking cautious steps and leading a horse with his right hand. In his left, he held a revolver. Its twin, Jed saw, rode on the man's waist. He wore a sweat-stained fawn hat with a gnawed brim pulled down low, shading the man's face.

What wasn't obscured by a gray-and-black-streaked, unkempt beard was red and puffed. And above that, the top of the man's face was obscured by his hat's brim.

Shirtsleeves with poorly folded cuffs flopped about the fellow's forearms, and he wore a vest that looked to have been brown at one time but had tanned with age and then seasoned with all manner of greasy spots and holes.

The man's trousers had not fared much better and were tucked into crease-worn, stovepipe boots. The overall look of him was familiar to Jed, but for the moment, he could not place him.

Nonetheless, he was either there as a curious man, but timid, too, and perhaps as such was not anything more than an annoyance, or he was someone up to little good.

Jed suspected the latter, as the fellow had a drawn gun and sort of skulked low and rounded as he walked, with trepidation about his slow steps and lizard-like turning of his head.

The fellow advanced toward the house, emboldened, thought Jed, because he saw no horses about the place, no sign of activity anywhere. What was he there for?

Jed aimed to remain hidden and find out. The folks in the house, after all, were beyond being hurt. Unless the man set fire to the place, there was little he could do. Or so Jed hoped.

Then the man stood up straighter, arching his spine, and as he pulled his head back a bit more, light crept beneath the low-pulled hat brim. Despite the shabby, bushy beard, Jed recognized the man now.

Chapter 16

It was Larry Chiswick, once the marshal of Glen Rose. Now, from everything Jed had heard about the man, Chiswick was a full-time drunkard. And from the look of him, that gossip and passed-along hearsay, which Jed usually didn't lend much credence, nonetheless seemed likely.

That said, Jed preferred to gather his own information and then form his opinions on a person or a topic based on his own first-hand experience. If it wasn't said to him or in his presence, he tried to discount it. And since he was now in the presence of Chiswick, he had to say that the man looked rough. Bloated and haired up, and far too red about the face.

As he thought all this, Chiswick completed his slight arching backward with a movement forward, then spat on the earth before him. It sounded to Jed as though the man had conjured up a wad of something foul, perhaps part of a lung, and was having a time expelling it.

The fellow's coughing jag subsided, and he dragged his cuff across his mouth. Judging from the drooped way he held his gun and the heaving of his shoulders, and from what Jed discerned was a faint whistling, wheezing sound coming from the man's slightly gasping mouth, Chiswick was decidedly not in the best of health.

Jed kept well in the shadow of the barn's corner and continued to eye the man. Again Jed wondered, what was Chiswick doing there?

Chiswick, meanwhile, shuffled forward and mumbled something, tugging the horse with a hard, quick snap of the reins, even though the horse appeared to Jed to be making better progress forward than the man.

Chiswick paused before the short hitch rail that flanked the left side of the little walk leading to the front door. He wound the reins around it once, then let the ends flop. Then he faced the door of the house for a moment, holstered his gun, and dug in his left breast pocket and tugged out a little sack of roll-your-own tobacco. He built a cigarette slowly.

Even at the distance Jed stood from the man, he saw that Chiswick's hands were anything but steady. Bits of tobacco tumbled from his efforts, and he heard the man bark a low curse. He finally got the thing built and rolled, the end pinched and twisted, and he stuffed it between his lips.

Finding a match was another slight project, it seemed. He finally got the thing lit with a shaking hand that made the flame dance and jounce, then he sucked deeply and with a greed Jed had seen many times before of one with deeper cravings than mere tobacco smoke.

The effort seemed at last to calm him, and Chiswick leaned against the hitch rail, the other end anchored by his hang-headed horse. Then Chiswick turned and eyed the house once more, now at ease and with fuller attention.

His gaze carried over the front of the little, stilled home. Then he sighed, and, tucking his half-finished cigarette between his lips, he used both hands to rummage in a cotton sack looped about the saddle horn.

He finally managed to get the thing off the horn and widened the drawstring enough to stuff a hand in. He withdrew it, clutching a half-empty bottle of whiskey. As soon as Jed caught sight of the label, he knew, beyond any doubt, although he had only this tenuous connection as proof, that Chiswick was the one who had, if not shot the Albersons, at least had been the one hiding in the scrub beside the roadway to the place.

His proof, which felt all but convincing, was the man's smoking, the results of which he found ground and stomped in the dirt back at the hiding spot. And there was the bottle, the empty one being Bold Branch, the same brand as the swill Chiswick was glugging back before him just then.

Not for the first time in the past few minutes since Chiswick's arrival did it occur to Jed that the man before him acted as if he knew no one would be about. As if he assumed nobody had yet discovered the bodies.

Could he be that obtuse? Surely, as a former lawman, he would have seen the fresh horse drops, the boot tracks, the hoofprints before the hitch rail. Yet these seemed to hold no interest for him. And what of Joel Funke's presence? Didn't Chiswick know the old man still worked for the Albersons? Indeed, Joel had lived there for decades. Everyone knew that.

Chiswick popped the cork off the bottle and upended it, and Jed saw the man's Adam's apple working up and down as if it were hitched to a pump handle. The action, which went on for far longer than any drink most men might indulge in straight from the bottle, forced a wince on Jed's face.

He knew of that whiskey, and it was nearly as bad as the gunpowder and snake squeezings that Merlin Sheldrake had been peddling to the tighter, more desperate souls in far too many public houses.

Chiswick belched, then sucked on the cigarette, finishing it in two long pulls, then tossed it to the earth, where it smoldered, a thick tail of smoke drifting up before pinching out. Then he chased the smoke down his throat with another long draw on the bottle before, with obvious reluctance, thumbing the cork back into place, although there was not but a finger or two left in the bottle's bottom.

Jed watched the fellow, wondering two things—when should

he make his presence known to Chiswick? And if Thompson or Doc Peters or Milchner should ride on in and surprise him, what might Chiswick do?

Jed listened with intention but heard nothing from the lane.

Chiswick made his decision easy for him, because the drunk, newly revived by the booze and smoke, walked to the front door of the house and, without drawing his gun again or knocking on the door, merely thumbed the latch and walked on in.

As if . . . thought Jed. "As if he knew what was in there." Jed whispered this and waited a moment or two before advancing on the house, his rifle cocked and held ready to fire.

He kept tight to the right side of the dooryard and arched his quick, silent-as-possible movements over to the cottage.

Jed reached the corner of the house and held there a moment, listening. The man was armed. He was drunk, but then again, Jed had seen a good many drunken men, especially that class of them he thought of as professional drunkards, who still functioned well enough. They were the ones who kept at their drinking, slow and steady, all day and well into the night, too.

So being Chiswick and being drunk meant he was certainly capable of aiming his revolver and pulling the trigger. But no matter how familiar he'd become with the effects of alcohol on his body, the man's reflexes were bound to be hampered.

This was not something Jed wished to put to the test, but he had to do something, and fast.

Jed held his breath, clenched his jaw muscles, and bent low, hoping he was crouching his tall frame down far enough that he would not be seen through the window from inside.

Deciding not to risk even that possibility, Jed dropped to his knees on the barely grassed soil and, suppressing winces as his kneecaps met with tiny but formidable rocks and such, he worked forward, still keeping that rifle aimed toward the door, a mere four feet ahead to his right.

Chiswick had swung it open more than halfway, leaving himself, no doubt unwittingly, with a nice wide span through which to look and then step on out, guns barking.

But Jed was now hearing something that changed his mind and gave him some small sliver of relief.

It sounded to him as if Chiswick had moved on deeper into the house and was now rummaging through the Albersons' scant possessions, slamming drawers and tossing things to the floor, from the sounds of it.

He was also muttering and offering up the occasional growl.

Jed also noted another thing—the air was close as it wafted out from the darkened space inside, to be expected, given the fact that two dead people lay inside. But there was something more, and then he knew what it was—the stink of an unwashed man.

It was no surprise that Chiswick smelled as bad as he looked, and that was saying something, indeed. The man looked as if he'd been shot out of a cannon in the midst of a raging battle.

There was on the air the bitter tang of stale sweat, stale cigarette stink, and stale booze. But what concerned Jed was the location of that mumbling voice. It still sounded as if it came from the back room—fine by him.

Jed knew what he wanted to do, then. He enacted his feeble plan and hoped it would not betray him, which he knew was entirely possible. In for a penny, he thought, not daring to whisper.

He gently eased his back against the wall to his right, and, still hunkered, kept an ear cocked while he slid up against the wall until he stood upright once more, bringing the rifle in close to his chest, the barrel aiming toward the sky. His knees both offered up a popping sound, and he winced, then he eased his face to the right, his cheek snugged against the door frame, and glanced inside.

Awaiting him was the same little kitchen as before, an area where Mrs. Alberson had concocted so many toothsome meals over the years for her husband, for Joel Funke, and for their visitors. The Albersons had never seemed to tire of receiving company, if Thompson's memories were any way to measure such things. And now . . . no more.

Jed held that way, still hearing Chiswick slamming about in the back room. Confident that he was safe for the moment, Jed squared off, lowering the rifle at the same time, and stepped into the room. His left boot complied with quiet, then his right betrayed him. It stepped on the small woven rag rug there, and a creak and squeak rose up from the planking beneath.

Jed froze and so did the mumbling sound from the back room. It held in silence for a good ten seconds, and so did Jed. But his rifle was aimed right at that open bedroom door.

Then he heard a slight scuffing, swishing sound, as if cloth rubbed other cloth, or perhaps leather. This was followed with a harsher but still soft, smooth sound. But it was a sound Jed was most familiar with, and did not wish to hear. It was the sound of steel clicking. The sound of a gun's hammer being eased back into a killing position.

Jed held still through this, but Chiswick did not. He was advancing, perhaps thinking himself stealthy and thus undetected. He was incorrect.

He kept on, and soon his gun and hand and right boot were visible, followed as he advanced by his hat brim and more of his body, arms and legs, and belly and beard. Soon he was almost fully revealed to Jed. Finally, long moments after Jed thought the man would stop, Chiswick seemed to catch sight of him.

"Hold it right there, Chiswick!" snapped Jed, keeping his cocked rifle leveled on the man, while stepping to his left and at the same time angling the width of his torso to the side, a thin attempt to present less of a target to the man.

Chiswick's reflexes were muffled by the booze as Jed had hoped, for the man seemed to dither. He seemed uncertain about whether he should pull the cursed trigger of his revolver, retreat back into the death room he was still half inside, or drop into a crouch and shoot it out right there and then.

In that scant moment, a thought flicked through Jed's mind that, were he in Chiswick's position, reflex would have driven him back and to pull the trigger at the same time, offering his threatener a parting shot, akin to a cornered wolf's warning growl.

But Chiswick did neither. Instead, he looked left and right, licked his lips, and faltered in everything he tried to consider. Finally, he groaned and held up his hands, the cocked revolver still gripped tight to the palm of his right hand. All he needed to do, mused Jed, would be to step to one side and at the same time jerk that arm down.

At their distance apart of a dozen or less feet, his bullet no doubt would find a fleshy resting spot in Jed's hide, but then again so would Jed's in Chiswick's.

"You move a muscle, so much as twitch, Chiswick, and I will do the thing I most dislike doing on this green Earth!"

Jed kept an eye on the drunk's face, knowing that any intention, any movement, began there. To Chiswick's credit, he did not utter a sound nor move a muscle—save for working up a wide sneer, as if he finally recognized who it was who had braced him.

Jed knew that the man reviled him. In fact, given what he knew of the drunkard of an ex-marshal, Jed suspected he held the top spot on the list of hated folks nested in Chiswick's sickened mind.

The big whiskey maker walked forward slowly, that rifle aimed square on Chiswick's chest. He stopped when he was still six or so feet from the man. As Jed's weapon was a rifle, he didn't want to give Chiswick the possibility of lunging at him and knocking that barrel aside somehow, and delivering a revolver shot at him.

"Now, Chiswick, keep both hands up and walk forward toward the center of the room. Yep, that's it. Now . . . stop! Right there! Yep, now, keep your gun arm to your right side and toss your revolver behind you to the floor. Do it! Now!"

"But . . ."

Jed could see that he had nudged a wad of fear into the man's mind. Good.

"But it's cocked!"

"Don't care. It's the only way I can trust you won't get any cute ideas, Chiswick. Besides, if it goes off, it'll be more likely to hit you than me."

"But, Stark—"

"Do it now!" Jed even managed to startle himself a pinch with such barking, not in keeping with his usual quiet demeanor.

Chiswick squinted his eyes as if anticipating a punch to the face and let the revolver drop, a bit to his side and behind him.

It hit the floor with a solid thump and lay still. Each man breathed easier.

"Now, Chiswick, get yourself over to the middle of the room like I said. Both hands up, palms facing me."

Again, the man complied.

"Good, now turn around, face that bedroom door, and get down on your knees. Do it!"

"What are you gonna do? Shoot me in the head?"

"We should all be so lucky. But nope, I want you to lay down, face first, and keep your back to me. Do it now, man."

"Okay, okay."

Chiswick lowered himself down, his popping knees only outdone by his groans. He finally got himself settled, and Jed kept his eyes on the man. He could not help but notice that he was in an even rougher state than he had first seen from a distance outside earlier.

The sole leather of the drunkard's boots was worn through

at the balls of the foot, and the chiseled-away outer edges of each heel were not helping the man's already ambling, shambling gait.

"Now face down, arms out to the sides."

"Aww, Stark, curse it, this ain't necessary! I wasn't doing nothing wrong!"

"Don't look at me! Keep your eyes on your task—and that task I have set for you is to lay face down. Now!"

The man complied, albeit with an increase in his grumbling.

"Keep it up, Chiswick, and I will shoot you and be done with it."

"Naw, you won't neither, Stark. You and me, we both know it, and so does everyone else. You're too much of an ol' fancy, goody-goody man to do that."

"I don't know what that means, but don't push it with me, Chiswick. Now, just lay there and keep those arms out to the sides."

"Yeah, yeah."

Jed stepped to the prone man's near side, Chiswick's right, and as quick as he dared, he slicked free from its sheath a long, bone-handled hunting blade. Jed shifted his rifle to his other arm and, keeping the snout of it close to the back of Chiswick's head, he reached for the man's left-side gun. It was fastened with a rawhide keeper thong, so he fumbled at getting it untied.

"You want a hand with that, Stark?"

"Shut it, Chiswick." Jed rammed the serious end of the rifle into the back of the man's neck and used the brief moment of surprise to wrench free the revolver. He stepped quickly away and slid the uncocked revolver into the back of his waistband.

"Now don't move, and keep those arms to the side, Chiswick."

He was about to ask once more what the man was doing in the house, and why he was out hiding in the bushes some time earlier, given the whiskey bottle and cigarette remnants, but he decided to keep his mouth shut. That was Thompson's business, after all, not Jed's.

That thought reminded him once more that he had been deputized by the marshal, not that such a thing mattered much at the moment. And that was the last thought he had before hearing the quick drumming of approaching hooves.

Jed walked backward to the door, still keeping an eye on the muttering Chiswick. He didn't trust a thing about the man, and didn't doubt that he had a hideout gun stashed somewhere about his person. Or a knife. Or both.

Jed risked a peek out the door and saw Thompson riding at a quick clip back toward the house, but no Doc or Milchner in sight behind him. Jed glanced back to see Chiswick, still stretched face down on the floor, but with his head quivering up off the floor, straining to see Jed and beyond. "Who's that?" he snarled.

"That? Oh, that's the law, Chiswick."

"Why? Hey, what are you doing here, anyway, Stark?" said the man.

"Not that it's your business, Chiswick, but anything I'm doing here, I guarantee, is a whole lot less suspicious than anything *you're* doing here. Now get ready to explain yourself."

"Ha! To that whelp? He ain't fit to shout at, let alone talk to! I taught him everything I know about law-doggin'!"

"That must have taken all of one, maybe two minutes," said Jed, feeling not a little annoyed with the crass mess of a man.

"One of these days, Stark, I'm going to take a full round out of you, you just wait! I'll—"

"You'll do what, Mr. Chiswick?" said Thompson, stepping into the room.

"None of your business, you!"

In short order, Jed told Thompson what he'd done since the man left to make his run back to Glen Rose. And then he told him of the mysterious visitor in their midst.

"Thanks, Jed." Thompson turned to face the man on the floor. "Don't go anywhere, I have to get something for you from the horse. I'll be right back." He smiled and winked to Jed, who suspected what the man was about to retrieve.

"If it ain't a bottle of whiskey, I ain't interested, Harley!"

The marshal strode back into the little kitchen with his hands behind his back. "Oh, it's something a whole lot more fun than a bottle of booze, Mr. Chiswick." He brought his hands around front to reveal a set of wrist manacles in one hand.

"No way! You ain't putting them on me, mister!"

"Oh yes, I am. And as I said, these are a whole lot more fun than whiskey . . . for me, that is. Jed, would you mind keeping that thing aimed at him while I put them on him?"

"Happy to, Marshal."

The foul words lobbed up and out of the drunkard's mouth were rank enough that Thompson and Jed both exchanged glances with raised eyebrows.

"I hope you intend to wash out for your mouth after that," said Thompson, smiling as he put the last steel bracelet in place and turned the key.

"These are cutting my skin, curse you!"

"I am sorry, Mr. Chiswick. What with this and that, I never have found the time to replace those. They are, after all, the manacles you left behind. As I recall, they were your favorites."

He didn't let Chiswick reply but stood, shoving up from his knees, and then bent and snatched Chiswick by the back of the belt and yanked the man upward hard, an action that surprised Jed.

"Now," said Thompson, ushering Chiswick outside and forcing him to lean against the hitch rail, then, with his revolver drawn, he motioned for Jed to follow him. They walked a dozen feet away, with Thompson facing Chiswick, revolver out and ready.

"I talked with Joel, who you'll be happy to know is still in the jail cell, as he requested. I didn't lock it when I left, but he reminded me, so I had to." Thompson's face took on the understandably gloomy look he wore before he left for town.

"Just remember," said Jed. "It might be for his safety, too. But now with Chiswick caught, well, I don't know what to think, Harley." Jed rubbed the back of his neck.

"Right, well, first things first. Joel suggested we bury the Albersons in their own plot, and as they are, in one coffin, as they were always inseparable anyway."

"That's a kind thought. But not dress them in their finery?"

"Be tough now, with all the stiffness that's set in, I imagine."

"True."

"We'll see what the doc says. He'll be along soon. Young Milchner will come in a bit. He wanted time to modify two coffins into one."

"Right," said Jed. "What do you want to do with him?"

"We question him. I hate to keep you, Jed. I know you probably have a pile of things to do today, but I could use you there. You saw everything that I didn't."

"No, it's fine."

Chapter 17

"Had to leave, didn't I?" he said. "Was out of whiskey."

"Hmm," said Thompson, his eyes narrowed and his head tilted to one side. Jed was beginning to recognize this as Thompson's thinking stance. Although he knew that the young man did not need any conjured way of standing to help his mental processes. He was a sharp knife. Always had been.

"Mr. Chiswick," said Thompson.

The manacled man snorted back a laugh. "Since when did you ever call me that, you whelp?" he chuckled.

"Since I can no longer refer to you as 'boss' or 'marshal,' Mr. Chiswick. Now, to get this straight, you were out and about, intent on visiting the Albersons."

"For some fresh eggs, yep," said Chiswick, still grinning.

"For eggs, okay. And you heard gunshots, two of them."

Chiswick's head bobbed in a nod of agreement.

"And you were startled, but of course not frightened, never that, and so you took to the wood, hence the empty whiskey bottle and the cigarette ground into the earth in there."

"Sure, yes, that's it. And then I saw that rascal Joel Funke riding lathered up on out of here, you know? Like he was, oh, I don't know, guilty of something."

"So you waited there in the bushes, crouching and concerned."

"You bet, concerned is the word for it. I'm a peaceful fellow and I heard two shots, that couldn't be good, now could it? After all, the Albersons weren't much more than Quakers when it came right down to it. And why would they be peeling off gunshots of a morning, or any time for that matter?"

Jed did his best to stifle a groan, especially on hearing the former lawman's description of himself as "peaceful."

Thompson ignored the man's questions and continued: "So you waited until Joel Funke rode by, making for town at a rapid clip, and then you took it upon yourself to investigate."

"You bet I did. Just because the dough balls in Glen Rose didn't think I was the man for the job any more, never mind that they had never had such a successful and kind marshal, why that didn't mean I ain't still a curious sort of fellow, you know?"

"What did you find then, Mr. Chiswick, when you arrived at the house?"

"Oh, Harley, don't be foolish! You know what I found, man!"

"Nonetheless, please humor me, Mr. Chiswick. Now, you found what inside the house?"

The drunkard sighed as if he were in a stage play, then rolled his eyes. "I found two dead folks. Shot in the head they were, right in their own bed!"

"And?" said Thompson.

"And nothing! Joe Funke killed them as sure as I'm sitting here, being likely the most honest man you have ever encountered in your little life, young man!"

Jed cleared his throat because he saw Thompson looking as if he might shout the man down in a moment, which was uncharacteristic of him and something that would no doubt delight Chiswick. And Jed Stark most wanted at that moment to give Lawrence Chiswick nothing at all, save for discomfort.

"Then why did you leave, but not go to town to report it, and then come back here when you thought nobody was going to be here?"

"Well, now, look, it's all confusing. . . . Oh, all right, I needed more whiskey. That's all. That's all I needed."

"And where did you buy it?"

"Oh, yonder at Haskell's Store, you know the one. Hey," he said, leaning forward. "Ask them and they'll tell you I was there for whiskey. I drank some there and bought the bottle and rode on back here."

"Why did you ride back here?" said Thompson.

"Because I thought I had best make doubly sure there wasn't anything odd about what I'd found earlier."

"Odd?" said Thompson. "What does that mean, Mr. Chiswick?"

"It means that, oh, I don't know, maybe I was wrong and they wasn't dead? You understand? I'm not all that comfortable with knowing if what I see will stick to be true, you see? I drink whiskey and I'm pretty good at it. But the stuff wears off right quick. I had to go get more."

"Yes, you said that. Okay, then, when Jed Stark came upon you, you were tearing the little house apart. Why?"

"Now, look," said Chiswick. "I wasn't tearing anything apart. I was only doing what I felt I should do! I was looking for a reason as to why Joel Funke would shoot his employers!"

"That is just what I would like to know," said the marshal.

"Huh?"

"Why would anyone at all want to shoot the Albersons?"

"Heck if I know," said Chiswick, looking at his hands, his face slightly redder than usual.

"Okay," said the marshal. "I have heard that you were in the company of one Dalton Majors, Mr. Chiswick. What can you tell me about that?"

"I am in nobody's company. I'm me and my own person and that's that."

"How did you get the money you have been spending on a horse and guns and whiskey and such? Especially when it's well known you've been out of paying work for a long time."

Chiswick's eyes narrowed and he snorted. "You mean since my badge was unlawfully ripped from me and my position as marshal was taken over by the likes of you!"

Thompson smiled and shook his head. "You know and I know that's not true. It's not the likes of me, Mr. Chiswick, it is me who is the marshal, who the citizens of Glen Rose chose instead of you."

"Liar!" Chiswick tried to shove himself up away from the rail, in an effort to launch himself at Thompson. The young man stood his ground even as Jed's big right hand clamped down on the drunkard's shoulder and shoved him backward.

"Easy, Chiswick. You forget there are two of us, and you are manacled, and we have guns."

The drunk slopped back against the rail and jerked his gaze toward the whiskey maker. "Oh, I don't forget nothing, Stark. Ever."

"Is that supposed to be some sort of a threat?"

Chiswick pulled on a long face topped with wide eyes. "Who, me? Why, Jed Stark, you do think the worst of folks, I declare it. Seems to me you ought to think better of your fellow man as you wind your way through this life."

"Oh, but I do just that, Chiswick, when my fellow man earns it. Sadly, that's something you never have done, and I suspect you never will. The only thing you do, and do well, I might add, is beg suspicion from others."

"What's that supposed to mean, Stark?"

Thompson stepped forward and leaned in closer to his old boss. "He means that you are and have been for a long time, Larry, a source of trouble and headache for everyone who knows you. Why else do you think your parents were always grumpy? Why else do you think your wife left you and took your child away? Huh?"

Jed was stunned. He'd never heard that Chiswick had been married, let alone had a child. And to add to his shock was the fact that Thompson, for the first time of which Jed was aware, was on the attack, bullying back and down the current scourge of their lives.

If anyone had earned the right to berate the fellow, especially Chiswick, it was Harley Thompson. Jed had heard some of the stories of what sort of public humiliations and needless cruelties the young man had endured as a deputy under Chiswick. Even those had been lightly mentioned and shrugged off by the usually docile, good-humored Thompson.

But Jed did not doubt, as most folks who knew the mild Thompson, the full extent of their truth.

There was a quiet for a moment in which the drunkard looked at the marshal with a blanched face and slack mouth and wide eyes.

"I . . ." Thompson shook his head and half turned away. "I am sorry, Chiswick. I never should have said that."

"I told you that in confidence, man." Chiswick's voice was oddly quiet, as if he still could not quite believe what he had just heard.

"I know, I know! You goaded me and I bit into it. Like a fish to a wormy hook."

If Chiswick heard Thompson, he didn't let on. He gazed at the gravel beyond his dusty boots. "As for the woman, well, she up and left because she was a city thing, too prim and such. Ill-suited to the life as the wife of a lawman. Boy would have turned out the same, I'll wager. Good riddance."

He looked up, eyeing the space between Jed and Thompson. "As for my folks, I expect they was bitter long before I come about. That's a fact. Some people just can't be happy, and that's it, that's all."

None of the three said a thing for a long moment. Jed knew that Chiswick's excuses were just that. And that Thompson's accusations were founded on fact. The young lawman could not lie if he had a gun to his head.

Jed was the first to interrupt the silence. He had things to do and so did Doc Peters, who from the clunks and murmuring within the house, was preparing to emerge soon.

"Chiswick, what were you looking for in the house? And are you working for Dalton Majors?"

Chiswick looked squint-eyed at Jed. "You the lawman now or did I miss the vote? Cause I would have voted ten times against you, Stark."

"He's not the lawman, Chiswick, but he did ask the questions I want answers to. And now. Or you're going to jail."

Jed suspected Chiswick was headed for the cell anyway, but he kept his mouth shut.

The drunk said nothing, but gazed once more across the yard.

"Fine," said the marshal. "Just so you know, unlike in years past, whiskey is not served in my jail."

Chiswick spat and said, "You think I care?"

"I think you will," said Thompson. "And I think it won't take long. Especially once that warm feeling that rotgut has given starts to wear off."

Still, the man said nothing. Finally, Thompson sighed. "Jed? You mind keeping an eye on this prisoner? I have to go talk with Doc Peters."

"Sure thing, Marshal."

As Thompson strode off toward the house and the just-emerging doctor, Chiswick, in a mocking, nasally voice, said, "Sure thing, Marshal!"

Jed remained leaning against the barn, his arms folded and his legs crossed. But he did smile.

CHAPTER 18

Marshal Harley Thompson stood in the sun of the south side of the street, out front of his office, enjoying a brief moment of quiet with Loudon Paley.

He and a pile of folks had returned from a graveside service at the Alberson place. Joel had made it a welcoming, if somber, affair, given what had happened to the beloved old couple a week earlier.

Joel had been released from jail the very minute Thompson had brought in Chiswick, given that the obvious threat to Funke's life, namely Chiswick, was now locked up tight.

Thompson had talked to the old man after the service, and Funke had told him that the Albersons had left the place to him to do with as he saw fit. Joel saw fit to stay right there and tend the critters until he could no longer do so.

He also had decided he would continue to live in the little home he and Rudolph had made out back of the barn. He wished to leave the house as it was for the time being. Perhaps one day, he'd said, he would give it to a nice young family that needed a home.

He had asked Thompson if he thought the Albersons would find that acceptable, and the lawman had said that it sounded to be the very thing they would wish for.

Now, back in town, Thompson turned to the man he was enjoying the sunlight with, Loudon Paley, and asked, "What do you think they want all that land for?" He leaned his left hip against the empty hitch rail, his arms folded over his chest, his fawn curl-brim hat tipped back as he squinted at the man with whom he spoke.

"Well," continued Thompson. "I mean I know that the folks who've been approached are saying that Majors's employer wants to start a cattle ranch. But from the sounds of it, whoever it is, he seems to be buying up more land than five ranches might need. Which brings me back to my initial question: What do they want with all that land?"

"Well, that I don't know yet," said Loudon Paley, "but something odd is in the air, something, dare I say, illegal."

"The killings, sure, they're mighty odd. But if you mean other than that, then that's a bold claim, Loudon."

The newspaperman nodded. "I know, and I don't say it lightly. But look here." He glanced to his right and waited for two women to walk by. They were moving slower than they had been, and their conversation had clipped off as they approached.

He noticed, too, that they glanced toward him and the marshal. Loudon pasted on a wide smile. "Ladies." He nodded. "Good day."

They stiffened, eyes wide, and mumbled something, then bustled on past as if he had tried to throw a bucket of cold water at them.

"You see what I mean, Marshal?" said Loudon.

"No, not really. Those two women always walk together when they meet up in town. Been friends for years. In fact, my own mother walks with them sometimes."

"Fine," said Loudon, glancing at the retreating shapes. "But what I'm getting at is the fact that this stranger's offers have begun to turn folks odd in this town."

"Odd how?" Thompson looked up and down the street. "Other than them slowing down, which I can only guess is them wanting to hear some sort of gossip they can spread around, I will confess I don't see oddness in it."

The newsman sighed. "Look, let's keep talking over a cup of coffee at the café, okay? I'll pay."

"Sure," said Thompson. "I have a list of things to do this afternoon, and a cup of hot coffee would go down well right about now."

They walked the few doors down the boardwalk to the Glen Rose Café and found it nearly empty of other customers, a far cry from the morning and supper crowds.

Once they were seated, Loudon jumped right back into where they had left off. "I admit I don't have all that much to go on. Not yet anyway, but I hope to soon. Or rather, I hope I don't. I'd rather be wrong about this. But if I'm not, then there may be headaches coming to Glen Rose."

The young lawman tried to suppress a sigh. He had known Loudon Paley for five years now, ever since the man had come to town from back East. And although he was good at his job as a reporter of information in and around town, and even into the outlying towns of Grindle, Finchley, and Tularetta, he also knew the man was not averse to raking up dirt where there was little need to do so. He wondered if it was a trick the man used in order to keep folks buying the next week's paper.

Sometimes, no matter if the story was about a local man who was mauled by a bull or a political office in Grindle, Paley could let his own speculation ride rings around the story's gathered facts. Especially if it was a quiet week in Glen Rose, which was the case more often than not.

"I don't mean to sound disrespectful, Loudon, or to presume to know more about your line of work than you do, but. . . ." Thompson scratched his head and settled his hat back on his full thatch of dark hair.

"Out with it, Marshal," said Loudon. "You think I'm exaggerating?"

"Well, maybe just a little. Stirring up coals and giving us more smoke than flame, if you take my meaning."

Loudon smiled. "I do, I understand, I really do. All I'm saying is you have to admit that that Dalton Majors fellow blew in to town and wasted no time in prowling the countryside and visiting people."

"No crime in that," said the marshal. "Some serious crimes happened after he left, sure, but I think we found the man." Thompson nodded toward the west wall, behind them. Loudon knew it was meant to indicate the jailhouse, where Larry Chiswick was in residence once again, this time as a prisoner.

"Has he confessed to anything yet, or implicated Majors as his employer?"

"No, not yet. He hasn't said much of use, in fact. He is not enjoying not drinking, by the way."

"I bet," said Loudon, thinking of how awful it would be if he couldn't have his nightly nip of Stark whiskey. "You cut him off cold?"

Thompson offered a tired smile and shook his head. "Even I'm not that mean, Loudon. I give him a couple of doses a day, just so he doesn't start howling and raving."

"You're a good man, Marshal Thompson," said Loudon. "Back to Majors, he seemed to have been systematic about his visits, judging from the routes he took and the places he visited. But sure, I'll grant you that visiting folks, even if they are strangers to you, is not any odder than most things a person can get up to in a day's time."

"But?" said the marshal, beginning to smile.

"But, the thing you might not know, Marshal"—Loudon leaned in closer, even though nobody was within earshot of them—"is that he made a cash offer to each and every place he visited."

"I do know that, in fact, Loudon. Most everybody knows that."

Paley nodded. "Sure, but do you know that he offered more than the average going rate for ranches in the area?"

"Yeah, I had heard that, sure. Even if it doesn't make any sense. Why would he do that? And who can afford to do that? And as I asked before, what does he want all that land for, anyway?"

"I asked Majors that very thing," said Paley.

"Oh, well, what did he say?"

"He said he didn't want the land."

"What?"

Loudon grinned and tapped his nose. "Majors doesn't want to own any land. But his employer does."

"Who's the employer, then? And why does he want to own everybody's land?"

"Funny you should ask me that, because I just found out who that very person is."

The marshal waited a moment, and when Paley didn't continue, he said, "And?"

"And it's not a he."

"A group of investor types, then? What do they call them, a consortium?"

"That's one word for such a group, yes. But no, this is not a consortium. Or a he."

"Who could it be then. . . . Wait a minute, you don't mean it's a woman?"

"Ahem!" said a stern voice behind them. Both men looked up from their table to find that Lilly had walked up behind them with her coffee pot. "And why, Marshal Harley Thompson, would you say that word in that particular tone?"

"Oh, Miss Chu, I'm sorry, I didn't mean anything by it, ma'am, I . . ."

As he spoke, the young lawman's face reddened a richer

shade than the bold red and white checked pattern of the tablecloth. Loudon and Lilly both could not suppress their chuckles for long.

Harley Thompson continued spluttering a sort of halting apology to her. "I only mean . . . oh, I didn't mean to offend. . . ."

Lilly wiped her eyes with a bare wrist and poured more coffee for the two men. "Relax, Marshal, I am kidding you. But I am curious to know what you are talking about women for. Hmm? Any chance we'll see you finally asking Callie Roberts to step out some day with you? A picnic, perhaps?"

It did not seem possible, but the young man turned an even deeper shade of red, a rich plum color that bloomed up from out of his collar and traveled right up to his ears.

"Oh, don't know, ma'am. I—"

Lilly realized she was close to some sort of edge with the young man and didn't like to see him squirm. Well, not much, anyway. "It's okay, Harley, don't mind me. I'm nosy, that's all."

"Yes, ma'am. I mean, no, ma'am. I mean—"

"And that's another thing," she said. "You keep calling me 'ma'am' and 'Miss Chu.' "

"Well, that's your name, isn't it?"

"Yes, but I'm not a century old, Harley. Besides, we've been friends a long time, haven't we?"

"Yes, ma'am. That is to say—"

"Then call me Lilly. Everyone else does."

"Oh, all right. Yes, ma'am. Miss Lilly. I mean—"

"Marshal," said Loudon, holding up a halting hand. "Let me intervene and tell you that there never has been a woman born who can be bested in conversation. Just nod and close your mouth and call it good, okay?"

"Right, okay, then," nodded the red-faced lawman, sipping his coffee.

"Good man," said Loudon. "Now, as to what I meant, well, it's just as I intimated. The ranch buyer and potential newcomer is indeed a woman." He lowered his voice and his head, leaning in toward the small table's center.

By then, Lilly had pulled out a chair and sat down with them, resting her coffeepot on the spare folded napkin. "Who is she?" said Lilly.

"As near as my resources have figured out," the newsman looked around him at the nearly empty diner. "The intended purchaser of all those ranches is none other than Mona Starret."

He leaned back, nodding, and sipped his coffee.

"Who?" said Lilly and Thompson at the same time.

"Who?" repeated the newsman. "You must be kidding me!" He looked from one to the other and saw they were most serious.

"Oh my," he said, sighing. "No one. No one at all. Save for the fact that Mona Starret is perhaps the wealthiest woman in the United States of America. And probably also of a large part of the world."

"Wow," said Thompson.

Lilly stood, hefting the coffeepot. "That's great for her, I'm sure, but why is she so interested in our little corner of things hereabouts when she could, from the sounds of it, buy land anywhere she wants to?"

"Now that's the interesting part," said Loudon. "Or at least I bet it is."

"Then you don't know," said Lilly, rolling her eyes.

"Well, no. That is to say, not just yet. But I'm digging, and my contacts back East never let me down."

"Why not just ask him?" said Lilly, nodding toward the door.

The marshal and Loudon looked in that direction, too. What they saw stunned them into silence. There, through the glass, and walking toward the diner, they spied no one other than Dalton Majors as he crossed the street, heading in their direction.

"Are you seeing who I'm seeing?" said Thompson, not shifting his gaze.

"Yep," said Loudon. "And I'll tell you something else, if he's back in Glen Rose, then if what I half expected to come true does indeed come to pass, he will have been accompanied by someone with far more import."

"Oh, for heaven's sake, what is it you are trying to say, Loudon?" said Lilly.

Majors reached the boardwalk out front and then angled to his right and kept walking toward the west end of the street.

"And what's he doing back in town?" said Lilly.

Loudon chuckled. "I assume he's here to continue making offers, paying earnest cash, and handing out promissory notes to all our local land-owning friends."

"And as to who I suspect will be with him, why none other than his employer, Mona Starret."

"The rich woman?" Thompson smiled as he stood. "I think we would know by now if someone that wealthy and important were in our midst."

"Hmm," said Lilly. "Self-important, you mean."

"Yes, well." The marshal slid his chair back, snug to the table. He laid coins down on the tabletop and grasped his hat off the seat of the unused chair to his right.

"Be that as it may," he said. "There have been a whole lot of suspicions raised and allegations made about this Dalton Majors and his dealings when he was last in Glen Rose, not the least of which was the Brighton shooting. But before I could question him, he disappeared. I think it's high time I talked with him."

"Hang on there, Marshal. Any objection to me tagging along?" Loudon stood up from his chair.

"Well . . ." Thompson cleared his throat and spoke in a bold and falsely deep voice. "This is technically official law officer business, Mr. Paley." He reached the door and turned the knob, then looked back. "But as a concerned citizen, I can't prevent you from standing nearby and listening in. I am, after all, your employee."

Loudon grinned and followed the young lawman out onto the sidewalk. "Bye, Lilly. I'll be back! I have to make sure our employee is doing his job!"

Lilly grinned and shook her head. "Of course you'll be back, Loudon." She shook her head as she walked to the kitchen. "You eat nearly every meal of the week here."

As she began working to clear up after the usual morning crowd, she considered the young marshal's parting comment about him being an employee of the citizenry of Glen Rose, which, although he said it in a joking manner, did not make it any less true.

It sure was nice to have a publicly elected official with a sense of humility about them, and enough grace to acknowledge that they were there to help and not to lord over everyone else the power of their position.

"A far cry from Chiswick," she said to nobody in the kitchen, wondering, for the first time in months and months, just how the man was faring. He had certainly earned every raw thing that had happened to him in the waning days of his holding the office of town marshal of Glen Rose.

Despite that, Lilly, and she knew that Jed felt the same, did not wish the man any further ill will. She knew he had crawled so far into a whiskey bottle that she doubted whether he would ever be able to find his way out of it again.

The thought of Jed, and by relation, his mama, Mother Stark, and known to her close friends as Minnie—company that Lilly felt honored to be in—brought a smile to Lilly's face as it always did.

She would be riding out there later to talk with Jed and tell him her good news. She hoped today's conversation with her husband-to-be would turn out better than the last one they'd had. Jed had been downright unreasonable, something she thought she would never consider thinking about Jed Stark.

"We'll find out later," she said, and began scraping the griddle. "How many more times will I do this?" she wondered aloud, blowing at her black hair as strands slipped down before her eyes.

Chapter 19

"Pardon me, Mr. Majors." Marshal Thompson sped up his gait to catch up with the trim figure in the off-white linen suit ahead of him on the boardwalk.

He was within a dozen feet, and unless Majors was hard of hearing, the lawman knew that he was being ignored.

The young lawman increased his pace and angled before Majors on the boardwalk. "Hold up a moment there, Mr. Majors." The marshal smiled as he said it, but his tone was bold and his eyes were dead serious.

The Englishman sighed. "Is this really necessary?" He looked Thompson up and down. "Deputy, is it? I am a very busy man."

Loudon came to a halt about four feet away from the pair. He'd known Thompson for about five years, well before he became deputy under former town marshal, Chiswick. As everyone who knew young Thompson could attest he was a kind-hearted young man, considerate and always ready to work to peacefully defuse a situation that looked to be lurching into dangerous territory.

And as his preference was peace, he did not condone nor resort to the regular use of the heavy-handed tactics of his former boss, Lawrence Chiswick.

Few were the instances when anyone could recall Thompson losing his temper. But when he did, people noticed, not least because he was still a young man, in his early twenties, and solidly built.

He also was well-practiced in his use of guns, be they revolvers or long guns. And although he was most reluctant to use them, everyone knew that Thompson had no hesitation should a situation call for such force.

Everyone knew this, of course, save for strangers in town. And the veteran newsman knew that Dalton Majors counted high on that score. How Thompson was going to react to this offensive newcomer, who knew? Loudon took one step backward and shuffled closer to the storefront to his left.

"Actually, it's marshal, Mr. Majors. Marshal Thompson. Which, I suspect, you knew. Perhaps it slipped your mind. While I respect the fact that you are a busy man, strangely enough, so am I. Odd we have that in common, hmm? Now"—Thompson stepped forward with his arms folded over his chest—"I will repeat myself. I require a few moments of your time, sir. It won't take long, I assure you. Won't you step into my office? We are nearly there, just up ahead of you, there on the left. See where the sign says, *Marshal's Office*? That's the place."

During this brief chat by Thompson, which Loudon thought might well have been the most he'd ever heard the soft-spoken young man speak all at once, he watched Majors's eyes. They began to narrow as he regarded the young, wide-shouldered lawman addressing him.

Loudon also saw that the Englishman's nostrils flexed and flared and his jaw muscles jounced beneath his smooth-shaven, bay-rum-scented face. If he clamps his teeth together any tighter, thought Loudon, he's going to grind them to powder.

"Whatever you have to say to me . . . Marshal . . . can be said right here, right now." Majors looked down and made a laborious show out of gently tugging on a swaying gold chain. In a moment, he had freed his gold pocket watch. He clicked it open with his other gloved hand and regarded the face. "You may have two minutes of my time, Mr., oh, pardon me, Marshal, Thompkins, was it?"

"Thompson," said the lawman. "Marshal Harley Thompson. And right here is fine. But I may well need more than two minutes. We'll see. Now"—he canted his head to one side and regarded Majors—"I will come to the point."

"Good, young man. My time equates with money. And I don't appreciate losing money on foolishness."

A cluster of three women approached from behind Majors, and he didn't see them.

Thompson said, "Pardon me, Mr. Majors, but in Glen Rose we always step aside for ladies." As he spoke, Thompson moved to one side of the boardwalk and lifted his hat to them as they sheepishly scooted by. The women moved by slowly and in single file, uncertain of what was happening there but not wanting to miss any of it.

Majors reacted as if someone had prodded him in the backside with a pin. He convulsed and snatched off his hat, stepping to one side without looking and bowing deeply at the same time.

Unfortunately, his frenzied efforts resulted in him backing into the last of the three slowly moving women. He planted a boot heel firmly on her own boot, and she shrieked, lost balance, and fell backward against the storefront behind her.

Majors spun, his arm out, eyes wide, as the other two women recoiled at the scene.

"My dear lady!" he shouted, bending low and trying to lend her assistance. A second ill-planned move resulted in his grasping, assistance-seeking hands groping the woman's bosom.

She shrieked once more, even louder, and lashed out, trying to slap him. She managed to swing her canvas satchel, half-filled with potatoes, high. It connected with the side of Major's head, and then one of the sack's two loop handles snapped, and the potatoes scattered across the boardwalk and bounced into the street.

The young lawman stepped forward and managed to part the two flailing figures, holding Majors back with his left hand and, with a finesse most appreciated by the woman and her two companions, he grasped her work-roughened hand as if he were thanking her for a lovely dance.

Thompson knew her, of course, as did everyone who was a lifelong resident of Glen Rose. It was Cindy Brullerton, and she was well known for her intolerance of foolish behavior. She was a middle-aged, unmarried woman who lived with her mother and father and seemed quite satisfied with that situation, as did her parents, mostly because she seemed to do most everything for them.

They had sold their herd of cattle some years before at a time when prices were high, and moved to town, where they lived a modest but comfortable life.

Her bosom companions, other than her clinging parents, were two widowed sisters, twice her age, who shared a home, now that they were both happily shed of their husbands. Most folks in town thought that poor dead Earl and Rupert were also relieved. In fact, it was said the two dead men were likely resting high above, playing harps and giggling at being freed of their earthbound marital bonds.

Their widows, Darla and Wanda, were kind enough ladies, everyone agreed. But their tightness with a dollar was the very fabric of local legend. They were rarely seen offering much to anyone that didn't result in something also being given to them. They were scrimy.

Bad enough, to be sure, as most Glen Rose residents knew, but the widows' biggest passion was gossip. And nobody in town was immune to their hard gazes and whipcrack tongues.

Cindy Brullerton had long known this about them and had always secretly counted her lucky stars that she was their friend. She knew what the alternative was, and it was painful and harmful. Yet in order to maintain their friendship, she was forced to contribute to the piling on of suspected flaws of others.

And now here she was, smack-dab in the middle of shopping with them on the main street of Glen Rose, when a man attacked her and seemed to refuse to leave her be. In fact, he went so far as to grope her in a way she had never been fondled before! It was all too much.

She should faint, she really should, thought Cindy. After all, she had already done the expected and had shrieked. Twice in fact. Then she had lashed out with a hard swing. Unfortunately, part of her shopping, the potatoes, had clunked and rolled away.

Yes, she thought. I really should faint away, and she fluttered her eyelids and sailed her hands upward, fluttering them nearly over her head and offering up a series of increasingly softer utterances, word-like, but that was all.

She sagged backward once more and let her head hang limp to her left side.

"My word!" shouted one of the sisters, brandishing a meaty hand, palm out.

By the time the strange man had realized her plight and subsequent intentions, Cindy Brullerton appeared to be well and truly unconscious.

"Oh no, oh no!" he said, still trying to roll to one side, his hands bent back at the wrists. He pivoted, landing hard on his right elbow, and howled himself at the same time as he collapsed on his right side on the boardwalk.

Marshal Thompson bent to help Miss Brullerton, being quite cautious as to where he placed his hands, and helped haul her to her feet. "My dear Miss Brullerton!" he said. "Are you hurt? Did he hurt you?"

"Of course he hurt her!" shouted one of the sisters, who by then had regained their senses and were advancing with walking sticks raised on the heart of the scene.

They bypassed the lawman, who appeared to be handling the situation as well as they could hope, given the fact that he was, so they thought, little more than a child. And they closed in on the strange man, Dalton Majors. Of course they knew all about the man, having worked with diligence to glean morsels of information about him and his dealings from his last trip to their town.

The first of the sisters to step beside the man, who by then was on his knees reaching for his fallen hat and cuffing it with his dusty fingers, prodded him with the business end of her stick. She shoved it hard into his side, not pulling it back away. "Explain the meaning of your boldness, sir!"

The other sister, not to be outdone, cut a shoulder in front of her sister and glared down at the wide-eyed, slack-jawed Majors. "Your victim is a dear friend of ours, and this will not be tolerated, sir!" She turned to her sister, and they shared a harsh nod of agreement.

It was about then that Cindy Brullerton, under the kind ministrations of the red-faced and nearly grinning marshal, fluttered back to life.

It took the marshal several minutes to quell the sisters, who were soon joined by Miss Brullerton, and soon enough all three women were in proper high dudgeon, howling about improprieties and how this sort of thing never happened back when . . . and there the ladies hauled themselves up short.

This sort of thing was far more likely to have occurred during Marshal Chiswick's time as town lawman, and they all knew it.

"Well, anyway," said Cindy Brullerton, smoothing and fussing over her already smoothed and fussed-over dress, "I . . . I shouldn't be attacked in the street! And by a stranger, no less!"

She looked to her friends for confirmation, which she received with closed eyes and knowing nods. "Quite right, quite right," said the sisters in near unison.

Marshal Thompson, on the verge of smiling the entire time, stood back and crossed his arms, waiting for the flustered folks before him to right themselves. Dalton Majors tried several times to apologize to the ladies, and to Cindy Brullerton specifically, but none of them were having any of it. In fact, Miss Brullerton, as the offended party, kept whipping up her palm as if she were waving to the man.

Finally, Thompson interrupted, laying a hand on Majors's sleeve. "What say we retire to my office, Mr. Majors. We'll leave the ladies to their . . . situation. I think your presence here is not soothing to them just now."

"But . . . but I can assure you"—he turned to the ladies—"and them, that it was a mere accident, that my intentions were, that is to say I meant no . . ."

"My word, Mr. Majors," said a woman's voice from the street behind the gawping, smiling Loudon Paley.

The newsman spun around to see, not a dozen feet away, and flanked by armed men, two on each side of one of the prettiest women he had ever seen. The marshal and Majors, and the three women, all looked up. Everyone else in the small but excited little crowd that the scene had given rise to all looked to the voice as well.

"Miss . . . ah," Majors broke free of the marshal's light touch and stepped down off the boardwalk, making for the woman. "I, ah . . ."

It was obvious, at least to Loudon, that the man was not about to utter her name before he reached her. It was also obvious to Loudon Paley, because of his inquiries and research, thanks in large part to the efforts of a few well-placed reporter chums back East, that he was able to recognize the stunning woman as none other than the very wealthy, and very pretty, Mona Starret.

CHAPTER 20

Within moments of her intrusion, albeit a *pleasing-to-the-eye* interruption to their proceedings, Mona Starret had managed to all but shut down the workings of Main Street, Glen Rose.

A brief but full silence descended on the street as everyone took in the woman and her entourage. And then Loudon Paley walked forward, his left hand extended and a smile wide on his face. "Let me be the first local to welcome you to Glen Rose, Texas, Miss Starret."

He was still a good eight feet from the mildly surprised woman when the four men who flanked her, two to a side, advanced and closed ranks before her, their dapper black wool suitcoats each parted to reveal shoulder holsters. Each held a hand poised halfway from their belts to the gun butts. None of them wore anything remotely resembling a smile.

Behind them stood Mona Starret and Dalton Majors, who had scuttled to his employer's side. As soon as the four hired men had presented themselves accordingly, Majors and Starret engaged in a hushed and hurried conversation.

Loudon paused briefly and then, still wearing the smile, pressed on ahead. He was wondering if she would be free for a meal at some point in the near future. And no sooner had he thought it than he gave voice to the notion.

All four of the stoic gun toters glared at him without letup, but behind them, he heard a snort, and not from a woman. It was Majors.

"Please excuse the man, Miss Starret. He is a local and is, shall we say, rather uncouth."

"Oh, but Mr. Majors," said the newsman. "While it is true I am a resident of Glen Rose, in fact, as for being uncouth, well, no less than four minutes ago I witnessed you barging into three of the finest ladies of our fair town."

Loudon glanced behind him and nodded, still smiling widely, at the women who had been doing their best and not succeeding at appearing as if they were doing anything at all but listening to the proceedings.

"Thank you, Mr. Majors, I will be the judge of who and who doesn't share a table with me."

Miss Starret strode forward, and the wall of four men parted in the center to reveal the woman to Paley. Once more, he was struck by her boldness and beauty.

He saw now that, not only was she among the prettiest of women he had ever had the honor of laying his eyes on, there was something more to her, a directness and boldness that most other people, men or women, did not possess. It was both impressive and a bit disarming.

"Miss Starret, I presume," said Loudon, gaining his speech once more, bowing and hoping that his hair, or what was left of it, was somewhat smoothed over. "I would be honored to break bread with you."

"No doubt you would," she said, smiling.

From anyone else, the remark could have come across as more than a little smug. From her, it was downright delicious, he decided.

"And pray, sir, how is it that you know my name, and I do not know yours?"

"Well, ma'am, that's because it is my business to know such things."

For a long moment, the woman's face was inscrutable, then she narrowed her eyes. "You are a newspaper man, are you not?"

"Your guess is as straight and as true as your presence here in Glen Rose is foggy and mysterious."

"Ah, a man with a way with words."

He offered a slight bow. "Allow me to introduce myself. I am Loudon Paley, proprietor and editor of the *Glen Rose Gazette*."

"How charming. I will take meals at my hotel at six o'clock in the evenings. Tonight, however, I am engaged." As if she had been expecting the question, Starret turned her head to face westward along the street, then nodded.

"It's that one, with the garish and poorly executed lettering telling all the world that the very business housed within is little more than a . . . hotel. How drab." Yet she said it with a smile.

"Ah," said Loudon. "The Glen Rose Hotel. A fine establishment. As well as being the only hotel in Glen Rose."

"Not for long, Mr. Loudon."

"Oh? And why is that?"

She smiled and shook her head. "You and the entire town will find out soon enough. Now . . ." She turned back to Dalton Majors, who Loudon could not help but notice had stood close by her as he glared at Loudon, seeming to seethe more with each passing moment.

As Starret spoke, she looked just past Majors, to her left, and saw Harley Thompson approaching. Again, the four men who had flanked her now shifted to the right.

Thompson stepped forward, thumbing the lapel of his brown wool vest and lifting the silver badge that rode there. "I am Marshal Thompson, and if you all wish to spend the rest of the day in our jail, admittedly a fine one for the region, then by all means continue to descend on me with blood in your eyes."

The odd statement hung in the air before them. They looked behind themselves at Miss Starret. Still smiling, she nodded once gently and they broke ranks. The marshal passed through, touching the brim of his hat.

"Ma'am. While I also wish to welcome you to our humble town, I am afraid I have a bit of business to attend to that involves your man here, Mr. Dalton Majors. In fact, we were in the midst of doing just that when you arrived. And I dare say, you all arrived with very little fanfare, did you not?"

"That is because we drove our own conveyances, one a modified work wagon laden with goods and gear, and the two others barouches loaded down largely with the six of us. They are parked beyond the other side of the street, near the stables. We will attend to them shortly."

"Fine, fine," said Thompson. "But I still need to talk with Mr. Majors."

"Oh, I see. What for? Has he . . ." She turned to face Majors. "Have you done something unlawful, Mr. Majors?"

"That remains to be seen, ma'am. I will also want to talk with you soon, as well." Thompson offered her a smile and she nodded, her catlike gaze causing him to redden about the face.

Still blushing, Thompson turned to Dalton Majors, who stood with his arms folded over his chest, glaring at the lawman.

"I am going nowhere, sir. Do you have any idea who you two . . . two men are addressing?" He looked from Loudon to Thompson and back again.

"Come now, Mr. Majors," said the marshal. "You wouldn't want us to show favoritism hereabouts, would you? Why, I'm not certain any of us would even know what that means, anyway. You, Loudon?"

"Me? Naw, I'm just a . . . what was that word he used? A local! And I might add, I suspect I am also a rube."

"Oh yes, well, there is that," said the marshal, still not taking his unsmiling eyes from Majors.

Their playful banter was goaded on by the fact that Mona Starret seemed to be enjoying herself. Finally, she said, "Oh, Mr. Majors, why don't you go along with the men, and return when you are freed from their local clutches."

She winked at Loudon and the young lawman, both of whom blushed again, a deep pink that rose up their faces from their collars as if blooming there.

"Then perhaps you would be so kind, Mr. Majors, as to visit the hotel. I will be there. Hopefully, Mrs. Dahl will have my trunks unpacked by then. Poor thing is getting old, perhaps such trips are no longer in her future. At any rate, you can update me on your exciting progress hereabouts."

She said this in full hearing range of the number of Glen Rose folks who had slowly pressed in closer to the core of newcomers.

Majors offered his employer a polite bow and a smile. "Very well, Miss Starret. I will do just that, and I will see you soon. I can't imagine any of this"—he lost his smile and wagged a careless hand at the marshal—"will take all that long."

"Very good, then." Starret turned and offered the onlookers a swish of her demure, decidedly not flouncy but decidedly expensive deep blue skirts beneath her matching riding jacket.

With her long, slender gloved hands, she beckoned the four armed men who not once in the proceedings had lost their deadly serious gazes. Their eyes seemed to take in everything and everyone all about them in the street, all at once.

She made for the hotel, gazing with quick clipped looks up and down the street, at the other buildings everywhere it seemed. The four men followed, spread out, each of them looking in opposite directions, as if they were expecting trouble from anywhere at any moment.

Maybe they have just cause to be so cautious, thought Loudon as he watched them all stride with purpose, away from the locals.

"Well, now, Mr. Majors," said Thompson. "Shall we?" He extended his left arm to indicate that the Englishman would precede him and make once more for the lawman's office.

Loudon fell in step beside Thompson. "That was interesting."

"Certainly was," said Thompson.

In a lowered voice, as they were but five or so feet behind the ramrod-stiff, scowling Majors, Loudon said, "I daresay we may get a fuller answer as to why she's here."

"If we don't with him"—Thompson nodded ahead, indicating Majors—"I have little doubt you will during your dinner date tonight with Miss Starret."

"Here's hoping!" Loudon winked, and the three men mounted the sidewalk, watched by the clusters of townsfolk, who were also swiveling their gazes up the street toward the receding party of newcomers with the bold woman at its heart.

"Now, Mr. Majors, please do have a seat. May I get you something? A nice cup of coffee, perhaps? Water? What will it be?"

"I want nothing from you, Marshal," said Majors, his nostrils flexing. "Save for you to stop wasting my time. I know when I am being detained wrongfully, sir."

"Oh, detained? No, no, no, that's just not the case, I can assure you."

"And why is he here?" said Majors, looking at Loudon, who had pulled up a chair and stood behind it, ready to seat himself close to the action whenever the other two men sat down.

"Oh, Mr. Paley, he's here at my request. A citizen witness, don't you know."

Loudon nodded, smiling. Knowing that Majors hated every moment of this made the moment so much sweeter somehow. He hoped they would get to the bottom of all this mystery and oddness surrounding the man's presence in town. It had to be far more than coincidence that the odd deaths of Henry Brighton, Deke Frakes, and the Albersons had occurred following his visits to their places.

Loudon was good and ready to begin fitting the remaining puzzle pieces together.

On the other hand, if what he suspected was taking place, well, that supposition only stoked the burning glow of worry kindling in his belly.

"Very well," said Majors, folding his arms across his chest. He looked up at the ceiling and sighed as if he were trying to make people in the street hear him. "I'll allow it."

Thompson traded glances with Loudon, each man wearing raised eyebrows. "Ah," said the marshal. "That's big of you, sir. And as much as I appreciate your benevolence in this matter, I don't need your approval to do much of anything, really. Now, I have a few questions for you, and I would appreciate, for the sake of expediency, if you would answer them succinctly and forthwith."

Majors regarded the marshal with what seemed to be surprise.

"Oh, we may be locals and rubes, Mr. Majors, but one or two of our forebears managed to smuggle a dictionary westward from civilization back East."

"Ah, yes, very well."

"Good. Now then, let's mosey back to the beginning of this saga, shall we? Why did you come to Glen Rose? Let's see, that was a month or more ago, I believe."

Another theatrical sigh preceded Dalton Majors's reply. "Marshal, what I do and where I go are none of your, or anyone else's, business."

"Maybe not most folks, but I'm a duly appointed lawman of this town, and as such, that gives me permission to ask questions that other folks don't have much excuse to ask."

"Be that as it may, marshal. I can see this conversation will get us nowhere fast. What I suggest," said Majors, reaching for his fancy hat and half rising from the chair, "is for you to mind your own business and leave innocent, money-spending visitors to Glen Rose well enough alone."

It was Thompson's turn to sigh. "The role of a marshal is, in part, to protect the people of his town. And the people of Glen Rose chose me to do that. I am certain you are aware of what transpired here a year ago with Merlin Sheldrake. All appeared to be settling down well and nicely, and it was a welcome relief, in fact.

"Then all of a sudden odd things began happening, at just about the time you decided to pay our humble town a visit, dangling far too good to be believable amounts of money and promising folks so much more."

"Surely, even if that was your business, nothing you said could be regarded as having unlawful qualities."

"That's true. But I found that not long after you left town, and in one case perhaps before you left town, one of the people you approached has died by an inexplicable gunshot wound, leaving behind a widow and a young child. And since then, an older couple, also approached by you, have met with an untimely end."

Thompson and Loudon both saw the thinnest of clouds of surprise pass over the Englishman's face. He blinked it away and narrowed his eyes and leaned forward. "Marshal, coincidence is not unlawful. You really are going to have to put more effort into your research about such unfortunate matters before you should even attempt to think about blaming me for such a tragic situation."

"Oh, believe me, Mr. Majors. I have done just that. And I have dredged up enough information about that poor man's demise as well as that of the two others, folks, I might reiterate, who also were offered freakish sums of money by you for their farms and lands."

Their conversation went on like this for some time, long enough in fact that even the newsman had begun to tire of it. But he kept his peace because he knew that Harley Thompson never did a thing without a possible end in mind. So Loudon listened and endured the protracted chat.

And although he asked the Englishman in various, repetitive ways for explanations as to why he was buying up so much land and why Miss Starret wanted it, Dalton Majors merely kept in place his slight, pasted-on smile and shook his head as if disagreeing with anything and everything he was hearing.

In the end, and although Thompson threatened Majors with a term in jail, Loudon doubted that the young lawman had the proof to back up such threats.

Finally, the marshal sighed, smiled, stood, and extended an arm toward the closed door that led to the street. "You are free to leave, Mr. Majors. For now. But rest assured, we will chat again."

"Very well, Marshal," said Majors as he walked to the door. "I look forward to it." There was no hint of a smile in his voice or on his face.

The Englishman opened the door of the office, and before he stepped out, he looked over his shoulder at Loudon. "Oh, Mr. Paley, about your possible visit with Miss Starret—why on earth she agreed to see you, I have no idea—she is a woman of money, high taste, and breeding."

"And I am, alas, a lowly commoner, yet I understand the honor, indeed, the privilege of merely being in her presence, and I will act accordingly. You may rest assured that should I be so fortunate to talk with her on behalf of the *Glen Rose Gazette*, I will do my utmost to present myself as better than I am. And I shall refrain from wearing sackcloth."

"Yes, well . . . see that you do! Good day." With that, Majors left, closing the door with more force than he needed to—the glass pane rattled in place and Thompson scrunched an eye, expecting he would have to replace the cursed thing and explain to the town fathers just why his budget included said expense.

The glass remained intact. Until the next time, thought the marshal as he exchanged a tired glance with the newsman.

"We are no closer to finding out any of the whys in this matter, are we?" said Loudon.

"Nope. And what a pompous jerk he is," said Thompson.

"But a pompous jerk affiliated with money. And that, apparently, makes all the difference in today's world."

Chapter 21

"You must be Jed Stark," said the trim, beautiful woman who had just stepped down from the fancy barouche. Dalton Majors had all but tumbled out of the buggy and then held out a hand to offer her assistance. She waved him off with a hard hand, and he shrank back as if he had been cut off at the knees. "And you must be Mother Stark."

Jed and Mama and Redeye had heard and then seen the slowly moving conveyance, a big ol' carriage from somewhere fancier than Glen Rose, that was for certain.

Jed stood with his arms folded over his chest, and Mama stood a few feet to his right with Ol' Shredder cradled in her arm's crook. Redeye held the ground between them, on point, with his top lip quivering and a slow, deep rumble building in his chest.

"And you must be Mona Starret," said Jed, offering a slight nod.

"I am pleased to hear you've heard of me." She began to stride forward, her left hand out in anticipation of a handshake, her eyes locked on Jed's and a wide smile adorning her pretty face.

"I'd stop if I was you, ma'am," said Jed. "Redeye here is not fond of strangers." The hound had advanced a slow half step, and his rumble had become an audible, steady growl.

"Yeah!" snapped Minnie. "And especially the uninvited type—and that means you and those goobers with you!"

Mona Starret held in place and let her offered hand drop to clasp the other, just beneath her bosom, Jed could not help but notice. He also knew that was a little ploy of hers to tempt him or some such.

"Mr. Stark and Mother Stark, please, allow me to speak for a brief moment."

"Go ahead," said Jed. Beside him, Mama said, loud enough for everyone to hear, "Why? We ain't interested in what she's selling!"

"Mama, please, be cordial. For one minute."

"Fine. I'm timing her, then."

Mona Starret licked her lips and gazed straight into Jed's eyes. "I can assure you that I have nothing but your best interests in mind."

"How do you know what they are?" shouted Minnie.

"Mama, please."

The stranger continued. "I will cut to the heart of the matter, as you already know from my employee's earlier visit"—she offered a weak gesture behind her in the general direction of Majors—"that I wish to buy your property."

"Why must you own it, ma'am?" said Jed. "If you're so bent on doing good for the region and having a big ol' ranch, do it anyway. As you well know, there's plenty of land available in Texas. Go buy some other place and leave us Starks to ourselves."

She closed her eyes a moment, her head canted to one side, and when she opened them, she eyed Jed again, but spoke as if she were explaining something fundamental to a small schoolboy.

"I'm afraid that won't work, Mr. Stark. You see, I need your land specifically. You see, Jed, from everything our research has told us, your water supply is the richest and freshest in all the region. For a good, long distance all around here, in fact.

"And besides . . ." She pasted on a wide smile and let her

eyes close to a half-lidded look, while at the same time licking her lips. Then she looked him up and down slowly.

Jed felt as if he were being stripped naked, one piece of clothing at a time. "Besides, Jed, I don't want to share. I own everything I ever want. I possess them. All the way, all of them or nothing."

"That includes people, too, I take it," said the big whiskey man.

"I wouldn't put it in such crude terms, but"—she shrugged—"sure, if that's how you'd like to see it. Although with you, Mr. Stark, I can definitely see a promising partnership forming."

She looked him up and down again, slowly, as if there was nobody else about them and they were both as nude as the day they were born.

Jed reddened, Redeye growled, and Mama stepped forward.

"Perfume the air all you want with your promises and money, you cheap, taunting honey, and tease all the menfolk about with your fancy face and your fancy clothes, but there ain't a thing you can say or do that would make a Stark pull up tent pegs and sell off this property! You understand?"

Minnie hoisted Ol' Shredder high and kicked back the hammer to full cock. "Now save yourself more of that hot air you seem so fond of blowing all over us and get back in your fancy buggy and leave us be!"

To Mona Starret's credit, thought Jed, while she did color up in the face a bit from Mama's words, the rich woman did not let slip from her pretty face that sympathetic smile. "I can assure you—" she began again.

Beside him, Jed sensed that Mama was puffing up even more like a wet hen and was about to touch off Ol' Shredder. "I'll handle this, Mama," he said in a quick growl. He stepped forward a stride.

"Hush up now, Miss Starret!" shouted Jed, cutting her off in mid-sentence. "I have had enough! Most anyone who knows me will tell you that it takes an awful lot to get me worked up. But you have managed to do it, ma'am.

"Now before you or that silly little English fella next to you say another word, just do us all, and I mean everyone in the state of Texas, a favor, and take your money and your greed and your wishes and desires and all those other fancy words you kept tossing at us and leave this property, now and forever, do you hear?"

That got to her. He saw it, and he was glad of it. She and Majors stood there before the carriage, eyes wide and mouths open, unmoving. Jed knew his face was a pinch red, and he did feel bad about shouting at her.

But the more he saw her, the more he knew that she was nothing but a rich, pretty woman who used both those qualities to get what she wanted in life, and who cared not a whit about the consequences. And that disgusted him.

He couldn't help himself, and he launched in again. "I've never talked to anyone, and certainly not to a woman, in that tone before, and I doubt I ever will again, for I intend to be surrounded only with friends from here on out for the rest of my days. And to my knowledge, none of the very few folks I can count as friends are greedy, selfish gluttons such as you! Now . . . go! Get gone!"

As he ended that second brief speech, Jed's voice rose in volume and size until everyone in hearing distance—Mama, Redeye, Mona Starret, Dalton Majors, and the silly little man in the carriage all grew wide-eyed and flinched as his words hammered into them.

When he was finished, Jed pointed a long arm at her, past her, past the barouche, and up toward the longer lane leading on up and out and away from Whiskey Woods.

It didn't take them long to load up and wheel around and make tracks. But as they turned, Dalton Majors leaned his pasty face out and looked back toward them and shouted,

"You'll regret this, Stark! No one says no to Miss Starret! She never loses!"

Mama brought Ol' Shredder up to her shoulder and touched off the trigger. The blast peppered the fancy carriage's backside, pocking the gleaming paint job and bringing a smile to her face and a whooping from her mouth.

"My word, Mama. If you don't beat all." But Jed was smiling.

Chapter 22

"What have you done, you idiot?"

"What do you mean, Mona?"

She gritted her teeth. "On top of that . . . that abomination of a meeting with the Starks, the blame for which I dump squarely on your weak shoulders—"

Dalton Majors tried to protest, but Mona Starret held up a slender hand that shook with rage. "Not a word of protest! In addition to the Stark mess, I have been hearing of killings. Killings! What have you . . . no, I don't want to know. But you had best make certain I am untainted by your . . . your efforts."

"I understand, and I can assure you, I have done nothing wrong. Anything I do is for you and for your happiness . . . Mona. And besides, anything that has been done can be blamed quite easily and perfectly on that fool of a drunk I hired to rattle cages hereabouts."

She paused, her drink halfway to her mouth. "You mean to tell me that your hireling is behind this recent spate of deaths?"

"Oh," Majors blanched. "Well. . . ."

"To say that I am unimpressed would be an understatement, you dolt. More than a few people in this freakish little backwater are already eyeing me with suspicion."

"But I thought you wanted the land, Mona?"

"Yes, of course I want the land, fool! Now more than ever, given that encounter with those backwoods savages! Yes, I want the land! And at all costs, or nearly so, yes, but under no circumstance do I want any nefarious or heavy-handed tactics to be traced back to me or to anyone in my employ. Is that clear?"

Majors nodded. "Yes, Mona. Perfectly clear."

"Let me once more explain something to you, Majors. Once I embark on pursuit of a thing, I do not alter course and I do not fail, Starks or no Starks. I succeed because I win. I win because I succeed. I eat people like the Starks for breakfast, is that clear, Majors? It's all very simple, really. And stop calling me Mona. I am Miss Starret to you, Majors."

"But . . . I thought that's what you said I could call you."

"That was then. You have forfeited that privilege."

"But the plans I mentioned for those buildings on Main Street, the café and such, you . . . you approve Mona, er, Miss Starret?"

She eyed him through narrowed lids. Finally, she sighed. "Very well, yes, this so-called town is nothing less than an appalling clot of buildings. I shall have them all burned once it is mine, anyway. I see no sense in wasting precious time. Do what needs to be done. But!" she held up one long, lovely finger.

"Do it only after my big, townwide meeting. The unveiling, if you will. Understood?"

Dalton Majors nodded. "Perfectly, Miss Starret." He smiled and bowed, and sighed inside as he took his leave.

I shall not let her down, he thought as he retreated down the safety of the hotel corridor. And once she sees that I am, indeed, the only man of her ilk who can get things done, and with none of it traced back to her, well, I do not see how she might refuse me then.

With a renewed sense of hope blooming in his breast, Dalton Majors set about to figure out how to accomplish this tricky bit of work before him. At the moment, his so-called hireling sat in one of the town's jail cells.

That the silly child of a lawman had yet to arrest Majors told him that, despite his booze-addled wits, Chiswick had not yet pointed a finger at Majors. This was good. But he needed the situation to be better.

He stopped outside a door farther down the hallway from Miss Starret's rooms and knocked. One of her hired guards, Priestley, the senior of the four, as it happened, answered. "Yes, Mr. Majors?"

"You're not on duty, then."

"No, the others are. I go on later."

"Good. Stand aside, we must talk."

If Priestley took offense to the Englishman's brusque manner, he showed no sign as he stepped back and welcomed Majors into the room.

Once Priestley closed the room's door, Majors said, "I find I have need of your personal abilities, Priestley. As I recall, you have knowledge of techniques of unlocking doors to locked premises, and the, ah, removal of certain items within said locked premises."

The man nodded once. "I do, yes. What would you like unlocked and removed, sir?"

Majors smiled. "A certain marshal's office. And within, a certain cell. And then the removal of the contents of that cell."

"Am I to understand these contents are a man, sir?"

"You are, yes. This is to take place after the townwide meeting Miss Starret is set to hold tomorrow at midday. This prisoner, an uncouth, unwashed, hairy brute of a man, is, to my knowledge, the only prisoner there at present. Bring him to the small stable behind the café. And if he acts belligerent, tell him I'll have whiskey waiting. And don't worry about covering up your actions—I shall personally see to it that a most sufficient distraction takes place."

Priestley nodded. "Very good, sir. Consider it all but done."

"Excellent, Priestley. See to it and I will not forget it."

The hired guard nodded once. "Sir."

CHAPTER 23

"Is everything ready?" Mona Starret looked at Dalton Majors.

"Indeed, mum, er, Mona, er, Miss Starret. The painted canvases are set to unfurl and display, and the contracts are in order."

"Very good. Now, stand aside and watch how persuasive I can be."

As Majors did just that, he marveled once more at the woman's inestimable abilities. He had long before seen what the Glen Rose townsfolk, nearly all of its residents, who had crowded into the saloon room—the largest space in the town of Glen Rose—were soon to see.

And without further delay, Mona Starret proceeded with her plans.

She paced the makeshift stage from which she looked down and over at the sea of faces, all staring back at her, begging her with their eyes to tell them what they wanted to hear: wealth and security were soon to be theirs.

She told them of her plans for the town, for the region, and for their lives. Each and every one of them was to be included, should they so choose to be part of what she promised them all would be "the largest cattle ranch in the world, yes, but not just that," she said, stalking back and forth and eyeing them and nodding, as if urging them all to agree with her.

"No, for the ranch itself that is but the base, the foundation of this bold venture. Starret City, for that is what this will be called, will consist of far more than a home for mere cattle.

"I have the intention to build a major railroad yard right here in Glen Rose. And world-class hotels for all the cattle buyers who will be coming and going and coming again. This will, of course, also require all manner of renewed and renovated and newly built facilities.

"There will be schools, a church, vast gardens, there will be dairies, butcheries, and so much more! Anything you can think of will be included in this plan, I assure you. My team has been working on this for many, many months."

She paused and let all of this information drift down and settle atop them like sprinkled fairy dust.

Despite her best attempts at incredulity and fervor, she saw by the confused looks on some of the faces that she was not yet reaching the dolts. "Let me reiterate that to date I have procured outright ownership of several thousand acres and have signed agreements to purchase many, many more ranches.

"If you are a landowner, or an in-town property owner and you would like to be among the many who have already had the good fortune and intelligence to sell to me, I can assure you, no, no, let me tell you that I can and will, right now, promise you that you will be given a figure that far exceeds fair current market value.

"Why is that, you ask? It is simple, my good, new friends. It is because I look out on this crowd, and I see not people in a town that has something I want. No, no, that would be far too easy. I have more money than anyone any of you will ever meet. I say that not as a boast but as a fact. I do not need to choose Glen Rose to settle in, no, no."

She hung her head and shook it slowly, continuing to rove

the stage, slowly from one side to another. "No, I have chosen Glen Rose because it is beautiful. It is where I have determined that I, too, shall spend my life. In other words, I plan on relocating here, friends."

She waited for the building cheers and applause to dwindle, just a bit, then she proceeded. "Did I mention that there will be ample and highly paid employment for every man, woman, and child who chooses to stay and contribute to the growth of Starret City? Indeed, the wages will be at least double what many of you currently earn. And as I will be the sole owner of all ranchland and cattle, I will, of course, absorb all of the risk. Think of that, my friends! You will earn more money than you ever have earned, and you will have none of the risk!

"Let me reiterate, this is all going to happen, my good people. With you, I sincerely hope. But it will also move forward without you. Either you can be rich, or you can live in increasing poverty and one day die alone and unhappy."

Just when she felt she had begun to turn the corner and had won the majority of them to her stated cause, she nodded, and two men advanced from the wings and proceeded to unroll three large canvas paintings mounted on separate easels.

Each canvas measured eight feet wide by six to seven feet tall and was painted in color. One was a map of the region as it was then, and the next showed how it would be after Starret City was built. The third showed a close-up view of the downtown as it would be once Starret's plans were enacted. It was nearly unrecognizable, but it was grand and filled with majestic multi-story structures, including a large one that sported a steeple, plus trees, lighted streets, and a massive railway station and depot.

The posters seemed to show an idyllic place, but not one that was much familiar to any of the Glen Rose they all knew and loved and in many cases had helped establish.

"Why here?" shouted one man.

Good question, she thought. And I'm about to give them the real corker of the situation. "Because this is where I want to be, plain and simple. And I am rich, and I want to do something for my fellow Americans that will help as many people as I am able. My long search led me to Glen Rose, Texas, and now that I have finally seen it with my own eyes, there is no other place I would rather be."

The questions and Starret's exceptional answers went on like this for another half hour, and Majors noticed that with each sweep of the minute hand on his pocket watch, Mona's grip on them grew tighter. Their allegiance to their current lives, and certainly to the Starks, diminished.

Finally, she let her arms drop, seemingly exhausted before them. This wonderfully wealthy woman had just told them that she intended to make them all wealthy as well.

She also wished to remove all headache from their lives and to give them high-paying employment and to build schools and stores and churches and anything else they might think of. And yet here she was, a humble woman standing before them, asking for their help.

"There is just one thing, the only thing, really, that will prevent any of this from happening."

She let those words shut them up, and they eyed her, all fully expecting her to laugh at them and tell them they were rubes and this was all an elaborate joke at their expense. But this she did not do.

Instead, she said, "Of course, that one thing would be that if a certain man, whom you all know, a landowner and descendant of one of the town's founders, were to continue his unreasonable belligerence in refusing to sell his place to me. His place was to be the very heart of the entire project, the spot on which I plan on building my very own home!

"Indeed, it is the one and only thing that will prevent any of this from happening. And it is sadly the hard-headedness, frankly, the selfishness of one family."

She let that sentence hang in the air while the people in the crowd looked at each other as if there was a skunk in their midst. Finally someone shouted, "Who, Miss Starret? Who would dare do such a thing?"

She put her hands to her face and slowly shook her head. "I daren't say the name, for fear of what their belligerence will bring to this town. But . . . but perhaps you all, if you can find it in your hearts to help me in this matter. . . ." Again, she let this last subtle question, delivered in seeming earnestness, hang in the air.

"Who?"

"It is . . . it is the Stark family of Whiskey Woods."

"The Starks? The Starks would dare do this to us all? Of course they would!" Soon, someone else shouted: "Them Starks always have acted as if they are better than the rest of us! And now they keep getting to prove it!"

"Well, I for one, am sick of it! Why our long-term well-being should be crushed and taken from us by one selfish man and his elderly mother! Ain't right, I tell you! Ain't right! I have had enough of the Starks and their scrimy, underhanded ways of doing things! No way am I going to let them do this to us!"

Starret held up her hands and quieted the roiling crowd. "Listen, friends. Please listen to me. Perhaps there is an amicable solution to all this!"

"Yes!" shouted Wanda Sue-Bell Hawley. "The Starks are smart folks, I'm sure they'll come to their senses."

A round of mumbles and a few random shouts of "Sure, they will!" and "Yes!" were soon drowned out by a raft of voices. One, a man's voice, barked louder than others, "Nah! Never will happen! They're wrong-headed!"

Mona Starret waited until the shouts rose to a peak once again, then quelled them from the stage with gentle, calming hand gestures and a sympathetic smile.

"Perhaps if you formed a consortium of the citizenry of

Glen Rose, then you could visit the Starks and ask them to reconsider, for the good of the community. For the good of you all." She held out her hands before her, spread wide, palms up, as if she were offering them a great gift. "For your children and grandchildren, and all the fine people of your families yet to come!"

They cheered her then. And Dalton Majors stood on the side of the stage just out of view of the crowd, his jaw hanging wide. Mona Starret half turned, caught his eye, and winked. Then she turned back to them, her hands clutched to her chest as if she were hugging each and every one of them.

"One last thing," she shouted over the din. Once it had waned, she said, "Might I suggest, and I speak from years of ample experience in the subtle pursuit of negotiation, that you show up in impressive numbers—always more persuasive that way, you know. And perhaps strike while the iron is, as they say, hot."

The brief pause was blown apart with the sudden shouts of the crowd as they realized the tycoon's advice was indeed sound. The bulk of the crowd boiled through the saloon doors and into the street out front, where they began the involved process of choosing leaders and those who would do the talking.

This took a mere ten minutes, after it was decided that Wade Whipple, owner of the town's most popular mercantile, and Horace Boone, the town's banker, should speak on their behalf. But that didn't mean the crowd of eager folks was interested in staying behind.

"Oh no, you heard the lady!" shouted some fellow.

"Yeah! We're all set to lose or win on the outcome of this!" barked another man. "So I say we all go out there to meet the Starks on their own ground!"

And within another half an hour, the majority of the town's residents, and a large assortment of folks who had made the trip into Glen Rose from outlying farms and ranches, mounted up on horseback and climbed aboard a dozen or more wheeled conveyances, from buggies to work wagons.

They all made their way, in some haste, spurred on by the fervor of Miss Starret's frenzy-inducing words and the promise of personal wealth bestowed by her on each of them.

Each face trekking eastward toward Whiskey Woods shone with that promise, eyes narrowed and glinting, and teeth set tight behind leers of expectation. They would have the Starks' participation, one way or another.

Chapter 24

As the meeting dispersed and frenzied Glen Rose citizens boiled forth from the saloon's doors, Loudon Paley stood at the back of the hall. He had begun the affair by jotting earnest notes of the proceedings so that he might offer a full rendering of it for posterity in his newspaper, perhaps in a special edition.

But as the meeting progressed, the newsman realized, as he listened to the wealthy woman and her intentions, and add to that her frightening guards and that smarmy Englishman, Dalton Majors, and the crowd's increasing and obvious immediate loyalty to her, his worst fears were becoming all too real, right before his very wide eyes.

He slipped out the doors just before the crowd and made his way down the boardwalk, eyeing the scene swelling like a bubble before him. He heard a child cry to his right. There, down below at the near edge of the street, stood Maeve Brighton holding Maisie.

"Mrs. Brighton!" he shouted, but although she heard him and looked about, she could not locate him until he made his way down the nearest steps and up to her. By that time, the crowd had all but engulfed her, and as he grasped her arm, she jerked away from him with fire in her eyes.

"Oh, Mr. Paley!"

"Mrs. Brighton, this is no place for you or Maisie! It's far too dangerous!"

"I was trying to get to that Starret woman or that Majors fellow, or both. I have a few things to say to the pair of them!"

"I understand, ma'am, but perhaps now isn't the best time. Here, let me help you figure this out. Away from this crowd. It's far too dangerous."

As he spoke, he tried to gently usher her out of the way of the shouting, sloppy mess of Glen Rose citizenry.

She was about to protest when a stout short-bed work wagon, pulled by a pair of equally stout, hard-stepping horses, rambled by them fast and far too close. Loudon managed to force himself between Maeve and Maisie and the wagon. It was so close that he felt the hub graze the back of his legs and the top of the wheel graze the middle of his back.

All the while Loudon forced the woman and her daughter back, away from danger. Any protest she might have made died in her throat as the wagon, driven by a red-faced man with a wild look, thundered by. The street filled with such activity, and people piled in and around the wagon and buggies.

"Let's get out of here!" shouted Loudon, ushering Maeve and her daughter away. Within moments, the street emptied, and the shouts and noises receded eastward as the crowd moved en masse toward Whiskey Woods.

Loudon guided the Brighton ladies westward along the main street, and then, when it looked safe to do so, they cut across to the opposite side of the street. "We should go to my office, at least until it's safe for you to make your way back to your place."

"But I have to see Mona Starret and Dalton Majors!"

"I understand, ma'am, but this is not the day. I can't tell you exactly how I know, but I can tell you that I feel there are, well, dangerous things about to happen hereabouts. Glen

Rose is not the safest place to be today, Mrs. Brighton. Please trust me."

She glared at him a moment, then seemed to sag a little and nodded. "Fine, then."

"All right, now let's get to my office."

Within minutes, they made it there, and shortly after he had poured cups of tepid coffee for them and had given Maisie a piece of a chocolate bar, the town grew even quieter. "Do you really think something is afoot, Mr. Paley?"

He didn't turn back from peering out the window down the long main street of Glen Rose. "I do." He did not explain that this feeling he had was far too reminiscent of how the town appeared and felt little more than a year before, during the Whiskey War.

They stayed quiet for some time, the momentum of the odd meeting washing over them. Loudon rummaged in his desk and pulled out his double-gun rig that he kept oiled and ready. He had never intended to use it again after he shot a notorious gunman, Pit Pritchard, during the Sheldrake incident. He caught Maeve's eye as he strapped them on.

"Just in case," he said, trying and knowing he was not succeeding well at conveying a light attitude about the guns.

Now the situation was once more tense, and he had the safety of his friends to consider. He gazed once more out the window. And then something far down to the right caught his eye. He squinted. There it was again.

It looked like a cloud, but it drifted up, up from . . . the front of the café? Even as he thought that it made little sense, he realized it was no cloud, but it was smoke. And smoke meant . . . *fire*.

"Stay here!" he shouted, yanking the door open. "There's a fire! I must check on Lilly!" Loudon dashed from his office door and ran eastward along the main street. He saw no one else on the street, at least not close by enough to shout to for help. Within moments, he had made his way to the café, and it was most decidedly on fire. By the time he reached it, sooty smoke had begun boiling out from beneath the front door.

As he reached for the door latch, he gave a quick look through the window into the dining area and saw flames within the kitchen, and the room was filled with gray and black smoke.

He yanked his shirt hard up over his nose and mouth and plunged into the mess.

The sound reached him first, a mere second before the clogging, cloying smoke. The flames crackled and snapped as if they were devouring dry sticks on a campfire. And in a way, he supposed they were, for the building, as were all on the street, was built of long-dry timber.

And he knew they could go up in minutes. He'd seen it all before, back East, covering such fires in cities. It would not take long for an entire building to collapse. At the same time, the flames would race outward, licking and biting into anything that might feed them. And that meant all the other buildings in downtown Glen Rose.

"Lilly! Lilly!" He shouted her name over and over as he made his way slowly, bent low and stumbling in the near-blinding smoke toward the kitchen.

He made it almost all the way to the back door that led to the alley behind the structures when the toe of his brogan caught something firm but soft at the same time. Loudon bent low and felt cloth beneath his hand. He patted it, and yes, it was a person! A woman.

"Lilly! Lilly!" He bent to her and raised her up by the shoulders. He was close enough now to see that, yes, indeed, it was his good friend. Her besooted face was sagged and her black hair hung loose and tangled about it.

And there was something more, something dark and wet smearing the side of her face. Blood?

He shook her lightly once more. "Lilly! Wake up, we have to go!"

But whether she was unconscious or worse, he did not know. She merely flopped as he held her. Loudon scooped her up and made the trip of the last dozen feet to the kitchen's back door and managed to thumb open the inner door.

The outer screened door was latched. He once more fumbled for the catch with his fingertips, then Lilly groaned, and he kicked at the door. It gave way with a shudder on the third kick, and he all but fell down the few steps and out into the lane.

Loudon carried Lilly as far out as he was able away from the building and laid her down on the earth. He reached into his inner coat pocket and tugged out a handkerchief. With it, he dabbed at the blood on her face and bent low over her, his ear close by her mouth.

He swore he had heard her groan before, and now he thought maybe he felt her breath.

Soon he was aware of something approaching from the west end of the alleyway, and he realized he and Lilly were not far off the laneway. Perhaps they wouldn't see them.

But as the shape approached, and as the fire in the café bloomed brighter and angrier and louder and wider, he recognized it as a horse towing a small buggy. It clopped at a quick pace right up to them, and there was Maeve Brighton and her daughter, Maisie, driving the thing.

Before he could shout to her, a loud cracking sound rose up from the café's kitchen, then a whooshing sound followed it, and a shower of sparks and a gush of air and smoke and flame shoved outward through the open back door.

Loudon knew that it would not be long before the entire run of buildings that made up the main street of Glen Rose would be gone. And that meant that they would most decidedly not be safe here.

Maeve jumped down from the buggy and rushed to his side, bending low over Lilly. She lifted her skirts and dabbed at Lilly's face, then parted the unconscious café owner's eyelids and looked at her eyes.

Maeve gave Lilly's cheeks a few sharp smacks and shouted Lilly's name close by her face. That did the trick, for Lilly Chu's eyelids began to flutter. "Wha . . . what happened? Are you"—she looked at them both and seemed to focus her eyes—"Loudon? And . . ."

"Maeve," said the other woman, smiling down at Lilly's face in her lap. "Do you know who you are?"

"Yes, of course, I'm . . . Lilly. Lilly Chu." The fire crackled and snapped, and another whooshing sound rose up. The heat, even at their distance from the conflagration, was becoming intense. "My café! My home!"

"I'm sorry, Lilly," said Loudon. "So sorry. There was nothing that could be done. It went up so fast."

She watched it a moment and shoved herself up to a sitting position. After a few moments of watching the fire, she said, "There was a man. A man in there. I . . . I left that foolish meeting to lock up, then I was going to ride to Jed to warn them. But then I heard a noise behind me, and I turned and there was someone there! He hit me, must have, for I went down. Hit me in the head, oh. . . . But I saw his legs, his shoes, fancy, light-colored trousers. . . ."

"Sounds like Majors," growled Loudon.

"Yes," said Lilly. "Might have been. I remember now, when I fell, I hit the countertop . . . my hands shoved things down, knocked a small jade figure my father gave me long ago, something he had given my mother. It hit the floor by my face. I saw it and I knew he was there, they both were, watching over me."

"Oh, Lilly, I'm sorry, I didn't see it. I'm afraid I can't go back in there for it."

She smiled weakly and shook her head. "No need," she said, holding up her right hand. "Here it is." She opened her balled-up fist to reveal a tiny, dark green figurine. It looked to Loudon to be a bit like a creature, maybe a dragon.

"It's the last thing I remember doing, seeing it there on the floor near me . . . grabbing it with my hand and then . . . I saw those men's shoes and trousers one last time, and then everything went black."

"Was there no fire when he hit you?" said Maeve.

"I don't think so, no," said Lilly. "Everything was okay. I'm always so careful of fire, so careful."

"Something tells me whoever he was, he set the fire," said Loudon. "This was no accident. No way."

"Are you well enough to ride in the buggy?"

"Yes, I have to get to Jed and Minnie."

Loudon shook his head. "I'll go there. You should go with Mrs. Brighton and Maisie. It'll be safer."

"No!" shouted Lilly, holding a hand to her temple. "No, I have to go to Whiskey Woods. I'll ride Poppy."

"No, not a chance, Lilly. Even if you weren't hurt, it's not safe. Things after that meeting, well, things are happening again."

"That's why I have to go!"

Loudon sighed, then spoke to Maeve. "I have to go to Whiskey Woods to help my friends. Mrs. Brighton, I think you and Maisie should go home. Can you take Lilly?"

"Yes, of course, we can help her, but we cannot go there, to our home. It's not safe. I just know it, Mr. Paley."

"Have you been threatened?"

"Not in words, no, but there were two black-suited men in the distance earlier today riding black horses. They seemed to be staring at our place, at the house."

"Starret's men?"

She nodded. "I think so, yes."

"Okay, but there might be danger out at the Stark place."

"I understand, Mr. Paley, but you and Lilly and the marshal are really the only friends I've, *we've* made here. And Mother Stark, she was so kind to us after . . . after Henry died. I . . . I would rather go with you, to help them. Please, Mr. Paley, I need to help."

Loudon looked from Lilly to Maeve to little Maisie back to Maeve, one hundred reasons why he should say no flitting through his mind. But then he saw Maeve's brown eyes. "Okay, okay. But we have to be careful. And please do as I say, okay?"

Maeve offered him a rare hint of a smile. "That's fine, then, Mr. Paley. Count on us." She lifted Maisie.

"And one more thing, Mrs. Brighton."

"Yes?"

"It's Loudon. But friends call me Loud."

"Very good, then, Loud it shall be. And I am Maeve."

"And I'm Maisie!"

They smiled, then the newsman helped them into the little buggy.

"But Poppy!" shouted Lilly.

"Don't worry. I'll ride Poppy and follow you. Give me a minute."

He hustled off and bridled the fidgety, dancing Poppy, then decided to skip the saddle and threw a blanket over her instead. Using a notched stall support for assistance, he climbed aboard the horse and guided her out and up to the others.

"We'll take the river route," said Loudon. "This buggy should be just narrow enough to make it. It'll be faster. But we have to ride hard, ladies." Loudon's voice was grim.

Lilly nodded.

"Then let's get to it!" said Maeve.

As they rode away from town, Loudon looked back and saw that the fire had indeed spread from the café to the two structures flanking it. He groaned and faced forward, patting his revolvers to make certain they were there and at the ready. For what, just yet, he did not know.

They cut southeastward toward the river and the old overgrown laneway, making eastward that cut well below the Stark place. With any luck, thought Loudon, they might make it there not too long after the townsfolk arrived.

Chapter 25

"Did you hear that?" said Jed, standing upright and narrowing his eyes. He looked toward the big cottonwood that marked roughly the end of the lane as it widened out into the dooryard.

He and Mama were sitting in chairs on the porch of his and Lilly's soon-to-be home, enjoying a few moments of quiet in the midst of events in town that were rapidly becoming frightening and more odd by the day. All because of the arrival of the land-greedy Mona Starret.

"From the lane?" said Minnie, looking in that direction, too, knowing that Jed's hearing was keen.

He didn't respond for a long moment, then in a lower voice said, "No, up the slope behind the tree."

They both held still, ears keen and eyes squinted.

"Are you sure you heard something?" said Minnie.

He nodded. "Yeah. Might've been a deer. But I'm not taking chances." He eased up out of the chair and made for the door. "Mama, come on in. We can't sit out in the open like this."

"You think it's that serious?"

"Maybe. But look what not wanting to worry about things got me last year. I need to start paying attention to the signs. Whatever they might mean and no matter how small they are."

Although she was a solid, independent person, Mother Stark was no fool. If Jed sensed the need to prepare for something, which likely included arming themselves, then there was real cause for concern. Jed was not one to strap on a gun lightly.

By the time Minnie eased in through the front door of the new home, which still smelled of fresh-sawn lumber, a scent that brought a smile to her face, Jed was in the middle of the room holding his rifle in the crook of his right arm and thumbing open his revolver with both hands.

"You keep the rifle here, and stay put. I'm going to ease on up that slope. It's likely nothing, but just in case."

He glanced down at Redeye, who was asleep on the rug by the table. There were times, more frequent of late, when the hound looked old, and this was one of them. "If he wakes up, keep him in with you, okay, Mama?"

"Yep," she said, annoyed at having to hole up with the dog and wait things out, but knowing that Jed spoke sense.

He sighed. "With all this foolishness that Mona Starret has brought on the town, clouding everybody's brains with promises of money, there's no telling what might be in the offing."

He didn't wait for Mama to respond, and it annoyed her, even though she knew he was right.

Jed handed her the rifle. "It's loaded and there are more shells there." He nodded toward a carton on the plank table. He walked to the door, then paused. "Look," he said, facing her as he buckled on his holster. "I'm not going to take any risks, I promise you. But now is the time for us to be vigilant."

He winked at Mama, and she said, "Jed, when it comes right down to it, it's just land. Don't get killed for it."

He stared at her for a long moment, then his face softened. "I know, I do know that. But if someone's sneaking around here, I need to know who it is and why they're doing it. I can't have my family living threatened. I just can't stand it."

She nodded.

"And, Mama? Stay put. I don't need to worry about you wandering around with that rifle, or worse, that cursed shotgun of yours." He grinned, and they both knew he was trying to make a joke. It was weak, but it helped.

Still, it flustered Minnie and she knew that, as Redeye was fast showing his age, so was she. At times. But they were still few and far between!

Once Jed crossed the open part of the yard, he felt easier, for the edges of the place were home to stacks of lumber, barrels, a wagon that he had been meaning to repair, and other bulky, large items. He bent low and paused behind each, his revolver out and ready.

A feeling of dread and familiarity came to him as he crept about the piled materials and equipment. Without invitation, his mind recalled the war, the cursed war, men sneaking and skulking and tracking and killing other men. And mostly because rich, powerful men thought it was the thing that needed doing.

He knew the foul war between the North and the South had been far more involved and complicated than that, but he, as had so many other men, had been mired in the guts of it, and it was difficult for him to keep a wide view of the thing.

All he knew was that a whole lot of people had died, as had so many beasts of burden. Acres and acres of once beautiful land, waterways, all of it and more had been savaged and ravaged by cannon fire and boots and blood, and he no longer had the slightest stomach for guns, killing, and brute violence.

He'd had to kill, and even when he sighted in on a man in blue, he'd whispered a small prayer of apology, for he knew he would be taking away the man's most treasured thing, his life. And in doing that, he would be depriving not only his victim but the man's wife, children, brothers, sisters, mothers, fathers, aunts, uncles, cousins, and friends of that man in their lives.

No, sir, the war had been an awful and sour thing that with

each passing year seemed to barely leave him alone. But if he had to say so, life since he had come to know Lil had grown smoother in all the good ways that he had before then assumed would never be open to him.

Now that he had tasted that, thought Jed as he made his way up the gradual slope, catfooting low toward the nearest thicket of scrub oak, there was no way he was going to risk losing it. Not to someone with ill intent in mind, no matter how much money they had.

Greed was greed was greed, and while there was air in his lungs and blood in his veins, this was one Stark who would not ever give in to such a glutton again, pretty woman or no.

The rough bark of the thickest tree felt oddly comforting against his cheek. He pulled in a deep breath, relishing for a brief moment the fruity, sour tang of the sun-warmed tree's skin as he thought about what he was going to do next.

He had few options. He needed to get up the slope, and he needed to do it without being seen and without getting shot if he was seen. It was also possible that there was nobody up there at all and that he had been hearing a critter and nothing more.

But he sensed that there was something shuffling and stepping somewhere up there and to his left, westward. He hoped it was as innocent as a mule deer wandering through and browsing for something toothsome in the thin duff of the forest floor.

Sure, it might well be that—nothing at all in the way of a threat. But his gut, and its tense twinges that seemed to work in tandem with his senses, told him there was something up there that should not be there.

"Okay, Jed," he whispered, so quiet he barely heard it himself.

Taking advantage for a last moment of the scant cover afforded by the trees, he bent low and leaned outward, his hat brim advancing before him at the height his belt buckle would be were he standing upright. He looked upslope, saw nothing there, and felt somewhat assured what he was seeing was indeed true, because the tree cover was sparse.

As with everything in life, this was a good thing for him and a bad thing for him. Good because he was able to see well ahead and know he wasn't in too much danger of ambush, and bad because he, too, would have no cover as he advanced upslope.

But he lived here, had all the years of his life, and knew that cutting upslope a bit farther to the east would give him the cover of that tumble of big, dull-edged boulders for a time. He made for it, angling upslope, eastward, and looking up and west as he dug in with his boots.

As he all but ran toward the rocks, he kept low and held the revolver ready in his left hand. He realized he'd not cocked it, and that would and could cause a fatal mistake.

He thumbed the thing back to half cock, and, as he closed the last dozen feet to the boulder pile, he swore he saw something up there, just behind the very next landscape landmark he had intended to then cut west toward—another, albeit smaller, jag of rock.

This one wore low, stunty pines clinging to the top and near side, their roots like the gnarled hands of an old-timer who spent far too long pounding away at the forge or swinging an axe.

What had he seen, he wondered as he pulled up, short and low behind the boulders. The red-gray lumps, solid in their presence, looked to be wedged into the graveled, scraggly hillside a long time before by a giant's jamming hand.

Jed didn't breathe in the seemingly long moments it took him to cover the last dozen paces to the spot where he felt certain he'd seen the man. For it had, he knew now without doubt, been a man moving in there among the rocks and bracken.

It would be a man holding a gun squarely on him, a man

who would shoot him quick and dead, given the way the spot was sited. The fellow would have the advantage of the high ground and would have certainly seen his approach, but there was nothing for it. Jed knew he had to get there and do it fast and hard and be ready to deliver to the intruder what the situation required of him—likely a bullet from his now fully cocked revolver.

He angled around the coarse upper corner of the tumbledown, his chest thudding with the concern and fear of this sudden unknown, the possibility that something he did not want to happen might well happen at any moment.

When he gained the spot, he found evidence enough of the presence of a man, and that gave him gratification, however cold it felt, in his conviction. He'd rather have not found a thing, or rather something that from his previous location downslope might have looked a whole lot like a man's profile or some such.

But no, here he found bootprints tramped, smeared, and ground into a patch of dusty earth, within the clutter of boulders. Where the man had been hunkered, spying and hiding, a sneaking beast intent on no good thing, was a grotto of sorts, accessible at the rear with a sideways, angling step, between two sizable, rounded lumps of sandstone that looked to have been there since the earth was a molten thing.

Jed's eyes cut back and forth between the northwesterly direction the man had taken when Jed rousted him, then glanced down to the earth within the boulders.

Yes, there were the bootprints, plain as the blue sky, worked into the dry earth. And what's more, within the clot of rocks was nested the mashed remnants of a roll-your-own smoke. It sat dab in the midst of a bootprint. The man had taken few pains to disguise himself.

This meant one of two things to Jed: the fellow was not expecting to be seen and then rousted, or he just plain didn't care if he was. But Jed was beginning to suspect who it might be.

No matter who, thought Jed, this did not sit well at all with him. For it meant the man had been hunkered here for a time, long enough anyway to smoke a cigarette.

Even as he thought this, his eye settled on yet another, then another, of the smoked remnants, all small, and all smoked right down to the nub, then smeared into the dirt.

Jed felt his gut tighten even more. He guessed he should at least be grateful the fellow hadn't set flame to the sparse forest thereabouts. But he was not happy, in the least, knowing the fellow had been there for quite some time longer than he had first suspected, and had been confident enough in his hidey-hole that he felt he could smoke as he wished.

Then, as if such things were part of a trail left just for him, Jed spied something shiny wedged between rocks. He adjusted his position, glanced up and all around once more, then back to the shiny thing.

It was a bottle. Jed reached for it, and with a quick tug, it popped free. It was a whiskey bottle. Empty and with no label and no cork. No doubt he'd find that somewhere thereabouts as well.

He glanced up and around himself again, then passed the mouth of the bottle beneath his nose. Rotgut. It smelled of sulfur and cloying scents, a foul mash of herbs the makers of such trash used in order to help give their foul, often deadly product a barely tolerable stink.

It was an interesting discovery, to be sure, and it all but guaranteed he knew who the fellow was who'd been spying on them—Larry Chiswick. But how? He was in jail. Wasn't he? Unless he'd escaped. Somehow.

Jed had found bootprints, an empty whiskey bottle, and cigarette stubs. Such things could have been left by half of the folks in town, or anywhere in the West, he reckoned. And taken separately, the leavings were of minor use to him, but for the fact that the former lawman had also left such things in the bracken and rocks not far from the Alberson place.

He glanced in the direction the rascal took off in, and saw no one, nothing in fact that might lead him to do what he did next. Tired as he was from the day's work, and from this fruitless, annoying chase, something inside, deep in his head and in his gut—that instinct thing again—told him he had to settle this long-standing score between himself and Chiswick.

He let go a small sigh, checked his revolver's hammer, and once more eased into a crouch, hunkering low as he made his way upslope and northwest. Before the day ended, he would regret this decision. But for the moment, something told him to follow that instinct, that it would lead him to some sort of situation with Chiswick.

He'd not made it a dozen steps when he heard a man's voice shouting: "Stark! Stark!"

At the first bark of his name, Jed seized in place, no longer feeling any lingering trace of doubt nagging him into thinking he was wasting his time, that there had been no way he was going to discover anyone in the upper reaches of the Stark woods. That had slipped away as soon as he'd discovered it was, with little doubt, Chiswick he was after, and who was after him and his loved ones.

"Stark!"

That ragged, raw, bellowing voice sounded as Jed would expect someone who drank rotgut and smoked cigarettes while sneaking about in the undergrowth might sound.

It also sounded as if the demon wanted him to reply. And so he would indulge this fool.

"What?" he snapped, clipping off the word and hoping it sounded to be everything the man's shouts were not—firm and bold and not diseased by drink or smoke.

"Ha!" shouted Chiswick. "Just trying to get a level reply from you, you coward! Cheat!"

Jed heard the words and felt the slightest ruffle of annoyance at the untruth of them. Their utterance told him the man was, as always, off the mark and making up foolishness. But why? Was he merely providing a distraction? For what? To draw Jed from the house. . . .

Jed felt a fast creeping coldness at the thought. His initial urge was to turn and bolt, make for the house, and check that Mama was all right. But that would leave Chiswick out here, armed and, as always, in a killing mood. No, that could not stand.

And besides, he thought, Mama was no wilting flower. No, Jed, he told himself. Spend the few minutes to deal with this verminous wretch and then hightail it back home.

Draw Chiswick out and keep him running his mouth, then he might get some answers, some resolution, although he knew this was a whole lot to ask for.

He needed to distract the fool so he might dash to better cover. As he stood now, Jed was barely concealed, dodging, as he had intended, between larger landmarks on his way, cutting up and across slopes.

"What are you talking about? And why are you spying on me, you lazy drunkard!" It was the best he could do without putting much effort into it. He was far less interested in insulting the man than he was in getting to a safer spot and getting closer to him.

He was nearly to another jag of old, dead timber and rock when the fellow barked again. "You say that to my face and we'll see what's what, Jed Stark!"

Jed jerked down behind the cover of logs and rock. Yes, it was Chiswick who the voice belonged to, and he knew now that the increased pressure to sell Whiskey Woods to Mona Starret was no longer something to shrug off.

Those irritating visits by Dalton Majors had been mere opening salvos.

But Jed had assumed, had hoped, that this would pass.

But it appeared now that it would not. It all smacked far too much and too close to the bone of the mess with Merlin Sheldrake.

"Here we are again," growled Jed as he pulled in a deep breath and, hunkering low, advanced on up the hill, hoping like mad that Chiswick's booze-addled mind was not able to draw a sight on him until he reached cover.

"Chiswick! You are reaching new lows, working for a snake like Majors!"

There was a long pause, as if the man were thinking something through. Jed suspected he'd surprised and bothered Chiswick by identifying him so readily. He was pleased that the way he had said it made it sound as if he knew who he was all along. Might somehow lead to the drunkard revealing something, any snippet of information, that might be of use.

"Stark! We been over this, you devil! Who I work for ain't none of your cursed business! I'm a free man, and I got a right to be where I want to be, any time I want to be there!"

Jed growled and pulled in a breath. He was about to shout how the man was, in fact, wrong as a man could be. That this land was off-limits to anyone but Starks and folks invited by them to walk across it.

But then Jed recalled something Mama had told him a few times over the years, something she believed but could not seem to adhere to herself, no matter how hard she tried: "You catch more flies with honey than with vinegar."

And that notion, food for thought, gave him an idea. He would try to honey-coat the situation, see if he might turn it from something antagonistic and useless instead to something of value to him.

"Chiswick! I'm sick of all this! Let's call a truce. Come on down to the shop, and we'll have a drink and talk things out! What do you say?"

Again there was a long moment's wait, as if the former lawman were thinking things through and was not very good at the thinking part. That was likely true, thought Jed, considering the man was slowly killing himself with rotgut liquor.

"Why don't you shut up, Jed Stark!"

Jed ground his teeth together hard. It was a mighty temptation to shout something that might set the man off, or maybe worse, give the drunk permission to flee. He was not so far away, and Jed suspected just drunk enough that Jed could give chase and likely gain on him, bring him down as a man might a sick coyote that's been terrorizing stock.

But Jed knew that would only result in one of them, or maybe even both, nibbling on lead pills, and that was not a thought that gave him any satisfaction.

Jed had no intention of doing something stupid that he would regret. And having been at the receiving end of a rifle's sights in the War and here and there since, the previous year, no exception, Jed figured his life was far too precious to risk. Even drunken bums get lucky shots once in a while.

He'd always known Lawrence Chiswick as a blowhard, but perhaps a better-than-average shot with a rifle and with his revolver. No, no need to risk it. "Okay, Chiswick. Fine. You go your way and I'll go mine, and we won't ever have to talk to each other again!"

This time the man's response was immediate and unexpected. Chiswick howled with laughter. "Know so much, do you, Stark?"

"What does that mean, Chiswick?"

"Means if you knew what was coming, you'd know I'd be doing you a favor if I put a bullet in your head right now, you fool!"

Jed cast all logic away from himself in that moment and, with molars still grinding hard, he growled and bolted up that hill straight at the spot he knew Chiswick to be, coward that he was, simpering behind a thick clot of trees and boulders.

Jed knew this land better than anyone alive, he reckoned,

having played on it and roved on it his entire life, first as a boy and then as a young man making meat for the stewpot and fire spit.

He wasn't about to respond to Chiswick with words, no sir, but he for certain wasn't going to let that sort of comment go unexplained. All thoughts of bullets with his name on them flitted away like startled moths as he gained traction with his digging boots, his revolver held out long before him, his lean, muscled torso bent low, but not so low he couldn't be seen from upslope. He didn't care. Chiswick would explain himself or . . . or what, Jed, he asked himself, without slowing.

He bit back on his obvious foolhardiness and kept on, his own footfalls on crunching and grinding duff and not quite masking the sound of his quarry's own fast-stamping feet.

Chiswick was running, then. Good, thought the big whiskey maker. Run all you want, but it won't make a whit of difference. I'll have you this time, you drunken lout.

Jed kept on, some sort of grim satisfaction weakly flowering in him, knowing that the ex-lawman was afraid of him. If he knew how I felt about that sick killer in this moment, how I've always felt about him, thought Jed, he would not have dared to come within five miles of Whiskey Woods.

Jed heard only his own boots grinding gravel then. He slowed up, knowing something was changed from the moment before. Chiswick had stopped.

Jed stopped and held his breath and cocked his head to the left, his stronger ear, the right, facing upslope and ahead. No sound. Jed was not by any sort of cover. Something, an inner tickle, perhaps the slightest of rustles of a shirt or coat folding as an arm drew back and raised. . . .

Something minor and that would otherwise go unheeded by him in a day's time nonetheless came to him in that moment, and even as he dropped, belly flat, to the dry, gritty earth, the scent of musty dirt and dust and the moldering pack of leaves and soil and twigs perfumed his nostrils as a bullet whiskered inches above his prone form.

Every scrap of his previous tossed-aside caution settled back on him like a heavy wool blanket, and he regretted letting the man's words burrow into his brain and cause him to act the fool.

Never give chase to a drunken man with a gun. Now here I am, thought Jed, face down in a clearing on my own land, pinned and being shot at by a vile drunkard with a freakish vengeance scratch to itch.

What on earth was happening here? From the scant information Chiswick had leaked at him, did that mean that the headache that was Mona Starret had truly already come to his own doorstep?

CHAPTER 26

"Jed Stark! You come on out here and talk to us! We demand it!"

"The only thing you're going to get, Boone, is a bullet up your nose! Now git while you can, you whining mess of a man!"

A rifle shot whistled out from a lowered window in the house, zinging low and fast over the heads of the crowd. Three women screamed, and several of the men whipped out their sidearms.

Just then, from down off the hillside to the north of the house, Jed long-legged it into the open, keeping far closer to the house than to the crowd, which had remained clustered a good hundred feet from the porch steps. He had never seen so many people at Whiskey Woods all at once.

"What is the occasion for this visit, folks?" he said. His voice might have sounded jovial, but everything else about him bristled with a seething rage. He knew exactly why these fickle so-called friends were here.

He held a drawn revolver and stood as menacing as any of them had ever seen. Jed Stark had always been a tall, rawboned, rugged fellow, quiet, slow to rile, and good-natured. But on this day, he seemed like a giant among them, for some odd reason.

He stared at them all with squinted eyes, marking their faces. "Phil, Mrs. Dibbs, Joseph, what's this about, then?"

There were mumblings but no one spoke. He heard Mama and Redeye walk out onto the porch behind him.

Two men, Horace Boone and Wade Whipple, both of whom Jed knew well, stepped forward, looking decidedly sheepish and uncertain of themselves. From behind them, somewhere in the crowd, a man shouted. "Get on with it!"

"Yes, ah, Jed, that is to say, Mr. Stark, we the people of Glen Rose have been, that is to say . . . we've been talking and—"

"You haven't been talking," said Jed. "I'll wager you've been listening to a certain woman make all manner of unbelievable promises."

"Then you decided to talk, all right!" shouted Minnie. "Shouting at each other about how rich you all could be if only the Starks sold their land to that . . . that painted heathen woman!" Her voice rose in pitch, and she cranked off another shot, straight up into the air.

A few children cried, a couple of women shrieked, and several men ducked low and hoisted their revolvers.

Jed held up a hand to quiet Mama, but kept his eyes on the crowd. "Now look, I know what you all want—for us to agree to sell our home and land to that Mona Starret."

Murmurs and head nods rippled through the crowd.

"Let me ask you this, then," said Jed, shouting loud enough for the entire mass of Glen Rose citizens to hear them. "If I came to your place, Boone, or yours, Whipple, and asked you to sell your home and land because a stranger from back East blew into town and promised that if you did I'd make lots of money, would you do it?"

"Well, Jed, that's not the same thing!" said Whipple.

"Near enough from where I'm standing," said the big whiskey maker.

To all their surprise, Mother Stark, with rifle on full cock and held in the crook of her arm, walked forward to the edge of the porch, and said, "When did any of you ever hear of something too good to be true ever working out? Huh?"

Nothing but murmurs and grumbling came in reply.

"Look," said Jed. "A Stark settled this land, and so it will always remain Stark land. And one rich stranger from back East isn't going to change that. Now . . . I'm done talking! Get off Stark land, all of you! Now!"

He raised his left arm to peel off a shot into the air when, from his left, down along the old, unused riverside trail that led to and from town, came shouts and the unmistakable sound of horse hooves moving at a steady clip.

Jed held the shot and looked toward where the river trail emerged from below the low swell leading to the river. Everyone else did the same.

Soon they were all rewarded with sight of a man on horseback and just behind him, a buggy and two, no, three people in it.

Before any of them could figure out quite what they were seeing, Loudon rode up near the house on Poppy, which Jed recognized. He bolted forward, shouting, "Loudon! Where's Lilly?"

But a glance toward the buggy, just pulling up, answered the question. There was Lil, her head bleeding, but sitting upright beside a thin, dark-haired woman in black, and between them sat a child, a little girl.

Before he made it to the buggy, Lilly stood in it, and shouted, "Downtown's on fire! Hurry! Town's on fire!"

She seemed then to have exhausted herself, for she sagged and began to wilt, collapsing, with luck, right into Jed's big arms. He caught her and spun, shouting, "Mama! Help me with Lil, she's been hurt!"

He raced across the yard and took the broad steps in two bounds. Minnie had already pulled the door wide for him to enter.

Loudon quickly led the horse and buggy and Poppy over to the low hitch rail set off to one side of the long porch, and ushered Maeve and Maisie up the steps. "Minnie will remember you," was all he said before turning and descending the steps, pulling his revolvers, and standing spread-legged about where Jed had stood.

By then, most of the folks from town had turned and were clogging the roadway on out of the ranch and toward town. They were shouting and cursing and all but turning on each other. A few holdouts stood in ragged clusters of two and three men, arms crossed and scowling at Loudon.

"I heard what she told you, and I see what you have all become! I've seen people in drunken city street fights behave with more decorum than you all! The Starks don't want you here, so leave! Now!" He raised his guns and thumbed back the hammers.

It didn't bother him much to do that to the few folks remaining, for he knew them all, and to a person, they were among the citizenry he would most suspect of such greedy activity, and not a one of them could be counted on in a crisis to help his fellows.

Behind him, he heard the porch door slam, then he heard not Jed's big boots, but a smaller set, though with no less stridency in their step. Soon he was joined by Minnie on one side and Redeye on the other.

Minnie held Ol' Shredder, and Redeye showed full fang and an urge to leap at the nearest person who did a thing save for retreat.

Loudon watched their faces and was gratified to see the men, raised eyebrows and tight mouths, turn to one another. As if by unspoken mutual agreement, those few leftover men turned and, in no seeming haste, began to walk away.

Minnie thumbed back the hammer all the way, and the steely, throaty clicks put a jolt of speed in their heels. The men bolted to their wagon and horses and generated a goodly amount of dust in making their escape.

"Chicken men, the lot of them." Minnie turned and walked to the porch. "Come on, Loud, let's see how your lady friend's doing with Lilly. I think I have some cookies for that wee one, too."

"Oh, she's not my—"

"Balderdash. Just give it time, it'll happen. Now come along, boy. You, too, Redeye!"

Loudon and the hound followed her up the steps, Mother Stark's soft chuckle reddening the reporter's ears.

CHAPTER 27

It didn't take long for Jed and Minnie to get the full story. With Maeve's help, and with Minnie plying little Maisie with cookies, it was determined—mostly by a flustered Lilly—that Lilly was going to be all right.

Jed refused to venture from her sight, but in a rare moment of calmness, he did thank Maeve for her help. He even brought her a cup of tea and introduced himself to Maisie, who could not believe he was so big.

Soon, however, Jed returned to fuming. And the more he heard of what Loudon and Lilly and Maeve told him of the meeting, then what Lilly told him about the doings at the café, locked into place a stonelike set to his features.

Jed Stark looked angrier than anyone could ever recall him looking, and he grew more so as the full story unfolded. "That's it! I'm going to town! Brace that filth, Majors, and give him a clubbing, then maybe I'll set him on fire, see how he likes it!"

In an attempt to calm him, Lilly said, "Jed, you're frightening Maisie!" He pulled in a deep breath and then let it out slowly. Then he bent to the little girl and, smiling, said, "I'm sorry, Maisie. I'm just a little worked up right now."

"That's okay, Mr. Fred."

Jed tousled her hair, then motioned to Loudon. "She can call me Fred or Jed. Anyone that cute can't be wrong. Hey, come outside with me for a minute, Loud."

They went out to tend the horses, and Jed said, "I need you to look after them while I'm gone, Loud."

"You think it's wise, leaving? You know what they're like in town just now."

Jed just stared at him, his jaw muscles working. "Somebody, likely that Englishman, tried to kill my Lil!"

"I know it, Jed, but he didn't succeed. Now, look, it wouldn't surprise me a bit to discover that Starret has sent her men out here to persuade you to sell, with bullets, if you know what I mean."

"Yeah, I expect so, especially after seeing all this." He motioned toward the empty yard, but Loudon knew he meant the townsfolk's gathering. "But I have to take the fight to them, keep them from my family."

"I understand, Jed, but I think we should all just stay put and wait them out. Besides, your family needs you here. Strength in numbers, right?"

Jed shrugged, but Loudon could tell he was reaching his friend.

"Might be best to let the townsfolk simmer a bit," continued the newsman. "They were easily swayed, sure, but they won't be that collectively stupid for long. I hope."

"Aw, I hear you," said Jed. "But it bothers me to sit back and wait on them. What if Starret and her men do try to hit us here?"

"Then you'll be here and not there—or worse. Your place is with your family and friends, Jed. And so is mine."

Jed looked at Loudon, and a small grin worked onto his grim face. "Family, huh?"

Loudon looked confused for a moment, then shook his head. "No, no, I meant friends. That's all, Jed. Friends."

"Okay, Loud. Okay." Jed sighed again. "Daylight will leave us soon. Maybe you could lend me a hand with the animals. Button this place up for the night, just in case."

"Sure thing."

"By the way, Chiswick escaped jail," said Jed. "We had a set-to in the woods a bit ago, but he vamoosed before I could get him."

Loudon stopped. "What?"

"Yep," said Jed. "Which reminds me, have you seen Harley?"

Loudon nodded. "He was doing his best to keep order in the street earlier. I was going to help him, but I saw Maeve and Maisie. There were wagons everywhere. I was afraid they'd get run over."

"Well, he's the lawman of Glen Rose, he's where he needs to be."

"No, Jed, I need to go back. He might need help. What if they clubbed him like they did Lilly and left him in the jail? That entire side of the street might be gone by now!"

"I'll go, Loud."

"Nope, not the way this is going to happen, Jed. Your family needs you and Harley is our friend. It makes the most sense for me to go. Besides," he said. "I'm not as hated in town just now."

"That's what you think."

"Bah," said Loudon, grinning and rushing to Poppy. "Help me up, you big brute!"

Moments later, Jed watched as Loudon, his best friend, aside from Lilly, and one of the quietly bravest fellows he'd ever met, rode back on out toward town, taking the river trail once again.

Back in the house, as Jed gathered arms and ammunition, he related what Loudon was up to. Maeve stifled a gasp and held Maisie as she looked out the window by the door, watching night come down.

"It's going to be a long, tense one," said Minnie. "I'm brewing up strong, black coffee, Stark-style," she said, rubbing the tall woman's back. "Loudon's one of the best men I know—but don't tell him I said that. Oh, he'll be back, mark my words. He's too ornery not to. And now he has more reason."

Chapter 28

Marshal Harley Thompson heard a crunching sound from the scrubby growth to his left. He was about halfway to Whiskey Woods along the river trail and hoping to get there in time to check on his friends, and hopefully to prevent any trouble between the Starks and any lingering townsfolk.

He hadn't expected a fire downtown to slow him up. But once he'd seen the fire brigade had gotten the blaze in hand before too many buildings had succumbed, he'd hopped on his horse.

Just as he was set to ride for the ranch, he saw the townsfolk returning en masse with shame and anger on their faces. And he didn't think it was directed at the Starks.

At the same time, he and the entire town saw Mona Starret and her fancy buggies and helpers all hightailing it on out of town, making eastward, no doubt, for Grindle and the train.

He thought he saw that cursed Englishman, Dalton Majors, clamber up into a barouche already well underway. Good riddance, he thought. And as for the townsfolk, none of them did more than throw ineffectual rocks at the retreating buggies.

He'd deputized Jimmy McCurdy earlier in the day, and the young man, who reminded Thompson a little of himself a few years back, had been a big help in keeping what order they could as the so-called committee had ridden out for the Stark place.

Once they'd seen the fire grab hold along that side of the street, it had been Jimmy who had checked on their prisoner and had run back out to the fire brigade, which Thompson had been helping, to tell him that the cell had been sprung and Chiswick was gone.

Thompson had had a moment of confusion, then anger, but he reasoned, at least if the entire block burned, he wouldn't have to deal with a prisoner, too. There was nothing for it, he'd just have to track the murderer later.

Now, with night coming on, Thompson wondered if maybe he should have stayed in town. But no, Larry Chiswick was still on the loose, and he despised Jed Stark as much as he loved cheap whiskey. If his former boss was headed anywhere, it would be the Stark place.

Thompson hoped he wasn't too late. The sounds he heard could be anything, from a mule deer to a lost steer to a . . .

"Well, look at what we have here," said a voice quite familiar to the young marshal.

Even as he spun his head toward the voice, Thompson's right hand tugged free his revolver and thumbed back the hammer.

"No, no, no. See . . ." Larry Chiswick stepped out of the brush, his own gun drawn and leveled on the marshal. "That's no way to greet an old friend. Especially one that taught you everything you know about the lawdog business!"

"Chiswick!" Thompson held his pose, his gun not quite pulled around the front of him.

"Yep, yep, it's me. And spare me your speechifying. I know what I am, I know what I done. Killed that farmer fellow in his field, did the same for my old pal, Deke Frakes, right in his kitchen! Hoo-ee! And I shot those two old folks, right in their bed, to boot!" He let out a sloppy, wet cackle. "Question is, what are you going to do about it, lawman?"

Before Thompson could reply, Chiswick said, "See, I got me one more task for my boss, one last party to convince to sell up, and then I'm gone, free, and best of all, protected by big money. And as we all know, big money is big power."

"I wouldn't count on it, Chiswick. Mona Starret and Dalton Majors and the rest of them all hightailed it out of town not long ago. Something tells me they won't be coming back to Glen Rose. In fact, I'm going to do my best to make sure they go to jail instead. Course, that might take some time."

It was worth all that hot air to Thompson just to see Chiswick's face turn four shades of purple. Then he wondered if he had overdone it.

His former boss was looking mighty riled, grinding his brown and green teeth as if he were chewing tough steak. Finally, Chiswick seemed to settle on something. "I despise you, you useless whelp, but I don't think I'll kill you. At least not today."

Chiswick laughed, a ragged, wet sound. "Now"—he waved his gun—"get off that horse before I change my mind and drop you right there."

Thompson was slow to move, and Chiswick shouted, "Do it now, curse you!"

The lawman leaned forward and swung his right leg up over the cantle, taking care to keep his gun low and held tight. With any luck, he might . . .

As soon as he was certain his left boot was free of the stirrup, Thompson launched himself backward, shoving himself with his left hand off the saddle, and turning as much as he was able in the maneuver. He hoped to collide with Chiswick and shoot before he got shot himself. But that was a big risk.

As he collided with the murdering drunkard, a gun fired,

the marshal's horse bolted, and both men collapsed in a writhing pile on the ground.

Thompson quickly realized it was not his gun that went off, because as they thrashed on the spiny ground, he caught sight of his gun, still on full cock, and still in his right hand. But Chiswick's gun was gone as the man was using both of his long-nailed, grubby hands, as well as his head and his teeth and his knees to do his best to gain the upper hand in this unexpected fracas.

As they fought, with Chiswick holding Thompson's gun hand high and away at the wrist, it came to the lawman in a flash that it was Chiswick's gun that had gone off, and if so, had it drilled a hole into him?

Thompson had no time for any more such consideration of his health, for he had his hands full. And then Chiswick made the fight even more difficult for the younger man. The stench-addled killer somehow wriggled and spun himself until he ended up sitting atop the lawman's gut.

The big, bearded face leered and laughed at him as Chiswick drove a fist hard and fast at Thompson's face, once, twice with surprising speed. Then, despite Thompson's thrashing efforts, Chiswick closed a big, filthy hand around the young marshal's upturned throat and squeezed. Hard.

Light and sound and hot pain flowered up before his eyes, within his head, and Thompson felt himself beginning to lose consciousness. If he did, he knew that would be it, the man who he used to let win at cribbage in the office would shoot him in the head and leave him for the coyotes.

The thought that such evil would, could quench the flickering flame that was his life worked like a blast of dynamite within Harley Thompson, and he mustered enough strength, even as he felt his consciousness fading, to raise his right hand.

He hoped he still held the gun, for he felt nothing there. With the last of his dimming sight, he saw the big, leering face of Chiswick staring down at him. Drool and snot ran from the man's mouth and nose and beard, and two wide, bloodshot eyes bulged at him, glee and rage mingling on the freakish face.

And just beyond that, up by the side of the man's shaggy head, Thompson saw his revolver, saw the barrel aiming upward, toward the sky. With all his waning ability, he willed the gun to aim downward, and then, as his sight pinched out, he heard a tremendous explosion, and then Harley Thompson knew no more.

Chapter 29

As Loudon thundered townward on the river trail, he heard a gunshot somewhere ahead. He hadn't ridden another hundred yards when, as he pulled a revolver and cocked it, he saw a horse trotting toward him, ears back and nostrils flared.

He turned Poppy sideways, blocking most of the scrubby trail, and the horse trotted right up to them and stopped, hanging its head close by and beneath Poppy's. As he eyed the trail ahead, Loudon reached for the horse's trailing reins.

It was then that he looked closer at the horse and recognized it as Thompson's beloved mount, Smokey. He hastily lashed the reins to the right side of Poppy's reins and rode ahead, gun held out before him, and then he heard another gunshot.

The trail wound along this stretch, and the brush and low forest cover crept close along the inland side, to Loudon's right. He hopped down and looped the reins over a snag of branch that he doubted would hold the horses for long, particularly if there were more gunshots, but he felt he needed to be on his feet and able to use two guns if need be.

He crept around a short, tight bend and saw an odd sight—what appeared to be two men piled atop one another, neither man moving. He advanced quickly, gun out and ready, and aimed at them.

"Harley? Harley!"

That's when he recognized the humped form atop it as Larry Chiswick. He moved closer and shoved him on the right shoulder. The man rolled and flopped to his left, then lay face up beside the other man.

The other man, who Loudon now saw, was Harley Thompson.

"Oh no, no, Harley! Harley!"

Loudon kept glancing from the lawman to the former lawman, until he saw that the entire side of Chiswick's head was a bloody, matted mess, with a puckered, seeping wound at its center.

Had they killed each other?

And then the man at his knees, Marshal Harley Thompson, groaned and coughed and wheezed and pulled in breath. In moments, he opened his eyes and in a raspy whisper, said, "Loudon? You okay?"

The newsman laughed and bent low and hugged his friend, helping him to a sitting position. "You're taking empathy to new levels, Harley."

"Huh?"

"Nothing, nothing. Hey, let's get you to Whiskey Woods."

"What about Chiswick?" said Thompson as he gained his feet, and Loudon fetched the killer's dropped gun.

"He's right where he should be, Harley. Right where I suspect he has wanted to be for a long time now."

With some effort and weak help from Thompson, Loudon managed to get the dead killer loaded onto Thompson's horse. Thompson rode ahead of him, and Loudon, riding drag, rode Poppy.

Some time later, and well after dark, they walked into the dooryard at Whiskey Woods.

Chapter 30

There were hugs and tears and the medicinal ministrations of Minnie and Maeve. A stiff drink of Stark's finest whiskey helped Thompson, in a raspy voice, to share what he knew.

With Larry Chiswick's handprint still bright red on his throat, Thompson said, "I think the people of Glen Rose realize, especially after seeing Mona Starret and her fancy buggies and entourage all hustling out of town, that they made fools of themselves, forgot what's important."

"Not for the first time!" shouted Minnie from her station at the stove.

"Nope," said Thompson. "But I hope for the last."

"Time will tell," said Lilly.

"Will she just get away with this, then?" said Maeve.

The room was silent for a long moment, then Loudon said, "I, for one, will do everything in my power to see that she and Majors get brought to justice. But I must say, Maeve, I think it will be a tall order."

"Why?"

"In a word . . . *money*. If you are wealthy, you can get away with anything in this country. Cynical, I know, but it has been proven over and over, and I don't ever see that changing."

Another long moment of quiet followed, then Thompson

said, "It's cold comfort, I know, ma'am, but Lawrence Chiswick, the . . ."

"Killer of my husband," said Maeve, her voice trembling.

"Yes, ma'am, that's the fellow. And of the Albersons and of Deke Frakes, too. He confessed of them all to me. Well, he's been killed, too, now. I . . . I didn't want to do it." He pulled in a breath and let it sigh out again. "As I said, cold comfort."

"No, Marshal Thompson, I understand. And it is sad all around, but I do appreciate the sentiment. Thank you."

He nodded and they all sat quietly, listening to the night.

As the ladies prepared a meal, Jed leaned forward and spoke in low tones to Loudon and the marshal. "Harley, when you saw Starret leave town, did you see those four men in black, those guards of hers, leave with her?"

Thompson sat a moment and thought back on that part of the busy day. After a moment, he looked up and said, "I saw one. That doesn't mean the others weren't in there, too, but . . . no, I only saw the one."

"What are you thinking, Jed?"

The big man didn't answer Loudon right away. Then he said, "I'm thinking we need to keep watch tonight."

"You reckon she left some of her men as a sort of last effort to win at this game?" said Thompson.

"I wouldn't put it past her," said Jed. "I think when we sent her packing, she was mighty angry. A woman like that, she has a big hat and a big head under it. Seems to me she'd do just about anything for revenge on us, if nothing else, for making her look, and feel, the fool."

"Okay, then, Jed. What's the plan?"

CHAPTER 31

Jed knew that vigilance was the key to them all surviving, at least until daylight brightened the corners once more. They needed to come through it unharmed, and morning was a long way off.

He decided to spend much of the night out at the fringe of the yard, with a blanket and his guns. He didn't think the three men, if that's all there were, would try much of anything at night, considering it would be dark, and they wouldn't likely be carrying lanterns. And they did not know the lay of the land. But he did.

Night came too soon for Jed's liking, but it did what it needed to, as it always had and would, his preferences not considered in the least by the wild world.

Loudon was also posted outside, and he and Thompson, who they decided needed rest first, would spell each other. Jed wanted no one to spell him, despite their arguments to the contrary.

He'd set up Mama, Lilly, Maeve, Maisie, and Redeye in the kitchen of the not-quite-finished, new ranch house.

Lilly was still weakened enough from the blow to her head and from the fire that, even though she protested, she slipped into sleep quite readily. Maeve, unequipped with firearms and the use of them, instead tended a fire and kept coffee and tea flowing.

She also ministered to Lilly and Thompson's injuries, and to Loudon's, as the fire had left him with raspy breath and a cough. Little Maisie was tucked up tight in a bundle of quilts on a big bed with Lilly.

Mama, as the one most able and proficient with a gun, sat with her back to a full log wall. From there she could see the windows to either side, and yet anyone without would have a difficult time seeing her. She also had a pot of strong black tea at hand, Ol' Shredder laid across her lap, and a stack of shells beside the teapot.

Redeye camped beside her and hadn't put up much of a fuss when Jed ordered him to stay inside. The dog sprawled on his favorite braided rug and commenced snoring.

Jed knew this was a sign that the old hound was aging and in less of a fiery hurry, as he had been in his youth, to curl a lip and point out an intruder. The big whiskey maker reckoned that the bullet wound the dog had sustained the year before also had a whole lot to do with Redeye's ease with staying put. He could hardly blame him.

It had been a much worse wound than they had realized at first, and he, Mama, and Lil all thought for certain the dog was not going to make it through. But, in keeping with his rebellious nature, Redeye had rallied, to the relief of all but the chickens, who regarded him as a bossy nuisance.

In the dark, Jed mused, in a half-joking way, that he'd always assumed the café would be the death of his sweetheart, because she spent so much time there and put so much of her love and effort into serving up fine meals for what seemed to be half the town and then some. But never had any of them imagined it would be gone, taken from them just like that, and Lil's home, too, upstairs from the café.

Since she started the business, Lil had built it up in a most admirable fashion, to the point where even many of the wrong-headed Glen Rose citizens, that is to say folks who think women should be baking bread and having babies, became instead regular customers.

She had bought the property years before when she'd come to town, alone and with enough money to open an account at the bank. The only reason Horace Boone, the banker, had allowed her to deposit her money there had been because it was a substantial amount.

She'd earned it all, Jed would later learn, on her own, buying and then selling for meager profits a handful of properties outside of San Francisco. But she had wanted to live back in Texas, where she spent much of her youth, as her mother had been a Texas ranch woman on a spread fifty miles north of Glen Rose.

Lil recalled her mother, who had died when Lilly was a young girl, speaking fondly of the two times she had visited the pretty little town of Glen Rose in her youth. Lilly kept those secondhand memories in mind all through those years when she was alone as a young woman.

They had been difficult years following her beloved Chinese father's death under mysterious circumstances. She remembered as a little girl telling him, with a grim look and a nod of conviction, as if she was one day going to right a terrible wrong, that she would at least see Glen Rose, and, if she found it to her liking, perhaps she might well settle there. Her father laughed and hugged her and told her she could do anything she could think of.

And now here she is, Jed thought. Ready to begin her life as a married woman, but without her business, the very thing that they had allowed to come between them in so many recent conversations. That the café, the source of some of Jed's vexation, was now gone left Jed feeling horrible. And he felt even worse about not being there for Lilly. He should have protected her somehow, should have prevented the fire, a fire that could have killed her.

How he might have prevented it, he knew not. But the thought of his beloved Lil facing that alone, knowing that she might well die, it was all too much to think about.

And now we're pinned down at our own spread, thought Jed.

The barest of the morning's early dawn light crept in enough to allow Jed to walk farther from the house. Being cramped up and awaiting evil to come to them was not his idea of living a life.

Jed checked that all the rest were up, awake and alert, as much as could be expected of them, considering what they had endured of the day before. Armed with a revolver, Jed slipped out the back door of the house and crept northward, forming a vague plan of action as he felt his way, as much out of instinct as by sight and touch. He had to at least try the usual locations where he figured a stranger might begin his sneaking attack on Whiskey Woods.

Of course he hoped he saw no strangers. He knew he was riled, and it would not take much more to set him off on a violent spree, hated as it would be by him. He had had his fill of such foolishness in the war, but this? This was different, and the one thing Jed had told himself he would take up arms and kill for—when folks of ill intent brought the fight to him and his family. And this they were doing.

Unacceptable.

A crashing, snapping sound erupted across the ravine to the northeast of Jed. His head spun in that direction, instinct tensing him even more than he had been. And relief, too, for he had been about to rise from his cover and low-walk along the small ridgeline making eastward.

From there, he could cut north as it narrowed at the box

end of the ravine. But this new sound, unexpected, bold, and loud, halted him in place.

Immediately following it, thanks to a breeze carrying from the north-northeast on over to Jed, just downwind of it by a couple of hundred feet, he heard the unmistakable sounds of the voices of two men, one shushing another. The second voice did not like that one bit.

If it wasn't the voices of two of the men he sought, now confirmed for him, Jed could have found it comical.

The sounds were a mistake, as if someone had fallen over on the bushy, brittle remnants of last year's twiggy rabbitbrush, while at the same time dislodging gravel and stone to scatter and clatter beneath his feet. The one who'd shushed him had every right to do so, Jed figured. But he was grateful for the warning.

It also gave him a location. And he bet it was that odd bowl of a trough just beyond the far low ridge. He had been there a number of times himself, often walking with a dog over the years, hunting rabbits for the stewpot. He had often wondered how that sandy-bottomed place, filled with boulders and stippled with clots of brush, could end up being shaped so.

He only noticed it as something different than the surrounding landscape because Mama had pointed it out on their many long walks together over Stark land when he was a boy.

She had explained to him that it was important to see the land not just as if you were looking at rocks and trees and such on the surface, but to look beneath those things living on the top, as she called it. See the curve of the land, how it dips and rises and flows, she'd say.

"Like when you watch the river a long time," a young Jed had said. "You start to see it isn't flat at all but full of big and little flowing bumps and hills and valleys."

He never forgot that. Probably, he mused now, because Mama had kissed him on the head and told him he was right up there with the smartest of the Starks. That put a jaunty kick to his step for a week.

Until he did something dumb and Mama pointed it out to him. Ha, he thought now, eyeing the spot he knew the sound had come from. But that's life. One minute you're a genius, the next you're falling over rocks and being told to hush up by your pal.

Jed kept low and edged back down the rise, confident no one was behind him, but not so confident in that thinking that he risked letting himself be seen in any open patches for long. The last thing he needed was a bullet between his shoulders. That would end it all right there, hard and fast.

There would be no life with Lilly, Mama would be lost in the world, well, maybe not quite lost, as the little woman was a force of all natural elements rolled into one, and then some. But no, he was not ready to die, not especially for some rich, crazy woman's greed.

Jed cut east, along the bottom of the ridge, with the little ridge to his left, flanking him and providing cover for him as he moved. Once he had traveled far enough, roughly two hundred fifty feet or so, he paused, listened, and heard nothing from above and beyond the ridge.

With this as his cue to proceed, he wormed his way, keeping low and pausing frequently, as a deer does in thick cover, holding every few feet to listen, head turning left and right, to determine if there were any sounds on the breeze.

In this manner, Jed was able to make his way back up to the top of the ridge, but easterly of his previous position. He looked to his left and across and waited. He was counting on the fact that whoever these men were, they were idiot enough to blunder about and make noise earlier, so caution was not something, even if they tried, they would be likely to employ fully.

Jed didn't have long to wait. Less than a minute passed before he saw, cutting almost directly down from where they had made all their noise, two men, both dressed in black, moving quickly and mostly without the skills and care of someone trying to keep quiet and hidden.

They were darting downslope, in a switchback fashion, too close together, raising dust and nudging loose washes and sprays and small cascades of rocks down the cobbly embankment.

They piled up at a point because the man in the lead apparently determined that, since he was covered by the man hugging his tail feathers, he might find shelter behind a rock from the eyes of the enemy.

Jed wanted to chuckle, for he was that enemy, and he was seeing them just fine. He knew that given the circumstances—an invasion of unwarranted, unasked-for, unruly, and uncontrollable forces, and on Stark land—he could shoot them, or at least wing them, disable them with a bullet, and be justified, legally and otherwise. After all, they were hunting him and his family, and that did not sit well with him.

But to maim or kill with a bullet when he was hidden from them? That was ambushing, and that felt wrong. No matter that he knew they would likely do that to him, without a worry. And that is precisely what they were hoping to do to him today.

But maybe not these two, thought Jed. They seemed like idiots. Still, idiots or no, he had to come up with a way to make certain they didn't scatter, thereby losing one in any melee he set in motion. He wanted them both as his prisoners. Could it be as easy as him getting closer and getting the drop on them?

As was often the case with beasts of the wild, there was no warning given by the startled mule deer that rose up from its place of rest, a brushy spot of cover down deep at the bottom of the ravine.

Jed saw it at the same time the two men did, he was certain of it. There was no way any of them could miss it. And it was a large, well-fleshed buck who looked to be in the midst of his prime years, given his coat and the already sizable rack of antlers at this date in the season, with rut still some months off.

None of that mattered much, and it only flicked through Jed's mind because he hunted deer now and again to make meat for the table. It was not something he enjoyed, but forcing himself to get up and away from the whiskey still was an infrequent but welcome occurrence in his life.

And so to see this bold buck bolt from its place of rest and cover, disturbed by humans, was a treat. The moment also proved, in its suddenness, to cause Jed Stark no small amount of grief.

The deer startled and fled, making for the eastern end of the ravine, a *not-quite-boxed-in* cornice that Jed knew afforded game to pass through via a ragged passage in the sandstone wide enough for a fat man to waddle through without quite scraping the sides.

While Jed was certain that was where the deer was headed, when it broke its cover, Jed had chosen that very moment to stand taller in order to try to get a sight line on the two men he was playing cat and mouse with. He wasn't certain if he was the cat or they were. He knew for certain he was no mouse.

But at that moment, as the big deer thundered through below Jed's perch on the slight ridge, the other men, as would be natural, watched the thing that had startled them as it bolted away.

And as Jed Stark was straight ahead and a pinch higher in their sight line, they saw him just fine. He managed to eye one of them, but the other stood upslope of the first and was blocked from Jed's sight by a clot of man-height brush.

"Hey!" barked one of the men, and he was promptly hushed and shushed by the other. Jed, too, had the same reaction, but his exclamation of surprise was directed at himself for his own stupidity. Now the two men knew for certain he was on them, and that they had been seen by him, perhaps for some time.

Each party jerked low and held. Then the two invaders began to do what such men in these situations do—they split up, each making for a different direction. Just what Jed did not want them to do. He bit back yet another criticism of himself for not dealing with them as soon as he had spied them. But what should he have done?

Growling low and grinding his teeth together hard, Jed shook off such thoughts, knowing they were less than useless to him, and instead kept low once more and dragged backward, taking less care than he had climbing up in scuffing his boots against rocks and whips of sparse bushes as he scrambled. He wanted to get good and away from where they suspected he might be.

He didn't think they were the most tracking savvy or woods savvy of men, but that didn't mean they were fully idiots. And they carried guns. Now he had to track them one at a time.

Jed checked his rifle and used the momentary pause to listen for the tell-tale sounds of men doing the same thing he was doing—creeping and stopping, creeping and stopping. He heard none.

They were not likely, individually or together, to have made it up the slight rise to his side of the ravine. Not yet. What is the plan, Jed? he asked himself. He ran his tongue tip over his dry lips and considered his situation, calling up and dismissing ideas with eyeblink speed.

Now that they were separated, he was not about to take them by surprise and rush them from above. Nor was he keen on the notion of waiting them out. That had never been his preference in life, no matter the situation. Thoughtful and at times perhaps slow, yes, he would accept that about himself, but not wholly passive.

No, he would meet them one at a time. And he would begin

to his right, to meet the man making his way eastward. It was a guess on Jed's part, but he suspected they would have split in that fashion, with one of them making his way west toward the mouth of the ravine. Jed would deal with him later, he hoped.

The other, the first he would tangle with, should be making his way up the ravine, and keeping out of sight by avoiding the bottom. Jed would keep to the same old game trail he was close by, which ran east, paralleling the ridgeline just above him to his left.

He was still plenty of distance east of them, and so he would take advantage of that and make it closer to the end. Where the trees grew thicker, he would risk a climb up and over, then descend into the ravine.

Once he reached the bottom, he would be hidden better than they had been because the trees, though stunty at times, and the grasses and brush, too, were thicker there, not to mention the clusters of boulders now and again.

The only trouble he could foresee having would be if the man did not behave as Jed expected, and wanted him to, in taking much the same path Jed would take, up a bit along the far side of the ravine. For there, too, the vegetation was thicker. But Jed knew the land and these rascals didn't, so he would keep that little nugget of hope in mind.

He would not count on it, but it might well help. In a death fight, every shred of possibility that tipped in a man's favor should not, he knew from experience, be discounted.

It took Jed no more than three minutes to make it close to the end of the ravine. He wormed his way up the slight ridge side once more, using thick rock and scrub cover to keep himself concealed.

At the top, he let his rifle barrel lead the way and followed with as much caution as he had ever used in such a situation. It would not do to pop up and feel a slug boring its way into his head, all because of haste.

Still, he did not dither, but kept himself low beside a great boulder, wider than it was tall. He crept forward, parting scrubby grasses with his rifle barrel, and inched his way into a position from which he hoped to see his quarry approaching.

He saw nobody. But he did hear something, a slight noise, little more than a slow-stepping deer might make, but the deer had long since bolted from the little ravine. Odds are this was his man.

There was a slight cracking as if a twig had been trodden upon. Then a long pause. Then a meager scrape, as of a stiff, twiggy branch against a man's sleeve or trouser leg. Jed waited, for the sounds were, no mistake now, drawing nearer, and just about where he had expected, or perhaps hoped, them to be.

That meant the man was less of a fool than Jed had originally thought. He could hardly complain, after all, as he was right where he wished to be, awaiting the man where he might catch him unawares and proceed without a gunshot delivered.

A little more, fella, he thought. Just a pinch more and we can talk. Or rather, I'll talk and you'll come up short, eyes wide, and arms raised.

That was how Jed hoped the situation would happen. He did not expect to hear a sound from behind him, the very direction he had foolishly assumed no one would yet be, could not have yet made it to. Unless there were three of them.

Jed suppressed a sigh and indulged instead in a silent swallow. He held still, for he was well and truly hidden. Although without looking behind him, downslope, he did not know if any part of him could be seen from below.

Nobody had yet told him to halt or to hold it or to not move. The moments dragged by. From ahead, and below, much closer now, he heard the man he'd been hunting continue to make his slight and mostly quiet progress. Jed figured he would see the man soon. He also knew that if he gave up his position, kneeling and hunkered by the boulder, he would surely be detected from behind and below, somewhere on the slope.

The man ahead began to make more noise, stepping with carefully placed but firm grabs with his boots up the graveled slope, scree beginning to drizzle and slide as he advanced. Jed knew the man had no choice but to make such sounds, for that was the only way up the slope.

Even cutting in wider switchbacks to gain the top of the ridge would not have lessened the sound all that much. Jed waited. Here is a fine situation to find yourself in, Jed Stark, he thought. Someone downslope of you who might come upon you any moment, and the man you're looking for just below you on the other side of the ridge, before you, who in mere moments will provide you with the perfect opportunity to brace him.

Jed knew that if he stood, he was all but certain to reveal himself to the one of the two he did not wish to do so—the man behind. And so, he thought, I had better stay right where I am and sit tight, at least for a few minutes longer. Somehow this mess might work out in my favor.

"Hold it right where you are, friend."

The glimmer of optimism that Jed felt puffed out like a windblown match, leaving his meager hopes drifting away like smoke. He didn't even dare turn around. He did, however, still see the man he had been after, not but forty feet downslope of him. The man thought the directive had been intended for him, for he paused and had begun raising his arms, a rifle held by the forestock in his right.

How could all this get any odder, thought Jed. And as quickly as he thought it, he dismissed it. In his experience, once you open the door to more and stranger experiences in life, somehow they scuttled on in. Some of them were good, many were not.

"You hear me, boy?"

Jed still did not turn, did not react. Something inside, that niggling voice that he had learned to pay attention to, at least when it first talked to him, often had something of use to say. And right now his little voice inside was telling him to stay put. The man wasn't about to shoot him in the back. He hoped.

A harsh, clicking sound told Jed that he'd maybe waited too long because that meant the man had just thumbed his weapon to full cock, one slight touch on the trigger and Jed would be rolling down the hill, backward, leaking blood and in a whole lot of pain.

He kept low and still faced away from the man, but slowly, slowly raised his arms out to the sides, his left holding his rifle. If he faced the man while doing that, the fellow might be more inclined to say that Jed had been trying to draw on him.

It must have worked because the man behind him advanced, slowly, his bootsteps, as with those of the fellow across and down from Jed, dug into the gravel, but he still kept his arms raised and did not move.

But the man behind Jed kept on moving closer. He seemed plenty confident that he was in full command of the situation. Jed didn't think so, despite the fact that he was in no position to debate the man's advance.

Another ten seconds or so, at this pace, and Jed would feel the man's rifle butt jamming into his back. He still did not turn, because a thought came to him. It was less than an idea at this point, but it was better than a stick in the eye. Mama was fond of saying that regarding the lesser but only available option in most any situation.

The man walked closer, and Jed kept himself low enough that he hoped he was still hidden. There was always the slim chance he'd not yet been seen by the man he'd been stalking. Jed doubted the man had seen him because he would have reacted by now, having learned that Jed had been braced by another fellow.

"Turn around, curse you!" growled the man behind Jed. His

voice was not one Jed recognized, but that hardly mattered to a man whose home and family were beset on all sides by strangers with nothing but greed in mind.

The thought of all of this stupidity being sugared down to dollars and power sickened him all over again, and he was determined to follow through with his meager plan. No more waiting. He tensed his jaw muscles, his teeth biting together hard in anticipation of what was about to happen. All he needed was another step or two from the man behind him, and then. . . .

He was given exactly that, and Jed felt more than saw out of his right eye corner that man standing right behind him, lording over him with a gun.

Jed, who had been kneeling this entire time, dropped hard and fast to his right hip, pivoting as he rolled, while at the same time keeping his rifle upright and swinging it to where he expected the man would be. As he spun, he jerked his long legs downslope, sweeping them in hopes of upending the attacker.

Some of what he did worked. He was able to pivot and keep his gun from fouling in the fall. And as he soon saw that it leveled dead-straight on the man. Just as well, for Jed's long legs connected with nothing save for a clump of brush, which proved to be useful to him only in providing leverage. He pushed against them and had that rifle aimed and ready to smoke.

His index finger was all but squeezing back on that trigger when he saw that the man he'd surprised, but not upended as he'd intended, had nonetheless been stymied enough by Jed's maneuver that he misstepped as he danced to avoid Jed's long legs.

It wasn't much of a blunder, but it was enough to jostle him and pull his attention for a moment from his quarry, giving Jed the perfect opportunity to shoot the man.

The big whiskey maker had just enough time to pull the rifle ever so slightly to the right, as the stranger refocused his attention and his gun's aim on Jed, sprawled on the slope not four feet before him.

The whiskey man touched his trigger and, at the same time, rolled to his left, once more scrabbling on the ground and heading downslope, away from the path the other man's bullet was sure to take.

Jed's intended shot found its mark right where he had hoped it would—hard and fast, right into the man's left shoulder.

That further fouled the fellow's own shot, which whistled well past Jed and drove into dirt twenty feet farther along the slope.

But nearly at the same time, a third shot slammed on the heels of the almost simultaneous shots of Jed and his attacker.

That third shot also found its mark, driving hard into the left side of the gut of the man Jed had shot in the shoulder. But it came from elsewhere, and Jed knew who, even as he spun, working the rifle for another shot as he gained his knees.

He watched the man he'd shot in the shoulder scream and jerk his rifle-holding hands up in the air. The gun spun from his grasp, and his head jerked to the left and back, then whipped hard to the right as the rest of him kept on moving, both from Jed's shot and from that other, third shot, barely discernible in sound from the first two.

But it was enough to let Jed know, in that snap of a moment, that there was a third shooter in this fracas.

The shot man spun, then stumbled straight back down the slope along the same path he'd taken moments before. He made it four or five feet before pitching forward, smacking hard face down with all his weight. And as he hit, Jed hoped for the man's sake that he was already dead or beyond caring and well on his way to death because he was not a small fellow.

Jed now saw that he was a tall and paunchy man, wide of shoulder and sloppy of ample gut. All that girth and meat seemed to concentrate into the man's top section. The fellow's head, the last thing to hit, slammed straight and true and hard and fast right on a sharp jag of black rock protruding a good ten inches from the earth, and angled slightly upslope.

The man's head drove hard onto that rock with such force that the unmoving, projecting point of stone emerged through the back of the man's head like a thing being birthed. It bloomed there slick and red, stringy-looking and glistening as if yanked from a dunking in a vat of gore.

From where he now crouched, on one knee, his downslope leg thrust hard into gravel, Jed saw the left side of the man's head and face. It appeared as if the man had been trying to eat the rock before it got him. From his angle, it looked to Jed as if the rock won the contest and took the man's mouth and nose with it.

The big brute lay that way, arms flung to the sides, and his thick legs lay straight, heels flopped outward. His arms, the hands of which were bent at odd angles, jerked and twitched. A long tremor pulsed from the man's right boot on up his leg and fizzled out, then the man lay still.

Jed heard gravel scuffing and glanced to his right, upslope, just in time to see the man he'd been tracking poke his head up over the ridge, his rifle held low by his belly. It seemed as if he had not expected to encounter what he was now seeing.

His gaze took in first the man stopped downslope away from him some feet below. Before he could raise that rifle back to a position of defense, Jed barked, "Drop that gun, man! Do it now! Now!"

The man looked to his left, still downslope of him but barely so, and saw Jed, secure on one knee and with his freshly cocked rifle aimed square at him.

"But . . . but. . . ."

"But nothing! Drop that gun!" barked Jed once more. "Or you'll get the same!"

Jed's words began to sink in, and the fellow's head nodded

sort of quick movements that didn't stop, as if he had some sort of nervous condition. His eyes popped wide, as wide as any on a man Jed had ever seen. And for good reason, Jed guessed.

The man bent slightly and let go of the rifle in his right hand, where it dropped a foot or so to the gravel at the top of the rise.

As Jed kept his gun leveled on the man and gained his feet, it occurred to him that if he had been that fellow, he would have just dropped back down the slope, gun in hand, and readied himself for a fight. But this man was either green to such a fracas, or he was well and truly thrown by what he was seeing.

"I . . . I shot Arnie!"

Jed walked closer, with slowness and with a hard sneer on his face. He felt every bit of it, too, for he was good and angry.

"We both did, you idiot," Jed growled. "Only he would have lived through my shot. Yours killed him. Remember that when it comes time to wonder if what you've been up to here on my land, on my ranch, was worth it."

The fellow looked from his big, dead pard over to Jed as if the whiskey man's words were just coming to him now. "Huh? You . . . but you're him. The one me and Jolly was tracking. We saw you."

"Yep," said Jed. "Now, down on your knees, or I will shoot you in the head. Do it now." He knew that what he was saying sounded brutal, but so be it. Nobody had to know he had no intention of shooting the poor excuse for a man in the head.

The man still looked so addled and shaken that he slowly lowered himself to his knees, easing into it, though, as if he had a tender back. Jed felt the barest hint of sympathy but was not interested in the least in offering the killer anything more than barked orders.

"Now, arms out to your sides and lay down flat, face down."

The man hesitated and looked up, finally, from his dead

pard to Jed with wide, wet eyes and a mouth twisted up as if he might begin weeping.

"You deaf, man?"

The man shook his head but did not comply.

"Then do what I said, or I will shoot you in the head. In very short order. And I will be justified in it."

"But . . . why? I didn't do a thing to you!"

Jed barked a grim laugh. "You have to be kidding me! You are trespassing on my land with the intention of hunting me and mine. You have just shot a man, but you had intended to shoot me instead. That's more than enough excuse for me to drop you like a hydrophobic dog."

"No," the man on his knees shook his head. "No, that's not true. I . . . I was hunting and I got lost, that's all."

"Oh, alone were you?"

The man hesitated, then said, "Yeah, you bet. That's all. Just lost."

"Then who's this Jolly you mentioned?"

"Huh?"

"You're a liar, mister." Jed stepped one stride closer, bringing him to within three feet of the man. It was a dangerous move with the potential for foul consequences, considering Jed hadn't yet stripped the man of his weapons, but this was no time to dawdle.

They'd already wasted enough time yammering. And that's when Jed realized the man was likely keeping him chatting in order to buy himself time so his pard might reach them. For surely the fellow had heard the shots and was even now making his way in their direction.

"One last chance to do as I say—lay down, face down, and spread your arms."

The man hesitated, and Jed saw that he had begun to lose that slight tinge of fear. Jed hated to do it, but he stepped forward a half step more and, as quick as a finger snap, he spun the rifle he'd had trained on the man's face. In the same movement, he spun the butt down and outward and pulled the barrel by the forestock close in toward him. At the same moment, Jed lunged at the man and slammed the smooth side of the outerstock into the man's head, just above the fool's left ear.

He was taught this maneuver and that location for smacking a man in the head hard and fast with something equally hard by a quiet but deadly, and far too serious, officer in the army. The man had rarely spoken but did much of his instruction in close-in combat by example and much pointing.

So dedicated was the man to this method of teaching that most of the newer soldiers, such as Jed, assumed the man was incapable of speech. This seemed to lend the man even more of an air of meanness, of showing he was most capable of cold brutality. And with this technique, he had pointed to that spot above a man's head, left or right side, and held up his revolver and ran his palm over the smooth butt of the gun.

He shucked his rifle and did the same with the butt, and also with the side of the stock. Then he had made as if he were going to drive that part of each of the guns quick and direct, right at the spot, in this case against Jed's head. He stopped just short of Jed's tender noggin and, in a low, even voice, with a gaze that did not waver, he said, "Drops a man." He snapped his fingers. "Like that."

A flash of memory of the man came back to Jed when he was in the midst of delivering a hard, snapping gun chop just above this intruding man's ear. His aim was a little low, and the stock caught the tip of the man's ear as well, smacking hard.

As the stock slammed into the man's head, he yelped, at first in surprise at Jed's action, then from the sudden and hot flash of pain flowering up the side of his head.

As the stock caught the tip of the man's ear, it pinched and smeared the flesh, forcing a burst of blood to fountain up, looking as if Jed had just thumbed a fresh cherry.

The man on his knees didn't remain that way for long. Even

as he yelped out a cry of shock and pain, his eyes rolled upward, showing white, and a quick burst of vomit burbled from his mouth. He pitched forward, his yelp, a strangled, gagging sound, dying in his throat as he lost consciousness.

As soon as he had felt the gunstock connect with the man's head, Jed knew it would do the job he needed done. He also knew it wouldn't kill the fellow, but between that split, bleeding ear, and the hard knock to the bean, as Mama would say, he was pretty certain this man was going to wake up feeling a mighty, throbbing headache.

"Didn't even have the fun of getting it with whiskey," said Jed, turning fast and dropping low into a crouch once more. He pivoted on the balls of his feet and repositioned the rifle into a usable pose once more, snugging the butt of it under his left armpit.

Within seconds, he was mighty pleased he had done so, for taking a first view of him, just cresting the berm to his right, Jed saw that it was the flopped man's initial pard, the mysterious Jolly, who Jed had seen him with earlier.

Jolly was staring straight at him, his gun extended and his arm held straight and true. Jed, too, held the same pose. They stayed that way for some moments, eyeing each other down the barrels of their guns. Finally, Jed said, "Your pals are done for, mister. I suggest you drop that thing and raise your arms."

"Oh, you suggest that, do you?"

Jed regarded the man's sneer. "Look, whatever thought you're having, let it go," said Jed. "It's not worth it."

Still the sneer remained. And then Jed saw that revealing thing, slight, to be sure, but there it was—that barest rise of an eye corner, the same with the mouth, and then the slightest movement of the man's gun hand.

All this told Jed one thing—the fellow was confident that he was going to win this thing. How much money had he been promised by that devil woman to see this thing through?

Jed thought all this in an eyeblink of time, and as quickly

knew it was kill or be killed, and he wanted, needed to be the one who killed, for he had far too much to live for.

He touched his trigger just before the other man did the same, and he heard his adversary scream, saw the man stiffen, and then jerk backward, collapse to the earth, and lay still.

Once more, a universal kindness had shone its light on him, for he felt no pain and saw no blood on himself. He regarded the man on the ground for a long moment, then he remembered that one of the men behind him, beyond the top of the rise, was still alive.

He began to turn when a man's voice behind him shouted, "Jed, look out!"

Instinct wasn't quick enough for the big whiskey man. He should have spun and dropped low at the same time. But he didn't.

But the voice behind him belonged to Loudon Paley, newsman, and he had moved quick enough, shot fast enough, barely, to keep Jed Stark from a bullet's killing path.

As Jed spun, revolver hanging from his hand, and not yet dropping into a crouch, he looked over the ridgetop with wide eyes to see the man he'd clubbed on the side of the head standing full height, head bloodied, arms raised as if he were at a tent revival, and a two-shot derringer gripped in his right hand, and a patch of redness welling beneath his shirtfront.

As if time had slowed, the man slowly pitched forward until he fell, full length as an axed tree might, then lay still.

Loudon appeared just behind the man and looked from the prone form over to Jed. He licked his lips, then, in his smoke-frayed voice, said, "You all right, Jed?"

Jed slowly looked from the dead man over to his friend. "I am now. Thanks to you, Loud."

Without another word, he strode up and over to his shorter, husky friend and wrapped him in a huge hug. "That's for saving Lil's life." Then he squeezed him again. "And that's for saving mine."

He let go of Loudon and looked at him hard. "We owe you everything. Thank you, Loudon."

As expected, an instant redness flowered up the man's neck, covering his cheeks and ears. He shrugged and smiled, but said nothing.

Jed draped an arm around Loudon's shoulder, and they walked down the slope and back toward the house. "Now this is a banner day. Loudon Paley is speechless!"

"Oh, now, hold on there. . . ." said the newsman.

"Ha!" said Jed, smiling. "Come on, let's do our best to turn this raw day into a great one, what do you say?"

Chapter 32

"Lil?" said Jed, looking down at her with tired but happy eyes and tenderly touching her bruised head. They stood off by themselves to one side of the fireplace.

"What is it, my dear?"

"Let's get married."

"I thought that was already decided."

He nodded, still smiling. "I mean right now."

"Now?" she said. "This minute?"

"Yep. Or maybe in two or three."

"But . . ."

"I asked him, and Marshal Thompson has the legal ability to perform the ceremony."

"He does?"

"Yep."

"Well, what about the house and—"

"It's not going anywhere without us. Look, Lil, there will never be a better time than now. All we have is now, don't you see? The past is done, the future isn't here, and when it does get here, it's the present, the now. So let's get married . . . right now."

Lilly looked around them at the small group of chatting people across the room, and she smiled. "You're right. And we are, at this moment, in the place I can't imagine not being in—our very own home. And we are surrounded by the people who know us and love us the best. I can't imagine anyone else who needs to be here."

"And if there are any others," said Jed. "Well, we'll just have to throw one big ol' wingding of a party. What do you say?"

He smiled down at this dynamo of a woman for a long moment, while she looked back at him, also smiling. "That sound about right to you, Miss Chu?"

"Yes sir, and that, Mister Stark, is the last time you or anyone else will address me by that name. From now on, it's Lilly Chu Stark."

"Perfect," he said.

"Perfect."

They kissed and then Jed made the announcement. Before he could finish, Mama Stark let out a whoop and shouted, "It's about time! Now we can get on with the grandbabies!"

Adding to that, Redeye bayed once, twice, then resettled himself on his rug in the corner.

The entire affair took less than ten minutes, with Maeve Brighton and Mama Stark sharing bridesmaid duties, little Maisie as the flower girl, using a handful of wildflowers and herbs from a small kitchen garden Minnie had planted out front for Lilly.

Loudon stood beside Jed as best man, and Marshal Harley Thompson officiated. Redeye yawned and stretched and led Lilly up the center of the big room to stand before the stone fireplace, now crackling with a low and friendly blaze.

Lilly's eyes widened and she held up a finger, then she fled down the hallway.

Everyone looked at each other, and then to Jed. He shrugged, his eyes wide. He was about to shout to her when Lilly returned and set a small jade figurine atop the mantelpiece. It was a smiling, good luck dragon.

"Okay?" said Jed as she settled next to him.

"Now we're all here," she said, smiling as wide and as full as she ever had. "The whole family."

When the ceremony had finished, Mother Stark toasted the happy couple. "To my sweet son and his darling bride, my new daughter, Lilly. May they be happier than any Stark has yet to be! And may they have lots and lots of wee ones so I can finally be a granny!"

Everyone raised glasses of Stark whiskey and they all shouted, "Hurrah!"

And the festivities lasted long into an otherwise quiet night.

TURN THE PAGE FOR AN EXCITING PREVIEW!

A LAWLESS LAND. A TEXAS DYNASTY. A NEW JOHNSTONE LEGEND.

From the bestselling Johnstones comes a blazing new saga of the American West. The epic story of the Hamlins of Luckenbach, Texas—and their fight to build a longhorn empire . . .

Caleb Ezekiel Hamlin arrived in Texas in 1850 with nothing but a handful of longhorns and a head full of dreams. Seventeen years later, his Circle H Ranch is thriving, his empire growing alongside the still-lawless town of Luckenbach. His ranch-born heirs—five sons and a daughter—are running the place now. They're known as "The Boys from Luckenbach." Each has a mind of their own—and their own way of dealing with the rustlers, robbers, and outlaws who threaten their home . . .

Jake Hamlin is the oldest and the toughest. When he's not butting heads with his siblings, he's trying to tame his wild teenage son. His brother Lawrence is the smart one who studied at Oxford and returned with lots of newfangled ideas. Their brother Elias served as a captain in the Civil War, while Rory got lured away by the gold rush. Then there's their sister Rebecca, who can rope and ride as good as any man, and finally the baby of the family, Jimbo. They might fight among themselves and forge their own paths. But when one of the brothers gets gunned down defending his sister's honor, the others come together—for justice, for family, for vengeance . . .

The boys are back in town. And they're out for blood.

Chapter 1

Eleanor saw him coming from a mile off.

The view from her kitchen window let her see a good way down the main road that eventually led into Luckenbach: a single rider coming at a gallop. She ran the rolling pin over the biscuit dough and watched him come.

He got closer, and Nate Wilson's stout form came into focus, Eleanor Hamlin frowned. Nate was Sheriff Gilmore's senior deputy. Now Eleanor felt anxious. Nate Wilson wasn't known to go miles out of his way just to make a social call, and nobody riding that fast ever brought good news.

Eleanor set the rolling pin aside, wiped her hands on her apron, and went out to the front porch to wait for him. She stood, hands clasped in front of her.

She gave up standing a few seconds later and lowered herself onto one of the benches. Forty-eight years old, and she was getting tired just a little earlier each day. Married at seventeen, she was still a strong, handsome woman, gray just beginning to streak auburn hair, blue eyes still alert but now with crow's feet at the edges. Work on the Circle H Ranch had been hard, but honest and rewarding. It was no kind of life for the weak or lazy.

But nobody had ever accused Eleanor Hamlin of being weak or lazy. It was just that the youthful energy of a seventeen-year-old had left her long ago. Joints were starting to creak. She rubbed her hands, already sore from gripping the rolling pin.

She could complain, but who'd listen?

Anyway, she wasn't the complaining sort.

Nate arrived, slid off his horse, and came to the steps of the front porch, removing his hat and wiping sweat from his forehead. He was a dull-looking man with a bland face and thin brown hair. The tin star glinted in the sunlight on his vest. He put one foot on the bottom step but didn't come the rest of the way up.

Eleanor stood. "Deputy Wilson."

"Sorry to be in a hurry, Mrs. Hamlin, but is Jake here?" Wilson asked. "I need to break some news."

"Jake's riding the fences with Jake Junior and a couple of the hands," Eleanor told him. "What news?"

Wilson rubbed the back of his neck, demeanor going awkward. "I hate to upset a lady. If you can direct me to Jake—"

"I'm not delicate, Deputy Wilson," she said. "Anything that concerns my husband, concerns me."

Wilson hesitated.

Then his expression went apologetic. "It's Jimbo."

Jake Hamlin didn't consider that he'd lied when he told Eleanor he was off to ride the fences. Not exactly. He and Jake Junior and his two best hands—Elmo and Mac—had set out riding fences exactly like Jake had said. But when they'd reached Parson's Creek, Jake had sent the hands ahead to finish inspecting the fences

Jake and his son Jake Junior—he preferred JJ to Junior—squeezed sideways through the gap in the barbed-wire fence, fishing gear in hand. The Hamlins had been the first in the county to string the barbed wire, and the salesmen had even given Jake a discount knowing the other ranchers in the area would follow Jake Hamlin's lead. It was that kind of family. Established and respected. Jake was proud of that but tried not to let himself get too proud.

Too much pride could distract a man from getting things done. Pride didn't put food on the table.

But today wasn't about barbed wire or family pride or anything but an overdue father-son talk. It was overdue, and at twenty, Jake Junior was too old for a good scolding. Jake knew that would only push the kid away. It had been difficult for Jake to suppress his natural urge to shout and lay down the law. That's how Jake had been raised, but he was smart enough to see there were times to go easy.

So they'd drop a few lines in the water, talk about fishing and bait and if it was too early in the year to catch big ones, eventually the conversation would shift to what Jake wanted to talk about.

At least, that was the plan.

Jake pointed downstream. "Where it widens. Current's not so strong, and it's a little deeper."

Jake Junior nodded. "Right."

A few skinny willows grew along the creek's banks, and they plopped down in the shade of one and began the pleasantly tedious task of fastening hooks and bobbers to their lines.

Parson's Creek ran for several miles more or less north-to-south and was the dividing line between the Hamlin Ranch and Chuck Logan's spread. He'd known Chuck since their daddies had been pals long ago, and the man had never been anything but the perfect neighbor. Jake spied a few of Logan's longhorns grazing in the distance.

The day would get hotter as it wore on, and they'd be glad for the shade. Maybe they'd kick off their boots and let their feet dangle in the creek.

Jake Junior passed the small pail of worms, and they both baited their hooks. A minute later, two bobbers floated in the weak current.

"Maybe we'll catch enough for dinner," Jake suggested.

Jake Junior grinned. "Then Ma will know we were fishing instead of working."

"She'll get over it if she don't have to clean them," Jake said.

His son laughed. "I reckon that's about right."

There was a moment of minor excitement when Jake Junior's bobber vanished beneath the surface of the water. He jerked the pole but missed hooking the fish.

"At least we know they're in there," Jake said.

They chatted about nothing in particular for a few minutes—the weather, a new bull Jake was going to buy, the new Methodist church being built in town. Preacher Abbot's shepherd had given birth to a litter of puppies, and Jake was thinking about getting one.

Jake reached inside his vest and came out with a small flask. "I guess it wouldn't be a fishing trip without this." He pulled the cork, took a swig, then handed the flask to Jake Junior.

Junior raised an eyebrow. "Oh yeah?"

"Go on."

Junior took flask and tilted it back.

"Cheaper than drinking in a saloon," Jake said. "Also a lot less likely to find trouble fishing down by the creek than hanging out in some saloon."

Junior gave his father the side-eye. "Someone told you, didn't they?"

"Luckenbach's not a big town," Jake said. "Now listen, Junior—"

"JJ."

"Sorry." Jake had to stop himself from rolling his eyes. "JJ."

"Who was it told you?" Junior asked. "It was that big mouth Clarence Meeks, wasn't it?"

"It doesn't matter who it was," Jake said. "You seem to think you're in trouble. You're not."

Junior's eyes narrowed with suspicion. "I thought I wasn't supposed to go into the Yellow Dog."

"Hell, son, you don't think I've had a beer with the boys once or twice in the Yellow Dog?"

As a younger man, Jake had been in there a little too often which was why he wanted to keep his son from wasting his time the same way. And it hadn't just been drinking. Jake was a big man who didn't take to insults, and there'd been too many problems he'd thought could only be solved with fists. And he could take a punch even better than he could throw one. As a hotheaded youth, he actually got to enjoy the brawls. A man likes to win after all.

But as Jake matured, he realized that a man's reputation was even more important than what he could accomplish with his fists. He'd learned slow and hard, but he'd learned.

And he was hoping to save Junior some time in the learning.

"What you do and what you tell me to do don't always match up," Junior told him.

"When you was fifteen, I told you to steer clear of that place," Jake said. "You're a man now. You can do as you like."

Junior waited. He knew there was more.

"Of course, doing what you like don't always mean it's the right thing," Jake said.

Junior nodded. "That sounds more like what I was expecting."

"I'm just thinking we're overdue for a talk," Jake explained. "You're not fifteen anymore."

"So it's okay to go into the Yellow Dog with my friends?"

"The folks that frequent the Yellow Dog are a decent enough lot," Jake told him. "But as you get older and travel around, you'll find saloons that are filled with bad men looking to take advantage of a young fella that's had too many drinks.

You get to talking too loud and laughing too loud, you'll attract the wrong kind of attention."

"It's just me and Scooter and Pete having fun."

"There's a line," Jake said. "On one side of the line is a fella having fun but cross the line and he starts acting a fool. It takes experience to know where the line is. A man needs to know to stay in control of himself."

"I know the difference, Pa."

"Let me come at this from another direction," Jake said. "You think Marybeth Macallister wants to take up with a man that spends all his money on whiskey in some saloon?"

Now Junior looked nervous. "I don't see what Marybeth has to do with anything."

Jake pulled his line in. The hook was bare. He reached for the pale and grabbed another worm. "She's a good girl from a good family."

"I know."

"What do you think her folks would say to your carrying on in a saloon at all hours?"

Junior frowned. "Marybeth and I . . . I mean, it's not like we're getting married."

"Any good girl and any good family will think the same thing."

Junior pulled in his line, and they both baited their hooks and tossed them back in the water.

"Does Marybeth know about Sally Lee?" Jake asked.

Junior looked surprised. "How did you know about—dang, Luckenbach *is* a small town, ain't it?"

"How do you think Marybeth would take it if she knew you were running around with a girl so . . ."

"Fast?"

"Well, I wasn't going to say that, but yes," Jake told him. "Don't you say it neither."

"What if it's true?"

"*Especially* if it's true," Jake said. "A young lady is responsible for her own reputation, but that doesn't mean she needs you making it worse."

"So what are you telling me to do, Pa?"

"This isn't about me telling you what to do," Jake said. "It's about some fatherly advice from an older, wiser man who used to be young like you are now. It's about deciding what kind of man you want to be. What you're going to stand for. That might sound like a lot to put on your shoulders, but if it was easy, we wouldn't have scoundrels and layabouts in the world."

Junior sighed. "I hear you, Pa. It might not always seem like it, but I listen."

Jake nodded. "Well, that's all I can ask, I reckon."

"And we don't seem to be catching any fish."

Jake grinned. "Then we don't have to clean them."

Junior chuckled. "You always could see the bright side."

The distant drumbeat of pounding hooves drew their attention. Jake stood, one hand going to shield his eyes from the sun's glare.

A rider approached, coming fast.

Junior stood next to him. "Who is it?"

Jake shook his head and kept watching until the rider came into focus. Then his gut twisted with anxiety.

"It's your ma."

"Ma?"

"She's veering this way," Jake said. "She's seen the horses. Leave the poles. Come on."

They returned to the gap in the fence and squeezed through just as Eleanor arrived. She reined in her horse. Her hair was windblown, cheeks flushed and glowing with a sheen of sweat. Jake and Junior both knew she wouldn't ride out all this way to find them unless something was wrong.

Jake took hold of her reins and stilled the horse. "What is it?"

"Jimbo's been shot."

Jake's eyes went wide. "What? How?"

"Some trouble in town," Eleanor said. "He's at Doc Morton's. If you cut across Chuck Logan's land, you can get into town faster."

"Junior, help me with this fence post."

Jake got on one side and Junior the other. They worked the post back and forth between them until it came loose. They lifted it out, the barbed wire sagging into the grass.

Jake mounted his horse. "Put that post back best you can for now."

"I'll come with you," Junior said.

"No, go with your ma," Jake told him. "If Jimbo's hurt bad, he won't be able to ride. Bring the buckboard. I'll meet you in Luckenbach."

He spurred the horse and splashed through Parson's Creek to the other side.

Jake took off across Chuck Logan's land at a full gallop, hoping he wouldn't get to Luckenbach too late.